DONKEY BOY

DONKEY BOY

HENRY WILLIAMSON

'Learning is not worth a penny
when joy and courage are lost
along the way.'   *Pestalozzi*

faber and faber

This edition first published in 2010
by Faber and Faber Ltd
Bloomsbury House, 74–77 Great Russell Street
London WC1B 3DA

A CIP record for this book is available from the British Library

ISBN 978-0-571-27108-5

To
John Middleton Murry

ACKNOWLEDGMENT

The lines from The Absent-minded Beggar by Rudyard
Kipling (pp. 243–4) are taken from *The Definitive Edition of
Rudyard Kipling's Verse* published by Hodder & Stoughton
Limited, and are quoted here by kind permission of Mrs
George Bambridge.

CONTENTS

Part One

JOY

Part Two

COURAGE

CONTENTS

PART THREE

THE WAY

PART ONE

JOY

Chapter 1

COMING EVENTS

IT IS A wonderful feeling to be alone in your very own house for the first time. Richard had visited the building in Hillside Road many times during its erection; but always with his exuberance diminished by the thought that while the builder and his men were there he had no right to consider himself the owner, or, indeed, to be there at all. The only free days had been Sundays; but of course it would not have done to be seen there on the Day of Rest. Not that Richard had any religious convictions about the Sabbath; he went seldom to church; but Sunday was Sunday, after all.

Now the builders were gone. A cheque for the balance of the purchase price had been paid to Wilton, Lemon & Co., and in due course the conveyance would be posted to him. At last he could insert the new latch-key on the ring, secured to a trouser button by a steel chain, into the lock of the front door, turn the key, and, pushing gently, feel it opening. There was a step up from the tessellated porch, and then he was inside his own hall, the key carefully withdrawn, and the bunch as carefully dropped back into his trouser pocket.

It was a Saturday afternoon in early March. The air was buoyant; gulls had been flying high over London Bridge, as though exalted by the impulse for renewal, for mating and nesting upon the marshes of the Thames estuary. Buoyantly upon the paving stones of the bridge black-coated men, suitably hatted of course, had moved in their tens of thousands to the railway stations upon the south side of the river. Exalted by thoughts of his new house, Richard Maddison had, with almost reckless extravagance, bought a first-class ticket for Randiswell station, on the South-Eastern and Chatham line, as that was nearer the house than Wakenham station on the London–Brighton and South Coast Railway, where he had a quarterly third-class season ticket.

The first-class fare to Randiswell was sixpence, a considerable

item in the budget of a City clerk: the price of three two-pound
loaves, half a pound of the very best China tea, a pound of
Windsor soap, or a hundredweight of coke. At London Bridge he
had decided, suddenly, to go by the low level—go hang to the
expense! Into the soft, clean upholstery of the carriage he had
settled with pleasurable excitement. The familiar smells of
Bermondsey were wafted through the open window, to where he
sat alone; they recalled with startling suddenness the last time
he had travelled on the S.E. and C.R. line, on the night of his
clandestine marriage, when Hetty and he were bound for their
brief honeymoon in the gamekeeper's cottage near Shroften farm.
The smells were of hops from the brewery, of tan-yards, of glue
and vinegar factories, predominant among them the acrid whiff of
sulphur—in an instant he was back again in the November night
of five years before: and feelings of humiliation at the wretched
secrecy of it all arose strongly in him, as his father-in-law's face
came to his mind. The sense of smell, almost atrophied in
civilised man, is nevertheless the most potent of the senses to
recall scenes in memory.

Richard Maddison, now past his thirtieth year, had settled
with himself as a creature of habit. He had travelled about four
thousand times to the City, to his desk in the Town Department
of the Moon Fire Office. About eight thousand times his boot
leather had pressed upon the flag-stones of London Bridge, on
his way to and from Haybundle Street. Each time he had been
conscious, in clear weather, of the rising sun on the right side of
his face as he went to work in the morning, and again of summer
heat, or winter hues of sunset, in the late afternoon as he returned.
To the sun, or its weak circular image beyond mist and smoke,
he usually doffed his hat, carrying it in his hand as he swung,
among thousands of others, across the swift muddy currents or
flooding tides of the river. Six days a week, except for Sundays,
Bank Holidays, and ten days' vacation a year, he worked in an
office, for about half of each year in artificial light.

During that time he had lived either in lodgings or a rented
house, always hoping to be his own landlord. Now he had
attained this desirable state: he was the owner of a £650 house,
one of fourteen in Hillside Road, Wakenham, built by the Antill
Brothers on a ninety-nine-year lease from the ground landlord—a
mysterious individual concealed by the term *Banker's Nominee*.

To this nominee Richard had contracted to pay £3 15s. per annum ground-rent for the next ninety-nine years, after which time the house would become the property of the ground land-lord, according to the terms of the agreement.

He had bought the house through his sister's husband, George Lemon, who lived in Epsom, and was a partner in a firm of solicitors in Lincoln's Inn. He had written to George Lemon only after some hesitancy and indecision; for his feelings of loyalty to other members of the family conflicted with his sense of no longer belonging to their world. In the end it had seemed the right thing to do, small as the value of the property was, to write a formal letter to his brother-in-law. George Lemon had replied most graciously, inviting Richard to luncheon at the London Tavern (he had fought against sleep in the Town Department of the Moon Fire Office that afternoon), and when they parted had made Richard promise to cycle over to spend the day with them at their place in Epsom any Sunday he cared to come.

Now, at last, he was alone in his own house, free to stand and enjoy his very own property!

Having closed the front door behind him, pressing the catch of the lock gently to save wear-and-tear, Richard hung his umbrella on the staircase railing by the post at the bottom of the stairs, and then put his silk hat upon the rounded nob of the post. He was now ready for a thorough inspection: but first—for everything must be done in proper order—he must sweep up the fragments of mortar and plaster on the floors, lest the surface of the wooden boards be impressed and injured further. Builder's men were careless beggars, with no respect for tidiness!

A month or so previously, Richard had brought over a bundle of newspapers and put them in a corner of the front room, re-marking to the plasterers that they might find them of use on the floors, but the hint had not been taken. Some had been used for lighting fires in the grates, with ends of planks and laths on which to boil cans of tea, he noticed. So Richard had made neat piles of waste-wood, for kindling his own fires later on; but these had disappeared. Always picking and stealing, the lower orders, he thought. Thank heaven they were now gone, and the place was his own!

Richard did not know that his action in collecting and storing odds and ends of planks had been resented by the two joiners, who regarded all waste wood as belonging to them—their perquisites. They had considered the toff to be a stingy cove, pinching their firing. Hadn't he got enough money to buy a fard'n bundle of firewood for himself at the grocer's?

After leaving the railway station that early afternoon, he had purchased a hand-brush and pan in a shop in Randiswell; and with these he intended to sweep up the dust and shavings in each room. He hoped to do some carpentry in the new house, and had already chosen the small upstairs room beside the bathroom for his own den. There he went first, and when he had swept a neat heap into the centre of the room, he sat on the floor, to enjoy a few moments of happy contemplation in solitude.

Should he keep his butterflies here, and his shelves of books, as well? No; wood-dust would get on them. He must think of another room for his very own personal things—his fishing tackle, sporting prints, dark lantern, butterflies, books, his breech-loader, green-heart rod, and cartridge-loading implements. And, of course, his special constable's insignia and truncheon!

He got up, and looked out of the window, with thoughts of possible neighbours. The room looked directly on to the semi-detached house next door. Across a short space was a set of windows precisely similar to his own, but all facing south. At the moment this house was unfinished; even so, a FOR SALE board on its post behind the privet hedge of the front garden was already displayed. It was a pity that the houses were built in pairs, but there it was: a poor man like himself could not pick and choose. At least he would now be away from Comfort Road, and the smoke of the railway cutting causing smuts to enter every window. The rainwater in the butt, too, had never been clean, since the catchment area of the roof collected much soot.

Here it would be different. There were but fourteen houses in Hillside Road, and they faced the Hill—forty acres of glebe land recently purchased by the London County Council, for over a thousand pounds the acre, and soon to be railed-in with spiked railings five feet high. Already various deciduous trees had been planted on the grassy slopes, and the view from the main bedroom, facing west, would be most welcome after the constrictions of being in a street with houses facing one another.

To the main bedroom Richard now went, leaping up three

wooden stairs to the landing. Here was a second door leading into a secondary bedroom, with a window facing east. This connected to the front, or west, room. It would be suitable for his own dressing-room—but then there was the question of the boy. Phillip was rising two years of age, old enough to sleep by himself, especially as there was now another little one on the way.

Richard swept the shavings of the bedroom into the pan, and shook them into the grate. Then he glanced around him with satisfaction. The western front was nearly all glass, for the floor ended in a bay of three windows. A fourth window, the upper half of a door, opened on to a little balcony, shared, unfortunately, with the house next door. A low railing divided the balcony, and the space there was only sufficient for one armchair, or two upright chairs at most. Still, Hetty would enjoy sitting there with Phillip, on summer afternoons when her work was done, with the green expanse before her. The sun would catch the balcony from the south, and be visible until it set in the west.

He opened the door, and stood upon the balcony. There on the distant heights of Sydenham stood the familiar Crystal Palace, glittering in the sun.

He felt exultant in his purchase. He was the owner of this new, clean house! Ninety-nine years to run! But to the job in hand. From the main bedroom he went into the dressing-room, to sweep up; and this being done, he descended the steps to the bathroom, the first door on the left past the head of the stairs. Here was much to satisfy the eye. What joy, to have a modern bathroom! Complete with water-closet, hand-basin with hot and cold taps, and new pattern of gas-jet: and the very latest design of bath, in no sense a boxed-in tub, but a real bath standing on four feet of iron cast in the shape of a lion's paws, well raised from the floor with plenty of space for cleaning underneath.

The happy expression on his face changed to one of vexation. The lavatory pan was foul, and stuffed with fragments of newspaper. He pulled the plug, the mechanism clanked hollowly, the water had not yet been turned on. He turned away in disgust, and went downstairs into the kitchen, and so to the scullery and the back door. This was locked, bolted, and chained; and having opened it, he went down three concrete steps to the yard below. Here, by a drain and under a spout, stood a rainwater-butt.

There had been a spell of hard frost recently, and a cake of ice lay on top of the water in the open butt; but it was not thick enough to have opened the oaken staves.

Amidst the building debris which littered the back garden lay a dented bucket, encrusted with white. Picking this up, he banged it to loosen some of the plaster of Paris, shook the flakes free, and returned to the butt. Setting the pail under the wooden faucet, he turned the tap. No water flowed forth. It was held by the vacuum, seen as opaque bubbles of air under the circular plate of ice.

He was about to strike the ice with a brick which he had picked up, when a peculiar sound made him pause. Could a curlew be singing over the field of withered yellow grasses beyond the garden fence? Listening intently, he heard the trilling notes of a curlew, or was it a golden plover? The notes appeared to come from the sky above the yellow brick face of the house: a series of remote bubbling notes. He went down the concrete passage between the outside wall and the creosoted wooden fence which separated the two houses, paused at the end, and listened. There was only the cawing of a rook in the elms beyond the garden. Most mysterious! Could his ear be deceiving him?

By the water-butt the sounds were audible again. The faintest of trillings; and then a creak, followed by a slight crack. Peering closely, he saw that a wandering bracelet of minute air-bubbles was threading its way under the plate of ice, scores of tiny bubbles following one another along a wandering course and disappearing at a certain point, where a stem of grass was frozen in. The battered plaster-pail was slowly receiving water from the wooden faucet below. So the mystery was made plain: the bubbles were making the singing noise, as they rose from the tap and found their way into the air again through the grass stem in the ice-cap. Now, as water trickled out below, they were like the reeling cry of a nightjar. The ice creaked, settling between the oaken staves; a grasshopper warbler succeeded the nightjar; then the rapid and near-inaudible ticking of the pipistrel bat alarmed, with glinting eyes and teeth, in its hole in the garden wall at home, seen by him and his brothers long ago. The reed-like trilling of the bubbles recalled the sunlit days of his boyhood, far away in the West Country. Richard sighed.

It was no good trying to recall those days, they were gone for ever; and looking at his watch, Richard saw that it was already two o'clock. Hetty would be expecting him any time now, but as the Saturday meal on homecoming was always a cold one, he would not be guilty of keeping her waiting. They had arranged to spend the afternoon in the new house, to decide where the furniture should go. It had been planned to bring a kettle and picnic basket for tea, with the boy; and Richard wanted to show her a tidy house, which was the main reason why he had come down to sweep up the dust in the rooms. He must dawdle no longer. With a blow of the brick he broke the ice. Water gushed from the faucet, with black fragments of old leaves. He had found the barrel lying in the field behind the garden during the late winter, and stood it in the angle of the wall, asking that a pipe be fixed from the gutter above. It would be useful to water the garden.

Carrying the bucket, which dribbled water from a split in its seam, upstairs, he flushed the pan, then returned for more. It took several douches to clear it, to his relief, for he had dreaded a choke in the pipe. At last the pan was white again, and presentable; and glancing into the other rooms, to enjoy a last glance at their freshness and clean ceilings and wallpaper, he went down the stairs, and let himself out of the front door, to pick his way down the little path with its border of rockery made of burnt lumps of yellow clay embedded with broken bottles, which had run into glass and fused with the brick in the kiln. Richard thought it a horrible rockery, but Mr. Antill the builder had, on pointing it out to him some weeks before, evidently been much pleased with the idea. "Makes a change, sir, don't you think?" he had asked, with some self-satisfaction. "My own idea, sir, I got it from the Crystal Palace one Saturday afternoon, when some young imps were making a cock-shy out of bottles with half-bricks."

Richard walked, in his rapid swinging lope, along Charlotte Road and was soon where it joined the High Road, and a little further on was Comfort Road, with the pawnbroker's shop at the corner. He walked freely, without the usual feeling of near-gloom, as he went down Comfort Road to his house at the end. Spring would soon be here; there was the garden of the new house to be laid out, a lawn to be made. It was but a small garden, to

be sure, and the subsoil of yellow clay began immediately under
the coarse and trodden grasses; but the top soil could be built up.
He had already noted, over the fence at the bottom, a mass of
leaf-mould, from the accumulation of elm-leaves fallen from the
tall trees above.

Richard had arrived, a week or two previously, just in time to
save a small elm that grew at the bottom of the garden. It was a
sucker from one of the roots of the big trees beyond. One of the
navvies, who had been digging the trench for the water pipe, was
about to cut it down with a hook, when he had stopped him. The
navvy had already helped himself to a faggot from the coppice
in the field, and wanted the sapling to complete the bundle. The
cheek of the fellow! He had been quite insolent, a man by the
name of Monk, who lived in Randiswell. And coming to the
end of Comfort Road, Richard put his hand in his pocket for the
latchkey, reflecting that soon he would be free of the constrictions
of walking up and down Comfort Road. He was still liable to hear
the odious cry of "Jesus Christ on Tin Wheels", when he cycled
down it, going into the country.

He turned the key, pushed the door, and was astonished to
hear the notes of a violin. An unfamiliar bowler and fawn overcoat, with velvet collar, lay on the chair at the bottom of the
stairs. The door of the parlour was half open. His son stood just
inside the room, his mouth open, staring at the player. Richard
took a deep breath. He recognised Hugh Turney, his brother-in-
law. He frowned. Why had he come, and at that hour? Had
he not warned Hetty that Hugh was an unfit person to have in
the house, particularly where there was a young child?

Hetty was in the kitchen, where three places for a meal were
laid upon the table. So Hugh was expected to sit at table with
them! Good God, what was she thinking about? But all the
Turneys were like that, impervious to any idea of what was right
and proper. He felt a desire to walk out of the house, to walk
away for ever. His wife was entirely untrustworthy.

"How nice that you are back, dear," said Hetty, with hurried
cheerfulness. "You must be hungry, and all is ready. I've got
some nice brawn, and some of your favourite mango chutney.
Did you see Hughie? He has some splendid news." Her cheeks
had gone pink, and she avoided looking at him.

"Oh," said Richard. He drew a deep breath. He was agitated.

He turned away, hesitated, then faced her. He turned away again to close the door.

"Why did you let him into the house?" he asked with lowered voice.

"Oh, it's quite all right, dear, please don't worry. He's quite cured of his arthritis. And he is about to enter on his new career. Please, Dickie, do not worry about him being here."

"But I do worry! And I do not believe in this arthritis story! Oh, very well, have it your own way! But don't say I did not warn you, if your son develops an incurable disease!"

"Hush, Dickie, please, Hughie may hear you!"

The violin music had ceased. Richard's face was pale. He breathed faster with agitation. "I've a very good mind to———"

With an effort he controlled the impulse to tell her that Hugh Turney did not suffer from arthritis, but from an unmentionable disease connected with the depths of immorality. Sidney Cakebread, Hugh Turney's brother-in-law, had himself told him so; but in confidence; and one's word was one's bond. How would his wife feel if her son were contaminated? But he had given his word, and so she would have to learn the truth from someone else. In his distress, Richard cried, after closing the kitchen door, "Very well, I wash my hands of the entire business! I am no longer master in my own house, apparently! You give me your promise not to allow your brother in the house, and at the first opportunity you break it! Do not tell me to hush! I shall not be hushed!"

Hetty leaned against the polished steel plate-rack above the kitchen range. Kettle-steam strayed by her shoulder. She had been dreading the return of her husband; she had been unable to ask her brother to go. Hughie had been so happy, having at last found the kind of work that he really wanted to do, after all the years of unhappiness with Papa, who had insisted on putting him into the family Firm.

Richard had turned to leave the kitchen when there came an excited banging on the lower panels of the door. A child's voice was crying out behind it. He opened the door, and a little boy ran wide-eyed into the room. He wore a sailor's blouse of white, with a broad square collar lined with dark blue lines, a pleated white skirt, white socks, and black button boots. He seemed almost overcome with some tremendous news.

"Ning-a-ning man, Mummie! Ning-a-ning man!" he cried, with shining face. Then, aware of a difference in his mother's attitude, and of his father standing there, he looked from one face to the other face; the eager attitude diminished, his thumb went into his mouth, and he began to suck it.

"Take your finger out of your mouth, Phillip," said Richard. As the child did not move, he bent down and pulled the hand with a movement almost abrupt. The child stood still on the linoleum floor, his eyes now round, as he stared up at his father so high above him.

From outside in the road came the strains of a barrel-organ playing *Il Trovatore*.

"Oh dear!" said Hetty. "He's late today. He usually comes on Saturdays before you get back."

"Ning-a-ning man!" exclaimed the child. "Penny Mummy p'e! Penny Mummy p'e!"

There was a glazed earthenware pot on the kitchen shelf where Hetty kept her small change. The child took the coin, and hurried away, full of eager delight to give it to the ning-a-ning man.

"Don't you teach your son to say 'thank you'?"

"I do generally, dear. Only he gets so excited when he hears music."

Richard also loved music; and he had not forgotten his own childish excitement when he had first heard a concertina played in the village street by a wandering sailor. The memory softened him, and he decided that he must be civil to his brother-in-law. Repressing a desire to say that Hughie's knife and fork and plate, and particularly his glass, must be washed separately in carbolic afterwards, he left the kitchen to greet the unwelcome guest with a moderate show of civility.

The guest had already left, apparently. Extra music was audible through the open front door. The fellow was showing off of course —he should be a music-hall turn. And going to the door, Richard received a surprise.

For Hugh Turney was a music-hall turn. Richard's reaction was one of disgust that any connexion of his could make such an exhibition of himself. Hugh Turney was bowing and scraping with the blatant gestures of a clown. He wore a yellow blouse with loose sleeves, a crimson cap with hanging tassel, silk knee breeches of the same colour, and yellow stockings with black shoes of patent leather with large silver buckles. His face bore no grease-paint; its usual pallor was accentuated by his dark eyes and black moustache, a larger moustache than when Richard had seen him last, and waxed at the points in what Richard considered to be a vulgar fashion. The fellow was a bounder.

Others apparently did not think so. The Italian organ-grinder, wearing a broken bowler, almost green with age, acid rain, and sulphurous fog, was grinning with delight. Phillip was jumping up and down, holding on to the iron gate. Mrs. Feeney had come out of her house below, having forgotten to put on her black bonnet, and was smiling at the gay sight. Children down the street were yelling to others, to run quickly. Across the way a door opened, and a very old man, his rusty double-breasted jacket and stove-pipe trousers hanging on his bony frame, moved slowly towards his gate with the aid of two sticks, while a great-granddaughter held him by a piece of greasy cord tied round his middle.

This was Matthew Pooley, a local wonder, who had received three telegrams from the Queen congratulating him on his last three successive birthdays; for he had passed his centenary, and now existed in the hope of his immediate relations that he would live to see the century out.

The old labourer was alive in only a small part of his mind and bones and sinews. A leathery moleskin cap covered his bald head. His yellow face was rutted as though the cart-wheels leading off the autumn fields of his past labouring had impressed themselves out of decaying memory upon his face. He stared shakily at the sight before him; he took some time to formulate a word; and then from blue lips a single sound fell, heard by no one. It was "Frenchie". The old man connected the sight of Hugh Turney with one of the great fears current during his boyhood—Napoleon Bonaparte.

As more people came to stare at the sight, Richard returned into the house, aloof and disgusted. It was only what might be expected of a Turney. Gone were his eager visions of leading wife and child into the new house that afternoon. He retired to his room upstairs, to continue with the packing of his intimate possessions, preparatory for the move during the following week. By then, Mr. Wilton had promised, the gas would be laid on.

In his particular room was visible another cause for exasperation. One of his boxes of butterflies, left piled by him in the corner,
each secured with string lest it fall open during removal and the
precious contents be destroyed, had obviously been opened.
The string had been cut. There it lay on the floor. Beside it was
the wing of a butterfly. Opening the box, while his long thin
nostrils distended themselves slightly, Richard saw what he had
feared, but not really expected to find: most of the fritilleries
within were damaged, the pins askew, bodies broken, wings in
fragments.

So Hetty had allowed the boy to play there, despite all that
had been said! It was monstrously unfair! She favoured the child
before himself! He knew, from bitter experience, that she would,
as soon as he mentioned it, find some excuse for it, even at the
cost of deliberate lies—her Turney blood showing itself. Why
could she never be frank and honest with him? She seemed
incapable of being straightforward. Richard sat on a cane-
bottomed chair and held his head in his hands.

What was the good of hoping for any improvement? She
would ruin the boy, who already was developing a whine in his
voice, as he followed her about, clinging to her skirts, usually
sucking his thumb, after he had thrown all his toys out of his cot.
The boy was growing up to be a namby-pamby. His mother
pandered to him. Had he not heard her talking to him, almost
crooning, abasing herself before him as he lay in his cot after his
evening tub in tepid water—Richard believed that hot water in a
bath had a deteriorating influence on human character. Hetty
had pleaded with him in his cot afterwards, bit of a boy that he
was, for a goodnight kiss! "Don't you want to kiss Mummie good
night, Sonny? Don't you want to kiss Mummie?" Then that
little bit of a boy remaining silent, until his mother's footfalls
reached the bottom of the stairs, when, of course, there were howls
of despair from up above. And what did his mother do but trip all
the way upstairs again, being entirely at the child's beck and
call!

There was a knock on the door. "Oh, come in." It was Hetty.

"Hughie is just going, dear," she said. "I thought you would
like to say how do you do to him before he departed."

"Oh, did you really, now? I suppose you haven't been telling
him what I said to you?"

"No, dear, of course not. He has to get back to town, for a rehearsal, he says."

"A rehearsal?"

"He is going to be Gonzalo, the Wandering Violinist, dear. He has a very important part at the Tivoli, and has to rehearse."

"I should have thought he had done his rehearsal already. How long has he been here?" .

"Only about an hour, Dickie."

"Did he come in that extraordinary garb?"

"No, dear, of course not! He changed in the front room."

This information caused Richard's lips to tighten; but he made no remark. He followed Hetty downstairs.

"Hullo, Hugh," he said, with a faint smile. "Hetty says you are just off. Won't you stay and take pot luck?"

"No no, old man, thanks all the same, but I never take luncheon," replied the other. Hugh Turney had changed back into tweed jacket and trousers swiftly; then the Wandering Violinist outfit had been stuffed into a gladstone bag, watched by Phillip, who peered at everything he did, from removing the large ear-rings clipped to his lobes to snapping the lock on the bag and drawing the straps through their brass buckles.

"Well, old girl, we must meet again when there is more time to have a chat," said Hugh as he pulled on his dog-skin gloves.

"I'll say goodbye, Hugh, and I wish you every success for the new venture."

"Thank you, Dick, I shall need it. Now will you give me your opinion—I've asked your noble son here, but he is prejudiced—d'you mind telling me which strikes you as the better name—Gonzalo the Wandering Violinist, or, more simply, Normo the Ning-a-ning Man?"

"Ning-a-ning man, Mummie! Ning-a-ning man come!"

"Yes, dear, he did come, but hush, Uncle Hugh is speaking."

"Well, if you ask my opinion, Hugh, to be perfectly frank, I do not feel myself properly qualified to give an opinion on the matter."

Hugh Turney hid his desire to scoff at this typical Dickybird remark. Hetty did her best to help.

"I like Gonzalo the Wandering Violinist, Hugh. At least I think I do. Though the Ning-a-ning Man is more homely, perhaps. Really, I like both."

Very helpful, thought Richard, as he withdrew from the group about the door-mat. He disliked prolonged farewells, especially by or outside an open door. He went into the kitchen, to find the stone jar of carbolic acid, meaning to go over, with a damp rag, every possible place which might have been touched by Hugh Turney.

At the gate Hetty was saying, "Don't leave it so long before we meet again, Hugh dear. Come one afternoon early, if you can, and we will have a picnic tea on the Hill, it is lovely up there. You know we are moving to our own house, don't you? So we shan't be here much longer."

"Yes, Mamma told me. You'll miss your old Ning-a-ning man, won't you, Pilly boy?"

The child stared up at him. "Bile inn, p'e, Uncle Hoo, more bile inn, p'e."

"He appreciates the broken-hearted clown, bless him," said Hugh, caressing the boy's hair with a hand. "Your boy's got the artistic temperament, Hetty—poor little devil."

"Yes, he loves beautiful things, I am sure. The trouble is, if he sees a thing which Dickie has interested him in, he immediately wants it."

"Don't we all? Well, not necessarily what your respected spouse, the Man in the Moon, is interested in, perhaps—but human nature is entirely based on imitation, Hett."

"Still, you won't be a naughty boy and take Daddy's butterflies again, will you, Phil?"

"No, no," said the child, earnestly. "Pilly naughty boy!"

"Dickie's butterflies mean such a lot to him—to Dickie, I mean," explained Hetty.

"And to Pilly boy, too, of course, if he sees them through his papa's eyes first. Imitation is the sincerest form of flattery! When's the other due, Hett?"

"In June, Hugh. Now, dear, I don't want to hurry you, but Dickie will want his meal. You know the new address, do you? Number eleven Hillside Road. Let me know how you get on, won't you, and don't leave it so long next time."

"Any news of Theodora?" asked Hugh.

"I haven't heard for quite six months, Hughie. I think she is still in Greece."

Richard was waiting, with his own bowl and flannel (which he had decided to burn afterwards) in the kitchen. The smell of carbolic had turned him faint, his interior already being in a state of interior bubbling due to lack of food, and incipient exhaustion. Would they never say goodbye to one another? Must they gossip their heads off on his threshold, like any other occupant of Comfort Road? Had they no idea of good form?

At last the door was shut, and Richard's feelings could be vented. Hetty tried not to show her tears as, standing in the parlour, while Richard wiped all possible places which Hughie might have touched with his person, she endured complaints about what, to her, had been a happy chance visitation. Her husband's attitude was inexplicable to her: a fuss over nothing at all.

"I gave you every possible hint that I did not want your brother in the house, did I not, repeatedly? And the moment my back is turned you flout my authority in my own house, and without a thought of possible consequences! If you care nothing for me, at least you should think of your little donkey boy, who is being spoiled by your indulgence to his every whim! Oh, I can see it happening! I am not deceived! Well, let me tell you this, once and for all! I will seek protection in a way you will not like if your brother Hugh comes here again! It is my duty to protect innocent life!"

Hetty stared at Richard in puzzlement, and fear. She knew he was exacting, and was easily upset, but she had not seen him in such a state before. What could be the matter with him? Was he ill, or sickening for some illness? Just because her brother had sat in the "Sportsman", the armchair in green Russian leather Mamma had given him for a Christmas present when they first came to Comfort House, he was working himself up into a rage.

"Do you hear me?" cried Richard, flinging the cloth into the pail of disinfectant. "Either you obey my behests honourably, or you leave my house! Yes, it has come to that! Do you hear what I am saying?"

His voice was thin and high with agitation. He was breathing fast. His face was pale and strained. What could have come over him? The child stood between them, looking up first at one face, then the other. His eyes were dull, almost mournful. "No, no," he muttered, and began to cry.

"Send the boy out of the room, please! I have something to say to you! You have only yourself to blame for what you are going to hear!"

Hetty took Phillip into the kitchen. The fireguard was up and fastened to its hooks. She lifted the edges of the tablecloth and laid them over the table. She hid the poker on the rack. She shut the cupboard doors. She locked the scullery door. What else could he touch, upset, break, and so make Dickie——? Perhaps he was hungry. She gave him a crust of bread, hastily spread with beef dripping. "Now be a good boy, Sonny, stop crying dear, and for goodness gracious' sake don't do anything to annoy your father. Mummy won't be gone long, play with your golli-wog, there's a dear little son." She left him sitting on the floor, the safest place, thumb in mouth, and clutching with his other hand a fragment of silk, part of an old petticoat of hers. To Hetty this was most pathetic: for she had not been able to feed him at her breast, and from an early time the piece of silk, called Hanky, had been the substitute.

"You may consider that I am being unreasonable, and alto-gether guilty of exceptionable conduct," began Richard, in a determinedly quiet voice, when she had returned to the front room. "So perhaps the time has come to tell you a certain fact. I feel it is my duty to communicate to you a certain fact, as it were under duress, for I am breaking a confidence in telling you; but since you do not seem able to accept what I ask of you in a loyal manner, I have no other alternative. Very well, then! I requested you not to admit your brother into this house for a very good and proper reason. You have thought he has suffered for some time from rheumatism, or neuritis, or arthritis, have you not?"

"Yes, dear, of course, naturally, I have believed what Mamma has told me."

"Well, I conceive it my duty to acquaint you with the truth of the matter, since, as I have said, you are not amenable to ordinary common loyalty to my requests. You understand what I am saying, I hope?"

"Yes, Dickie, but please do not keep the suspense much longer. Phillip is crying. I don't think he knows you, dear, when you are angry, and he does so love you, really he does."

The baby was kicking inside her; and the kicks seemed to be also upon the front part of her brain. She tried hard to keep back tears.

"Well, let me tell you this, Hetty, your brother Hugh is suffering from something highly contagious. I am not at liberty to say what it is, but the nature of the disease is that it would be gross dereliction of duty on my part if I did not show every concern for the welfare of, not only Phillip, but of yourself, and myself as bread-winner. I suggest that when next you see Sidney Cakebread, you ask him to tell you, for he is my informant, and as he is a gentleman, I accept his word without question."

"Yes, dear, of course, naturally. I had no idea, I assure you——"

"Well, I am glad that you are at last aware of your responsibilities in the matter. Now if you have thoroughly washed your hands, may I please have something to eat? And do please, I beg of you, accept what I ask of you in future."

"Of course, dear, I am so very sorry. Now I have the food all ready, a nice broth on the hob, and then some brawn with your favourite mango chutney. I must go and see about it. I hope little Phillip has been good."

"Why should he not be good? There is no need for such anxiety. A boy will be a boy, you know. By the way, did you cut the string round one of my butterfly boxes?"

"No, dear, of course not!" Hetty was emphatic. "I have kept Phil out of the room, dear, when I could, but he goes in because he wants to be like you, you know. 'Daddy's things, Daddy's things' is what he is saying all the while you are away, dear. I am sure it is not the things so much, Dickie, as that you showed them to him, and he sees them as part of you."

"Oh, come now, that is pure Irish blarney! Naturally a child is inquisitive, and wants to acquire property as soon as it can! But the law of meum et tuum has to be respected, and the sooner a child realises this, the happier for all concerned."

"Yes, dear. If you will excuse me, I will see about your meal. There is a letter for you, I think from your brother John."

"I'll finish this job first, and be ready in, say, ten minutes."

Hetty escaped, with relief, to the kitchen. And there, oh dear! "Sonny, Sonny, what have you done now! Oh, you are a trial to me, really you are, my son!"

The boy had got hold of her pair of scissors, and with them was sitting on the floor, cutting up a copy of *The Daily Trident*. With a feeling almost of horror Hetty read the date—Saturday, 16 March, 1897. It was that morning's paper!

Fortunately at that moment Mrs. Feeney called over the garden fence, to enquire about the scrubbing out of the new house, and so Hetty was able to ask her if Mr. Feeney would get another copy as soon as possible from the shop by the station.

She returned to the kitchen to find that Richard had come into the room, seen the damage, and picking up Phillip, had set him across his knees, and lifting up his skirts, struck him several times sharply on his thin little bottom. The boy screamed so much that he had difficulty in uttering the word "Mummy!" as he held out his arms to her. He seemed to be choking. The shock was great, because it was the first time he had been struck, or punished at all. Hitherto Daddy had been someone huge and kind and safe, a familiar presence promising wonder and fun. "Daddy! Daddy!" he cried, for the familiar presence he had lost.

Chapter 2

GEOLOGICAL PARALLEL

Richard, upon reflection, after his meal, regretted that he had not kept a stiff upper lip in the matter of Hugh Turney's visit; he was ashamed because he had behaved weakly. After all, Hetty had not known the full seriousness of his condition; and he himself had shown Phillip how to cut out pictures to be pasted upon a screen lat:r, for the nursery in the new home. Ah well, things would be better in the new environs of the Hill.

With these near-optimistic reflections he set out that afternoon with his wife, pushing the child in the mailcart. The boy's sailor suit was now complete with a straw-hat with *H.M.S. Defiant* on the band. They were going to visit Lindenheim, as already to himself Richard called the brick and slated semi-detached house. The gate was not yet in position, but the posts were set. Later he would get a painter to put the name of his mother's old home in Germany on the top bar, in white letters. The gate of course would be green. A hedge of privet was to be planted by the builder, as part of the agreement.

Hetty was delighted with the house. She had seen it during the building, several times; but now that Dickie had the key on his ring, to unlock the front door, it was really a home, their own little house. Knowing that he would be hurt if she did not share his ideas about every room, she was ready to agree with all he said. But to her surprise he asked her first for her ideas about the arrangement of the rooms.

While she was wondering what to reply, he declared that the withdrawing-room downstairs must have new curtains, and contain her own furniture; that the end room, with its french double windows, opening on to the steps leading down to the garden, must be the sitting-room.

"Yes, dear, it will be nice for you to be quiet here in your Sportsman armchair, to read your paper when you come home, and not be disturbed by me or the children. They can be with me in the kitchen."

But Richard would not hear of this. She must not think of herself merely as a servant, a maid of all work, a nursemaid. No, the children would be looked after by Minne, and they would sleep with her in the eastern bedroom, above the sitting-room.

"Minnie?" exclaimed Hetty, in surprise. "Do you mean the Minnie who was your own nurse?"

"Yes," replied Richard. "I heard from John today. As you know, Minne has been with him since Jenny died, but his housekeeper does not get on with her, apparently, and so Minne is leaving. He asked me if we would like her to come to us, now we have a larger house. Minne can look after Phillip, and this will enable you to get some proper rest at night. You need it badly, and so do I."

Richard, whenever he had spoken of his German nurse to Hetty, had praised her for steadfastness and kindness, and so Hetty had a picture in her mind of Minne as a wonderful person. And as Dickie liked her so much, surely it would be the very thing to have her with them. But could they afford it? She must say nothing to disappoint him.

Hetty knew that her husband was not earning very much money. He was not yet able to afford a proper meal for himself in the middle of the day. She occasionally peeped into his diary, where every expenditure was recorded, and occasionally one of his thoughts. *Ought I to give up smoking?* he had written recently. He spent $4\frac{1}{2}d$. a week on an ounce of Navy Cut, one of his few pleasures. He had started to smoke after his father's death had brought him a little money. What the sum was she was not sure, but as he had bought the house out of that money she supposed he could not have much left. He allowed her twenty-five shillings a week for the housekeeping, including her own and the baby's clothes; and as she had to pay Mrs. Feeney the charwoman out of this, she imagined that Minnie's wages would have to come out of her weekly allowance as well. Oh dear, she did not see how it could possibly be done!

"Well, what do you think? It would give you more leisure, and I might even give you a bicycle for your birthday present if you are very good," he said indulgently. She could see that he was pleased with the thought of his old nurse coming.

"My brother John had generously offered to pay Minne's wages, twenty-six pounds a year. They are not exactly wages, you understand, but rather in the nature of a pension to an old and faithful servant and friend of the family."

"Yes, dear, of course, naturally. But, Dickie, do forgive me mentioning it, but I cannot help wondering if Minnie will think perhaps that I am so different in my ways from what she has been used to, dear. Otherwise I am sure it is wonderfully kind of you to think of help for me."

"Don't be so humble, little wife," said Richard. "How would you like to play tennis at the club? You need more social life, so do I. And Minne's coming will enable us both to go out more."

But Hetty was still anxious within. The past two years had been a time of almost ceaseless work. She could not fully realise what Dickie was saying.

"Yes, it will be wonderful with Minne in the house: she is a woman of high principles and standards," went on Richard. "It will be something new for her, a little house in the suburbs. But there, things have changed greatly for her since she left her native Bavaria with my mother after the brutal Bismarck had killed her father and brothers in the war."

Hetty looked at Sonny, sitting on a soap box. He was eating, as an especial treat, a sandwich of Gentleman's Relish. His large blue eyes were upon his father; she knew he was taking in all Dickie said—if not the words, at least the feeling behind them. How nice it was when Dickie was in a calm mood!

There were to be no further upsets that day, even when the child added to the wandering stains of water on the stairs and bathroom floor, deliberately, his father declared. Had the little cuss not pointed at them with his finger as they wobbled, with the movements of the battered pail, upon the floor, and then added to them in imitation?

"He's only a little man," said Dickie, and lifting the boy up, carried him to the proper place. There, of course, nothing happened, perhaps because a little black spider was struggling upon the surface of the water. The child was absorbed in the sight. His father held down a piece of newspaper for the insect to climb upon, and then opened the window and put it on the sill, saying that spiders were good insects, eating up disease-carrying flies.

"Yes, my boy," said Richard, addressing his son, as they were having tea in the kitchen, 'you have to thank not only a donkey, but the Prussians for your existence here today. For if Bismarck had not decided to federate the German states and principalities, by fire and sword, perhaps I would not have been here, and then most certainly you would not."

"Noo house pider," exclaimed Phillip, pointing upwards to the bathroom sill above the kitchen window.

"By Jove, the boy has got the bump of location," exclaimed the proud father. "He knows the direction of the bathroom! And not yet two years old."

Hetty looked at the child proudly. "He takes after his father," she said, "don't you, Sonny?"

The child got off the box to seize his mug of milk and gulp it. Then he hastened out of the room, and they heard his boots clumping up the stairs. Richard followed, stepping over him, to shut the bathroom door. He did not want any imaginary spiders being rescued. Nor any of the bedroom windows shattered by pieces of wood. So the explorer was carried downstairs again, and re-seated on the soap box, and told to contain his impatience.

Richard became reminiscent as he sipped a mug of tea.

"When I was a small boy, we children were always led to say good-morning to our father and mother by Minne. The boys had to bow to them in turn, and the girls to curtsey. And this was repeated in the evening, before we went to bed. But you"— to the child—"you little donkey boy, you crawl whithersoever you will, you peer and pry everywhere, little fingers picking and stealing, as though by divine right. Don't you? Come, confess now! Who went to Dad's butterfly box, and cut the string? Who took Dad's silver fritillaries off the pins, and broke them? Why, Dad was keeping them for you, you donkey, for when you are bigger, when you will care for such things, and see in them memories of the woods and hills of your genesis."

The child understood little of what was said, but he felt the feeling coming from Daddy. Daddy was the one who played with him and showed him wonderful daddy-things out of boxes and drawers and off high shelves. The spanking was entirely for- gotten; indeed, the condition by which it had come upon him had no connection in his mind with Daddy. His recording nervous consciousness had been shocked at the time; fear and pain had momentarily broken its continuity; but as Hetty had said, from the idea of her brother Hugh, it had not been Daddy hurting him, but something outside and beyond Daddy. Which indeed was the truth, the rare clear truth that many centuries before had been expounded by Jesus of Nazareth: an instinctive truth, a primal truth. A child's mind is instinctive, through its feelings, which are of its parents.

Hetty's mind likewise was instinctive; she felt happiness flowing into her when Dickie, who was by nature kind and careful, spoke like that to his son. She thought of her child as Dickie's son; it was her dearest wish that he should grow up to be the companion that he needed.

After tea Daddy got down on his hands and knees and pretended to be a dog chasing a little donkey. He went slowly, flapping his hands on the bare boards, moving slowly and lumberingly, lest the boy be over-stimulated. The game went on, with frequent meetings between dog and donkey, to avoid any prolonged suspense for the little one. Sometimes the dog flapped and thumped away with the excited donkey in chase; after a reassuring hug, the pursuit was reversed. It went on round the doors of the rooms and down the passages. The house resounded with the child's delighted cries, until Richard made a mistake. He hid in the coal hole, and came out suddenly and so frightened the donkey, who was transformed into a screaming baby that would not be comforted until his mother had him, sobbing convulsively, in her arms, to draw the square of silk over his cheek. Immediately into mouth went the thumb, silk clutched in the other hand. Sonny was safe.

Richard went away to look at the garden; but the light was beginning to fade; and the cawing of rooks in the row of elms behind the bottom fence seemed to him harsh and noisy.

He was walking up the little slope towards the french windows when a door opened in the lower house, and over the garden fence a tall thin man with beard and gold spectacles looked out. He bowed, and bade Richard good-day in a voice of extreme gentleness. The bow and greeting was returned. Nothing more. Richard was relieved. It was proper that a near neighbour should keep his distance, it augured well for the future.

A few minutes later, from the south window in the sitting-room,

as already he called it, Richard saw his neighbour again. He
wore the usual frock coat and black tie with starched linen collar,
and this time apparently his wife was with him, a small woman
with a mass of ginger-coloured hair piled on her head. She was
so small that the top of the pile appeared to be well below her
husband's shoulder.

"That must be Mrs. Bigge," said Hetty, glancing through the
pane. "Mrs. Feeney does for her, and said I would like her very
much."

"Mrs. Bigge!" exclaimed Richard. "Extremes certainly seem
to have met in that marriage!" and he laughed at his joke. So
did Phillip, because Daddy was laughing.

When, a fortnight later, the Maddisons were installed in
Lindenheim, Mrs. Bigge of No. 10—Montrose was the name on
the sky-light over the door—became at once a friend of Hetty's.
She came in during the first morning, and offered to bring her a
cup of tea.

"You won't mind a little body like me not leaving a card on
you first, will you, Mrs. Maddison? I am my own card, I always
say. Well, I hope you will like your new home, dear. And what
a dear little boy you have, to be sure! Do you mind me calling
you 'dear'? I am very nearly old enough to be your mother,
you know."

Mrs. Bigge's voice was broad and deep, in odd contrast to her
small size. "Yes, Mrs. Feeney has told me and my dear hubby,
that's Mr. Bigge, Josiah is his name, all about you, so I feel
like an old friend already. We have a daughter, Norah, still at
school, but finishing this year, when she hopes to get her licen-
tiate of the Academy of Music, to be a teacher, you know. Does
your little boy like music? Mr. Bigge, that's Josiah, plays the
harp, but only to amuse himself, not professionally, of course."

Hetty was delighted. "Then we will be musical neighbours,
Mrs. Bigge, for Mr. Maddison plays the 'cello, or used to before our
marriage. I have always hoped that he would take it up again."

"Well, dear, I am sure you are very busy, but if you want
anything, don't hesitate to pop in and tell me, will you now?
We are all on this earth to help one another, and pass by the way
once only. You will want good fires, won't you, to dry out the
house? Do you know any of the other neighbours, dear? Well,

I expect you will soon enough. The couple below us are called Groat, he is a master in a school in Deptford. His wife, poor thing, has one glass eye, her brother shot it out when she was a girl, with an arrow, playing Indians, and now for the rest of her life she has to wear a glass one. So don't be put off her, if she appears to glare at you if you meet her in the road; it is the glass eye glaring, not her own one, dear.''

And with this neighbourly information Mrs. Bigge hurried back into her own house, leaving Hetty happily ironing on the new kitchen table, her range burning brightly and the flue turned to heat the hot water in the tank over the bath. She was delighted that now she had hot water out of the tap, as well as a copper in the scullery for boiling on washing day. Mrs. Feeney was coming on Mondays to wash for her, and to clean up the house, as well as a half-day on Wednesday mornings.

The boy's second birthday anniversary was approaching. Coltsfoot was in flower among its grey soft leaves in the clay of the garden, part of which lay in hardening regular lumps turned up by Richard. He dug, as in everything he undertook, with extreme thoroughness. He had noticed some navvies digging a trench for the water-pipe during the past winter, and observed how their corduroy trousers were hitched by a strap below the knee. Inserted into the strap on each right leg was a scraper, like a flat wooden spoon. They had dipped their spades in a bucket of water before each thrust of the blade, to help ease off each stiff clot. That was the correct way to dig in clay, so Richard had copied them. He had carved a wooden scraper, but fastened it on the handle of his spade, by a flat spring he fixed there. He dipped the blade in water, he heaved up a clot, he slid it off sideways. Impossible to get any weed-roots clear of such a solid, cold, sticky lump, so the idea was a bare-fallow: the sun to bake them: then later he would sprinkle compost among them, and after a favourable rain and a period of partial drying out, he would tap them with a fork, and they would surely disintegrate.

His son watched him digging, and using the wooden scraper. He remembered where Daddy's spade was placed after use, up against a corner in the wall of the house, and went into the garden the next morning, a Monday, to do likewise. The spade being too much for him, he concentrated on the scraper. He prodded the clay with it, squatting intently, for a while; he was digging

with a spade. He splashed it in the pail, and dug until he remembered his golliwog, and went indoors to get it. In the
kitchen the piece of wood became a poker, to be put between the
bars of the kitchen range, as he had watched his mother doing.
He drew it forth alight; it hurt his finger; he dropped it with a
yell, and ran out of the room. The glowing end fumed on the
stone base below the range.

Hetty was making the beds upstairs. After a while, the boy
came back, remembering the Daddy-thing. He gave it to Golly
to dig with, and at six o'clock it was floating beside him in his
night-night bath, before the kitchen fire. It went with him, being
a Daddy-thing, and therefore part of his life, with Golly and
Hanky in his cot. His mother took it from his hand when he was
asleep, and, not recognising it, burnt it on the open fire, which the
range became with the side flaps pulled out, ready for Dickie's
homecoming.

That evening, going out with goloshes over his boots to do some
digging, Richard missed his scraper. He spent the best part of an
hour before twilight in wondering where he could have put it.
He returned indoors perplexed. Was his memory beginning to
fail? Where *could* he have put it? Again and again as he read the
Daily Trident his mind wandered to the little piece of carved wood.
He asked Hetty if she had seen it when she was in the garden.

No, Hetty had seen nothing like it. Eventually, unable to settle
to the newspaper, he lit his dark lantern and went prowling in the
garden, again without result. When he came into the house once
more, the boy was crying, calling "Daddy, Daddy!" from his cot.
Touched by the appeal, Richard went upstairs to be with him,
feeling concerned lest he might have had a nightmare. The child
was sitting up, wild-eyed, sucking his finger which had a blister
on the top. He had dreamed of everything being red, a deep
glowing red, the ning-a-ning man, the ning-a-ning man's hat, the
ning-a-ning, and all the houses. What puzzled him was why
Mummie and Daddy were not red, too.

Richard went to his room to fetch a bar of Callard and Bowser's butterscotch, his favourite sweetmeat. Returning to the cot,
by which Hetty was sitting, her cheek against the boy's soft,
warm hair, he took his ivory-handled pen-knife from his waistcoat pocket and, holding the silver bar across the palm of his left
hand, gave it a precise blow to crack it clearly across. While he

was unpeeling the fragment he again spoke to Hetty about the missing scraper.

"Where could I have mislaid it? Did I put it back in the clip? Surely I did. Can you recall if you noticed it on the handle of the spade as you passed that way? Who hung out the washing? Not you, surely, in your condition?"

"No, dear, Mrs. Feeney hung it out. I did not notice it, I am afraid."

"Are you sure you know the piece of wood I mean?"

"I think so, Dickie. It was what you were carving by the kitchen fire the other night, wasn't it?"

Then with a start, which was received by the boy, Hetty realised that it must have been the piece of wood Sonny had been playing with during the day. It was what he had pushed between the bars of the fire.

As his mother looked at him, the child's eyes opened wider, feeling her anxiety, though he had no notion of the direct cause of it.

From within the safety of her arms the child looked at the world-filling face of his father. He understood what he had been saying, but did not connect it with his own digging, the splashing in the pail, the poker: he had forgotten the Daddy-thing, with Golly and Hanky safe in bed with him. Looking at Daddy's face, he had the same feeling he had had from the Daddy-thing, and now from the Daddy-sweet he sucked, removing it between finger and thumb to look at it for the greater pleasure of putting it back in his mouth.

The child did what the father did because his wonder was stirred and he was happy with all he saw Daddy doing. The small man coming to see the big man, the son tottering on his feet with joyous cries towards the father, the child approaching with arms held out for balance, his mind showing itself in his eager face and attitude, the idea of Father and the idea of Father's things, which the son was beginning to know as things apart, though very close together. So interest in Father was, as consciousness grew, less than the interest in Father's things; even so, all were Father.

Thoughts of and for Father came into the son's mind as geological strata were formed upon the earth, in surge upon surge of energy, impressed by following feelings: the uniform layers of slow sedimentary life, alike with the faults and breaks of fiery upheaval,

involving criticism, fear, resentment and, finally, schism. This
had happened in Richard's young life; it was to happen, without
the father's knowledge, in Phillip's young life.

Richard used to say at this time, "He is after property, the little
rascal!" as a joke. Later, it became no joke.

Walking about the house in the mornings, the child imagined
himself to be that wonderful thing, Daddy. Thus he sought
Daddy's pipes in the rack on the wall above the table, near
Daddy's green armchair, and though the smell and taste checked
him, he put one of the curved briars in his mouth as he sat in the
chair being Daddy. Then "Book! Book!" he said, and got down
to fetch one from the pile in the downstairs lavatory, and carried it,
pipe in mouth and goloshes dragging on his feet, to the armchair.
Pipe in mouth, newspaper held upside down, one rubber over-boot
still held by a foot, he was Daddy reading Book to Mummy.

Creeping to the open door, Hetty listened to a recognisable
rigmarole.

"Julibee julibee Ol' Q'een bike bike bike haha haha bile inn
ninganing ding dong penny bike bike book no no! F'ee T 'ade
donkey boy Daddy man in Moo', all gone, all gone," while she
thought, Oh, Sonny loves his father so much.

Richard's bicycle stood in the lavatory. In admiration and
emulation of Daddy, the child spun the pedals, tried to make the
cyclometer go click click click, tried to climb up and tinkle the
bell. He clambered on the lavatory seat. Tinkle tinkle tinkle was
heard by Hetty in the kitchen. There was a cry, a clash of metal,
and then wailing. The emulator had slipped, pulled the cycle
over, and was wedged in the porcelain pan.

"Oh, what have you done, Sonny! You must never never *never*
touch your father's things again!"

"No, no," he agreed, solemnly, holding up arms to be raised
from the otherwise immovable position.

"Daddy's things, not for Sonny! Daddy will be angry if you
are a naughty boy, Sonny!"

He grizzled with the feel of cold water, the big white slippery
hole, and Mummy cross with Sonny.

"No, no! All gone, all gone, all gone!"

"That's a good boy. You must not touch Daddy's things,
Sonny, for Mummy's sake."

"No, no," he repeated, with earnest solemnity. She removed socks and shoes, washed his feet and dried them, and took him up to his cot. When he was safely settled in with Hanky, Golly, and Thumb, she returned downstairs to see if any of the enamel, or the plating of the handlebars, had been scratched. With relief she saw that no damage had been done to the precious Starley Rover.

The child did love the father. One of his joys was to get into bed beside Daddy and Mummy on Sunday mornings. He lay between them, Golly beside him, with no thought of Hanky. Once Richard tickled him for fun, but the child's laughter came to the verge of hysteria, and so he did not do it again. He was careful not to include the child too warmly in his affection, and so the child never merged as it were into the father, to draw from him the vital warmth, to become one flesh, the basis of natural feeling. Richard was too scrupulous; he was also shy; the child did not want to snuggle into him, so he responded likewise. He felt, when he saw the child wanting to be cuddled by his mother, a little out of it.

One morning when he put his head near the child's, which lay on the mother's shoulder, Phillip pushed him away. Immediately Richard withdrew into himself. Soon afterwards he got up, and without a word went into the next room, to dress and go downstairs, and so to dig in the garden. He felt that neither wife nor son wanted him.

As a fact, the child's action was wholly instinctive, as was his habit of imitating his father. Later, the child's habit of seeking his father by imitation in acts with his father's things was to be observed and misinterpreted and checked as a bad habit; then to be punished as the vice of stealing, under the commonplace thought of *spare the rod and spoil the child*; and by this punishment the natural feeling for his father was sealed-off, and the son became, at an early age, as aggrieved in spirit as was the father.

The child cried easily: he could laugh, too, until the tears came. But his grief went deep, the tears pouring in silence down his face. His Aunt Dorrie discovered this, and sometimes pretended to cry, just to see Phillip's eyes grow round, his face to pucker, his tears to run. Hetty begged her sister not to do it; for the child's strength, like Dickie's too, she said, could easily run out.

Chapter 3

A MIND OF ONE'S OWN

RICHARD told Hetty, before Minne came, that she was a sensible, practical woman, who would bring up the little fellow to be himself.

"Like a vegetable, with its own juices well inside its skin, and a hardened skin, too, to protect him from the pandering of others."

Hetty supposed that the "others" were herself, Dorrie, Mrs. Feeney, and Mamma—all of whom had, in one way or another, been the subject of his criticism. She herself had been accused of making Sonny a namby-pamby, because, when he was restless at night sometimes, and had lost Hanky, he called out to her to hold his hand through the bars of his cot. "'An' Mummie, 'an' Mummie, 'an' Mummie," the plaintive voice requested. This had sometimes kept Dickie awake, and he needed his eight hours of sleep every night.

"Leave the child alone, it is only a bad habit, wanting to cling to you, and the longer you keep it up, the more he will require it."

"'An' Mummie p'e, 'an' Mummie p'e, 'an' Mummie p'e," the voice often pleaded in the darkness of the night room, faintly lit by the wan beams of the lamp-post half-way down Hillside Road.

Once the *please* touched the father.

"Dash it all, he is being polite, so we must not disappoint him," and Richard got out of bed, tall and thin in his long white nightdress, and took the boy into bed beside him. "Anky! Anky!"

"You don't want that old rag when you have Daddy to keep you warm, Phil," whispered Richard. He held him against his chest, but the child was restless, and being told to lie quiet, tried to do so. He lay unnaturally still, while Hetty suffered beside him, knowing his feeling of being held against his will, almost of imprisonment. Tears flowed in the room of wan slatted light penetrating the venetian blinds.

Back into his cot the child went, with a warning to lie still and go to sleep like a good boy. But the good boy, now in disintegration of darkness, became the naughty boy. Silent weeping broke into sobs.

"'An' Mummie p'e, 'an' Mummie p'e, 'an' Mummie p'e!"

Hetty herself was lying unnaturally still, keeping back her tears. A prolonged sigh from Richard; an edge of irritability in the voice pronouncing, "Tomorrow he must be put by himself in the next room. He will have to learn to rely on himself sooner or later." He tried to settle to sleep; but detecting misery all around him, finally sat up in bed.

"What, are you crying, too? Oh, my lord! Two cry-babies together!"

"No, Dickie, I was thinking of the Old Queen. I don't know why, but she came into my head. She must be so very, very weary."

"Oh, rot! What has she got to do with it?"

Hetty summoned up her resolution to say, "Perhaps I should sleep alone with Sonny just now, dear. I think he is teething. And he is so very very nervous by himself."

Richard promptly got out of bed. "It is your husband who will have to be banished, I can see that!" He opened the connecting door between the bedroom and the dressing-room. "Now you will be able to hold your best boy's hand to your heart's content!" he called out. The connecting door was closed.

Minne, or Minnie as she was called, arrived a fortnight later. She set herself to work within ten minutes of her arrival. Everything she undertook she did with all her energy. Hetty soon found that Minnie wanted things done in ways different from her own. Minnie had a passion for an almost disconcerting cleanliness.

From the front door to the beginning of the path between the burnt glass-and-clay border was a passage called the porch. It was covered by a glass verandah supported on iron posts standing on a low brick wall above the Bigges' equivalent passage below. The porch was paved with terra-cotta pavors, a dozen yards of them. Minnie decided that these must be cleaned daily. She not only swabbed them, as Mrs. Feeney had done twice a week, but she scrubbed them with carbolic soap and hot water. Only thus should the *hochgeboren's* path be cleaned. In black bodice and voluminous yellow skirt, Minnie on her knees scrubbed and scrubbed, before wiping each octagonal pavor smooth and dry.

It was the same in the kitchen. She was respectful to Hetty, she observed a punctilious regard for what she was asked to do; but she did it her own way, until soon Hetty felt she was no longer mistress in her own house. Minnie seemed to imply that everything Hetty did was done in a wrong manner. Boots must not be cleaned in the scullery, for the dust would settle on the plates in the wooden rack above the sink. They must be cleaned outside, on the steps, above the pit where the coke was shot by the coalmen, who carried their bags all around the outside of the house.

There was an iron-framed gas-stove beside the kitchen range. Minnie cleaned this several times each day. No bicarbonate of soda must be put in the greens. Ach, their goodness would be killed! Of course the greens-water must be used for stock. It was good for baby. Greens-water! Hetty usually carried the cast-iron cooking pot round the corner, and with the lid pressed against the greens, poured the smelly water into the rainwater drain beside the corner where Dickie's garden tools stood in a row. This is what cook had always done at home, for to pour it away into the sink caused a bad smell in the pipe.

Then no fat from the roasting pan must be poured into tea-cups, to stand and harden in the larder. Fat must be poured into a special basin, kept for the purpose. It was bad to peel potatoes. They should be scrubbed, and roasted in their jackets, to retain the goodness.

Minnie washed her hands a score of times a day. If she so much as lifted Phillip into his go-cart, or tall feeding chair, she would wash her hands before doing anything else. Mrs. Feeney must not bang mats against the wall outside, to knock out the dust. Mats must be taken down the garden, laid on their faces upon the site of the lawn, and assiduously tapped, tapped, tapped, with a stick, to loosen the dust. Thus the soil would be improved. Minnie seemed to have inexhaustible energy, and an undeviating desire for cleanliness, order, and correctness. Every time she blew her nose on a handkerchief she washed her hands. That was perhaps right, but why did she make life so hard for herself?

Minnie slept in the eastern bedroom, with Phillip in his cot beside her bed. One afternoon, when Hetty went upstairs, she was surprised to hear Minnie sobbing behind her closed door. The sound was audible down the passage, with the four doors along its length, the last of which was the night nursery.

Hetty hesitated, drawn by the desire to comfort Minnie. But what if Minnie wanted to cry alone? Had she said anything to hurt Minnie's feelings? Hetty decided that she ought to pretend that she had heard nothing.

The puzzle of Minnie remained. Why did she insist on working so hard? Was it, as Dickie had said, because she was a German, with higher standards of cleanliness and order than those of the rest of the world? Minnie was quite old, of course; she must be fifty at least. Old people were different from young people. Her own papa was fifty-six next birthday; Dickie's Papa had died at fifty-three, and his mother at fifty-one. Minnie had been in England since she was a young girl, with Dickie's mother, so she must be nearing fifty.

One evening, when Hetty heard the sounds of crying again, she walked softly in her slippered feet down the passage and listened at the door. There was a double sound of weeping, or rather a lesser moaning accompanying the crying; and, somewhat agitated, Hetty knocked on the door, saying, "Are you all right, Minnie? May I come in? Is anything the matter, dear?"

After a pause the door was opened, and Minnie's red eyes and wet smiling face greeted her. Behind her, Sonny's face was a picture of woe.

"What has happened, Minnie? Why is Phillip crying? Has he been naughty? Surely not."

"Oh no, Gnadige Frau!" said Minnie. "He is so anschaulic, he is sad because his pflegemutter is sad, that is all. Ach, mein lieber Phillip, here is your real mother come to see you, so weep no more."

He did not seem to want his mother. "Won't you kiss me, Sonny?" Hetty pleaded. He stared at her, then turned away his head. "Ah, he is forgetting me already," she said, shaking her head slowly.

"Ach no, Gnadige Frau," said the German woman. "It is not so. It is the pflegemutter who is to be forgotten. Always this is so in my life, Gnadige Frau. First there are the kinder of the wohlgebornen baronin, but they grow up and leave me, all my dear Fruhjahrsweizen! Ach, and the Dinkelweizen——" Minnie was happy again now, remembering her earlier years at Rookhurst. "The Dinkelweizen bringing them butterscotch into the nursery, he was so kind a big brother to Viccy and Dora, and to Hilary, mein lieb' Ganschen!"

Hetty did not comprehend the German words, but she understood the feeling of them. So that was the reason of her tears; how very natural! Minnie loved the little children she had brought up, only to lose them! A real mother had the same feeling, too, for Mamma had often said, "Ah, Hetty, if only all of you were small again!" and she would sigh. Charlie her eldest, grown up and gone away, and never writing any letters; and nowadays, said Mamma, she seldom saw Hughie. Dorrie and her little ones were near to her, that was a blessing; and Joey the youngest was living at home, going up to Sparhawk Street in Holborn every day, for on leaving school he had gone into the Firm. Yes, she understood Minnie's feelings about her charges growing up, and being lost to her. Minnie must be lonely, too, being in a country so far away from her own people. She must be as kind to Minnie as she could be. Minnie was one in a hundred, really.

Dinkelweizen—what a curious name for Dickie! Whatever did it mean? Hetty did not like to ask Minnie, so she waited until Dickie was in a good mood after his dinner that night. He had carved another scraper, and was pleased because he had seen a thrush singing on the top of the elm tree at the bottom of the garden.

Then Richard told her that his nickname with Minnie had been *Dinkelweizen*, "Bearded Wheat", and that his youngest sisters, Augusta, Victoria, and Theodora, had been *Die Drei Fruhjahrsweigen*, "the Three Spring Wheat Stalks". Hetty began to feel that they had come from a world of enchantment, of Grimm's *Fairy Tales*, so different from her own as a child. Fancy Papa, or Mamma, calling Charlie, even if he had a beard, which would have been black of course, Bearded Wheat! Or Dorrie or herself a Spring Wheat Stalk! She began to smile as the picture of Dickie grew in her mind, his long face swaying on a stalk in the wind, his beard growing upwards into his hair, as the wind swayed him to and fro, to and fro, and as a thin leaf-like arm slowly came up from beside the stalk to hold on his top-hat, she broke into laughter. Mr. Dinkelweizen, no longer the Man in the Moon, but the Man in the Corn!

"Well, what is the joke? Do share it with me."

"Oh nothing, dear, really, only my fancy."

Seeing his face, "Really, Dickie, I was not laughing at the nickname. It is really a very beautiful idea. I have only met Theodora of your sisters, of course, and I love her very dearly, for she is my great friend. An ear of wheat is very beautiful, I am sure, and with the corn-cockles in it, and the blue scabious of June." Scabious was the colour of Dickie's eyes, a dreamy blue, the blue of the summer sky. The Man in the Corn, so different from other men!

Hetty felt the tears brimming in her eyes, at the picture of Dickie as a head of bearded wheat, a man in a fairy story locked in the corn, crying voicelessly with the wind for freedom; Dickie in the cornfields around her when she was a child, waiting to be set free by love; Dickie as a spirit among the butterflies and herb-fields of Cross Aulton, and the scent of lavender when the old roots were being burned on the bonfires of autumn. She brushed a tear off her lashes.

"Come come," said Richard, watching her from the green leather armchair. "What an odd lot you women are, to be sure! You are all the same," he went on tolerantly. "Minnie was turning on the water-works yesterday, then the boy followed suit, and now you! There must be something in the atmosphere of this house. The yellow clay holds perhaps the water from draining away." He returned to the pages of his familiar *Daily Trident*.

Later, having set aside the newspaper, he suggested a game of chess. They sometimes played at night, but Hetty had not yet won a game. However, it gave something for Dickie to think about, and she was always hoping that a sudden brilliant move of hers would enable her to call out, "Check mate!"

But not tonight. As they were sipping their cups of cocoa, brought in on a tray by Minnie, Hetty said, "What does 'ganschen' mean, Dickie?"

"What? Oh, 'little goose'. Gosling. That was Hilary's nickname, and I think I shall apply it to you."

"Yes, dear," said Hetty, gratefully, feeling herself to be a little nearer to the world of her husband and Minnie. She kissed him on the top of his head, as he settled comfortably into the arm-

chair, to read his paper during the half hour of peace before he
would follow Hetty upstairs to bed.

Despite his affinity to Minnie, *The Daily Trident* was Richard
Maddison's only companion, of like mind with himself, in his
house. It shared his inner life. Its pages, particularly the
articles on the English countryside, bicycling, gardening, fishing
and other sports and games, made him feel that he enjoyed a full
life as he read the pages in the train to and from London Bridge,
keeping the best of them for the armchair at night, together with
the first pipe of the day in one or another of his several briars.

The Daily Trident had appeared in May of the previous year.
He had purchased a copy of No. 1 out of curiosity. For weeks upon
the hoardings around the station, on end walls of various houses
and warehouses, behind the glass fronts of empty shops had been
displayed yellow posters on which large blue and red letters
announced *The Daily Trident*, "a penny newspaper for one halfpenny". At first he had dismissed them as vulgar and flamboyant,
and repeated to Hetty what he had heard in train and office,
that it was an amateur affair, engineered by a young Irish
journalist. But one morning, as he was crossing London Bridge,
together with thousands of others upon both pavements, two
donkeys had moved by the kerbs on either side, each led by a
figure in white. Upon the flanks of each small grey reluctant
animal were hanging yellow boards, in red and blue lettering
declaring, *I do not intend to read The Daily Trident.*

For days the animals were to be seen, walking lethargically
upon sett-stone and wooden block of various London streets,
until one morning many men in white coats at every corner it
seemed, were selling copies of the first number of *The Daily
Trident*, getting rid of them as fast as they could collect and pouch
brown copper coins bearing the heads of Queen Victoria, William
IV, the Georges, and even a small greenish ha'penny, on its face
the words *The Anglesea Mines 1788*, and on its rim *Payable in
Anglesea, London or Liverpool.* Richard secured his copy with this
antique but legal coin, which he had received in change somewhere, and folded it carefully for inspection of its value later on.
His own paper was *The Morning Post*, the only true Tory newspaper for him.

The first thing he read, during his luncheon interval of forty minutes, decided at once for him that it was the sort of paper he had always wanted to read. It startled him. There was the truth about Mr. Turney, his father-in-law, to a T! Later in the evening of the same day he cut out the piece and gummed it upon the fly-leaf of his pocket diary.

STRANGE DOUBLES.

VERY ORDINARY PERSONAGES OFTEN MISTAKEN FOR ROYALTIES.

There is scarcely a distinguished personage in this country who has not a living counterpart who delights in copying all his peculiarities of manner and speech. The moment a man acquires prominence people are accustomed to search for any marked characteristic that he may possess, and when these are found in individuals resembling him in features and figure, identification becomes difficult, and errors frequent.

Not so very long ago our Embassy in Paris was greatly perturbed by the information that the Prince of Wales had landed at Calais. During the three hours that elapsed between the departure of the mail train at the port and its arrival at Amiens, telegraph wire and Channel cable had carried many electric dots and dashes of the Morse Code between the City of Light and our own Foreign Office.
. . .

"And I bet everything I possess that the impostor was Mr. Thomas William Turney!" had muttered Richard to himself, recalling the story Hetty had told him in the summer-house of her garden, before they had decided to be married in secret, owing to the choleric opposition of her respected parent. The story was that she had been coming home from her school in Belgium, when upon arrival at Dover, Mr. Turney, on hearing that the Prince of Wales was expected from Paris, had had the cheek to walk off the boat before all the other passengers, and passing down between the lines of cheering people, he had raised his hat to left and right, while smoking a large cigar. The impostor had reached the train waiting in the station with hands in pocket and bearded chin held close into his buttoned ulster, in order to be lost among the crowd.

That story, for his son-in-law Richard, illustrated the entire

character of the old man. Mr. Turney was an impostor—a hum-
bug—a hypocrite—a charlatan—a bogus fellow. Had he not
brazenly assumed the coat armour of the extinct Norman family
of Le Tournet, while his son Hugh, according to Theodora, even
claimed to be the heir to a barony in abeyance? That was the
family he had, in a period of loneliness after Mother's death,
married into!

Now, towards the end of the third year of his marriage,
Richard Maddison had arrived at the conclusion that no spiritual
or mental communication with Hetty, or with any other Turney,
was possible; and since he knew no one else, apart from the
fellows at the office, *The Daily Trident*, with its reiterated, almost
pronged policy of fidelity to King, Country, and Empire through
the triple virtues of Faith, Hope, and Vigilance, was the bed-
fellow of his mind. Let radicals call it the Yellow Press; he knew
the truth when he saw it: he had a mind of his own in such
matters.

Chapter 4

DIAMOND JUBILEE

"MINNIE Mummie, Minnie Mummie, Minnie Mummie!"

Hetty stopped at the head of the stairs. The plaintive voice almost whispered down the passage. Sonny was in his cot. The door was half open. He was frightened when it was closed.

"I am just coming, Sonny. Mummie just coming."

"Minnie Mummie, p'e."

The word *minnie* meant a kiss. Or an embrace. Or security, affection, safety. Hetty knew this. She loved Minnie now, the two women sometimes embraced. It was sad that Minnie was soon to go away. Her father was ill and lonely in the Black Forest country, and at last his only daughter was going home. She would wait to see the Gnadige Frau safely delivered of her little one, and strong again on her feet, before she left.

Minnie's father had had a stroke, and she must not delay the journey. Such tears, such a commotion of feeling! She must return to her dear father. Bayen called her to the smell of the pine trees once more, to the yoked oxen; but never, never would she forget her little ganschen, her little gosling who was *not*, as his pappy declared, an eselfunge, a donkey boy!

Much as she loved Minnie, Hetty could never bring herself to tell her her own secret name she had for Sonny—Little Mouse. For his eyes were round and big, like those of the little mouse which had so terrified her in the front room at Comfort House, before she knew what it was, when it had opened the sitting-room door one night before her baby was born. She had watched it gathering wool from the mat for its nest, and taking it down the hole by the pipe in the floor. But Hetty had given away her secret unwittingly. She had asked Minnie what was the German word for mouse; and Minnie exclaimed, "Ach, the small mouse among the corn is what he is to you, his true mother. Haselmaus! His nest bound to the Dinkelweizen!" And Minnie had laughed merrily with Hetty, while Phillip jumped and laughed with the happiness in the faces above him.

49

Now Haselmaus was wanting his true Mummy!

Going along the passage, Hetty opened the door. Little Mouse was standing up in his cot. Golly was flung on the floor, beside Hanky. She stooped with difficulty to pick them up. Beside them was a child's book of lithographed pictures, *Streuvelpeter*, which Dickie had given him for his birthday present, with the words in English. (Would he have bought it if he had known that the Firm had printed the book? There was the name at the bottom of the last page, *Mallard, Carter and Turney Ltd., Sparhawk Street, Holborn, London, E.C.*)

There was something about the book that faintly distressed Hetty, with its pictures of the stumps of poor Peter's thumbs dripping blood after a tailor's shears had snipped them off, because he had sucked them; it might have happened to Sonny, and all because she had not been able to—— Still, that was life, she supposed. Habits of carelessness or forgetfulness did lead to frightful fates, sometimes. But was not Sonny too young to think of another boy being carried into the air, shot by a fox, or drowned over a quay? Would it not frighten Sonny, and perhaps give him nightmares? But Hetty had not dared to speak like this to her husband; she had hardly dared even to think it to herself.

Having comforted the child, who had thrown out his cherished objects in order to bring her to him for a kiss, she settled him down in his cot with a piece of barley sugar, with Golly and Hanky beside him, and Thumb ready to follow the sweet. Before leaving the room, she hid *Streuvelpeter* on the top shelf of the cupboard, under her folded piles of disused clothing that she was keeping to make into clothes for the children.

She went slowly along the passage, and down the stairs to the sitting-room, to rest, for her labour pains were upon her.

Minnie had already gone to leave a message at Dr. Cave-Browne's, and to warn Mrs. Birkett, the midwife, in the High Road beyond. Mrs. Bigge next door had promised to keep an eye on Hetty. Every now and then she called out, quietly but cheerfully, from her back door, into the open southern window of the Maddisons' sitting-room.

"Are you there, Mrs. Emm? Are you all right, dear? There now, of course you are! Now tell me, would you like me to pop in and make you a nice cup of tea?"

Hetty would like nothing better. The little woman went on, "Josiah, my hubby, says I am an inveterate popper, In and Out Again he calls me; but it's best to be neighbourly while we can be, don't you think, dear?"

"Oh yes; thank you ever so much for coming in," replied Hetty, laughing with relief, because Mrs. Bigge as a popper seemed so funny. She thought of a vetch pod popping in the sun; Mrs. Bigge's shape was that of a pea pod, from her square-piled hair to the square-cut end of skirt above black button boots. Mrs. Bigge noticed Hetty's glance at her boots, for she said:

"No trailing dust on my skirts, dear; why bring part of the street with you into the house? Let them have their fashions, and I will have mine." Mrs. Bigge's personality popped like a black vetch pod ripe in the sun. And like the pea in bloom, she was fragrant; and then Hetty turned away from her fancy. She was in pain again.

Through the floor came a faint thud. Down the stairs floated a cry.

"Minnie p'e, Minnie p'e Mummie, Minnie p'e Mummie."

"Ah, the little pet!" exclaimed Mrs. Bigge, popping out of the chair. "Is it his rest-time-dear? If not, let me bring him down, dear. Aunty will take care of him." She went up the stairs, calling out in her deep voice, "Auntie is coming, dear! Auntie is coming! I know where you are, in the end room; many's the time I've heard your little voice through the open window. It's your new Auntie, dear, just coming!"

Mrs. Bigge went smilingly to the boy. He stood clasping the wooden rail, a mournful look in his face that went straight to her heart. A tear lay on one cheek. Then she saw the reason: the boy had messed himself.

She lifted him out of the cot, and carried him into the bathroom. "I'm just giving his hands and face a little wash, dear," she called down the stairs. "He'll soon be right as rain."

"Oh, thank you, Mrs. Bigge."

She ran some water into the basin and washed the boy, wondering why he was so very thin. Was he getting enough food? She had some cream-buns, and would bring one in for him.

"Do you like cream buns, dear? What would you say if Auntie were to give you a nice cream bun?"

The child did not reply. She lifted him down from the basin; he was rigid, holding himself away from her. She sat him on her knee, and dried him on a towel that smelt faintly of tobacco and bay rum.

Down in the kitchen, Hetty wondered what was going on up in the bathroom. She heard the water-closet rattle, and the flush of water.

"A little accident, dear, my little pet has had, but we have put it all right, haven't we?" said Mrs. Bigge, arriving with the child in her arms. " He is such a good little man, aren't you, dear?"

The child was less rigid. He had a dread of messing himself, nearly as great as his dislike of being placed upon his small round enamel pot, that so restricted movement when he felt he *must* move. He was afraid of movement at times. When he had slept in the cot beside his mother sometimes a terrifying loneliness had overcome him; but he had been afraid to call to her to bring her over him, for the safety of her face, because Daddy might be cross with Mummie.

When he had called to Minnie from his cot beside her, Minnie had taken him into bed with her. She had cuddled him. Minnie was too hot, and her arms stopped him from moving when he wanted to. "Oh, do lie still, lieb' ganschen, and let Minnie sleep." So he would lie still, rigidly motionless. Perhaps Minnie might realise that her gosling with the faraway blue eyes was weeping in silence, but why was that? Ach, perhaps he had a tummy-pain! His head was hot. So at six o'clock next morning there was another ordeal, a brown thick liquid to be swallowed out of a cup, with a horrid smell, called licorice powder. And after his bread and milk for breakfast, Minnie had sat him on his pot, while changing her yellow skirt to a black one. Then putting on cloak and bonnet, she said he must be quick, quick! for the storch was coming today, to bring him a little brother, or a little sister. And she must go for the good doctor, and he must be quick, lieb' ganschen.

"Try, dear one, try, *try*——" and Minnie made a growling noise, which was to stimulate trying.

Nothing had happened. She put him back in the cot, telling him to be a good boy while she was gone, and to try not to call Mummie, as Mummie was not well. Minnie would not be long. Minnie would come back to her little gosling.

Try meant being good boy on pot, try was what he did in pot. Minnie come back. Ganschen—gosling—little mouse—Sonny— Donkey Boy must do big try in pot for Minnie, lie still for Minnie Mummie, oh-be-quiet-ganschen.

Then the pains again, loneliness, pot pot pot, Minnie p'e Mummie, Minnie Mummie, Minnie p'e, Minnie come p'e; all voicelessly in his mind.

At last, in fear the child sent out his calls for help. First Golly, then Hanky, then "Minnie Mummie!" Overwhelming shame, grizzling and sobbing, until Auntie made it all better again. Clean, clean! He trusted himself to Aunty Bigge, sitting serenely in her arms.

And when Minnie came back, jump jump jump for joy; and a horse came with a big man in a cart of black and a man with a black bag came in and said "Hullo, little fellow, how are you today, it seems only yesterday I was launching you into the world, now be good boy and don't annoy", and Mrs. Feeney came and Mrs. Bottle Black Drink came (Phillip watching the midwife pouring out porter from a flagon and refreshing herself) and Mummie was in bed and he must play in the garden. He went to look at Mrs. Bottle Black Drink in the kitchen. She was not there, but her bottle was. He took what he thought of as its hat off the bottle's head, and after poking his finger in the neck, licked it, not liking the taste; but fascinated by the black pouring, he tilted the bottle on the floor. It was nice black splash. Having splattered it about, he remembered Daddy-things, and hurried out into the garden.

He found the scraper, and did some digging and splashing and then what Daddy did and was a Goodboyanddontannoy when he stood the scraper against the wall beside Daddy's spade, Daddy's fork, Daddy's rake, Daddy's trowel, Daddy's hoe. And it was nice and safe with many people-faces in the house and no one telling him he must not, and new Auntie's cream bun. And Daddy kissed him and silver sweetie went *crack crack* with Daddy's white penknife and told him he had a little sister and Phillip thought that was the new name of the sweet and liked little sister and Grannie gave him new shiny shilling for his money box which rattled and he went by-byes with it and Golly. And Hanky goodasgold.

That evening Richard did not see the wooden scraper standing in line, so neatly with the other garden implements; for Minnie, seeing it first, had fastened it back in its place on the handle of the spade. Hetty had told her of the previous scraper, and of the trouble it had very nearly brought.

The Hill, once a place where a fellow might walk with some degree of privacy, was fast becoming spoiled, in Richard's eyes. The forty acres had been fenced in with iron railings. There were gravel paths, iron gates at the various entrances, notice boards with the rules and regulations of the London County Council printed upon them, and varnished over against the weather. There were seats at intervals. Upon the crest a bandstand now stood.

Hither on summer evenings swarmed the masses, as Richard thought of them: the great unwashed from the slums on the low ground south of the river. Hundreds, thousands of men and women arrived with pale-faced unwashed brats in mailcarts and soap-boxes on wheels every Thursday evening during the summer, to hear the Band playing. Sometimes a breeze brought the strains of brassy music as he toiled during the long evenings in the garden.

The little garden, in size between five and six square poles, was Richard's delight. He had a pet hedgehog which lived in the rough grasses and old leaves at the bottom of the fence. It ate the big black slugs, and could be seen, and heard, rustling and grunting in the twilight. It came forth to a saucer of milk. There was a brown owl, too, that flew in the half light to a branch of one of the elms in the waste land over the fence, where was a black soil he dug up and tipped over in pailfuls, for the making of a meat-soil. Otherwise it was a deadly kind of land he was trying to convert for vegetables and flowers.

The first thing he had done was to dig up the top spit, for a bare fallow. Now the yellow clay was baked hard, the ends of bindweed roots brown and withered in the clots turned up by the spade. Ugh, ugly London clay! Soil of fogs and bricks, rows of brick houses being run up everywhere by the jerry builders. The view from the Hill, which he crossed every day to and from the station, was becoming ugly. There he was, part of it all. Gone were the hopes of Hetty on a bicycle beside him, pedalling into the countryside. He must go alone; or not at all.

On Thursday evenings the crest of the Hill swarmed with shouting children, unwashed faces, pale and grimy, little girls wearing hats and coats and boots cast-off from their elders. In the late twilights of the summer evenings the southern slopes held their scores of dark and faceless couples lying unmoving in the grass: an objectionable, almost an offensive sight. For Richard liked to be alone with his thoughts on the Hill; he never thought that perhaps the couples on the grass had similar ideas.

On Thursday evenings the great attraction was the Crystal Palace firework display. From the ridge a couple of miles or so distant rockets arose and broke into sprays of colours, inducing from the dim slopes long-drawn *oo-hs!* and *ah-ahs!* of wonder and admiration. The swarming of the masses out of their sunless streets was a sign of the times, the end of an age, the beginning of the masses becoming vocal. Already agitators were busy. On Sunday afternoons, by the oak on the eastern part of the Hill, speakers ranted and held forth on the woes of the workers, and more than one red flag was unfurled. Richard had gone up one Sunday to listen, and had told Hetty, on his return, that all he had heard was prejudice, ignorance, and soap-box hot-air. Still, it was letting off steam, and free speech was the Englishman's right. But the utter rubbish that was spouted there! The usual socialistic nonsense, that Jack was as good as his master! Liberalism under Gladstone had paved the way for Labour agitation, which led to Socialism, and so to the terrors of class-warfare and Communism.

"Yes, dear, of course, naturally," agreed Hetty, half-listening, while thinking that at times he was rather like one of the speakers round the Socialist Oak himself.

One June evening of that year the Hill was transformed. For weeks a great bonfire near the bandstand had been building. Faggots and branches of trees, tar-barrels in the middle, a mass as high and compact as a house, for the Queen's Diamond Jubilee. In the twilight Richard carried his son up the wide gravel way beyond Hillside Road, planted on either side with may-thorns, to see the sights. He left pocket-book, all money, and watch and chain behind; and carried his oak walking stick on his arm. Minnie was to have come with them; but at the last moment was left behind. Burglars might take advantage of the celebrations to break into the house. Hetty must not be left alone with the baby. So Richard went with Phillip in his arms, the boy wrapped up and wondering what was to happen: something exciting, he could feel. And it was all strange and frightening, all red like his sleep-pictures, called nightmare by Mummy, when the ninganing man and the ninganing and all had been red.

The flames ran up the forty-foot bonfire and soon all the people were moving back from the big red. The wood was crackling and the tar-barrels roaring, and all the faces red in the fire light. Shouts, cries, all the sky on fire—he hid his face by Daddy's tickling beard and cried for Minnie. Before he took the child home, Richard went apart from the crowd of many thousands of people with gilded faces around the perimeter of heat, turning his back upon the great roaring fire, the sparks coiling and whisking hundreds of feet into the air. He walked to the southern crest of the Hill and looking across the lights of houses and streets below, saw many beacons burning far away. There were nearer fiery tongues leaping upon Honor Oak Hill and Sydenham and Shooter's Hill, with smaller speckles all the way to the North Downs. Chains of beacons ringed the base of the London night to Hampstead and Highgate and distant Hainault and Epping. His imagination took fire; he thought of the tongues of flame from Poldhu in Cornwall to Dunkery Beacon on Exmoor, a living girdle of flame from the hills of Cranborne Chase and the Great Plain above the grey spire of Salisbury Cathedral to Portsdown Hill and eastwards to Ditchling, in Sussex; onwards to Wrotham Hill and Caesar's Camp above Folkestone in Kent: the midsummer night filled with fire along the coasts of England, far north to the pikes of Northumberland and the remote grey capes of Scotland. Great Britain was aflame! Sixty years a Queen! Nearly into the Twentieth Century! He was the father of a son and daughter in the greatest nation on earth! Could it all be possible?

"Look, Phillip, bonfires everywhere, for the Old Queen!"

"Mummy p'e Daddy, mummy p'e Daddy".

Richard sighed. Fancy forsook him. With memories of his boyhood *gone for ever and ever*, he walked in the ruddy twilight down the broad gravel to his home again, the child quiet against his shoulder.

He was taken up to bed at once, and Richard said he thought

he would return upon the Hill, for it was an historic occasion; but feeling suddenly weary, he settled in his armchair, and read the Golden Extra of *The Daily Trident*, printed in gilt letterpress for the Diamond Jubilee. He had an evening paper, too, which he intended to put away, for his son to read when he was a man. That day the old Queen had driven to St. Paul's Cathedral for the service, which had taken place on the steps, because she was too weak to get out of the State Carriage.

Well, it was the end of an age all right; and another near-terrifying thought came to him, that almost before life had begun, he was approaching middle-age. Next birthday he would be thirty-two. How far away seemed the holiday in North Devon with brother John and Jenny, Theodora and Hetty, and the baby in its specially made wicker basket. Could it have been only two years ago? And had Jenny been dead only five short months? Jenny, so beautiful and wise and calm, the one he had, from the moment he had seen her, loved with his soul, was dead; and John left with a baby son, one year and eight months younger than Phillip. She had died in childbirth during the gale that had swept all England last December, the same night that the Chain Pier at Brighton had collapsed in the storm. He had cried as he walked to the station after he had read John's telegram.

Richard sighed and closed his eyes; then started up, as a cry came from the kitchen. At once he thought of burglars; his hair twitched coldly on his neck; he thought of his special constable's truncheon which he kept inside his desk. He went to the door.

It was nothing, Hetty assured him, nothing at all. "I was only startled for the moment, by the sight of a mouse."

"You are becoming a nervous little thing, aren't you?"

Richard was never irritable now that Minnie was with him. Minnie and Richard often talked and laughed together about the old days. He showed her his cases of butterflies, and she peered at them, murmuring at their beauty and precision in line. She was devoted to Richard; she was able to endure an alien living mainly through him, the only one left to her. She was almost selfless, almost entirely subordinated to his feelings. His true, or inner living, was held in affection for Minnie; and the rows of pinned and mummified insects were as real to her as to him.

Hetty had cried out because suddenly as she was suckling the baby beside Minnie a mouse had appeared on Minnie's lap; and before she could say anything, Minnie had sprung up and with a shake of her skirts had jerked it into the open grate. It had screamed in the flames and tried to run over the hot coals. Hetty had hidden her eyes. How could Minnie do such a thing?

Minnie was now living for the day when she would see her Fatherland again. She thought London was the dirtiest and cruellest city in the world. The filthy streets, the untidiness, the careless ways of people, their acceptance of low standards, and above all, the look in the faces of the children seen in the streets, all blank and worried, had given her *heimweh*, homesickness for the clean and orderly countryside of her childhood. Truly the Englanders called their country the Motherland, for they treated it as so many treated their wives, with no *mitleid*, and often with unkindness. How she had suffered for her poor *hochgeboren baronin*, her father and brothers killed in the war, and then a cruel Englander for husband! But God in His Mercy had taken her, and surely her spirit on its way to Heaven had gone back to Lindenheim, to the beautiful schloss on the side of the hill, where she belonged.

So Minnie departed. Richard obtained leave to see her off from Liverpool Street Station, on the train for Harwich and the Hook of Holland. The outside porter from Randiswell came up with his trolley to take her corded wooden box early one morning. When the moment came, of parting from the place that Minnie could not bear, a place neither of the town nor of the countryside, suddenly Minnie looked stricken. Fortunately at that moment Mrs. Bigge popped out of her front door, beaming with affection, and trotting up the porch, put her arms round the older German woman and hugged her.

"Pleasant journey, dear, and don't forget us, will you? We won't forget you, and your beautiful yellow skirt, will we, Mrs. Maddison? Nor will dear little Phil, in a hurry, with his 'Minnie Mummie', bless his little heart. Well I must not keep you, I've left my iron on the gas-ring, so tootleoo, and give my love to Germany. I've never been there, but I know it is very beautiful."

With a wipe of an eye and wave of hand Mrs. Bigge hurried away down the front path lined with candy-tuft and London Pride growing in the rockery, with some fleshy cactus-like plants,

and so into her own house again. And there her face was, between
the Nottingham lace curtains of her front room, beside an
aspidistra, ready to smile at last farewell to Minnie.

Mrs. Bigge was much affected at the departure. For Hetty,
too, the occasion held a sense of desolation; and for a terrifying
instant it seemed that every time you said goodbye it was bringing
death a little nearer. Every parting was a kind of oblivion;
every tick of the clock said goodbye. How very sad was change!
You met people, and places, and then—goodbye! Very shortly
the dear, dear house in Cross Aulton would be in other hands,
for Mamma had said that Pappa was thinking of giving it up,
it was far too large, now that only one child was left at home,—
Joey already grown up, and in the Firm!

Her face smiled, her lips quivered, her eyes were bright with
unbroken tears. Oh sonny, come to Mother, hug Mother, hold me
close dear little son, she thought to him. You, little son, who have
such large serious eyes, Little Mouse, you understand, don't you,
Sonny? We'll be together when Minnie and Daddy have gone,
won't we, Sonny?

Phillip was sitting on the stairs, looking at the scene through
the bars of the banisters, his mouth down at the corners, very
quiet in the immensity of so much movement.

"Ach, how can I go, how can I leave you all, whom I love
so dearly?" cried Minnie, laughing and smiling, when the last
moment was come, and the door wide open. Ach, mein lieb'
ganschen, will you not miss your Minnie? How may I go now?
And the lieb' dark-eyed Mavis, so called because the Dinkelweizen
heard a drossel, a thrush, singing on the top of the little elm-tree
at the bottom of the garden! That was just as it should be,
naturlich! For all true things come only from Nature. It was his
German blood. Ach, the Englanders were at heart like the
Deutsche! Had not the good Queen married a German
hochgeboren Prince, noble Albert? Then why was it that she was
leaving all her dear freunde und verwandte—her kith and
kin—for what after thirty-three years must now be entirely new
and strange? Duty, duty called. Auf wiedersehen! Auf wiedersehen!
Auf wiedersehen! Grüsse Gott! Hetty, Mrs. Bigge, and Phillip
watched the two turn the corner—a last wave of the hand——

Hetty walked up the porch crying. Phillip was crying too.
They sat down in the kitchen and cried together, mother clasping

son. The house would never be the same again. Ah well, she must try and be worthy of all that Minnie had taught her, keeping the larder and scullery neat and fresh and clean as Dickie liked all things to be. And then as she was wiping away tears from two faces, both smiling again, there came a ring at the bell in the corner of the kitchen ceiling, and Phillip was excitedly pointing out the red signal behind the glass of the box and saying, "Front door, Mummie, front door!"

"Open it, will you please, Sonny? I think it must be Aunty Bigge."

He ran to open the door, and there stood Mrs. Bigge, with a steaming pot of tea in one hand.

"New Auntie come, Mummie, New Auntie come!"

"Yes dear, it's your new Auntie who loves you! I thought a little company just now would be the very thing for us both," cried Mrs. Bigge, cheerfully. And at once life seemed to be flowing again.

"Ah well, we must make the best of it, mustn't we, Mrs. Bigge?"

"Yes dear, and what you need now is a nice sensible young girl from 'Old Loos'am' down in the High Street. That's what they call Miss Thoroughgood, of the Agency. I would not wish to interfere in your affairs, of course, were it not that your own mother lives so far away."

"Thank you, Mrs. Bigge. Mamma did think of moving nearer, now that all her children are flown, except the youngest, she says."

"Yes dear, she was telling me the very selfsame thing on the day little Mavis was born. And I said to her, 'Mrs. Turney, why not move into Hillside Road, there is a house vacant right next door, where you can keep an eye on your grandchildren.'"

"Oh Mrs. Bigge, I expect she will have forgotten all about it by now!"

Mrs. Bigge misinterpreted the anxiety on Hetty's face. "No, don't you believe it, dear! Why, she said she would talk it over with your Papa. Cross Aulton is a nice place, I've heard, but too far away from you for your Mum's liking, I gathered. It is nice for a girl to have her mother near, especially when she has such an understanding one as you have, dear."

"Yes, Mrs. Bigge." Hetty was in a flurry. Mamma next to her would be too good for words, but—what would Dickie say?

The baby was crying in the crib upstairs. "I must feed the baby now, if you will excuse me."

"Goodness gracious, and I must go back to my iron on the gas ring! It will be red hot. Well, don't hesitate to let me know, dear, if you need anything. Just rap on the back window with the bamboo cane I have leaned against the fence, it will save you having to come round to the front door."

Papa and Mamma living next door! Whatever would Dickie say? Oh, pray that Mrs. Bigge would not mention it to him, if she spoke to him over the fence while he was gardening! But poor Mamma! How awfully ungrateful she was, not wanting her own mother, who had felt for her as now she was feeling for her own little daughter. But it was not that she *really* did not want her. Mamma would understand.

Mrs. Turney did understand. She arrived later in the day, knowing that her daughter would be feeling a little overcome, with two babies alone in the house. It was a happy inspiration that brought her over, she could see by the look in her darling's face the moment she opened the front door.

Sarah remained with Hetty until shortly before six, on her way to spend the night with her elder daughter Dorrie. She had told Hetty a little of her worry about Dorrie, for her marriage to Sidney Cakebread was not going very well. But with four little ones to be considered, perhaps things would come right; one must always hope for the best, and leave such matters in God's hands; and Sidney Cakebread was a good man, in every sense of the word.

Seeing how Mamma was worried, Hetty did not say anything about the idea that she might be coming to live with Papa next door.

Chapter 5

"OLD LOOS'AM"

WITH A feeling of optimism Hetty next morning set out with Mrs. Bigge to pay a visit to the Domestic Servants Agency of "Old Loos'am" in the High Street. Hetty had every confidence in leaving her two babies in the care of Mrs. Feeney. She would only be gone for an hour and a half at the most, so there need be no worry about Mavis waking up hungry. Her next feeding time was two o'clock, and now it was only just after half past ten. She could allow herself two hours, with safety.

Hetty carried the shopping basket she had bought at Hyères on the Riviera, ages and ages ago it seemed to her, more than four whole years had passed since that remote, faraway time. Ah well, she sighed thinking of the untrammelled joy of her girl-hood, everyone had to grow up. Had she not her dear husband instead, and the dearest little son in the world, and the loveliest baby daughter with brown eyes, to whom Dickie had taken with such delight? It was strange how Sonny did not appear to have any interest in Mavis: could he be jealous? Dickie crooning over Mavis, she had observed, caused him to hide under the table. Dickie laughed, thinking it funny.

Mrs. Bigge and Hetty walked down the asphalt pavement of Hillside Road. The petty cracks of the dark surface were already pierced by bindweed, now showing its pink flowers from the clay beneath. "Aren't they pretty?" said Hetty. Mrs. Bigge agreed. She carried a shopping basket of wicker, from the basket-maker in Randiswell, who soon would be gone now: for a row of new, modern shops was to replace some of the older, weather-boarded cottages of the hamlet.

Hardly had they turned the corner of Hillside Road into chestnut-lined Charlotte when a man, walking down from the hill, opened the gate of No. 11, after a quick counting of the houses downwards from the top of the road. He walked under the glass porch and rang the bell. Mrs. Feeney opened the door.

"Why good morning Mr. Hugh! Mrs. Maddison has just

gone out, only just this minute. I wonder you did not see her going down the road, sir. She is with Mrs. Bigge from next door. They're going down to the High Street. You will overtake them quite easily, if you hurry, Mr. Hugh."

"How are you, Mrs. Feeney? Well, I hope? Two of them, you say? Perhaps I'd be in the way."

"No, Mr. Hugh, I'm sure they would be delighted to see you. Mrs. Bigge is very nice, you'd like her, sir."

"Right, I'll vamoose. See you later!" And with a waggle of his straw boater Hugh Turney was gone.

He walked quickly down the road, and at the first bend he saw them below, where Charlotte Road ended in Randiswell Lane. He walked faster, not wanting to lose sight of them. Hurrying round the corner, he came upon them unexpectedly. They had stopped on the other side of the road, and were looking at a small shop with second-hand furniture on the sidewalk outside it. They had not seen him.

Acting on an idea, Hugh Turney walked back the way he had come. As soon as he was round the corner, he pulled something black from his pocket, which he fastened by two loops over his ears. It was a false beard.

"Eh bien, mesdames!" he said, with the gesticulation of a stage Frenchman. "Alors! En avance! Maintenant pour la plume de ma tante!"

Setting his boater at a slight angle, and perking up the waxed ends of his moustache, Hugh Turney advanced with a slightly mincing step, swinging a malacca cane with one hand, the elbow of the other arm raised, as though he were carrying a bouquet for a lady. In this guise he passed his sister and her companion on the other side of the road. Proceeding onwards he came to the Railway at the corner by the station, where, seeing that the two women were some distance behind, he entered through the ornamental glass-panelled doors and called for a brandy and seltzer. This he sipped while watching for them to pass beyond the window.

The publican, a fat man in shirt-sleeves, standing behind the bar, suddenly uttered a loud belch of gas, which had generated from an excess of raw onion, white bread, and gorgonzola cheese.

"Comment?" said Hugh.

"Pardon," said the publican. "I gets the wind, see." He spoke in a feeble, sorry voice.

"Vraiment," replied Hugh, stroking his false beard. "Il y a beaucoup de mots vrai parlé de l'estomache."

"'Ow much?" asked the publican.

"I remarked that many a true word is spoken from the chest," replied Hugh, removing the beard to feel the point of his chin.

"Oo d'yer fink you are? What's the game, trying to be funny?" enquired the publican, in a rougher, rousing voice, as more wind broke from him.

"I am Gonzalo the Wandering Violinist, and I am, alas, trying to be funny," replied Hugh.

"Well, you can 'king well start doin' some wanderin' nah, you poncified little tich," roared the publican, now in possession of his full self. He made as if to lift the mahogany flap in the bar counter, to chuck out the sauce-box.

Bearded once again, Hugh swallowed the rest of his drink. "Bonjour, petit pomme de mon oeil!" he cried, and with a bow, backed out through the door, leaving the irate man staring at his retreating figure.

Over the bridge Hugh caught up with the others, and slowed his pace to a saunter, keeping half a dozen yards behind them, swinging his cane and now walking with splayed feet, his jaw dropped in the guise of a simpleton. "Ah ha, my old Alma Mater!" he cried, gazing at the red-brick Public Baths, with the tower in front. "Ha ha, they'll never get me in there any more. Scrub, scrub, scrub for a week, and they discovered my shirt. Scrub, scrub, scrub for another week, and they found my vest. Scrub, scrub, scrub until all the brushes were worn out—but they never found me!"

"Don't turn round, dear, but there is a strange man behind us," whispered Mrs. Bigge; whereupon Hetty turned half round, to see for a moment what appeared to be a bearded Frenchman. "Cross the road, dear, he is following us," whispered Mrs. Bigge, a little later.

The Frenchman followed.

When they came to the High Street, Mrs. Bigge said, "Look in the shop with me, dear, we can then give him the go by."

The strange man also stared in the shop, a little behind them. A tram rattled slowly past in the middle of the street, pulled by three dejected horses in line. "Ve Anglais zont a nation of har'nimal loveurs!" exclaimed the Frenchman.

Mrs. Bigge nudged Hetty, "Don't look at him, dear, he is either trying to scrape acquaintance, or else escaped from the Infirmary." This was a local institution recently erected by the Metropolitan Asylums Board.

They walked on down the High Street, relieved that the stranger was now some way behind. Outside the Domestic Servants Agency, Mrs. Bigge said, "Now dear, you go in, and tell 'Old Loos'am' that you require a girl to train. Do not offer more than eight pounds a year, mind. That is the proper wage. If you agree to pay more, Miss Thoroughgood will only get it out of the girl in registration fees, as she calls it. I'm just going down to the butcher's to buy my hubby some tripe, it's his harp night. He likes tripe for supper with onions before the practice in the front room with Norah. Hullo, that fellow's still hanging about. What do you suppose he's after? There, I did not mean to alarm you, dear. A foreigner, by his appearance, and you know what foreigners are. Perhaps he's come over for the Jubilee and lost his way. Ah, he's found one way, I see," for Hughie had turned into the Castle, for another b. and s.

"Thank goodness he's gone. I'll come back for you here, dear, and mind now, don't be put off by Miss Thoroughgood's manner or appearance. She is a stuck-up old thing, she can't forget the old days of Macassar Oil, she was Mr. Roland's housekeeper. You know, Roland the Macassar Oil King, that's why they call her 'Old Loos'am', he used to be the big man round here, fancied himself as the Squire." And with a sudden "Here, give us a kiss!" Mrs. Bigge hugged Hetty, sang out "Tootle-oo," and hurried away.

Miss Thoroughgood's Domestic Servant Agency was in one half of a shop, the other half being what Mrs. Feeney would call a snob's shop, and Hetty a boot repairer's. Miss Thoroughgood, when away from her office, liked to think of it as a bootmaker's. Rows of misshapen foot-gear stood on a high bench before the leather-apron'd snob and his assistant. A continual knocking and banging accompanied Miss Thoroughgood's particulars of her servant girls' ages, religions, references, and experience.

Hetty entered the shop, and after a brief glance at her, Miss Thoroughgood continued writing. In the glance she had observed

that the caller was dressed in a clean but old-fashioned style, and
judged her to be a governess in search of employment. Hetty
was wearing her boater hat, with a blue serge shirt and short
jacket with a rolled-back collar faced with white. Under the
jacket was a plain white blouse topped by a high starched collar
and a dark blue tie. A good class of young person, thought Miss
Thoroughgood, and the thought induced her to say, in a regal
tone of voice, as she continued writing, "I will not keep you a
moment, young woman."

Banging of leather sounded through the partition. When it
stopped Hetty heard the scratch of the steel pen upon the paper.
Miss Thoroughgood appeared to be cogitating upon some matter,
for her muttered words were audible. "Now let me see." Miss
Thoroughgood picked up some cards. "H'm. Yes. The Very
Reverend H'm-H'm recommends—but she expects twenty-five
pounds, and board wages when the family is out of Town. Too
demanding. H'm. Major the Honourable H'm-h'm requires—
does he now! Not if I know it, the old ruffian! I won't keep you
a moment, young woman. Hopeless, hopeless! What *do* they
expect for eighteen pounds a year nowadays? Why, in Mr.
Roland's time, when Lord Dartmouth called to see him——"

The banging was resumed.

Miss Thoroughgood was a big woman, grey and puffy, looking
as though her body was composed largely of white bread, which
indeed was the case. The body, except for the hands, ears, and
small areas of skin behind the neck, was covered by a façade.
She wore a wig, her eyebrows were painted black and her lips
red, her face was powdered, the cheekbones rouged, the rims
of her eyelids were blackened with a mixture of lamp-carbon and
gum arabic. Above all this, like a Martello tower in defence of
the façade, was a hat that held Hetty's gaze in fascination and
wonder.

As she was staring at it, Miss Thoroughgood appeared to read
her thoughts; for the black-rimmed eyes looked up, while the
rest of the ensemble remained immobile, as she said:

"I shall not be very long. I have just to finish my letter to the
wife of our mayor."

"Oh, I have plenty of time, thank you," replied Hetty.

Miss Thoroughgood smiled, unexpectedly revealing long
yellow hare's teeth. At once Hetty thought of the Mad Hatter in

Tenniel's illustrations to *Alice in Wonderland.* As for the hat, Hetty had never seen anything like it. It was of purple plaited straw, wreathed with two ostrich feathers, one pink and the other black. They were connected in front with a rosette bow of mauve silk, displaying a large paste buckle. From the back of the hat arose several willowy aigrettes. Various sprays of artificial flowers, including marigolds and forget-me-nots, were secured upon otherwise bare places of the plaited purple straw. Two humming birds were mounted, one on either flank, upon the superstructure, which was underpinned by ten-inch hat-pins of blued steel, with globular black china heads.

With this armour of her soul Miss Thoroughgood faced the disintegrations of the new age and of her body.

"Are you new to the district?" she said, her pen pausing.

"Yes, I am in a way, though my——" Hetty was going to say 'husband', but Miss Thoroughgood cut her short, with a question.

"Then you know the Quaggy brook?"

"I don't think I do," replied Hetty, puzzled. What an extraordinary question!

"Then you will never have known Loos'am as it was, and as it ought to be, young woman," Miss Thoroughgood managed to say, through the tapping and thumping of the snobs. "Let me tell you that I myself have often picked wild flowers upon its banks, but where are those banks now? They are making an artificial canal-bed of concrete, and taking our brook under something they call an Arcade—what could be farther from Arcadia, indeed?"

"Yes, I am afraid they are building everywhere today."

"And what buildings! Look at our High Street, look what is happening to it. Architectural splendours of the Caroline and Georgian periods are almost daily being torn down, and the rubbish of the modern jerry-builders being run up in their place. The tragedy is, no one seems to mind. Do you, for instance?"

"I love old things and old places," said Hetty.

Miss Thoroughgood looked with new interest at the face before her, appraising candid brown eyes and child-like smile. A nice face, a fresh face.

"I will take down your particulars in a moment," she said. "That is, if you are not in a hurry?"

"Oh no, Miss Thoroughgood."

"In the old days," she went on, "when proper standards of conduct were imposed from above, let me tell you, there was not this frantic hurry——" She drummed her fingernails on her desk. "Really, what one has to put up with nowadays——" Her face seemed to sag; her other hand clutched her side; her eyes closed as in pain. Hetty wondered if she were ill.

With a deep sigh Miss Thoroughgood recovered herself. "Where was I? Oh yes, of course, the Quaggy is being put underground, for a terrace of so-called modern shops, I hear, with wide plate-glass windows, for the display of goods, for one and all to gaze upon. In the old days, let me tell you, shops were *shops*, and people went *into* them to select their purchases. Nowadays we are, apparently, to be confronted with wide plate-glass windows, for all to gaze upon, and the lowest of the low to be tempted to covet goods which can never be theirs. Do you think that can be right?"

Hetty began to see why the strange old-fashioned personage was nicknamed "Old Loos'am". Miss Thoroughgood went on to say that though the Borough had changed for the worse, she prided herself that she did not change with it. Had she not for forty years been housekeeper to Mr. Alexander Roland, whose Macassar Oil had been used upon most of the Crowned Heads of Europe—and some in Africa, too, but of course they did not count? Had she not been an associate of Mr. Roland, who had been responsible for the innovation of an entirely new word in the English language? Did her listener know that an entirely new article of domestic use had come about because of Mr. Roland's world-famous oil?"

"Of course, the antimacassar!" exclaimed Hetty.

"Exactly!" declared Miss Thoroughgood. "And now let me ask you what has taken the place of Macassar Oil? Bear's Grease! Or rather, imitations of it which the public are exhorted in advertisements to refuse! That it can so easily be imitated shows the nature of the stuff that has, in the modern manner, imposed counterfeit and sham in place of what was once old-established and true!"

Miss Thoroughgood went on to say that the large house over which she had once presided on the Rosenthal estate, with its cedars and peacocks and wide lawns, where Mr. Roland had lived like a gentleman upon its several acres of grounds and gardens, was now being covered by the boxes of jerry builders.

Miss Thoroughgood did not say that she had been the house-keeper, nor did she voice her abiding disappointment that she had been left, in his will, only £10 for every year of service with her late employer. With part of the £420 she had bought a small house in the High street with a shop-front; and in this had opened an office wherein she considered that her status as gentlewoman, and her experience in managing a retinue of servants would be invaluable to those of her own class. But something had happened to her own class; it seemed to have vanished, and in its place was —what? People who thought themselves above their station, just as the rows of little semi-detached villas had replaced the dignified houses of the days that were no more. And what sort of people were they who came to her Agency for servants? The majority of them were nobodies, with their aspidistras in the front rooms.

Through the banging of leather, the tapping of nail, the treadle of stitching machine, "Old Loos'am" concluded her attack upon the present.

"I call this the Age of the Aspidistra. Why, in our palm court at Rosenthal, we had, let me tell you, six castor-oil ferns as tall as some of the new houses! In those days everyone who was anyone had a butler, footmen, and it goes without saying, a carriage and pair. Today modern Loos'am, which pronounces the place with an 'ish', just as licorice is nowadays pronounced lickorish, comes to my Agency for what? 'A young, untrained girl'! That shows what pretentious nobodies are swarming over Loos'am today! Now then, to business. You require a post as a nursemaid to a superior family, am I right?"

The banging and knocking from the other half of the shop stopped when the door opened, striking a bell, and a slim, straw-hatted and black-bearded man came in. He bowed to Miss Thoroughgood and swept off his boater.

"And how may I be of service to you, if you please," as Miss Thoroughgood's towering hat was inclined with suitable hauteur towards the newcomer.

"Ah, mademoiselle, veuillez me dire, s'il vous plait, parlez vous français?" enquired Hugh, hoping to high heaven that the old buzzfuzz didn't.

"Non, monsieu." Miss Thoroughgood looked non-plussed.

"Eh bien, then I must wait for a *Baedeker*," and the supposed Frenchman spread his hands.

"You speak a little English, I presume?"

"Ver' little, ever so tiny, ma'mselle." The speaker's manner was uneasy. "I vill vait for diction-aire, yes?" He swept off his hat again. Miss Thoroughgood looked at Hetty significantly. The hammering had not been resumed. Gratefully Miss Thoroughgood thought of the nearness of the snobs, should a lunatic have come in to attack her.

"Now," she said, importantly, turning to Hetty, "Tell me what it is you want."

"I was wondering if you know of a little maid to live in, and help with a little boy, and take him out in the mailcart for walks sometimes."

"Oh, I see. I beg your pardon! Your face is so young and fresh, I was deceived! You require a junior nursemaid. What other staff do you keep?"

"I have a woman who comes in to clean one half day a week, and a full day on Mondays for the washing."

"And that is all, is it?"

"Yes," said Hetty, blushing.

"You are married, of course."

"Oh yes," smiling. "And I work in the house, and do the cooking. A young girl to help, generally, is what I require."

"That ees what I require, too!" cried Hugh. "Madame, permit me to—'ow do you zay it—to con-grat-u-latt you on your magnifique Paris Theatre Bloos!" He swept off his hat, and bowed once more.

Miss Thoroughgood looked startled: then she glanced down at her blouse, which covered her from waist to chin. She was flattered by the attention to it, for it had been bought for the Jubilee celebrations, only after considerable and intermittent desire and rumination. From close against her adam's apple to below the collar-bone was a gauzed yoke, with imitation pearl encirclement in several tiers, joined to an extensive shoulder frill in fine pleated muslin by a festooned band of mirror velvet, sprinkled with cut crystal cabochons. Miss Thoroughgood thought it most *distingué*. It gave her a feeling of being Society, with gay huzzars and gentlemen of the Household Cavalry about her; for upon the flanks of her Jubilee blouse were extended battlemented epaulettes of black jetted guipure over an underlay of ruby satin. Miss Thoroughgood had bought it specially for the garden party given by the Mayor and Mayoress, on the afternoon of the Jubilee celebration, together with an equally impressive hat. When Hetty had come in, Miss Thoroughgood had been writing her letter of thanks.

"Madame, I hoffer my sairvices to the young lady as valet and mailcart garçon to push, push, push—like this—you watch me pushing, ver' steady push-man——" and pretending to be pushing a mailcart, Hugh opened the door, closed it with one hand while with the other holding an imaginary handle, and disappeared beyond range of the window.

"He's been drinking, obviously," remarked Miss Thoroughgood, nodding the assembly of flora and fauna piled on her head. "He was no Frenchman, but some conceited nobody. His manner was all put on. Now, let me see what I can do for you. Nothing at present, I am afraid, for your requirements. But girls keep coming in, and I will send you the next one who registers with me. About sixteen pounds a year? Will you be prepared to pay that for a reliable girl?"

Hetty blushed again with embarrassment. Sixteen pounds a year! She said lamely, "I really do not know. You see, Mrs. Bigge, who recommended you to me——"

"Mrs. Bigge? Do I know a Mrs. Bigge? How do you spell it? With two gees, or one?"

"I think with two gees, Miss Thoroughgood."

"Well, I know a Mrs. Legge, with two gees, but not a Mrs. Bigge, with two gees. The Legges, I need hardly say, are a very old family connected with Loos' am. Our late Vicar was Canon the Honourable Legge, of course, brother of the lord of the manor, the Earl of Dartmouth, you know. Yes, the Very Reverend the Honourable Legge left us recently, on preferment to the bishopric of Lichfield."

"Yes, of course, I remember," said Hetty, hoping that she would not giggle at the picture of the Honourable Legge as a leg walking off by itself! Oh, dear, she must not laugh. She managed to say, "Of course, naturally, I remember. Mrs. Birkitt, the midwife, was also with Canon Legge, she has told me about the little Legges."

At this point she collapsed with laughter. That naughty boy Hughie had returned, wearing the false beard under his chin, in the manner of Brigham Young the Mormon. Holding up a finger as though he were preaching, Hugh said, "Do forgive me, dear lady, for not recognising you just now—I was but recently disguised as a gee with four legs—the usual number, you know— and right well I needed every one of them, for my enemies are hot in pursuit of me—I must away—Time waits for no man," and bowing yet again, with a sweep of his boater, Hugh retired.

"A joker," said Miss Thoroughgood. "It was obvious to me from the very first that he was an impostor. Frenchmen have little pointed beards. No, I was not taken in. Is he known to you, Mrs. — Mrs.?"

"I am Mrs. Maddison. He is my brother," replied Hetty. "I have not seen him for a long time, ever since we moved into our new house. He is always up to some joke or other."

"Your husband, or your brother?"

"Oh, how silly of me, my brother of course! Mr. Maddison is in the City."

"Indeed. Well, let me take your address, and I will see what I can do for you." She wrote down particulars. The hammering began again. Hetty paid a shilling fee, and accepted Miss Thoroughgood's *dictum* that £16 a year was the correct wage to offer. "The cost of living has gone up, you see," she said, playing with a silver pencil, her eyes on the desk before her. "There will be no further fees to be paid by you, of course, if we can suit you."

Hetty hesitated. Miss Thoroughgood, looking up and smiling her yellow hare-tooth smile, said, "Well, shall we say thirteen pounds, for a good class girl? Very well, good morning to you, Mrs. Maddison."

Hetty was glad to be outside. Hugh and Mrs. Bigge were waiting for her. Hugh insisted on taking them to coffee in a place with the words, GOOD PULL UP FOR CARMEN painted on the wall below the glass window. "You get the best coffee and dough-nuts in London in such places," he said. "But it is best to bring your own tin-can out of which to drink it," he added. "Well, perhaps I've made a mistake this time," he continued, sipping the greenish liquid. "They make the soup in the same crock as the coffee in this house, I fancy."

"Go on, drink it up," growled Mrs. Bigge in her deep voice. "It's hot, and I find it very tasty."

Hugh looked at her with interest. "Bravo," he said. "Spoken with the spirit of emancipation!"

Mrs. Bigge thought how happy Hetty looked. Poor girl, she was not properly appreciated by her husband. He would never unbend sufficiently to do what they were doing. "My!" she said. "If Josiah could see me where I am, he would think I have kicked over the traces!"

"What a wonderful character the old girl in the Agency is," said Hugh. "You know, Hetty, I want to stage an act on the halls, and the trouble is, I see so much about me—everyone I see, almost, is funny. I worked out an act, to include Little Old Carlo, the Ning-a-ning Man, complete with monkey and barrel organ. I as Gonzalo, the Wandering Violinist. I found a chap to play Carlo, but the music halls won't look at it. They want their crude beery songs. I think there is a future for sketches, comic characters not too far apart from real life—rather on the Dickens lines. But managers are the very devil—if you'll excuse the term, mar'm. They've no imagination. They want the same old gags and forms. They're like 'Old Loos'am', conventional. My lor', she's a character! She out-bowers the bower bird. Talk about fin-de-siècle! She is the midwife of the twentieth century, that rig-out."

Mrs. Bigge enjoyed herself greatly. He was such a refreshing young man, full of ideas.

"Yes," went on Hugh. "I must work out an idea, to use characters one meets with, as Dickens did. But managers are so fixed in their ideas of what they imagine the public wants. Oscar Wilde has blown a hole in the old convention, letting in fresh air, and I want to carry on for him—poor fellow, he's done for himself, I fear. He's rotting in a Paris garret. If I had the cash, I'd cross the Channel and seek him out and give him a wonderful dinner, just to let him know that it isn't everyone who's shocked by the exposé. Anyway, the man in his work, and his work is witty, and by heaven, if good christians are the salt of the earth, poets' wits are the pepper."

"Is that the Oscar Wilde whose trial filled 'The News of the World' a little while ago, Mr. Turney?" enquired Mrs. Bigge.

Now for it, thought Hugh: the old girl's liked me so far: now see her face fall. "Yes, ma'm," he said.

"Oh," exclaimed Mrs. Bigge. Then, "Did you know him, Mr. Turney?"

"Unfortunately not, ma'm, I had left the 'varsity when he honoured the Fin de Siècle with a visit. For had I been present, I would to-day be able to stand in the drawing-rooms of the assured and to claim, with another blackguard like myself, but also a man of genius, unlike myself—I refer of course to the celebrated Frank Harris—that Wilde remains my great friend."

Hetty was a little apprehensive, so she said, "My brother is a joker, Mrs. Bigge, and does not really mean all he says." She remembered Dickie reading her bits about the trial from *The Morning Post*, from his armchair, during several evenings in early spring, two years before. She remembered it well, for he had on the table beside him several envelopes containing seeds, left out from planting in the garden of Comfort House. She recalled a phrase Dickie had used. *It is all pure filth, of course.* Hetty had not known exactly what had happened, to cause such a trial, but ever since then the name *Oscar Wilde*, whenever she had heard it spoken or come across it in the newspaper, had repelled her, for the name conveyed to her an atmosphere of coarseness, badness, depravity, violence, and terror. Hughie's words, therefore, had hurt Hetty; so she did not want to believe them.

"I can see you are more than a fair weather friend," said Mrs. Bigge.

"Yes, of course he is, aren't you, Hughie?" cried Hetty, in relief. Then, to change the subject, she enquired if he had seen any Shakespearean plays lately.

"No," said Hugh. "But I have seen some of a new fellow, George Bernard Shaw, who is going to count quite a lot in the future, you mark my words. Do you read 'The Saturday Review,' ma'm?"

"No, Josiah takes 'The Daily Chronicle,' and we borrow 'The Church Times,' and sometimes 'The British Weekly,' so we are not in the swim of the Arts at all, Mr. Turney."

"But Mr. Bigge plays the harp beautifully, Hughie. Hughie plays the violin, you know, Mrs. Bigge. Yes!" she cried, happily, "He is very musical." She was excited to be nearing the prospect of seeing the house again, and Sonny and the darlingest little Mavis. It was time to go back.

"My Josie plays every Wednesday evening, here's the tripe for his supper," and Mrs. Bigge, stopping at her gate, held up the shopping basket. "Well, dear, it was a nice walk down to the High Street and back, I enjoyed myself hearing so much interesting talk from your brother. May I call you Hugh, young man? I am very nearly old enough to be your mother, you know."

"Yes, but only if we were children playing at 'Mothers and Fathers', ma'm! Please call me Hugh, I love it. And please believe me when I say that I am doubly glad that I came to visit m' sister today, for I have not only seen her, but have met one of her friends who, like herself, is of that rare quality which never ages—the quality of the eternally young in heart." And sweeping off his boater, Hugh bowed as he held open the gate of "Montrose" for Mrs. Bigge.

"Thank you, Hugh."

"And now, in the twinkling of an eye, I travel from the land of the haggis to the land of the sausage—from Montrose to Lindenheim——" as Mrs. Bigge let herself into her front door. "Well, old girl, I haven't enjoyed myself so much since we were all together at Maybury. You know the guv'nor is giving up the house at Cross Aulton, of course?"

Hetty was startled. "Oh, Hughie, when?"

"At Michaelmas next, I understand. So Dorrie told me. I spent the night with her. I'll tell you all about it later. Well, Mrs. Feeney, the bad penny has returned! Hullo, whose voice do I hear in the distance?"

They listened at the foot of the stairs. From far off came a gentle, plaintive cry.

"Minnie mummie, Minnie mummie, Minnie mummie."

"Just coming, Sonnie dear!" called up Hetty. "Has he been a good boy, Mrs. Feeney?"

"Oh yes, mum, as good as gold. So has Mavis, not so much as a stir while you've been gone. I took a peep now and agen, just to make sure she wasn't face down in that pillow Mrs. Cakebread sent you, ma'm. But she was rightsides up."

"OO-ee come mummie, Oo-ee come! Bile-inn tweedledee, bile-inn tweedledee, p'e mummie!"

"Straight from the lap of the gods!" said Hugh Turney.

"There's my public, Hetty, d'you see? The next generation! When the cursed modern idiom is swept away, all the pretentiousness, the façades, the hypocrisy of our age. Eh, Mrs. Feeney, whatsay?"

"There'll always be sweeping away of somp'in', Mr. Hugh. Now would you like a cup of tea, mum? The kettle's boiling. I've washed and hung out the diapers, mum."

"I think I would, and I am sure you could do with one, Mrs. Feeney. Hughie? All right, Sonny dear, Mummie is just coming! Be patient a little longer, dear. Hughie, go up and see Sonny, will you? He loves you so, he recognised your voice as soon as we came into the house. Tell him I'll be up soon."

Hugh went upstairs. Soon the boy's laughter followed, with joyful shouts and imitations of the violin, followed by bag-pipes. Hugh did this by holding back his head, thus stretching his neck, and with a finger and thumb closing nostrils, gave forth a nasal whining of varied pitch interrupted by taps on his adam's apple. Then in rapid succession he was a trumpet, a banjo, bassoon, drum, and other instruments. All the while his audience was standing by the cot-rails, its face responding to the artiste's every mood and gesture. There was a pause. "Enough of onomatopoeia, Phillip my son. Now we will have something decent. Poetry. How about the Ettrick Shepherd Lad? He ended up, like all poets, in a mess,

'Bird of the wilderness, Blithesome and cumberless, Sweet be thy mattins o'er moorland and lea——.'"

Fixing the child with his eyes, Hugh continued, while a feeling of sadness arose in him, *"Emblem of happiness, Blest be thy dwelling place—O, to abide in the desert with thee."*

He sighed. Phillip stared at the saddening eyes. Affected by the boy's attentive pathos, by the line of his sensitive mouth, drooping at the corners, by the feeling of wild moorland purity and spring-water, Hugh's voice became wild with longing as his spirit took possession of him. It became most tender, rising and falling in soft modulation.

> *"' Wild is thy lay and loud*
> *Far in the downy cloud*
> *Love gives it energy*
> *Love gave it birth.*

Where on thy dewy wing
Where art thou journeying?
Thy lay is in heaven
Thy love is on earth!
O'er fell and fountain sheen,
O'er moor and mountain green,
O'er the red streamers that herald the dawn!
O'er the rainbow's rim,
Over the moonbeam dim,
Musical cherub sing
Soaring away.
Then when the gloaming comes
Low in the heather blooms
Sweet will thy welcome and bed of love be.'"

Intently with the child's dark blue eyes upon him, Hughie concluded with slow intensity,

"'*Bird of the wilderness, blithesome and cumberless,*
O to abide in the desert with thee.'"

He closed his eyes, overcome by his feelings, which were of himself ever exiled from Love, in the luminous and tender vision of the spirit of Theodora, whom he had not seen since the christening of the boy two years before.

Hetty came into the room. "Oh, Hughie, you have been making Sonnie sad, look, there is a tear on his cheek. He is so easily upset, and must conserve his strength. He isn't very strong, you know."

"My dear sister, I merely recited James Hogg's 'Skylark', and drew a tear for beauty. He will thank me later on, for opening his eyes at an early age to the true values of the world."

"Yes, Hughie dear, please don't let what I said upset you. There, I was perhaps a little over-anxious." Phillip's eyes were now eagerly fixed on a paper bag she was opening. Out came a stale bun, one of four for a penny. Not only was this an economy, but they were better for the digestion, Dickie said. The boy seized the bun, and began to munch it.

"What do you say, Sonnie?"

The boy gulped, and said slowly and clearly, "Danke schön, mummie." Hughie laughed. "By Jove, he's got his wits about him, Hett!" Phillip laughed too. With bright eyes he repeated, "Danke schön, mummie p'e!"

"Minnie taught him to say it."

"What precocity! I'll put him in my act. The Ning-a-ning man, old Loos'am, Dick the Melancholy Lamp-post—dressed as such—playing the 'cello in the shades—Good God, what an original act!—then the Spirit of the Streets, of joy and heart-break!—Gonzalo! The Quick-change man with violin, and Sonnie just to watch and register what we put over the footlights. He can be dressed as a monkey on the barrel organ; we'll be billed as The Lost Spirits! Lost Spirits in search of a home in the Temple of Art! Don't say anything now, I must make some notes."

Hugh wrote rapidly in his notebook. He seemed to be weary afterwards. He sighed. "Well, all good things come to an end. I must be off, old girl."

"But you've only just come! You'll stay for some lunch?"

"I never eat in the middle of the day, thanks all the same. I must go, really. I've been writing lyrics, and must take one to a man I know, who's in with one of the leading publishers. Good-bye young feller, au revoir, auf wiedersehen, tootle-oo. You want to put him in long trousers, Hett old girl, he's a big boy now, too big for skirts. That long hair too, over his shoulders. Bless me, no one would know whether it was a little girl or not, unless the wind—

> "'There was a bonny Scotsman
> At the Battle of Waterloo
> The wind blew up his petticoats
> And showed his——'"

"Now Hughie, whatever you do, you must not go teaching Sonnie things he may repeat to his father, for goodness gracious sake!" said Hetty, with a nervous laugh. "I'll make you some cold mutton sandwiches, they won't take a minute, and you can eat them in the train if you are in a hurry.

"But do try and stay longer next time," she said down in the kitchen, carrying the saddle of South Down lamb. "I see any of the family so seldom nowadays, or anyone else, though one or two people have called. Do you remember the nice Mr. Mundy, the vicar of St. Simon's? He called, with Mrs. Mundy. He told me there is likely to be a new church built in Charlotte Road, but I shall never give up Mr. Mundy at St. Simon's."

"Well, you won't be lonely very much longer, Hetty. What does Dick say about it—the proposed move of our respected parents?"

Hetty did not understand.

"Didn't you know the Old Man was moving to this district?"

"No Hughie. Oh dear!"

Hetty had to sit down.

"I'm dashed sorry if it came as a shock, old girl. Yes, the Old Man's bought several properties in the neighbourhood, as an investment, so I heard from Mallard the chairman of the firm. Naturally I concluded, as the family is leaving Maybury, that the Old Man intended to come here to be near you."

Chapter 6

RICHARD'S BOHEMIAN EVENING

RICHARD enjoyed the first summer in his new house. He had joined St. Simon's Lawn Tennis Club, and now it was a habit, and a pleasurable one, to spend two evenings a week on the grass court adjoining the parish hall. Here was an oasis from the dry hot smells and sights of the City, from ammoniacal heat reflected from asphalt and sett-stone, the dust of dry horse-dung in nostrils and eye-corner, the everlasting clatter of hoof and rolling wheel.

At half-past five, while the sun was yet high in the west, he left the main doors of his office building in Haybundle Street and set out, one amidst thousands, for London Bridge, carrying his straw boater in hand as he swung along optimistically. He liked his work, his colleagues were, he considered, a thoroughly decent lot; and there was much less etiquette and decorum than in the old days of Doggett's in the Strand. There the rules about dress had remained rigid; the frock coat, the tall hat, and the umbrella were still *de rigueur*. Now in the summer he wore a jacket of black vicuna material as befitted his position and responsibilities, and a black waistcoat with grey, black-striped trousers of the same durable cloth.

Twelve minutes after leaving Wakenham station, by way of worn wide flagstones and gravel paths of the Hill, he arrived with his swinging stride, hat in hand, down the wide gravelled way to Hillside Road: twenty yards on asphalt, and the garden gate of Lindenheim clicked, and Hetty heard the familiar whistle as he walked under the porch: she heard the key in the door and the jingle of the bunch dropping into his trouser pocket, as in the hall he wiped his boots, dry and clean though they were, by habit on the mat at the foot of the stairs. Then the hat hung on its peg, and the folded *Trident* laid upon pegs above it, ready for the armchair later on.

While Hetty was preparing his evening meal, Richard went upstairs to take off his City clothes, first having turned on the cold tap of the bath, and then, in carpet slippers and dark blue

dressing-gown, he locked himself in the bathroom, for a refreshing immersion. This was something to be looked forward to all
the afternoon, cool though it was in the marble and mahogany
ground floor of the Town Department. Beautiful cold water,
aa-ah! as he sat down and then, raising knees and shifting body
forward, preparatory to extending his length and submerging,
that was the moment! He was primitive man in his original
element, according to Darwin. Was this the water of the river
Thames, or its tributary the Lea? Whence was it drawn? Perhaps
from deep wells in the chalk below the clay? He must remember
to ask Mr. Mundy. There was a knocking on the door.

"Dad, me come in. P'il good boy now, p'e, Daddy."

"Just a moment, old chap. Just a moment."

Richard dried himself on the hard Turkish towel and secured
it round his middle before slipping back the bolt. Phillip came
in, with a penny boat which his mother had given him—Hetty
had got it in exchange for three jam-jars from a man with a
barrow, in Randiswell hamlet. The jars had to be taken down,
for of course no barrow man would be allowed up Hillside Road;
nor would he venture to come, knowing his place. Hillside Road
was not Comfort Road.

Richard looked forward to his meal in the garden room, the
french windows opening upon what was to be a lawn from next
spring onwards. Now it was undergoing a bare fallow; and very
bare it looked, covered with cracked spade-slabs of hard yellow
clay. Still, the compost of leaf-mould was heaped under the
elm sapling at the bottom of the garden; the leaves were green
upon the trees; tomtits visited its branches for hanging green
caterpillars, and beyond was the field which was said to be without title deed or owner—a delightful piece of waste land, too
steep for building, grown with long grasses and here and there
a wilding thorn. Sometimes a kestrel hung over its slopes for
mice; butterflies drifted there. It was *rus in urbe*, Mr. Mundy,
the vicar, had declared, cycling down from the Hill to see how
Hetty was getting on that afternoon—the countryside verging
upon the town.

"Well," said Richard, now wearing his brown-striped white
flannel trousers, white shirt and tweed jacket, "well, I must be
thinking of my tennis", as he folded his table napkin neatly
beside his plate, with seven prune stones aligned on the edge. He

had already recited the inevitable, "Tinker, tailor, soldier, sailor, rich man, poor man, beggar man——" and laid down his spoon. Phillip, opposite him, beside Hetty, was a soldier for the occasion, since three prunes were deemed by Richard to be "enough for his little economy". However, the child had plans for taking both Daddy's stones and Mummy's stones, together with his own, to bed with him that night. "It will be the usual couple of sets, I suppose; and Miss MacIntosh will partner me against your good Vicar and his lady. What a pity Minnie has gone, for otherwise you would be able to come and partner me."

Hetty had often heard from Richard about Miss MacIntosh, the secretary to the Vicar, who helped him to run both the Antiquarian Society and the St. Simon's Lawn Tennis Club. Hetty had seen her on one occasion only, when she and Dickie had been invited to tea at the Vicarage. Hetty remembered her red hair and white skin from that occasion nearly three years before: she had been a little afraid of her. Why, she could not tell; but Hugh, who claimed a knowledge of anthropology, had explained that it was the natural dread of Celt for Dane. The Danes, like the Vikings, were killers, Hugh had declared.

Hetty said, with a little laugh, that she was afraid her tennis days were over.

"Cheer up!" said Richard, giving his prune stones to Phillip. "When the new maid comes, perhaps she will turn out to be reliable, the pearl beyond price, and then you must accompany me. It is a pity to waste your racquet. I see a string has gone. You should have kept it, as I told you, in the top of the cupboard in the kitchen."

"Yes, dear, I am sure you are right. But I think it was a mouse."

"But damp tautens the gut, and causes it to break. A mouse, indeed! What mouse would gnaw the gut of a cat? Why, it would be a cannibal!" and Richard laughed at his joke. Phillip laughed too, because his father was laughing.

"See, even the boy laughs at you. Give him your stones, Hetty. Now then, my boy, see if you can determine your fate!"

It *was* a mouse, she was sure. The same mouse that she had found in the last of her Christmas puddings in the larder. It had eaten a hole through the cloth and down to the bottom of the basin. Head first, it was asleep, after eating itself too fat to get out. At least it looked like it, for the mouse's tail-tip had been sticking out of the hole in the cloth, a very dirty little mouse. She had carried the basin to the bottom of the garden, and left it there; and returning an hour later, there the mouse was, still asleep, lying head down in the hole. So she had shaken it out, and it had run into the compost heap. And Hetty had burned the rest of the pudding, to get rid of the evidence. Thank goodness Dickie had not seen it in the larder!

Richard helped his son to determine his fate. Since he had given seven stones, making ten with Phillip's, and Hetty had added six, the boy's fate was decided—a thief! He looked quite pleased, with sixteen stones on his plate.

"Well, I'll be off on the Starley Rover, Hetty. Home about nine forty-five. We'll have a game of chess when I return, shall we?"

"Yes, dear, if you like."

The Starley Rover lived in the lavatory next to the sitting-room, against the wall. Propped against the other wall was the violoncello in its case, never opened nowadays. The small room was used as a store; Richard had fixed a couple of shelves there.

Soon, with cycle clips securing trouser bottoms round his ankles, Richard was walking down the flinty surface of Hillside Road, to mount a score of yards from the bottom and pedal away up Charlotte Road, and so to the tennis club eight minutes later.

"Ah Maddison, here you are! Now we shall have our match, what? Mrs. Mundy and I will, I hope, have our revenge for last Tuesday evening's debacle!"

"But I have only just arrived, sir, perhaps somebody else would care to play before me?"

"We have all played, and now for some of your cannon-ball services, to help commote the liver!"

Soon the white ball was passing to and fro under the lime trees whose honey had long been taken by bees and flies. Richard alone of the four played without a hat. His partner, Miss MacIntosh, was in white as usual, from tam o'shanter, jacket with leg-o-mutton sleeves, pleated skirt touching the lawn, to white canvas shoes. Richard felt himself to be in fine form, he was exhilarated to be in her company, though he was on his guard, being a little scared of her. He had to restrain himself from playing with the dash he felt capable of, since his opponent was both clerical and elderly, and therefore scarcely one to be the recipient of his fastest cannon ball service. When it came off, this service, delivered with pear-shaped racquet from the top of extended arm with all his strength, was unreturnable, so far as the other male members of the St. Simon's Lawn Tennis Club were concerned. Since Richard was over six feet in height, the ball descended a steep incline almost invisible over the net, to flick the forecourt dividing line within an inch or two of the chalk, whence, curving onwards, it passed the immobile opponent waiting tensely well beyond the back line, while he was still looking at the white puff of the strike upon the grass. If propelled at one particular angle of the racquet it swerved to the right; if upon the reverse, to the left.

But Richard could not bring himself to serve his cannon-balls to Mr. Mundy, despite the request for no mercy. "All is fair in love and tennis, Maddison!"

This remark, recurring again and again to his mind, discomposed Richard a little, behind the austere expression upon his bearded face. Did Miss MacIntosh give him more than a partner's glance of her green eyes, as she crouched slightly upon the back line, ready to drive back his service should it be returned?

Mr. Mundy was a player resourceful as he was steady. After it had seemed that a ball was beyond returning suddenly a lob would soar up almost to the height of St. Simon's grey tower, around which the shrill-whistling swifts chased one another; or the ball was cut sharply across the net, spinning upon its bounce or darting away unexpectedly. His underhand service, too, was deceptively gentle, the ball upon arrival within the forecourt liable to break away unpredictably. He was a cunning old fellow, thought Richard.

"Come come, Maddison, no favours to my cloth! Play your hardest, sir! Oh, well volleyed, Miranda! Upon my soul, you would be a match for the brothers Renshaw! 'Vantage out, to server. Your turn, my love. Oh, pretty to watch, pretty to watch! Ha ha, caught you on the wrong foot, Maddison! Game to us, my love, and set! Well played, Mrs. Mundy! Now let us all partake of some cool lemon squash under our linden trees, and enjoy a well-earned rest."

A row of deck chairs stood along one side of the court, in the shade. By them was a table with glasses, a bundle of straws, and a carafe of pale yellow liquid, in which ice floated, beside a dish for pennies. The money was understood to go towards the Girls' Friendly Society. Richard dutifully placed his penny in the dish, and bore his glass and straw to a chair three seats away from Miss MacIntosh. There he pretended interest in the single between two young women wearing straw-boaters pinned through their hair, whose mis-shots were the cause of some mortification to themselves, judging by the half-repressed "O-ohs", and "Oh dear" that accompanied the gentle parabolas from their spoon-like scooping.

"Come and sit nearer, my dear Maddison. I notice that you do not reverse your racquet for the back-hand volley, nor for the back-hand drive. I have not seen it done since Major Wingfield in the early 'seventies took out a patent for his new court which, as you may recall, was the shape of an hour glass."

"My father was a friend of Major Wingfield, sir, who taught him the stroke."

"Now that is most interesting. That must have been before the All England Croquet Club took a viper to its bosom, and admitted tennis playing to its sacred precincts! Do you play croquet, a sport much in decline since our young Amazons have preferred to beat the rubber ball rather than the wooden one. What do you think, Miranda?"

"I think both are good games, Vicar." Miss MacIntosh rose to speak to Mrs. Mundy, who was leaving the garden.

"You must come over with your lady wife and take a turn with us at the hoops," went on the Vicar. "Tennis to commote the liver is an excellent thing before preparin' one's sermon, but croquet is more the game for the family, helping to keep it together. No doubt you recall many happy hours spent with your parents and brothers and sisters with mallet and ball?"

"Yes, sir, croquet can be capital fun."

"Now tell me, how do you like your new house?"

But Mr. Mundy appeared not to be listening to Richard's answer to the polite enquiry. He seemed preoccupied with other thoughts. He glanced sharply in the direction where Miss MacIntosh had disappeared with Mrs. Mundy. The two women had gone through the gate at the end of the tall laurel hedge leading to the road upon whose grey-flagged sidewalk Richard strode morning and evening to and from the station.

"Ah, yes, the Antiquarian and Archeological Society! I have been meaning to ask you if you would care for me to put

your name forward. I recall our most interesting talk on the Hill
during the sledging, in the winter of 'ninety-five, do you remember?"

Richard thought that Mr. Mundy had done most, if not all,
of the talking on that occasion. "Yes, I do remember it well, sir."

"Well Maddison, we are watching a phase of history, of
geological history. Like a crustacean, modern man is raising
the subsoil all about him. In other words, we are witnessing an
extension of the Industrial Age; and to me personally, it is a
great pity that the absorption of our neighbourhood into the,
I might say perhaps not with untruth, horrid County of London—
as apart from the City of London, which has an historical soul of
its own—Yes, a great pity that the modern trend should obliterate
with advancing rapidity so many of those oases dear to the antiquarian. Therefore I hope that all, to whom the history of our
parish and its environs is of interest, will forgather for the
purpose of acquiring data for our local history, in the coming
season of winter. I refer, of course, to the Wakenham Antiquarian
and Archeological Society, of which I am honoured by being the
President. In a nutshell, would you care to join us?"

Richard kept a straight face. He thought of the prune-stones,
and Hetty's face; he thought of all the antiquarians, diminished
to insect-size, all hiding in a nutshell. Suddenly he felt extremely
well-disposed towards Hetty.

"Do not decide now," the Vicar added, misinterpreting the
look on the young man's face, "there is plenty of time to think it
over. The subscription is nominal, a half-crown the year. We
have several members, including one or two of the working
classes, good steady fellows, artisans who have decided that their
spiritual needs are met in St. Simon's rather than the chapel
recently erected at the bottom of Twistleton Road. For them the
question of subscription is met by a rule that permits the appointment of honorary members. We have lectures in the dark months,
with lantern slides. An urn of tea and some buns provide an
occasion for friendly intercourse after the lectures. This coming
season, some of our younger members have asked for dancing.
We must not always be Dryasdust: a little frolic helps to commote the liver!"

Richard wondered if Hetty had been telling the Vicar that he
was interested in archæology. She was quite capable of agreeing

with him in the matter to such an extent that an entirely false impression would be given. It was not fair! The thing was being done against his will, he was being press-ganged into it. What *had* Hetty been saying to Mr. Mundy? For obviously the Vicar had an entirely false impression of himself! He must be careful not to commit himself; the next thing, he would expect him to attend his church, or even to sing in the choir. And with a start he heard Mr. Mundy say, "I hear you are musical, Maddison. Do you sing?"

Fortunately at this point the return of Miss MacIntosh, co-incident with the court being vacant, provided a change of thought in the Vicar, too, judging by the expression on his face. The white Amazon, whose confident stride revealed upon a splendid figure the absence of corsets, was approaching from the opposite side of the court. For Richard her return induced a stealthy excitement, concealed behind the austerity of his expression. As she came near he rose to his feet, preparatory to offering his chair; she anticipated his intention, and with a friendly smile inclined her head, and sat down between him and the Vicar.

"I am preparing Maddison for induction into the Antiquarian Society, my dear," he said. "Miss MacIntosh," turning to Richard, "is a young woman of parts, being our good secretary and organiser. Yes, as I was saying, very soon the gravel pits, the ditches, the water-courses of the district will have disappeared. So we must to work to make our records for those who are to come after us, before all is covered by bricks and mortar. History lies in layers upon the surface of the earth. Recent history, of the last few thousand years, is very near the top. A fascinating subject. Why, we might even discover another mammoth!" He patted the hand of Miss MacIntosh.

"Yes, do join us, we need some new blood, Mr. Maddison. Our expeditions are quite good fun."

Her glance met Richard's across the profiled dark blue chin and red face of the Vicar; she lowered her eyes after a slight flicker of the lids had sent a wild excitement through him. Richard contained his breath, not wishing the Vicar to observe the quickening he felt. But he did not think to control the delicate movement of his nostrils, which the Vicar observed.

"Yes, I think I would like to join the Antiquarian Society, sir."

"Good man. Well, Miranda," placing his hand firmly on her

knee as he prepared to rise, "I think we should be returning to
the study to finish our Ruridecanal Report. No doubt the Club
will be seeing you again on Saturday, Maddison? I shall not be
here: Saturday is m'sermon. And when we are playing together
again, you must forego all consideration for my grey hairs, and
serve upon me your fastest service! We must match you in a
single with Miranda here. She has a formidable top-spin drive
upon occasion, as befits a past champion of Somerville."

The Vicar stood up. Richard stood up, too.

Miss MacIntosh lifted her eyes to Richard's, and modestly
lowered her gaze a moment after. With a pang he watched
them depart. After the next set was finished, it was time to be
going home. The net was relaxed, and hung upon its wire. Good-
nights were exchanged. He was left alone.

He felt the evening, the world, suddenly to be empty. Shrilly
whistled the swifts as they screamed around the church tower
which arose grey, as though fossilized, into the pale and remote
sky. The clock hands were at eight. It was nearly September;
soon the linden leaves, dry and listless in the August heats, would
change colour, and be falling from their parent trees. Well, there
was nothing for it but to go home. And taking his bicycle, he
wheeled it to the sidewalk of worn grey square stones, took a final
regretful glance at the empty court, before pushing off in a direction opposite to that from which he had arrived.

What had he done? He did not want to join the Antiquarian
Society. He did not believe in any religion. He had merely
wanted to play tennis, chiefly as a means of keeping fit; and now
he was being treated for all the world as though he were a
stalwart of St. Simon's. It was a deliberate trick of that young
woman to get him into the Church! Half-crowns were not so
easily come by, that he could afford to dispense lightly with one
of them. That was what came of permitting a woman to arrange
a man's affairs, or to *interfere* in a fellows' doings, on his behalf.
Hetty must have been drawing the long bow to Mr. Mundy
about his interest in country matters, exaggerating some of
his remarks to her about the geological formation of the Hill—
which he had read to her in the first place out of St. Simon's
Parish Magazine, written by Mundy himself! That's what
women's minds were, grasshoppers, jumping to any fortuitous
conclusion. And ringing his bell, Richard turned the corner of

Twistleton Road and pedalled down the slope towards Pit Vale.

He did not want to go home. The thought of home was hollow, vacant, grey, meaningless, without life or soul.

Ting-a-ling-a-ling! Racquet under one arm, straw boater on its safety-cord attached between brim and buttonhole, tilting uncertainly in the wind of descent, Richard, feet on rests fixed to the front forks, began to travel fast down the slope into Pit Vale. One hand was ready to grip the brake-lever which would press the plunger with its rubber pad upon the humming surface of the front tyre—and deposit him upon the tramlines and granite sett-stones if he applied it too suddenly! *Ting-a-ling-a-ling!*

Richard hurtled down the slope, his boater now waving on its cord behind him. A small boy shouted, "Whip be'ind, guv'nor!" Another chanted, "Old iron never rust, Solid tyres never bust!" A dog stood in the road as he whizzed on downwards; a dog with dingy white coat, tail between legs, a weary look about its face. *Hi! hi!* The damned thing cringed, and shifted only at the last moment from the horse-dung it was eating, recently dropped by a weary horse, one of three abreast hauling a tram up the Vale.

The evening was fine; green lakes among red remote islets covered the western sky. He alighted across the road from the entrance to Mill Lane, at the junction of the Randisbourne with a tributary called the Quaggy. In the pool where the streams met were several chub, or used to be; and he peered over the parapet, hoping to see one. Not much hope nowadays, with more and more filth being poured into the little river!

After looking in vain, he went on down the street, coming to where it met with the road coming down from the Heath.

Here stood a new stone fountain with a circular drinking rim to which iron cups were chained; and below it a trough for horses. Richard always remembered it as the place where he and Hetty had seen the horseless carriage pelted with horse-dung during a Sunday walk soon after they had set up house together. There had been only a lamp-post then, he remembered; now it was a fountain, with lamps above it, built for the Queen's Diamond Jubilee, with the name of the Obelisk. Feeling thirsty, he went to drink; but not out of any one of the iron cups, for fear of disease. He sucked in water from the stream that fell as he pushed the iron button.

"Nice day, guv'nor," remarked a short man in brown and

black striped costermonger's clothes, with a flash of six pearl-buttons sewn on the outer hem of his bell-bottom trousers. He hopped up beside Richard and took a heavy iron mug and filled it for drinking. "I like a nice cool drop o' wa'er, too, specially arter the beer. Best wa'er sarfer river comes ou'er this 'ere Obelisk."

"Well, it's the same water everywhere, provided it comes from the main. And that comes from the river Lea, so I am told."

"Yus, but the marble cools it in this 'ere Obelisk, and that's what makes the difference, see?"

"Is it marble, or granite? In either case, the water comes out of the ground, through an inch pipe, probably, tapped from the main. It's the ground that cools it, surely?"

"Blime guv'nor, what's the idea o' argyfying over cold water, guv'nor? I likes it arter the beer, see? Beer dries me tongue and froat up like. This 'ere Obelisk water wets 'em again, see? That's all, guv'nor! Good night!" And the little man in close-fitting flap-pocket coat and bell-bottom trousers, human cock-sparrow, climbed into his barrow and was drawn away on it by his donkey.

"There's ignorance for you," said Richard amiably to himself. "And what, and why, is this fountain called an obelisk? Why not a catafalque, or a pyramid? The best water south of the river comes from a misnomer, by way of a pipe of one inch bore, possibly three quarters of an inch. Ha ha," and he laughed to himself. He felt a new man after his drink. The odd thing was that the water did taste differently from that at home.

It was a wonderful summer night, there was a magic quality in the approaching twilight. Far, far away in the west, remote beyond the outlines of roofs and chimneys, the sunset lingered among green lakes studded with rosy islets. There in the glory of the heavens lay the Happy Isles, the Hesperides, an archipelago of the mysterious sky. It was as though the flower-girt coral isles of the Polynesians were reflected as in some camera obscura of the wondrous universe. As he stared at the sky, Richard's mind came down to earth, to less heart-stealing thought, as he recalled the Harvest Homes of his boyhood. It was harvest weather down there in the West. He could see the fields of corn cut and stooked, lying in golden chequer upon golden chequer under the downs and upon the sun-hazed plain of Colham. He saw the white owl and the yews of the churchyard, and Mother and Father in the chalk, and Jenny his brother's wife, so young, so lovely, dead in child-birth, Jenny who had surely been as near to being divine as it was possible to find in the world, lying beside them.

With a whisper of "Ah well!" Richard turned away from the country of the lost, telling himself that he was now in Kent, or a part of it, as much a captive of London as he was. Then upon his being, Medusa-like, came the image of Miranda MacIntosh, her hair the colour of those far peaks and islands of the sunset, her eyes the hue of the sea; and as inhuman.

The Starley Rover rested, held by a rat-trap pedal, on the granite kerb of the fountain's base. Richard stood on the steps, deprived for the moment of direction. His knees felt weak; an interior ache filled the hollow of his ribs. He ached for beauty to descend upon his being, a beauty wherein he would find peace, rest, and—Nirvana.

He leaned against the fountain, the so-called Obelisk, while the torment of suppressed desires of his being gave him, as the light of the summer evening deepened above the Borough, and the trees darkened and the first stars were visible, and the first lamps were lit, a feeling of being in another world. He felt homeless, and heavy with lack of hope. The new house was not really the home of his spirit; he was pretending to himself all the time. Ah well, one must make the best of it; life was a tragedy.

With this conclusion he pedalled away from the Obelisk, passing inns which recently had been rebuilt for the purpose of taking more profit from beer and porter, whiskey, rum and gin: buildings of brick and glass, of flaring gas and tables of mahogany with heavy cast-iron legs and frames, nearly indestructible. It was the age of the brewer becoming a gentleman, together with other big tradesmen. Songs, shouts and laughter came from The Plough, The Duke of Cambridge, The Roebuck, and The Joiner's Arms.

He came to the Clock Tower, also built to commemorate the Jubilee. It stood at the parting of two ways. The money raised by subscription for its erection had run out before it was finished, causing the omission of a series of panels bearing coats of arms. It was a case of either the clock or the arms; and the clock was more useful to those who, by necessity, cared nothing for the past. Away with the old century, let it die, and give place to the new, that was the modern spirit.

The trees in the High Street were due to come down, he had heard; everywhere was building and expansion. The new advanced woman was part of it all. Miranda MacIntosh, she was a brazen huzzy, she was Scots, she was a disturbance. If only a fellow dared . . . no no, what was he thinking, it was unthinkable, confound her, he went to the club for tennis, not to be looked at by sea-green siren's eyes. Jenny, Jenny! Was he like his own father, who had kicked over the traces, and gone to the dogs, because of drink and women. *His own father*—the disgrace of it—was that why he himself had such—such——. Father's deathbed repentance; but nothing could ever undo the shame, the disgrace, the ruin he had brought upon the family. Miranda—what a name —in itself something beyond the pale, something luring, like the Lorelei in the Rhine, who drew men down to drown, with promises of inhuman delights. O damn Miranda! Was he some stripling boy, that such thoughts should find him their prey?

He pedalled slowly by the White Hart. Should he call in for a glass of beer? There was no harm in that; and he was not likely to be recognized. No, for one glass might lead to another. A game of chess . . . what was the good of playing with Hetty, who would, or could, never really exert herself to try and win? It was a farce. His whole life was a farce. Making a garden out of a few square yards of London clay! O damn it, what was the matter with him? Miranda had got into him like an octopus. The white skin, the breasts showing movement beneath the white bodice, the show of leg to the knee, almost as she turned to take a back-hand volley, what a woman, what a mate. Alone with her on a South Sea Island, he would teach her to ogle a married man! Secretary of the Archæologists' Association, more like the Harlots'! And by now feeling completely disgraced in his own eyes, and that he might as well go the whole hog, Richard stopped at The Castle, a hundred yards or so before the turn up to Randiswell; and wheeling his cycle into the passage leading to the various doors marked Jug and Bottle, Public Bar, Private Bar Saloon and Billiards, he set it up against the end wall, and without further ado pushed upon the ground-glass-panelled Private Bar and asked for some cider.

"Don't keep it, sir," said a man with eyes almost concealed in a smile, a man in shirt-sleeves kept off his wrists by rubber bands, as he raised his boater, then set it on his head again at the original angle. "Porter, stout, bitter, mild in wood, Bass, Worthington, Guinness, Reid's, Raggett's, Truman's, Allsopp's, Courage's in bottle. This is a free house."

Feeling the fellow's eyes unbearably upon him, Richard said the first name that came to him. "Raggett's, please."

"Nice evening, sir. Been playing tennis?"

"Lawn tennis," said Richard, not wanting to encourage conversation. The place smelled of stale beer and tobacco smoke.

The publican turned to say, as he drew a cork, "You'll pardon me mentioning it, I hope, but I notice by the shape of your racquet it is a tennis racquet, and not the new lawn tennis shape."

"You are quite right," exclaimed Richard. "It *is* a tennis racquet."

"Originally for use with soft leather balls stuffed with feathers, and sometimes horsehair, so I understand."

"Do you play, yourself?"

"No sir," replied the landlord, with a giggle, "I've got some old copies of 'The London Illustrated News,' and was reading about it only the other day."

The publican wiped the counter before putting down the glass of stout.

"Threepence, if you please, sir. It's up a ha'penny since the Budget."

Richard buttoned his jacket across his watch and chain as the door opened and two women in black bonnets and dresses came in. The landlord's eyes grew to narrow slits as he smiled again, the straw hat being lifted and replaced while his face assumed the faint suggestion of being Chinese.

"Two half quarterns of gin, Freddie," said one of the women, in a voice familiar to Richard, who had turned his face to the mahogany partition. He had recognized Mrs. Cummings and Mrs. Birkett. What would the landlady of his bachelor days, and the midwife who had attended Hetty, think of him being there?

He soon found out, when feeling himself discourteous, he turned round, simulated surprise, and raised his boater, slightly embarrassed by the thought of the landlord having just done the same thing.

"Why Mr. Maddison, it is a pleasure to see you out and about, and in the Castle, of all places!" exclaimed Mrs. Cummings. "What a small world it is after all, I was only talking of you to Mrs. B. as we were walking past the Public Baths just now! 'I never see Mr. or Mrs. Maddison nowadays,' I said, 'they never asked me to the christening of their little son, but then Mr. Maddison was always so reserved a gentleman, Mrs. B.,' I said. How are you keeping, and how do you like your new house? I suppose all those years you lodged with me, and I always tell people you were the nicest gentleman I could wish to have under my roof, all those years with me seem nothing now you are happy and secure with your wife and family."

"You must come round and see us when you can manage it, Mrs. Cummings. We have another baby now, I expect you know, thanks to the skill and care of Mrs. Birkett." He bowed slightly to Mrs. Birkett.

Mrs. Cummings looked significantly at the glass on the counter. "Do you see what I see, Mrs. B.? Father is keeping up his strength," and both women laughed. "Raggett's Stout! You must excuse us laughing, Mr. Maddison, but it is an old joke between Mrs. C. and me, how you brought your little wife home that evening, some months off her time, those bottles of Raggett's all ready for the happy occasion! We've often had a quiet laugh over it, I hope you will not be offended, Mr. Maddison?"

"Oh no, of course not. Well, how are you, Mrs. Birkett?"

"Very well, thank you, Mr. Maddison. How is the little one progressing?"

"Very well, thank you, Mrs. Birkett. The mother is able to feed the baby this time."

"Well, here's a health to her, Father," and Mrs. Birkett raised her glass of gin and hot water with a slice of lemon in it. Mrs. Cummings followed. They drank.

The landlord appeared to be interested. So he was; but chiefly in the hope that the meeting would lead to more custom. It did; for Richard considered it the thing to do to offer them another drink. They accepted at once. He decided to have beer this time. He ordered himself a pint of strong Burton ale. Why not, indeed?

It had an exhilarating effect on him. The evening became alive, in that he lived in the present. The tennis had been good fun; Mr. Mundy was doing his best to keep the true values of the country alive; Miss MacIntosh was a gay and natural lassie from the Highlands. He began to speak of his butterflies, while Mrs. Cummings exchanged a wink with Mrs. Birkett. They expected to be amused; they were enchanted. Freddie the landlord leaned nearer, the better to hear what the gentleman was saying, while marvelling at education. Richard told them how Painted Ladies and sometimes Large Coppers flew miles across the seas, with the rare Camberwell Beauty; how the herb fields in North Surrey were, in summer, acres of pure colour; and thither came Fritillary and Admiral, Marbled White and Blue Adonis. How one collected not for the sake of acquiring rare specimens, but as talismans of future happiness. Mrs. Cummings wondered at the change in him from the reserved young man she had known before, and declared that the alteration was due to his marriage.

"Wonderful what the right partner will do to a man, or to a woman for that matter, eh Freddie? What do you say? Come on Freddie, try and be as interesting as Mr. Maddison!"

The landlord's eyes were smiling within the enclosing lids. He did not reply, but still smiling, lifted his glass and sipped. It was water; a customer in the saloon bar adjoining had just paid threepence for a half-quartern of gin for him.

"Come on Freddie, you've been married, haven't you?"

Freddie tittered. His eyes were mere slits. Then he spoke.

"It's the cup that cheers, don't they say?" and slightly lifting his boater once more, he moved away to attend to a customer in the saloon bar. The public bar, at the other end, was served by a big stout man in leather apron and thinning forelock plastered with oil flat on his brow. Noises of shouting and raucous laughter came from there. It was snug in the small enclosed Private Bar.

"Well," said Richard, "it has been most pleasant meeting you two ladies. I called in on my way home from lawn tennis, for some cider, but they had none. Still, this ale is excellent. It is the first time I have entered a public house in this part of the world, but I must say, it is a pleasant experience."

"Now let me stand you a short one for the road," said Mrs. Cummings. "Come on, dear, one more. It isn't every day Mrs. B. and I have the pleasure of hearing anyone talk like you do, you know."

"Well, I have left my wife all alone——"

"She'll manage all right, don't you fret. She'll know you've been in good hands, when you tell her. We know our Mrs. Maddison, don't we, Mrs. B.? Why, if you searched the wide world over, you'd never find a more naturally understanding or warm-hearted little woman like the one you've got. And such a delightful sense of humour! You'd never believe it, unless you heard it."

Mrs. Cummings' words had a subduing effect on Richard. His social sense made keener through the drink, he felt an implied reproach in what his old landlady had said. Hetty was subdued when with him; she was happy and humorous when he was away. He had suspected it, of course; and when away from her he had often told himself that he must be more patient, and not allow the fact of their differing standards to affect him; but somehow, whenever he had been with her all the good resolutions had made no difference. She did not seem able to learn.

"Let me stand you a gin, or a whiskey, for old times' sake," urged Mrs. Cummings. "Then you can go back to your little wife, and please to give her my best regards."

"I will indeed. Now if you will excuse me——"

"Not until you have drunk the Queen's health, I won't hear of it! Why, it isn't many times in our lives we shall be together again in the sixtieth reigning year of the best Queen England ever had, God bless her."

"God bless her!"

"The Queen, God bless her!" Freddie lifted his hat once more and then sipped water. He drank spirits only in the daytime when travellers calling for orders having first enquired after his health, always invited him to have a drink with them. In the evening he took the money from happy customers and drank only water, for the sake of his liver.

It was dark when Richard wheeled the Starley Rover into the High Street. Having no light, he walked home. The stars were now thick in the sky, the moon was rising. It seemed that the hamlet of Randiswell, even the laughter and shouts from the garish Railway, and the way up Charlotte Road, were part of the freshness and inherent decency of human life.

Hetty had cocoa keeping warm on the gas stove. She was surprised and delighted with his happy face. It was lovely to have the messages from Mrs. Cummings and Mrs. Birkett.

He lay back in the armchair and stretched out his legs, and then his arms, yawning with mouth wide until he remembered to cover it with his hand. And soon upstairs, to wash teeth and hands and face, and into relaxing cool nightshirt. Hetty was glad that he wanted to sleep in her bed; she lived only that he, and others about her, should be happy.

Had she known, while she was giving of her ultimate gentleness to him, that he was imagining her to be red-haired, green-eyed, milk-white of brow and neck and cheek, she would not have resented it, having accepted within herself, as she had for some time now, the truth that she could not, of herself, make Dickie happy.

But what she did not understand was why, after she had given herself to him, he was almost always, the following morning, querulous, and critical of her in one way or another. The more she submitted to him, as was her wifely duty, the more irritable and fault-finding he became. Once, having inspected her larder, and complained of food allowed to become stale, he became so angry that, despite her efforts to conceal her hurt, she broke into tears. This caused him further upset, and a measure of contempt, that she had avoided, as he declared, the issue between them by taking an unfair advantage. Were there blowflies' eggs on the remains of the leg of mutton, or were there not? That was the issue! Did she wish him to die by eating tainted meat, and perhaps herself and her precious little coddled son as well? Then it behoved her to be more scrupulous in her regard for them all!

What Hetty did not understand was that Richard was chronically under-nourished, for he ate nothing between breakfast and his evening meal, except his tobacco-tin of marmalade sandwiches. He was economising for his son's education, among other responsibilities.

In distress Hetty left the room, and went upstairs; and like a child she sought relief in the company of another child. "Oh I cannot bear any more, Sonny, I cannot bear any more, I cannot —I cannot," she sobbed.

The little boy stood up in his cot watching Mummy crying because Daddy was ur-ur-ur-ur-ur to Mummy—the child who learned by manual-visual imitation of everything his parents did: and as Mummy cried and clasped him he cried too; and when Mummy was gone he stood up in his cot, clutching silken Hanky in one hand, Thumb in mouth for desperate reassurance, Golly pressed to his nightshirt; and as he listened it was more and more as though a thorn had begun to pierce the large-seeing eyes filling half the face and serving the mind of the soft-bony creature, the mind that was being formed by visual-aural records in the back of the skull, an imaginative cave stored with the records of its living, which was also that of its family, and of its forebears.

Chapter 7

RICHARD HAS A SHOCK

ONE morning a girl was sent up by Miss Thoroughgood's Domestic Agency. She rang the bell worked by a current from the big glass salammoniac cells on the shelf in the coal cellar, and when Hetty went to the door she was standing there unsmiling and unspeaking. She had a sallow skin, with eyes as black as her hair. Her hands hung down limply by her side.

Sitting in the kitchen, uncomfortably on the chair, the girl was not communicative. Hetty gave her a cup of tea. She took it without a word. Her high button boots were old, too big for her, and cracked. So were her oversize jacket and skirt, which were obviously cast-offs. Hetty was disappointed. She had been imagining a smiling, enthusiastic girl, blithe and hard-working, one to be trusted in all matters. Perhaps with a name like Florabell, or Hyacinth, or Margaret, or Celandine—for often Hetty's thoughts went back to Cross Aulton, and the herb fields which she saw with such radiant sadness in memory.

"What is your name?"

"Mona Monk, mum."

"Oh." After a pause Hetty added, "I see. Well, Mona, have you had any experience?"

"On'y runnin' errands for Missis Bevy, and at 'ome workin' fur me mum, mum, and mindin' me li'le bruvvers an' sisters."

"Do you like children? I have a little boy, and a baby daughter."

Mona stared at the floor.

"Do you like children, Mona?"

"I dunno, mum."

Hetty's heart sank. Mona Monk seemed well-named, poor girl. She did not think that Dickie would like her appearance, or her manner.

"You don't dislike children, I suppose?"

"Only some," said Mona.

"Do you think you would like my little boy, Mona?"

"I ain't sin 'im yet, mum."

Hetty laughed. At least Mona seemed to be truthful.

"How old are you, Mona?"

"Fourteen, mum."

"Can you cook anything?"

"I ken fry spuds, an' make a nice cupper char."

"Oh." Hetty wondered what that was. Then Phillip came into the room, carrying his gollywog. "This is Master Phil, Mona."

The girl stared. The child stared at her. Mona smiled. He smiled, and went to her. She touched his head. "Ain't 'ee pretty, mum?" she said, looking up at Hetty. The face, suddenly winsome, touched Hetty's heart.

"Well Mona, if you will be a good girl, and try and learn, I will think about engaging you. You would want to live in, of course?"

"Would I hev me own bed, mum?"

"Of course, Mona."

"Then I wouldn't hev to sleep wiv no one else?"

"Oh no. Sonny will be in his cot, and the baby sleeps in a cradle in my bedroom. Would you like a rock bun?"

The girl grabbed one. She broke off a piece and offered it to the boy. He took it, saying solemnly, "Danke schön."

Hetty explained what it meant. "You see, Mona, it is good manners to say 'Thank you' when people give you something."

Mona's face looked closed-up again.

"Would you like another cup of tea?"

"No, mum, it's quite all right."

"You should say: 'Thank you', Mona."

Mona stared at the ground. A silence followed.

"Did you hear what I said, Mona?" asked Hetty gently.

Mona nodded. Her black hair hid nearly all her face.

"Then what do you say?"

Mona's head went lower. The tattered black straw hat, with its faded ribbon, began to shake. A grimy hand covered her eyes. She was crying.

"Please don't cry, dear. I did not mean to be unkind. You must not mind me telling you, you know; I am only trying to help you." Poor little girl, Hetty thought, what thin legs she had. Her black thread stockings, loose on her broom-stick legs, were torn.

"Why are you crying, dear? See you have made Sonny cry, too."

At last the girl said: "I didn't mean no harm, mum."

"Of course not. But you should say 'Thank you' when someone gives you something, that is all, Mona."

"But you didn't give me nothin', mum."

Hetty was mystified. Then she laughed. The boy laughed. "How silly of me, of course you were right! Only say 'No, thank you' if you don't want anything, and 'Yes, thank you' if you do."

"I'll try, mum, if you give me another charnst, I swear to Gawd I will. Don't turn me away, mum. Me Dad will belt me."

Hetty was all compassion. "Very well, Mona. I will give you a chance. Did you talk about wages to Miss Thoroughgood?"

"Yes, mum, thank you."

"What wages are you asking?"

Mona said quickly, "I must not ask for less'n five shilling a week, mum."

This was far too much, thought Hetty. And yet it was the only girl Miss Thoroughgood had had come to her for weeks, according to Miss Thoroughgood. Far too much, five shillings a week for an untrained girl. Hetty said she would let her know, and Mona Monk departed.

Mrs. Turney was coming over from Cross Aulton to visit her daughter the next day, and Hetty told her mother about Mona. She had taken quite a fancy to the girl, she said.

"Well then, dear, suitability is half the battle. If you consider her to be suitable, do you engage her, and I will pay half her wages. Thirteen pounds a year is a great deal to pay a little maid, but if it helps to keep small brothers and sisters, I will not grudge the money, dear."

So when Mona came up the next morning, Hetty said: "Very well, I will pay five shillings a week, Mona, and you will live in, and have half a day a week. Mr. Maddison will expect you to be in at nine o'clock. You will go home on your afternoons out, won't you?"

"Yes, mum."

"Very well. You can start next Monday, for a month's trial. I will provide you with cap and apron, and a black frock. But you will be expected, of course, to provide your own underclothes, boots, and stockings, out of your wages."

"Yes, mum, thank you."

"Now, take a rock cake, Mona, before going home to tell your mother, I am sure you are hungry." Hetty held out the plate.

"No, thank you, mum."

"But aren't you hungry?"

"It ain't my turn to eat today, mum."

Of course: many poor families could not afford enough food to go round.

"Well, dear, it *is* your turn today now, so please don't think you are taking anyone else's share."

Hetty had found out from Hern, the grocer in Randiswell, that the girl's father had been a soldier, but now was a navvy, digging ditches in the yellow clay for water and drains of new houses. The Monks lived in Mercy Terrace, beside the line in Randiswell.

Hetty gave Mona some cold mutton and bread, which the girl ate ravenously, and then complained of a pain. She and her brothers and sisters seldom had meat to eat, it seemed.

"Of course, when you are here, Mona, you will have your meals every day."

"Cor," said Mona.

"Cor," said Phillip, standing there, watching and listening.

Richard was told the news on his return that evening, when Hetty saw he was in happy mood. The last few days had been close and oppressive; but a thunderstorm had cleared the air during the afternoon.

"Now you will be able to come with me to the Tennis Club dance," he said.

"Oh Dickie, I have not danced for ever so long a time, and have nothing to wear!"

"Your cream silk dress, what is wrong with that, pray? You look very nice in it."

"But the half-bustle is out of fashion, Dickie. However, I could have it altered, and no one would know. There is a good sempstress in the High Road, near Mrs. Cummings. Or I have heard of a little woman in Randiswell."

Hetty was surprised at the idea of Dickie even thinking of going to a dance. What had happened to change him? Of course, it was the exercise, and the nice friends he had made.

"They are a pleasant lot of people in Twistleton Road. We had a hand or two of whist this evening, during the thunderstorm, in the Vicarage", he told her, when he returned from the club that evening. "Mr. Mundy suggested it, he is the old type of sporting parson, and I must say more to my idea of what a clergy-man should be. Mrs. Mundy gave us some peach brandy, and very good it was, too."

Although he had taken the news of the servant girl coming without any fuss, Hetty was not easy. She had doubts about Mona Monk, and was apprehensive of Dickie's effect on the child when he saw her. But there, she was sure she would improve with proper food and kindness; and it was a good augury the way she had taken to Sonny.

Hetty was relieved that Richard seemed happier. During the past week he had more than once found fault with her. The Christmas-pudding basin, which she had put behind the water-butt, well away from the scullery, meaning to give it a good soak before washing it in strong soda-water, had been found by him, and an explanation demanded. When she had told him about the mouse he had been angry, declaring that if she had not been so careless she would have seen its traces on the larder shelf before it could have time to eat its way to the bottom of the pudding.

Then—and oh, she felt such shame, she could hardly bear to think if it—he had discovered that she put her menstruation napkins, to keep them hidden until she could wash them later in the morning, tucked under the steel laths of the mattress. Sonny had found one when crawling under the bed while she was cooking Dickie's breakfast, and he was dressing after his cold bath. Oh dear, he had made such a scene. He had gone on until she had broken down, though she had tried not to; and Sonny had clung to her skirts, also crying; then he had accused her of playing on the boy's feelings in a manner to estrange him from his father. It was quite untrue; she would never dream of doing such a thing; but Dickie had not believed her.

He had left the house without his breakfast; and she had not had time to make him his usual sandwiches of bread and butter and marmalade, in the tobacco box. So he had been starved all day, and it was entirely her fault. And when he had come home half an hour earlier than usual, the chops in the perforated zinc box standing on the copper of the scullery for coolness had gone off; and when she was about to put them in the pan he had smelt them; and there had been another disturbance. She should have anticipated them going off in the thundery weather, he cried. She should have cooked them; they were quite nice cold, provided they were eaten at once, and not left for days and days to get stale. And if she had done so, he was just as likely to have complained of the cold meat on his plate. How many times had he not said, "What, cold mutton again? Aren't there any other varieties of cooking in your repertoire? How about savoury rissoles, or Lancashire hot-pot for a change? Surely you have benefitted a little from Minnie's tuition?" It was best not to say anything, her replies only made him worse, he seemed to take them all as evasions. But often by the time she had washed the baby's diapers, bathed Sonny and put him to bed, tripped up and down the stairs a dozen times to his plaintive, "Minnie mummie, Minnie mummie, Minnie mummie, p'e," cleared the sitting-room of his toys and tidied the place up, tidied herself and washed and changed from her working clothes and put her hair in order, and perhaps soothed the baby crying with wind-pains—oh well, when Mona came perhaps she would have more time to do things in the way Dickie liked them done. It was all very difficult; he was away all day, and had no idea of what extra work the larger house involved.

Richard, on the other hand, regarded his day in the City as a grind; the street noises and constant movements wore upon ear and eye; pleasant anticipations of returning home, of seeing Hetty and the odd little boy, whom he dearly loved, and the baby, who had become Mavie, a personality to him since she had smiled at him, of a quiet and pleasant meal with Hetty in the cool sitting or garden room, of work in the garden afterwards, at carpenter's bench in the spare room upstairs, or tennis at the Club—to Richard his homecoming at evening was always keenly anticipated, and being insufficiently fed during the day, he had not the resistance to disappointment. He received a salary of sixteen pounds five shillings every half-quarter, and the investment of his remaining capital, after house and furniture had been paid for, produced a further fifty-six pounds per annum. For years his mind had been set on the need to save every possible penny,

against illness or other contingency; and by now the habit had
become a satisfaction in itself. He kept a record, in his meticulous
handwriting, of every halfpenny spent, and balanced his books
at the end of every month.

Mona was afraid of "The Master". She cowered within herself
in his presence, over-awed and often tongue-tied. Her attitude
discomposed him, made him withdraw into himself, with the
effect of mutual tension.

Phillip formed his feelings from those in the house: he responded, like any other young child, to the spirit of his human
surroundings. During the day he was generally happy and
interested; there was wonder in all things, keen delight or
apprehension in the unexpected. Aunty Bigge often came in,
first rattling the brass flap of the letter-box, to be greeted with
a little dance of joy. Mrs. Feeney's black bonnet wobbling up
the path or seen approaching up the road from Mummy's bedroom window as he helped her to make the beds by standing in
the verandah out of the way, gave him equal joy.

Good-boy-don't-annoy watched for Milk-oo man, too, and
Basket-grocer man, and Butcher-man stripey-blue apron and
wooden sheep on shoulder (the wooden trug, with two handles at
each end, looked to the child like the half a split sheep hanging in
the butcher's shop in Randiswell) and Black Coal-man with black
horse and waggon, and Ning-a-ning-man with ning-a-ning
wormy up the road (organ-grinder hauling barrel organ up the
steep road from kerb to kerb, in a series of zigzags).

In this manner, being good-boy-don't-annoy, he helped his
mother to make the beds on fine mornings, by keeping watch on
the balcony beyond the open door. He watched the sparrows on
the roof above, chattering and quarrelling, the cats in the gardens
below, the people who came and went out of the houses up and
down the road.

He stood there with his new friend in his hand one morning,
inside its box. The new friend was a woodlouse. It was a sad
moment when, having given his friend a bath, he pulled the
plug and his friend went down the hole that gurgled like Minnie
snoring.

It was through his small son that Richard came to like Mona.
One day he overheard her saying to him, as she put on his coat
before taking him out in the mail-cart one Saturday afternoon,

"You're a lucky boy, Phil, you don't 'arf know 'ow lucky, your dad don't never belt you or your mum."

"Pill lucky boy."

"Yus, and you're lucky to 'ave Mona to 'old your 'and in the darkness, too."

" 'An' Minnie-mony-mummie."

"Say 'Fank you, Mona', like a good little boy, in German."

"Danke schön, Minnie!" he cried, for this was now a joke.

"Now say it properly. Say 'Fank you, Mona', in English. Go on, say 'Fank you, Mona!' "

"DANKE SCHÖN, Minnie!" shouted Phillip, with great glee. Then appearing unexpectedly round the door, there was Daddy holding up a silver-papered bar of Callard and Bowser's cherry toffee.

"And what have I here for a good boy?"

"Tiff-tiff, Daddy got tiff-tiff!"

The silver paper was carefully removed; the ivory-handled knife taken from the waistcoat pocket; the bar tapped across the middle. One half for Phillip—"What do you say, dear?" urged a kneeling and anxious Mona. "Danke schön, Farver!"

"And a piece for you, Mona."

"Oh fank you, sir!"

"Don't bite it up, suck it and so save your teeth."

"Yes, sir."

"Yes, sir," echoed Phillip.

"Now take the boy on the Hill, Mona, and do not let him touch any dogs, and don't speak to strange men, will you?"

"No, sir."

"No, sir."

"You funny little chap!" said Richard, picking him up and hugging him, before going to sit in his deck-chair in the back garden, well-pleased with life.

It was a warm September afternoon, towards the equinox. Yellow leaves hung among the dull green of the elms in the waste land beyond the creosoted garden fence. Mr. Bigge, over the dividing fence of the lower garden, was making a rockery. The boundary fence being his, he had nailed above the posts wooden extensions to which he had fixed supporting wires for Virginia Creeper. He wanted privacy in his garden, having on two occasions overheard his neighbour speaking to his wife in a tone of voice that distressed him.

Richard did not suspect the reason for the extremely soft-spoken, evasive Josiah Bigge wanting to secrete himself in his garden. He thought that Mr. Bigge did not wish to be overlooked, a feeling he could understand. There was the five-foot high fence between his own garden and that of No. 12 above, a house at present unoccupied. That garden was overgrown with weeds. All he knew was that the FOR SALE board by the front garden gate had been removed some weeks previously, so presumably it had found a purchaser.

Had Hetty seen anyone looking over the house? he had enquired of her the previous Saturday afternoon. Hetty had dreaded the question; the thought of it coming from Richard, one day, had affected her milk; and when at last the question had come, she replied evasively, and made an excuse to leave the room soon afterwards.

Richard did not notice her concealed agitation; and finding her a little time afterwards in the front room, sitting on the sofa by the open window, where the leaves of the aspidistra risped slightly in the dry breeze, he thought she was resting there; and mindful of her needs while nursing the baby, he made some remark, and left her alone. He did not know that she was feeling sick with apprehension, indecision, powerlessness. O, sooner or later Dickie would have to be told! If only she could summon up sufficient courage to tell him!

Now, a week later, as the quarter day of Michaelmas approached, Richard was about to find out for himself who his upper neighbour was to be. The revelation came while he was lying in the deck chair in the garden, his face held to the sun standing high in the south-west over the slated roof of the Bigge's house.

It was half an hour before tea; and after tea he was going to change into flannels for the Club. On the following Saturday the tournament was to be held, the last meeting of the season. Then —goodbye to summer! How swiftly the year had flown! Soon the mists of autumn would collect the smoke of London—four hundred tons of it dropping on Greater London every day—into cold, clammy, muffling fogs. For a moment the thought was appalling; but he consoled himself by thinking that there would be the meetings of the Antiquarian Society, and Whist Drives, and lectures with slides of the Magic Lantern. He had not had a real holiday that year, deeming that the expenses of the baby's coming did not justify himself taking one; but long rides into Kent and Surrey on the Starley Rover, and tennis most evenings had been ample compensation, he told Hetty. It had been a wonderful summer.

"I am so glad, dear," said Hetty. "For you have worked so very hard and did deserve a real holiday." She herself had had none at all, unless the fortnight in bed after having Mavis could be called a holiday. Sometimes, by what he said, Richard seemed to think it had been.

The air was still. Josiah Bigge over the fence worked quietly and industriously; only his old gardening hat, of faded Panama straw, the black band a little frayed with age, was occasionally visible, as he rose up to stretch himself. Mr. Bigge never turned in the direction of his next-door garden. Richard was well content with him as a neighbour: a mutual bowing, raising of hats, elementary weather reports—beyond such things the worlds of the two men did not meet.

Richard, with closed eyes, basked in the heat of the sun on his face. This was his idea of bliss. His temples, cheeks, neck, wrists, the backs of his hands clasping the wooden arms of the deck-chair, were brown. He felt the sun entering his being through the lids of his eyes: he was of the sun itself; surrendered to his god, the sun. He drew a deep breath of contentment, sighed himself away upon celestial radiance. An omnipotent, sempiternal power seemed to be bearing him away from ordinary living to a realm delicious with a warm peach-like sleep, in remote lands of blissful solitude.

In memory of the peaches on a southern flint wall of his old home at Rookhurst, Richard had planted a little peach tree in the flower bed raised above the gravel path on which his chair stood. Its thin branches were trained against the fence. There had been no blossom on it that year; it had been planted out late; but in his mind he could feel the warm flushed fruit, soft with softest down, hanging there in another summer—a token, a link, an assurance.

Afar off he heard the ringing of the front door bell inside the house. The french windows of the sitting room were wide open. The further door of the sitting room was open, for the summer air to wander at will through the entire house. He heard Hetty open the front door. He heard voices. He waited in a calm suspense; almost indifferent: and hearing nothing more, lapsed once more into radiant ease, his head now leaning to one side. He would resist no more, he would yield to drowsiness and sleep.

In the front room, Hetty was in conversation with her mother. The door was closed upon the new carpet seldom trodden upon, the two new armchairs seldom sat in, the maple-wood Windsor table in the centre, the half a dozen upright mahogany chairs with black leather upholstered seats standing in various places by the walls, seldom used. There was a piano in one corner; a maple-wood side-board by another wall; a Chippendale side-table with china-ware on lace doyleys; photographs in frames; a bowl of pot-pourri, made of rose-leaves from Cross Aulton; another bowl filled with lavender-seed also from Surrey to balance it. There were Red Indian moccasins of moose-hide entirely sewn with minute coloured beads, brought from Canada by Hetty years before, when she and Papa had gone to see Charley in Manitoba; a clutch of prairie hen's eggs in a basket; a whip-poor-will's egg.

There were pictures on the walls, Dresden china figures on the mantelpiece, and other gifts and possessions valued as in a museum —for this was the drawing room, the best room, the front room where almost formal visitations were made. And here Hetty was closeted with Sarah Turney, who had arrived unexpectedly with Thomas, her husband, to look over the house next door with a view to living there.

Outside the open middle window, beyond the clipped privet hedge, a familiar horse and carriage was drawn up. Hetty had first seen them from her bedroom, where she had gone to feed baby. Her feelings were such that she had dreaded she would faint. Through the open door of the balcony she heard her father's voice speaking to Jim, the coachman; then to her Mamma. She had heard Mamma asking Papa to go into the empty house, saying she would join him before very long.

Thomas Turney, who with grim humour knew how Richard would probably take the news, opened the front door with the labelled key and entered his new house for the first time. He had bought it, with several others in the neighbourhood, for investment, through an agent employed by his solicitors.

Hetty, biting her nails, had felt unable to go down even when she heard the front door bell ring; but fear of Dickie going first to the door had impelled her to run down the stairs. She was pale with her emotions.

Sarah tried to comfort her. Sarah had done her best, in her gentle way, to indicate to Tom what their daughter's feelings were, while assuring Tom that otherwise Hetty could not but be happy that her mother and father had decided to move nearer to her. But could it not be one of the other three houses he had purchased? There were two in Charlotte Road, and the third near the bottom of Hillside Road.

Before coming to No. 12 Hillside Road, Mr. and Mrs. Turney had visited the other three. Washing on a line visible from the window of a downstairs room had decided against the first; children's voices in dissension over the garden wall another; the lower house in Hillside Road had its front door cheek-by-jowl with its neighbour; none of them was satisfactory.

The front door of No. 12, with its stained glass leaded panels on the upper half, opened to his key. He went in, liking the sound of his feet on the new bare boards. It was compact, delightfully small and would be simple to run after Maybury. He opened some of the windows in the front room facing the sun, and let in fresh air, then went down the passage, with its three steps, to the room with its farther end almost entirely open to the east, with tall french windows. Thistles, docks, and stems and sprays of seeded, yellowing gix, grew outside against the lower panes of glass.

He opened these windows, approving the view of the steep slopes of grassy hill over the back fence. Five bedrooms up above, two good rooms downstairs, one east, the other west—open ground beyond both. He cleared his throat, and spat into the tall mass of deciduous weeds, unaware that, on the other side of the fence, his son-in-law was extended there, half-asleep.

Lying in the deck-chair, Richard was content. His mind moved from warm, nectarine drowsiness, and hung suspended, without definition or thought or self, as on a thread from the sun.

He became aware of movement through dry grasses, a remote crackling of stems and stalks far away over the harvest-hazy plain of Colham. And then a blackness seemed to be where the tawny blood of the sun had floated him, shutting out all but the heat-sense directly in front. He felt the blackness immediately behind his head, and a presence there without definition: and as clear thought returned upon him, he was aware of being regarded over the wooden fence. This was the fancy; for no presence was audible there, except by the cessation of movement through dry grass. He waited, disbelieving the fancy.

Then with a start he heard a voice calling out behind him, "How d'ye do? Having a rest in the sun, eh?" Preparatory to raising himself out of the canvas slump of the chair, pressing upon the creaking wooden arms to turn around, he heard the soft, apologetic tones of Mr. Bigge coming from between the wires of the lower fence's extension. "Oh yes, yes, how do you do," and Richard saw in front of him the faded Panama raised as the bearded, bespectacled face bowed several times in succession. Richard remained still.

"My name is Turney, sir!" said the voice behind him. Richard smelled cigar smoke.

The gentle, mellifluous voice in front replied, "My name is Bigge, sir. How do you do," and the head bowed its little bows again.

"I expect you know my daughter and grandson, eh? And my son-in-law here in the chair, I've disturbed his nap. Well Dick, how are ye? I expect Hetty has told you her mother and I are thinking of coming to live here?"

Mr. Bigge, after further bobbing, discreetly disappeared from view. Richard got on his feet, and shook the hand of Mr. Turney over the thin branches of the young peach tree extended, cruciform, upon his side of the dark wooden fence.

Chapter 8

ANTIQUARIAN ANTICIPATIONS

RICHARD DID not play well at St. Simon's Tennis Club that
evening. In his depressed state he allowed himself to be inveigled
into a doubles game with three members previously unknown
to him; and this despite the fact that Miranda MacIntosh was
sitting, alone in a row of deck chairs, racquet in hand, waiting to
be greeted and invited.

The Vicar was not present; in his study not far away he had
composed, and now was rehearsing, another of the celebrated
sermons that induced in Hetty, and in hundreds of others of his
congregation, such enthusiasm. For Mr. Mundy, who at Oxford
had revealed a talent for dramatic acting so obvious in his
friends' eyes that they had lamented its loss to the stage, knew
how to move and impress his audience by the controlled and
directed use of his own emotions, which were varied and experienced.

When the doubles game was over, another four, including
Miranda MacIntosh, played a long and close set. There being
no others to play when that was finished, except the waiting four,
Richard played again with his former partner, for their revenge,
he said. While they were playing Miranda MacIntosh said
goodnight to the three sitting members, and left, to Richard's
disappointment.

What was he thinking of, he asked himself. Apparently it was
not of the game he was playing; for he and his partner, Miss
Danks—who played every ball underhand and avoided all
volleys as unladylike and certainly would not have dreamed of
serving overhand and so expose her person like Miss MacIntosh,
of whom Miss Danks thoroughly disapproved both as woman and
as secretary to the Vicar—were soon beaten.

During the week that followed, Richard looked forward to the
tournament, and particularly to the idea of inviting Hetty to
accompany him to the Club, for the end-of-season tea. There was
to be a special table laid under the trees to carry many good

things, he said, including a large bowl of her favourite *compôte de fruit*, and an equally large bowl of Cornish clotted cream. This Miranda MacIntosh had confided in him.

He did not ask Hetty until the Friday night, keeping it to himself all the week as a surprise; and then he learned that some of the Cross Aulton furniture was to arrive the following day, and that Hetty had promised Mrs. Turney to be there to tell the men where to stand the various pieces. Richard felt acute disappointment; but said nothing. He had wanted Hetty at the tournament to prove to himself that Miranda MacIntosh meant nothing to him, and to help resolve for him his own contrary feelings.

In the tournament the Maddison-MacIntosh partnership collapsed in the second round. They were beaten by a pair he had thought of previously as rabbits. He did not attempt to serve his cannon-ball service, and played generally without spirit.

The Vicar, who won the doubles with his wife as partner, wondered what had occurred so to upset the young fellow. For obviously he was depressed, judging by the aloofness of a manner, the more pronounced by an almost punctilious politeness. Manners makyth man indeed, but mannerisms indicated that all was not well with the soul. Here was a young man who had yet to come to know God, thought Mr. Mundy, as he set off to prepare his sermon after tea. It was St. Michael and All Angels, he remembered. He would like to preach on the theme that a man came to God by way of St. Michael and all Angels, these being the instincts and senses of man. He had read his William Blake, and also the revolutionary works of Havelock Ellis—both behind the shut door of his study.

The Reverend (and reverent) Ernest Hamilton Pepys Mundy in youth had sailed before the mast round the Horn, he had seen blue whales blowing upon the ocean main of Melville's Moby Dick; he had made his way across more than one continent, driven on by an austere and self-denying quest for God. Then, after his travels, he had returned for ordination, working by choice as a curate in a poor East End working-class district. At the age of thirty he had married, and been given the living of St. Simon Wakenham. Possessed of private means, he had been able to help the poor of his parish practically, and gradually

it had come to him that the spirit was almost entirely an emanation of the condition of the body.

The soul was the divine spark, which was given and taken away;
but body and mind were of the earth. Yea, verily the earth, the
very soil, was the mother of man, and woe to mankind when that
truth was overlaid, and forgotten! And by the selfsame section
of the population which was the most complacent, self-satisfied,
and assured that all was for the best in the best of all possible
worlds—the middle-class mind emanating from expanding in-
dustrialisation and increasing money profits therefrom. The
modern multi-headed Midas, everything it touched was turned
to—soot! One could but fear this mentality, which had buried
its natural instincts under a pall of respectability; and for more
than one reason. But if discretion were the better part of valour,
it certainly was the only hope in a middle-class parish.

Mr. Mundy had a secret. He loved the young woman who
was his amanuensis, and she responded with like naturalness.
And why not, indeed? The Bible itself, if one excepted certain
glossed and falsified passages in the Jacobean translation—such
as the captions in the *Song of Solomon*—had none of the modern
constrictions about natural love!

Even so, Ernest Mundy was troubled by an occasional sense
of guilt that disturbed him. After all, every man was a child, a
reflection of, his age. His wife, dear woman, was content to
live her detached existence, as his very good friend; and while
he was not guilty of such bad taste as to confide his satisfaction
with Miranda to her, he suspected that she knew about it, and
regarded it with unconcern. Had it not made him, in every
way, a better man? Until the coming of Miranda MacIntosh,
he had slowly felt himself to be withering away, to be dying
on his feet with ennui. She had saved him. Was not God
love?

This tolerance shown to himself was of the same tolerance
shown to others, an understanding of the problems and per-
plexities of others, which revealed itself in his sermons: the
essential tolerance and fairness of Jesus, as exemplified by all
his teachings. Never once, he was wont to declare, did our
Lord say 'Thou shalt *not*'. Christianity was positive, it was almost,
in a modern advanced term, muscular. It was a religion, a way
of life, for manly men. Beset by an old restrictive order based

on fear and revenge and deadlock, the teachings of the Son of Man were divine in the sense of the clarity and generosity of God, the Father, all-seeing, all-knowing, all-understanding. God was love, and it was no sin to love one another—but this was perhaps a little too advanced for his contemporaries, so, having understanding, the Vicar limited his sermons to the spirit, not passing beyond into the feelings of the human heart. Even so, he was disapproved of in some places. He was a student of William Blake, a little known eccentric Cockney poet and artist, whom his age had declared, by its own faults of judgement, to be mad. The proper study of mankind was man—in other words history, ever present, for the past lived in the present, and was of it: and the history of man's achievement was in the earth, in the soil, in the arms of the mother of all living. Almost, he would like to say, in the arms of Eve!

And having more or less familiarised himself with what he would preach on the morrow—though to be muffled a little in the pedantic idiom, confound it, lest he set one and all about his years—Ernest Mundy, scholar of Winchester and graduate of Christ Church of the University of Oxford; mast-and-yards man; prospector for gold in Australia; backwoodsman in Canada; barman in San Francisco; ordained priest in charge of St. Simon Wakenham, and President of the Antiquarian Society; aged sixty years and weighing ten stone eight pounds for the past twenty years, returned to the presence of his wife and friend, Ethelburga, and that of his secretary and rejuvenator Miranda, who surely was the equal of her namesake character in the most sweet and true play ever written—*The Tempest*, by William Shakespeare. The Rev. Mundy felt like leaping over the gate when he saw again the figure in white through the hedge, and heard once more the singing swoop of Atalanta's racquet.

He seated himself beside the queerly repressed, almost stilted young man whom he wanted to help.

"Yes, my dear Maddison, the lowest formation exposed in our district is the chalk which is the uppermost member of the Cretaceous system, which, as you know, concludes the Mesozoic Geological Period".

And the uppermost member of the Turney family, thought Richard, concludes the happy Hillside Road period.

"We are always in the process of history. Where will we be—
where will our bones be—the very stones of St. Simon!—when the
Atlantic over-runs its present bed, and where we stand now is
sea bottom once again?"

Presumably our bones will be submerged, thought Richard.
He was conscious of Miss MacIntosh, in the finals of the Ladies'
Singles, serving over-arm, a very Amazon among the ewe-
flock, led by the bell-wether of—a tea urn!

"A greyish mud," continued the Vicar, warming to his subject,
"is in course of deposition on the floor of the North Atlantic.
This is the Globegerina ooze, the Globerinae being, as you are
aware, a large genus of the order Foraminifera. Probably this
ooze, accumulating in the light-years of universal time, will
eventually displace the waves, and so constitute the chalk formation of a yet unborn continent, of which our bones will be in
part foundation. And talking of foundation, which to all
mammalia is a good square meal, will you give us the pleasure
of your company at supper tonight?"

Feeling himself to be extremely daring, and in some way
disloyal to Hetty, Richard accepted.

"Good man. This Globegerina ooze is now being deposited
at the rate of a foot every hundred years. If the chalk at Dover,
say, which is a thousand feet deep at least, was deposited at the
same rate, then but a hundred thousand years was occupied in
the deposition. Rather alarmingly rapid, is it not?"

"I can feel the weight of an entire new range of hills, the New
Atlantis Downs, pressing upon my skull, Mr. Mundy."

The Vicar approved this reply, indeed he was delighted. He
was a lonely man, despite his popularity based on the practice of
geniality and consideration for others. There were not many of
his own class living in the neighbourhood, and though a man
was a man for a' that, it was pleasant to be in the company of
one's own sort now and again: and the fact that Richard Maddison's grandfather and great-grandfather had been at college
in Winchester was a thought predisposing him toward the young
man beleaguered in the suburbs like himself. How he would
be execrated, in the blessed neighbourhood of Wakenham, as
hypocrite, Adamite, Pagan, free-thinker, seducer, and even
blasphemer, if his thought and private life were suddenly
exposed, as in a camera obscura! Bless his sweet Miranda!

To Richard the supper party of six people in the Vicarage was a wonderful evening. If only his father had been like Mr. Mundy he thought as, seated next to Mrs. Mundy, he ate Bradenham ham with pickled pears and drank a hock wine from the Moselle valley. The name on the label upon the tall slender green bottle startled him—*Liebfraumilch*: he had never heard of it, or seen it, before. And in a parson's home, of all places! It was rather crude, like all German humour. He replied politely, almost carefully, to Mrs. Mundy's remarks. She thought he was nice but dull. Richard felt he was dull; but the wine warmed the cockles of his heart, bringing back within the open empty shells, open as little wings of partridge chicks flying, or flown, to eternity, the authentic bivalves of the mud. Cockles, cockles! Boyhood holidays upon the sea coast, ragworm casts and cockle holes streaming with chain-bubbles of air as the tide came in over the flats. How the cockles in the mud rejoiced as the water returned to them! The sea that was life to them, the vast flats where little stint, greenshank, and dotterel piped and flitted, and beyond, the great liners coming up Southampton water from the Orient, from the Americas! Mr. Mundy filled his glass again. And as though reading his thoughts, he said, "A good little hock, this, warms the cockles of the heart, my boy."

But all Richard could say was, "Yes, indeed, sir."

On Richard's other side sat a vivacious young girl, named Flora Gould. She was dark, with violet eyes, and a face of beautiful contour. She was affianced, he understood, to the young fellow opposite him across the table, who dressed and looked like a cavalry officer, with his dark hair parted in the middle, and his gaily brushed moustache, the ends of which now and then he twirled between finger and thumb. Their parents lived next door to one another in Twistleton Road. Flora Gould and Gerard Rolls were to be married in the coming spring. Unknown to Richard, Mr. Gould, a leather merchant with a tanning yard in Bermondsey, had bought the topmost house in Hillside Road for his daughter's wedding present.

"To our bones!" said the Vicar, raising his glass. "To our universal mother Eve, the earth! From the ooze we came, to the ooze we return!"

"Come, Ernest," remarked Mrs. Mundy, "No time like the present."

"The present, m'am, is a flux of the so-called past. We are but the descendants of Protozoa, Foraminifera and Radiolaria, of their testas sunk to the sea floor, impregnated by lime and silica, to become chalk and flint. To the Thanet sand that covered them, flushed there by the sea!"

"Really, Ernest!" said Mrs. Mundy indulgently as to a child, as she raised her glass.

"To the Antiquarian Society, and happy days to come!"

"Do not forget my Dorcas Society!"

"Of course not, my love! Are not the Woolwich and Reading beds superimposed upon the Lower Tertiary Thanet sands?"

"It is a little obscure to me, but no doubt there is a connexion, Ernest."

"Verily so, my dear Ethelburga!" The Vicar raised his glass. "For William Blake wrote that Nature was the Devil—and a Devil not so far removed from the empyrean, I might add— and Darwin proves the evolution of species, and so science may soon prove the inculcation of matter with spirit and the soul— that will be a great day when religion and science join hands."

"In the Dorcas Society, Ernest?"

"Assuredly so, my dear Ethelburga; for the Dorcas Society arises in good works for the poor; and the poor are of a lower stratum of society; and society is human, and the human mammal has its basis in geology. We are but the rocks in animation; we are but dust from dust, with the flowers of the field. But I cannot improve on the major poetry of the Old Testament."

The Vicar spoke with mellifluous charm, tipping his empty hock glass as though it were a planetary sphere uncertain of its axis after Higher Purpose had launched it into space. He looked up suddenly towards Richard, peering over the top of imaginary spectacles.

"Cockles, Maddison, cockles! First the great sea, the wine-dark sea long before the coming of the grapes of Aeschylus and Virgil; and descending from the sublime to the particular, the sea covering Kent, Surrey, Sussex, part of Hampshire, Essex, Suffolk, part of Norfolk—extending over what now we call the German Ocean—together with the Bristol Channel, and north-west France—the sea which deposited, in our own small locality, what we now call London Clay. Vast rivers fed this sea, which was warm in the cooling of the earth, and overcast by fogs——"

"Are you going to join the Antiquarian Society, Mr. Maddison?" Violet eyes looked with frank friendliness into Richard's.

"If I am not black-balled, Miss Gould. I have one grey hair, discovered over my right ear this very morning, and so I am just qualified." Richard thought this remark somewhat funny; then before he could wonder if it implied discourtesy to his host, the Vicar exclaimed, as he went round with the tapered bottle, "Fortunate youth to be the possessor of even one! Mine have long since been returned to geological impulse."

He went back to his chair at the head of the oval table, and poured himself a glass of wine.

"Above the Thanet gravel lies the Woolwich bed. This gives us our local character and no doubt colouring on occasion; it is the bed on which we lie, and within which we lie, which both supports and encloses our mortal shells. In places it is a red and purple mottled clay——" Richard thought of the face of Mr. Turney, and chuckled to himself—"elsewhere blue, flaky, estuarine clay containing layers of shells of cyrena cuneiformis, a bivalve somewhat resembling the cockle—and here we are back where we began, at the cockles of the heart." And his hand rested a moment affectionately upon that of Miranda MacIntosh.

H'm, said Richard to himself.

Then Miss MacIntosh said with engrossed seriousness, "Were not some teeth of sharks found in a new road being excavated beside the Randisbourne, Vicar, quite recently?"

"Yes, Miranda. And—greater triumph!—we excavated, with them, some thigh-bones of Bostaurus, the great wild ox Urus of Roman historians. Who knows, my dear Maddison, that this calcined relic was not the direct progenitor of the famous wild cattle still kept at Chillingham in Northumberland? We have also found bones of the long-faced wild black ox, resting on clay at the base of a gravel bed rolled by the stream, and obviously deposited in an eddy. But that is not all! One condyle of the longest bone was *sawn* off!"

"How was that done, do you suppose, sir?" enquired Gerard Rolls, caressing his cavalry moustache opposite Richard. Mr. Rolls was by occupation a traveller in bristles.

"With a saw, of course, Gerard, what else would it be done with, do you suppose?"

"Yes, but what *kind* of a saw, that is the question to my mind,

Vicar," and the young man gave an upward fondle of his own natural bristles.

"A saw is a saw, I have seen saws in butchers' shops, and choppers, too. The men bang them down so hard on the wooden blocks, they soon chop them away. Don't you agree with me?" and the bright dark violet eyes of Flora Gould were turned winsomely to Richard's.

"Yes, but did the ancient Britons have saws in those days—before the Bronze Age—am I correct, sir?" Richard, flustered by such eyes, appealed to Mr. Mundy.

"Let us hear your views, Maddison," replied the Vicar, "Let us hear all sides to the question. Miss Gould has seen saws in butchers' shops. Are we all agreed? Ah yes, someone may enquire, but were there butchers' shops and were they equipped with saws in those days?"

Fortunately for Richard, Miss Gould supplied the answer.

"Well, the Romans had houses with hollow walls, up which heat from fires passed to heat them, and Papa says they were wonderful people, so they must have had saws."

"Mr. Mundy is speaking of the Pleistocene Age, dearest," said Mr. Rolls, tolerantly, across the candle-lit table.

"But he said the bone was *sawed* in two, so it must have been sawed, you noodle, you!" and Miss Flora Gould blew her lover a kiss over the wavering flames. "Silly billy, that proves my point, doesn't it, Mr. Mundy?"

"Yes, my flower of evolution. The clay was derived from the decomposition of felspathic rocks, and the river or rivers—of which only our small Randisbourne and its tributaries remain—some alas—" and the Vicar looked sadly round the table—"shortly to be enclosed in sewers for evermore—where was I?"

"You were going to tell us who sawed the bone, I think, Ernest," said his wife.

"I am coming to that in a moment, dearest Ethelburga. Meanwhile, the London Clay Sea must needs have passed through regions where such rocks are exposed. Sir Charles Lyell thought it was a large river which drained a continent lying to the west or south-west of Britain."

Here Richard saw a chance to raise himself from the obscurity of ignorance.

"Atlantis—the lost continent!"

"Yes indeed, Maddison. Now not to tease the ladies further, let me say at once that a little while ago we had the greatest pleasure in finding in the Randisbourne gravel on Reynard's Common a small saw made from a thin flint-flake, by which the operation in question might have been performed. Marrow, extracted from the larger bones of mammals, has ever been a *bonne bouche* to primitive peoples."

"I always eat the marrow in my chops," said Flora Gould. "It gives me energy!" and she waggled a forefinger at her lover, then blew him a kiss.

"It gives you those bright eyes, my dear. It was, judging by fragments in our little museum, in most cases obtained by the simple process of smashing off the condyles; but the longer bone probably fell to the lot of a chieftain who preferred to have his marrow free from splinters. But how his slave, with that little flint saw, would deal with marrow bones of Elephas primigenius, the Mammoth, or of the Great Two-Horned Woolly Rhinoceros, we must leave to conjecture, even as I now observe that our gracious hostess is preparing to leave us, gentlemen, to our filberts and wine."

And Mr. Mundy, followed by Richard Maddison and Gerard Rolls, arose dutifully to his feet, while Richard hastened to open the door, with a correctly perceptible bow, for Mrs. Mundy.

Chapter 9

"LONDON PARTICULAR"

On a late November night the first fog of the winter descended upon London. Matter floating from factory louvre and domestic chimney during the windless hours of a hazy day fell with the afternoon condensation of moisture upon river, roof, and cinder flat. As the hour of four was struck upon the cracked bronze rim of Big Ben an acid mist in the half-empty streets began to corrode oppidanal prospects sombre as steel-engravings. The lamplighters stepped rapidly upon their rounds; carriages of the leisured classes, coachmen in front and tiger-boys behind, drove their masters and mistresses homewards to roaring red coal-fires, and themselves to comfortable quarters above stable and mews. Street vendors by shallow and tray in the poorer districts cursed, but remained with their wares exposed above the gutter; thieves rejoiced; within thousands of counting-houses and offices middle-class anxiety increased behind thoughts of policies, bills, cover notes, invoices, and other patterns of commerce expressed in paper and ink.

Richard Maddison, glancing out of the tall glass windows of the Town Department of the Moon Fire Office in the City, hoped that a pea-souper would not come down, at least before his train reached Wakenham station; for that evening he was giving a lecture upon 'Local Lepidoptera' to the Antiquarian Society. The very idea of it during the preceding weeks and days, had given him quaking moments akin to panic; for he had never so much as made a speech in public in his life before. And a lecture to last one hour, without magic-lantern slides! He tried to forget it, and to concentrate entirely upon the policy he was preparing from its proposal form.

He sat on a tall mahogany stool against a long mahogany desk or counter, one of several clerks seated likewise along its length. A ground-glass partition divided the counter into two sections, by which opposing faces were concealed from one another. Above the screen arose porcelain globes supported on lacquered brass pipes, out of which issued gas, by means of improved non-corrosive jets. The pot-bellied stove by the far wall, beside the messenger's lodge, gave forth a steady radiation of heat. It was, by the clock above the inner swing doors before the main entrance, a quarter after four o'clock. The rumble of wheeled traffic opposite the Royal Exchange down the street had sunk to a deeper growl, as the pace of the vehicles was slowed.

"Looks as though we are in for a London particular," remarked Journend, the pleasant little colleague on his right.

"Yes," said Richard, "I am afraid you are right," glancing up before continuing his work.

Outside the London day was decaying rather than dying. Westward the sun was still visible above the Houses of Parliament, a livid orb in the manufactured air. Gradually the enwreathed rim was sinking to wreckage upon the pinnacles of the building which had constituted itself guardian of the free world served by navy and merchant shipping paramount upon the seven seas. Through the poisonous atmosphere the sun's colour was as of the redness of dyed tainted meat offered for sale in the poorer quarters of London.

With the sun's disappearance there arose as out of sweating paving-stone, sooted building, wet bedunged asphalt street, and dripping branch of plane tree supporting puffed and dingy-rock-dove—the pigeon of the Londoner—an emanation as of solar death. Sulphurous whiffs caught the breathing; acid inflamed the membranes of eyes; detritus lodged under lids, inflamed haws, to be removed, if the muttering pedestrian were fortunate, with hook of nail or rubbing of finger-tip. The pea-souper dreaded by Richard, together with nearly two million other Londoners, was beginning to drift in slow swirl and eddy into the streets from the direction of the Thames estuary. It was to be seen billowing past the street lamps, enclosing them at once in clammy thickness; it moved upon central London from its gathering places over the industrial east both north and south of the river, as though sucked upon the tide moving in from Gravesend and the marshes of Sheppey and distant Nore. At six o'clock, when it was at its most dense, more than four hundred tons of organic and inorganic matter were in suspension within the area called Greater London; double night lay upon the City, more terrible because it was made by man who least desired it.

At half-past six the southward march across London Bridge of black-coated workers was at its greatest press. The granite sett-stones of the road between the sidewalks bore the grind and percussion of thousands of iron wheels and shoes. Lamps were visible but a pace distant and then as yellow spots within cocoons. Richard walked, worsted-gloved hand over mouth and nose, with coat buttoned and collar up against pickpocket and cold. The starched cuffs of his shirtsleeves were encased with white paper; a muffler was round his neck. Coughs were audible everywhere in the bobbing ranks of benighted travellers: these were the only human noises, the only complaints, as though amplified by the mechanical hoots and blares of foghorns upon the river below.

The bridge itself was in movement. The mass of masonry was transmitting into the flood-tide constant vibrations from its submerged piers which shrimps and prawns resident in the weed clustered to the sterlings periodically discerned with their feelers: the vibrations of tens of thousands of human feet, of multitudinous wheels hooped with iron beating upon flag-stone and granite sett. The tide of human beings was crossing the tide of Thames, the one on the ebb to the suburbs, the other to the German Ocean.

There was inevitable delay in both the higher and lower levels of the railway station. Great jets of steam screeched from the safety valves of delayed engines, the noise momentarily decapitating the body hurrying to find a seat, peering into carriages already packed tight, with men standing between wooden seats covered with hard, dull and durable upholstery. Tobacco smoke reeked with fog; fifteen men unspeaking, almost unmoving—like the train. It was inevitable. It could not be altered. It had always been, and always would be.

Reports sounded muffled down the line. Richard, standing with the top of his head not far from the pale blue flame in the glass cover in the middle of the roof, was thinking that he could not possibly be at St. Simon's hall at eight o'clock, washed and changed and having supped. Would the train never start? What train was it? No matter, the fog had upset the entire time-table. Should he go directly to the hall; or go home first?

The feeling of being unclean decided him. The membranes of his eyes were inflamed, specks of carbon and metal felt to be enormous and untidy in their irritation. He would go home first, wash and change his clothes, and have his supper later. Why had he undertaken to give the damned lecture at all? There was no time for that sort of thing any more: butterflies belonged to youth gone past.

At last the train started. Standing figures braced themselves against the jerk following the guard's whistle; thereafter was dull endurance, amidst the detonation of signals, until finally the train stopped at the familiar, but ghostly, station. He hurried out into the cold murk of the night, walking as fast as he dared, hands held out before him, up Foxfield Road leading from the station to the Hill. It was already twenty minutes to eight.

He walked in the middle of the road, to avoid blundering into iron railings and scraping himself against brick walls of gardens. As he climbed up Foxfield Road the fog became less dense, so that the lights on lamp-posts began to be visible a dozen yards away. Fumbling along as fast as he dared, he crossed Twistleton Road, coming to Cranefield Road, and the next turning to the right would lead up to the gates of the Hill, which would be lightless.

The fog was thinner as he came to the end of the last rows of houses. He could see an occasional rectangular blur on either side of him. He stepped high over the kerb, and felt the pebbles of the gravel of the path under the thin leather soles of his boots. He must get them repaired; it was false economy to wear them through to the inner sole.

A colder air was in movement upon the Hill. He felt a wet mist condensing upon his eyelashes. A star was visible overhead; the black trunks of the elms where the rooks nested in spring, and where once he had seen a Camberwell Beauty in the beam of his dark lantern, loomed on his right hand. He felt easier: he would just have time to wash and change, and return for his address. Any ruffians accosting him, as on the occasion when he had lost the Camberwell Beauty, would have another man to reckon with, he assured himself, as his chin thrust itself forward and the hair on his neck rose. Richard never passed the elms without memory bringing before him that scene of nearly five years before.

The path forked to the right beyond the trees, passing the dark square of the West Kent Grammar School. Another couple of hundred yards, and he would be at the top of the broad way leading down to Hillside Road.

He was half-way down the gulley when he heard the sound of someone sniffing. Recently seats had been placed by the London County Council on both sides of the gulley, against low iron railings enclosing plantations of hawthorns on the steep slopes above. Someone was sitting there alone. Richard had just passed the seated figure, pale blur of face, when he heard sobbing. He stopped; and was about to pass on, mindful of the foolishness of interference, when a strangled voice said, "It's only me, sir."

"Is that you, Mona? Is anything the matter?"

There was no reply. Drippings from the bushes pattered down.

"Mona? What are you doing there? Are you alone?"

"Please sir, yes sir. Oh, oh," and unrestrained weeping joined the melancholy patterings from the trees.

He walked to the seat, saying in a gentler tone, "Come, do not be afraid of me. Do you not feel very well? You ought to be indoors on a night like this, you know."

"I ain't doin' no wrong, please sir. It's—it's me half day off, please sir."

Poor little thing, thought Richard, his heart touched. "Well, I am afraid it is not a very pleasant one. It is yours to do what you like with, of course, but then you are not very old, and we cannot have you getting pneumonia, you know. Come along, there's a good girl. You should not be alone on the Hill. Come along now."

More sobbing. "I dursen't, please sir. Missis is angry wi'me. I couldn't help it, please sir."

"Oh, some little trouble? Well, it cannot be so serious, I am sure. Mrs. Maddison is not one to be angry very long, Mona." He thought that perhaps she had broken a plate or cup, or even dropped a tray.

"Come along now, be sensible. It is hardly a night for a dog to be out." The girl did not move. "Well, if you will not come, I suppose you will stay there." He moved away, his sympathy lessening.

A despairing cry came out of the murk. "Gawd's sake, sir, don't go and tell me farver, sir. He'll kill me, sir."

He began to feel impatient with the girl's hysteria, as he thought of it to himself. "Come along, Mona, I am sure you have not done anything really very bad. What is it, a broken plate or a cup? Well, that is not very terrible. Just come along

home now, and I will try and put things right for you. Come
along there's a good girl, you must be very cold, come in and
have a cup of hot cocoa by the kitchen fire."

"Thank you, sir. I'm sorry, sir, I didn't mean no harm, sir,
promise you won't tell me farver, sir?"

She was in such a state that Richard promised. She followed
him, sniffing and blubbering, down the broad gulley, through the
spiked iron gates padlocked open, and so to the asphalt pavement
of Hillside Road.

Richard let himself in with his latch key, and whistled as he
opened the door. Hetty came out of the kitchen. "Go on in,
Mona, there's a good girl," she heard him say. "We must not
let the fog come in, must we? Wipe your boots on the mat,
there's a good girl—heels and sides, and then the soles. Well,
Hetty, I found your little helpmeet sitting on the Hill, and
thought it was time she came in. I must hurry back for the
address; have you some soup all ready?"

"Yes, dear, some Scotch broth, it won't take a minute. I'll put
it on a tray, and bring it down to the sitting-room."

" I must wash first."

"Yes, dear, I'll have it all ready for you when you come down."

When he came downstairs he went into the kitchen to change
his boots. Mona was sitting, in coat and hat, on a chair by the fire.

"Come, cheer up, Mona," he said, "you must not go around
looking like a wet week, you know." Whereupon Mona hung her
head, and began, once more, to weep silently.

Carrying his other pair of boots, to warm them by the sitting-
room fire, Richard, with concealed impatience, went down into
that room, waiting in his armchair while Hetty poured out a
bowl of broth.

She remained anxiously quiet while he sipped the welcome
soup. She did not want him to be upset in any way before the
lecture, which he had been preparing, with the aid of his note-
books and various volumes containing hand-coloured woodcuts
and plates, during the past few evenings. She knew that it meant
a great deal to him. And how glad she had been that Mamma
was next door, to advise her what to do about Mona. Mamma
had suggested telling Dickie when he came back after his lecture.

"Your little maid of all work is not very happy, what is the
matter?"

"Yes, dear, she is a little upset over something. I will tell you of it later, it really is not very important."

"Then if it is not very important, why mention it at all?"

"Yes, you are quite right, dear, it was stupid of me. Would you like some biscuits and cheese after the broth?"

"I haven't time. Well, you women are contradictory creatures, I must say: you arouse a man's curiosity, and then you refuse to say anything about the cause of it. What is the mystery, pray?"

"Only a little trouble Mona has got into, Dickie. Really, I did not mean to worry you at all. I sent Mona home, to tell her mother, and have been expecting to hear from her."

"Got herself into trouble, has she? If you mean what I think those words mean, I should not call it a little trouble. She is scarcely turned fourteen, too. Is that what you mean?"

"Yes dear, I am afraid so."

"Then she will have to leave this house immediately!"

Mona was listening at the top of the three stairs, her heart beating rapidly. Earlier that evening she had gone into the Randiswell Recreation Ground for the purpose of drowning herself; but thoughts of Phillip, whom she loved as her own, had come between her desire for death. The voice of master, which had given her a little hope as he spoke to her out of the fog, was now cross. There was no more hope. Mona turned back into the kitchen, put her arms upon the scrubbed deal kitchen table, and broke down. She would drown herself in the river.

In the sitting-room, while Richard drank his soup, Hetty was grieving, as she had many times before, that she was seldom able to utter her real thoughts to her husband. She knew by now, and had accepted it, that she must always be very careful what she told him. He was so easily upset. Her main thought before and during the first year of their married life had been of concern for him; her thought had been mainly directed to thinking of ways and means by which he would be pleased. Alas, that so many of her good intentions had turned out the other way! If she tried to keep things from him, that would upset him, she knew; he called it suppression of the truth. And if on the other hand she told him something that had happened, he was just as likely to complain that she was incapable of managing her own affairs. Talking this over with her mother—nothing of it must be told to

Papa, of course—Hetty had eased herself of a condition that at times had given her nervous headaches. Sarah had given her daughter comfort by her own confession.

"Yes, dear, we all have to suffer our husbands. Perhaps to be silent is better than to try and explain. Then there is always prayer."

"Yes, Mamma, I do pray, every day, that I shall not do anything to upset Dickie."

But there were some things Hetty could not tell even her mother. She could not think of them, even, without mental flurry and evasion. And the latest of them, and to her mind the worst, was the shocking things she had found out about Mona.

Three mornings previously, Hetty had gone into the end bedroom at eight o'clock, all being quiet in the house, thinking that Mona had overslept. It was a Sunday morning, and the alarm was not wound on Saturday night—on week-day mornings it went off in Mona's room at half-past six—because Richard needed an hour's extra sleep. Mona was supposed to go downstairs at a quarter to eight, on Sunday mornings, and bring up a small pot of China tea on a tray, with two cups and saucers, a jug of milk, a plate of thin slices of brown bread and butter, and *The Weekly Courant*, which had been thrust through the letter-box. This was the ritual of Richard's Sunday morning, a little luxury he allowed himself once a week. He looked forward to it at eight a.m. precisely. The brown bread and butter had to be cut the night before, by Hetty, and kept fresh between two plates. He would not have Mona, probably with unwashed hands, cutting the bread.

Hetty had found Mona asleep, and Phillip asleep beside her, one arm lying across his body. The bedclothes were disarranged, as though she had been tickling him, which was forbidden. Also, she was not supposed to have the child in her bed, by Richard's orders; for she was a developing girl, and neither Hetty nor Richard considered it proper that a young boy should see any exposure of her body. Hetty had instructed Mona that she must always take off and put on her clothes behind a screen that stood in the room for that purpose.

What Hetty saw shocked her deeply. Phillip was lying on his back, part of his night-gown rucked up, so that his thin legs were exposed and part of his bluish-white stomach. It was not the

sight of that which shocked Hetty, but the fact that Mona—it
could only have been Mona—had tied one of her small red hair-
ribands in a bow round the private part of the little boy. Her
own little child, her dear little Sonny, to be treated like that by
Mona, whom she had utterly trusted! Thank God the boy's
father had not seen it!

Hetty removed the riband, praying that Sonny would not wake
up. Her prayer was answered; the boy slept on. Gently she
covered his legs with the night-gown, and dropped the creased
riband on the rug by the bed, so that Mona might think it had
dropped off one of her plaits, and so have no recollection of her
action.

But more was to come. Could she believe her eyes? Surely it
could not be her fancy? Mona was lying on her side, only a sheet
of the bedclothes covering her above the waist; and to Hetty it
appeared that she was bigger than she ought to be. Perhaps it
was the fold of the blanket lying across her that gave the suggestion of a mound? Animated by anxious curiosity, Hetty gently
tugged at the blanket to straighten it and saw that Mona's bigness
just there was not a fancy. At that moment a dark eye opened and
Mona was looking at her. The girl sat up, muttering; thrust
away the hair from her brow and said, "Oh mum, I overslepp
misself, oh the master's tea——"

Hetty said nothing about it to Mona that morning, or the rest
of the day, but on the Monday afternoon, two hours before
Richard was due to come home, she said that Mona must have a
bath, using the same water in which Phillip, and then the baby,
had been washed. And making an excuse to go into the bathroom while Mona was in the bath, Hetty saw that the girl was
pregnant.

Before saying anything to her, Hetty consulted her mother.
Sarah said that the best thing to do was to have a quiet talk with
Mona, and advise her to tell her own mother on her next after-
noon off.

"Your own experiences, dear, will enable you to know what to
say to the poor child," remarked Sarah. "She is so very young,
only fourteen, dear me. She is such a good girl too, you can see
that by the way she cares for your little two ones, Hetty."

So on the Wednesday, after a dinner of cold mutton, and the
rest of the potatoes and greens of the night before fried up

together warm and brown, and some hot jam tart, Hetty spoke to Mona, who hung her head and began to cry at once.

At three o'clock she left the house, going down the road in the direction of Randiswell and her home in Mercy Terrace. And Hetty knew nothing more until Richard returned, late because of the fog, with Mona that evening.

Richard was putting on his coat at the foot of the banisters by the front door, the dark lantern having been lit, more from an idea of romantic companionship in the forthcoming ordeal of the lecture than for finding a way through the fog, when there came the noise of knuckles knocking on the coloured glass panes. He opened the door slightly, on the chain, and a woman's voice said breathlessly, "Is our Mona 'ere? Are you the master? 'Im as put it acrost our Mona will 'ave to pay, that's what I come to say, to get what is 'er rights!"

"Who is it, Dickie?" called out Hetty, in anxious tones behind him.

"I do not know," he replied, and turning the screen of the lantern, shone the beam on the sad face of a prematurely-aged woman.

"I think it must be Mona's mother, dear."

"Oh," said Richard. "I'd better turn up the gas." It was usually turned low for economy. He slid the dog of the chain out of its groove, and opened the door.

"I think I had better have a talk with Mrs. Monk, dear," said Hetty. "You go to your lecture, Dickie," she added, with an attempt at calm, "I am sure everything will be all right."

"So it't'd better be!" cried Mrs. Monk. "It's a shime, an' the man what done it will 'ave to pay, Mr. Monk will see to that!"

"Why are you talking to me in that tone of voice?" said Richard, for the woman had addressed her remarks directly to himself.

"Mrs. Monk is not herself, Dickie," said Hetty. "Pray go to your lecture, it will come all right. I will see Mrs. Monk, perhaps it will be best to leave it to me, dearest."

But Richard was not going to leave Hetty with what he fancied to be a violent woman. It was plain to him now what was the implication.

"I must ask you to explain your attitude, Mrs. Monk," he said. "No, Hetty, I cannot leave you: I shall have to abandon all idea of my address, there is no help for it. Here, come into the kitchen; we shall awake the children if we talk here in the hall. Please wipe your boots on the mat, Mrs. Monk."

"I'm sure I never intended no offence, sir." Mrs. Monk wiped her boots vigorously. She was overawed to be inside such a house, of whose splendours she had heard from her daughter. She was now beginning to be afraid.

Hetty rose to the occasion. "Let me make you some cocoa; it is a cold raw night, Mrs. Monk. Mona, put on the little kettle, there's a good girl, fill it up from the big kettle on the hob, and set it on the ring. Mr. Maddison has to give a lecture in St. Simon's Church Hall, and must not be late. You go, dear, Mrs. Monk and I and Mona will have a talk together, and decide what is best to be done."

Richard hesitated. His experiences in the district had given him a profound distrust of the lower orders. He was trying to make up his mind—a man already unsure because of lack of sufficient food—when a sudden thumping on the door and a shout without decided the question of go or remain, for him.

The scene that followed was one to be remembered with recurrent agitation by Hetty for many years, until greater events beginning seventeen years later shook, and altered, all of Hillside Road and the district circumadjacent to the Hill—the flux of consciousness extending to those known to her, even to far places of the earth, involved in an almost universal upsurge of human violence arising from repressed human instincts. On this November night of 1897 there were blows on the door of No. 11 Hillside Road when Richard refused entry to Mona's father. The blows were followed by the shattering of stained and leaded glass, and hysterical screams from the kitchen. Richard went to the door and fastened the brass chain on its catch, and then slid the bolt into its socket. Having turned out the gas, he ran down the three steps, lantern in hand, to the sitting-room. Pushing up the roll-top of the desk there, he seized his truncheon and whistle.

Meanwhile the front door, its latch having been turned by a bleeding hand thrust in the space of broken glass, and the bolt pushed back, was receiving heavy blows as the weight of the body outside was hurled against it. The screws holding the chain were torn out of the wood; the door was burst in and was only saved from fracture against the wall by the coats hanging from their hooks on the rack.

By this time the children upstairs had been awakened by the noise. The screams of Phillip added to the upset as Monk the navvy, drunk on gin and porter from the Railway, pushed his way into the kitchen, tore off his shapeless cloth cap and hurled it upon the oilcloth, while the terrified women cowered back. With a bellowing cry of "Where is 'e, the 'kin' bleeder? Stole 'arf 'er wages, the 'kin' bastard, and put it acrost my litt'l gal, 'e 'as! By God A'mighty, when I done wiv 'im—where's 'e gorn, Jes' Chris' on tin wills? Coward, 'at's what 'e is, 'kin' coward run away! I'll get 'im, if I swing for it!"

Monk pulled off his coat, spat on his hands, loosened his belt, and went towards the passage, down which Richard had disappeared.

"Oh please do not!—Dickie, Dickie!—O my children!" and Hetty wrung her hands.

Then she heard the noise of the sash-window in the sitting-room being flung up; and a long-drawn *Fran-nn-nn-aa-aa-nn*—the twin discordant blast of a police whistle. Lantern in one hand, truncheon in the other, nickel-plated whistle in mouth, Richard was summoning help through the fog.

He drew a deep breath; blew a second blast; inhaled deeply again, as he secured the cord of the varnished wooden truncheon, with the arms of the City of London painted upon it, around his right wrist; and summoning up himself, with lantern in left hand, walked resolutely towards the kitchen, his nostrils wide, his hair feeling to be standing up on the back of his head. He felt entirely calm, events were happening outside himself.

Monk the navvy spat on his hands again, and was holding fists before face and head preparatory to the crouch and rush when the tip of the hard-wood billet, coming up with a flick of Richard's forearm and wrist—the old Indian club twirl—struck him under the chin and not down upon his head as he had expected. Immediately he collapsed in a loose heap.

More whistle blasts into the fog. Answering blasts and shouts. Footfalls upon asphalt, upon the tiles of the porch.

"Hullo, sir, had some trouble? We know this customer."

Monk was hand-cuffed before being hauled to his feet, whimpering. He was frog-marched into the hall. More oaths as he was pushed through the door, more blows; and the sobbing of Mrs. Monk and Mona in the kitchen audible again.

The delinquent was flung down upon the little lawn in front of the house. He pitched face-first over the burnt-brick rockery, there to lie and await the hand-ambulance.

By this time other front doors down Hillside Road had opened —"Montrose", "Chatsworth", "Knebworth", etc. Voices came from the fog. One preceded action: Mrs. Bigge, shawl over Assyrian style of hair-dress, beset with pins and clasps after the mid-weekly wash, popped into "Lindenheim", and at once went upstairs to Phillip, calling out as she hauled herself up by the banisters, "There now, little man, there now! Aunty Bigge is coming, Aunty Bigge is coming, to tell you about Goldilocks and the Three Bears!" Hetty was already with the baby.

When it was over—the statements written into books, the wheeled and hooded cart brought and the man taken away prostrate under the brown canvas, strapped across feet, middle, and wrists—Richard pasted brown paper over the shattered leaded panel of the front door, while Mrs. Bigge, in the kitchen, had a cup of cocoa, wide-eyed Phillip in her arms.

"I hope Josiah is not upset by it all, perhaps I ought to pop back into the house and see." Gallantly Richard escorted Mrs. Bigge to the front gate of "Montrose". From the notes of the harp coming from upstairs, it appeared that Mr. Bigge was undisturbed. Thanking her for her good offices, Richard returned to his own house, with no further thoughts of his lecture.

Which, as it turned out, was in accordance with the thoughts of other members of the Antiquarian and Archeological Society; for owing to the extreme density of the fog, only Mr. Mundy and Miss MacIntosh, who had but to walk a hundred yards or so, arrived at St. Simon's Hall that night.

The next evening Miss Thoroughgood called, asking to see Mr. Maddison on particular business, in private. Richard saw her in the front room, behind the door shut for about five minutes. Afterwards Miss Thoroughgood left with raddled face, and Hetty heard her thanking Richard profusely as he let her out of the front door, and saw her down the dark porch and awkward path to the gate. Hetty did not ask what Miss Thoroughgood had said, nor did Richard tell her.

In due course local newspapers printed accounts of the

proceedings at Greenwich Police Court, where a remand was made; and later still, the details at the Quarter Sessions. Richard appeared as a witness on both occasions. The accused man declared on oath that his daughter had told him that her employer had not only interfered with her, but had kept back half her wages, paying only half-a-crown a week. Hetty denied this, saying she had paid Mona five shillings every Saturday. Medical evidence was given that conception had occurred before the girl entered employment as a domestic servant. An earnest member of the Society for the Elevation of the Poor was permitted to give evidence of extenuating circumstances. She said that there were seven children in the family, which was one of three families occupying a three-bedroom'd house in Mercy Terrace. The Monks occupied one room. Monk had always been a good husband and father until he had experienced a prolonged period of being out of work, for no fault of his own.

Mrs. Monk was not required by law to testify against her husband, nor was Mona brought into the witness box; so the charge of incest, known by the court missionary and others to be common enough in such rookeries of the poor, was not made. It was sufficient that Monk had committed the acts of burglary, assault and battery, with intent to do grievous bodily harm. He was sent to penal servitude for the maximum number of years.

Richard was deeply mortified by accounts printed in the newspapers. He never went back to St. Simon's Tennis Club, nor did he attend any further Antiquarian Society meetings. His feelings about the matter may perhaps be indicated by the fact that, when his quarterly season-ticket expired on the London, Brighton railway, he changed to the South Eastern, going to and returning from Randiswell every day, in order to avoid passing down Foxfield Road and the parish hall of St. Simon Wakenham. And he never told Hetty, or anyone else, what Miss Thoroughgood had told him in confidence: that she was suffering from skin cancer, and had charged Mona an excessive commission of half her wages, as that was the only way she could pay the doctor's bills. "Old Loos'am", as she had been known, died in the Infirmary half a year later, and was buried in the graveyard of the parish church.

PART TWO

COURAGE

Chapter 10

HETTY IS ISOLATED

THE may blossom was white on the thorns upon the Hill, as though to adorn the first springtime of the new century. Leaves of silver birch and elm hid the black branches of winter; the grass was a deeper green, like the colour painted upon the spiked iron railings enclosing the forty acres of the Recreation Ground. Hetty had planned to dress the two children in their best clothes— Sonny in white sailor suit and Mavis in the silk frock she had made for her—and take them to Greenwich, to visit her favourite Aunt Marian; but on rising that morning she felt ill, and wondered if she were going to have one of her bilious attacks.

She was so obviously unwell, head hot and cheeks flushed, that Richard ordered her to remain in bed, saying that he would get his own breakfast. The porridge was already cooked in the double-cooker, and had only to be heated under the gas. Rashers of streaky bacon were in the larder. Hetty prayed that Dickie would not be upset if he found any food that he considered stale on the shelves; and she started to get up, but felt so giddy that she climbed back again into bed, shivering.

"I shall be quite all right, Dickie." Thinking of the children, she felt relief that Mamma was next door. "Mrs. Bigge will come in, dear, if I want any help. I'll take some nux vomica, perhaps that will put me right. No, dear, I don't feel like—I mean I don't want any breakfast. Just a cup of tea, thank you Dickie. Sonny and Mavis only have a plate of porridge each, and then a slice of bread and butter with marmalade."

"I know, I'm not entirely unobservant, Hetty!"

"No, dear, of course not. My head aches a little, I can't think very clearly." Her eyes shone with fever. "Oh Dickie, please don't bother about getting the children's breakfasts, on second thoughts. Sonny has never dressed himself alone, dear."

"Well, it's time he learned! A boy who cannot dress himself, at his age, indeed! I've never heard of such a thing!"

He went to the door and called down the corridor, "Phillip, are you awake?"

"Yes, farver," a thin voice floated back.

"What are you doing?"

"Nothing, farver."

"Then get up, at once, and dress yourself!"

There was no reply, so Richard, in dark-blue dressing-gown and carpet slippers, went down the corridor to the end bedroom but one. On the way he turned on the cold tap for his morning tub.

"Come on, old chap!" he said to the boy lying in bed. "Are you feeling seedy, too?"

"No, farver."

"Then get up!" He stripped back the clothes, revealing the thin child lying curled up with a golliwog, and a loudly purring brindled cat, in his arms.

The boy stared at his father. Something in the stare penetrated to an inner feeling of the man, who almost against his will heard himself speaking with an abruptness that he did not really intend. Indeed, Richard never really intended to be censorious or critical; but gradually the habit had formed.

"Now you know very well it is forbidden to take Zippy to bed with you, don't you?"

When the boy did not answer, but continued to stare with full dark stare, the inner feeling seemed to leap out of Richard and he said severely, "If you do this again, my boy, you will have to go to bed and have only bread and water for a day! I will not have you grow up in deceit! Come on, up with you!" and he gave the boy a slap on his bottom.

The cat stretched itself and yawned, while the boy began to cry.

"Oh come on, Phillip! Cannot I say anything to you without you turning on the water-works? Be a man! Look at Zippy, he doesn't start crying because he has to get up. Zippy, Zippy! Come on then, old fellow." With tail erect the brindled cat walked over the bed, and rubbed its neck against Richard's knuckles.

"Oh, come on Phillip, stop snivelling! Anyone would think you'd been ill-treated, the way you respond to a slap! Why bless my soul, I hardly touched you. Your Mother is not very well, and so you must be an extra special good boy to-day, and look after your Aunt Isabelle when she arrives. It's time you had a cold tub in the morning, I started them before I was your age. Come on, I'll give you a swish before I have mine."

He led the boy into the bathroom.

"Come on, now, off with your nightshirt." The bath was a third full, a quivering oblong of pale green coldness.

"Now then, in you go, like a man. Come on, climb over by yourself. Don't stand there shivering, and for heaven's sake don't start grizzling again! Come on, don't be a mamby-pamby!"

Hetty was listening. The bedroom door was wide open. She had heard the slap, the overbearing voice, the whimpering, and wondered anxiously what Sonny had been doing to upset his father. She knew how the boy had adored his father, and had felt after the birth of Mavis that his father did not want him any more. It grieved her to think that during the past year the boy had become noticeably more shut-in upon himself. At times it seemed to Hetty that Dickie had forgotten how he, in his boyhood, had felt when *his* father had been cross and impatient.

The bathroom window was open at the top. Richard believed in plenty of fresh air. It was a calm summer morning outside. Through the drawn-down top of the window a starling was visible on the chimney pot of the opposite house, belonging to Mr. Turney. Richard always thought of his father-in-law as Mr. Turney, as invariably he addressed him as Mr. Turney. Thomas Turney's sons addressed the Old Man as "sir"; Richard had done the same to his father; but to him Mr. Turney was Mr. Turney, an individual he could not respect.

This feeling, of course, was shared by both men towards each other, since it had its existence between the two.

Richard had an affection for the starling. Its bronze-green sheens glinted in the sun as it sang on the rim of the warm red chimney pot. It wheezed and shivered its wings, as, with opened upheld beak, it turned from side to side, like a singer on a concert platform. Its song was composed of mimic cries of its surroundings—yodel-like *Milk-o!* cry of milkman, clatter of tinned milk cans, plaintive cry of kestrel hawk that hunted over the Hill, ringing cry of tomtit, bark of dog, *zec-zec* of carter to horse, the thin wail of a violin—even the noise of Mr. Turney clearing his throat in his bathroom opposite! Richard greeted the bird, in his mind, as a friend, every morning. He knew that the starling was throwing off into the sky its joyous greeting to the sun, the expectations of its mate's sky-blue eggs hatching, and food in the cabbage fields of Randiswell—and then Richard's happy communication with the herald on the chimney pot was liable to be broken by the actual noise of Mr. Turney clearing his throat at the wash-basin, sniffing diluted Sanitas up his nostrils, and gargling. Richard was too sensitive to close his own bathroom window, although he did not want to hear the vulgarian noises of his father-in-law; nor for Mr. Turney to overhear the private noises of his own ablutions. Any moment now Mr. Turney would be entering his bathroom.

"Come on, old chap, no use shivering on the brink! Under you go! Why, you're not half a man! At your age, I and your uncles used to swim every morning, summer and winter, in the Longpond at home."

Richard believed this; as a fact he had learned to swim at seven years of age.

Phillip was standing unhappily in the bath. He was afraid of the deep mass of greenish water below him. He was greatly apprehensive of being shattered by the cold. Richard lost patience with him. He bent over the bath, placed one arm under the boy's knees and the other around projecting shoulder-blades, and lifted him up preparatory to laying him flat on his back. But the child clung to him. He was rigid with fear, his mouth open, his eyes terrified.

"No, farver, no! Please don't! No, farver! I beg your pardon, farver!"

"Let go, boy! Don't be such a blue funk, Phillip! Why, you'll have a wonderful glow afterwards. Come on now, let go of my dressing-gown!" The father spoke sharply; he had lost patience; his wife's indisposition had ruined his morning routine, and pleasure in the exhilarating cold tub, which he took every day of the year, attributing to it his absence of colds or any other illness.

He pressed down the clinging boy. Phillip cried out, tried wildly to claw himself up. His head bumped on the curved rim of the iron bath, and he began to cry. The father lifted him out, covered the shivering little wretch with his towel, and dried him.

"What a fuss over nothing, my boy! There now, don't you feel better?"

He had come to the conclusion that his son was a cowardly sort. Did he not tell untruths, sometimes, it appeared, for the sake of untruth, when really there was nothing to be gained by it? Hetty was partly responsible, of course; she spoiled the boy, by giving in to his every mood.

"Now toddle along and show Mother that you can dress yourself like a big boy! You *are* a big boy, you know, you are five years old. You must look after Mother today, and Mavis. And when Aunty Belle comes, you must be on your best behaviour. There now, you won't be afraid of cold water any more, will you?"

"No, farver."

"And tomorrow, if you are good, I'll let you give yourself a cold swish, after I've had mine, all by yourself. What do you say to that, eh?"

"Thank you, farver."

"That's right, old chap. Now toddle along and get your clothes on, and perhaps if you are good today, when I come home tonight I'll give you, as an especial treat, some cherry toffee."

"Thank you, farver."

The boy hurried away back to his bedroom. Richard, as was his habit, shut and bolted the door, to enjoy the privacy and refreshment of what he called his tub.

As a special treat for breakfast, he cooked some bacon for Phillip. The two had the meal together in the kitchen. Richard was a little keyed-up because he had taken, for him, a bold decision. He would ride on the Starley Rover to the City. This would enable him to leave a message at Dr. Cave-Brown's on the way. He had not cycled to his work for two years, and so the prospect was cause for some trepidation. He had never yet been late at the office—whether in the old days at Doggett's in the Strand, or now at the Moon Fire Office in Haybundle Street—during all his years in the City, since the age of seventeen. And he must not spoil that record of punctuality.

Having taken his wife a second cup of tea, he lifted out his bicycle and departed down Hillside Road on that enamelled and nickel-plated machine, straw hat held under arm lest it blow off in the rush of air down the short and flinty hill to the corner, and then up the slight slope of Charlotte Road to the doctor's.

Phillip watched him out of sight from his mother's bedroom
window. Then he turned and said to his mother, "I'm the man
now, Mummy."

"Yes, dear. You will be a good boy, and not touch any of your
father's things, won't you?"

"No, Mummy."

The idea having been put into his head, Phillip promptly
went down the steps from the landing to Father's work-room. It
was a wonderful place, full of strange and exciting things. He
tried the handle, and found the door locked. He returned to his
mother's bedroom.

"May I float my birf-day boat, Mummy, in the barf?"

"Yes, dear, if you promise not to make a lot of splashing."

Hetty thought with relief that Mrs. Feeney was coming for a
whole day today.

"I don't want Mavis to come, Mummy. She interubbers
me."

Mavis could now walk. She lived much of her life in the cot
and the high chair which Phillip had vacated. She was now
asleep, having had from her father, whose delight in her was as
obvious as his disappointment with his first-born, a bowl of
warm bread and milk, called sop.

Hetty lay with aching eyeballs. She felt sick, her head ached.
She shivered. What could she have eaten? Or had she caught
a chill. Thank goodness, Mrs. Feeney would be here any minute
now.

Phillip put in the plug, and turned on the taps. The fire was
not alight in the kitchen, so no hot water could scald him, thought
Hetty, or be wasted. His Aunt Victoria had sent him a little
yacht from Holborn for his birthday, on behalf of his godmother
who was living in the Aegean, making a study of the country of
Homer and other Greek poets, preparatory, it was understood,
to coming home and starting, with a friend, a school for young
gentlewomen in the West Country.

Happily Phillip sailed his boat in the bath. He experimented
with extra sails from the toilet roll, extra masts with toothbrushes
from the rack above the soap dish, and with the soap for its
own sake, together with the tooth glass. It was interesting to
transfer water in the glass from bath to lavatory pan. He tried
to sail the yacht in the pan, and to find out what happened when

he clambered up and pulled the plug. Obviously the form was disintegrating, for next he sought out Zippy, to give that cat a cold swish.

This being done, the cat yowled and fled, looking unusually thin, and leaving a string of water on the linoleum of the landing and the carpet of the stairs. Philip knew where it had gone to, its hide in the cupboard under the stairs, where brooms and brushes were kept, with smelly cloths—Phillip knew every one of the smells—for polishing and cleaning wood, stone, and metal.

Having pulled Zippy out of the cupboard, Phillip was wiping him in the scullery when there was a knock on the door. He went to the door, recognising the knock of Mrs. Feeney. He knew all the other callers by the way they rang the bell, knocked, or, when it was Hern the grocer, who was deaf, both rang and knocked.

"Why, what have you been doing with the cat, Master Phil? My goodness, the poor old moggy's as wet as anything! What have you been doing, eh?"

Mrs. Feeney went straight into the kitchen, put her bag on the board under the dresser, and began to untie the strings of her bonnet.

"Zippy had a barf, Mrs. Feeney. I did too, with Farver. I've been sailing my boat. Mummy's ill in bed. So don't make too much noise, will you?"

"Oh? I'll be going upstairs then, to find out what's the matter."

"You won't make any noise, will you, Mrs. Feeney?"

"Go on with yer, Master Phillip, it's you that mustn't make the noise!"

Mrs. Feeney loved her Master Phil. Had she not helped to bring the little dear into the world? Mr. and Mrs. Maddison were a special master and mistress to the charwoman. She had the highest regard for both of them, based on Richard's invariable courtesy to her, and on Hetty's sweetness and confiding kindness; and also, though Mrs. Feeney did not realize this, on her own not unexceptionable integrity. Mrs. Feeney always worked her hardest and best. She was invariably cheerful, and always grateful for all and any little extras in the way of stale pieces of bread, cold potatoes, bones and pieces of mutton fat, old clothes and hats, old newspapers, that Hetty gave her. She did not ever stand on her rights, as the phrase went; she knew only her duties.

For a shilling, Mrs. Feeney worked a half day of five hours.
A whole day was eighteenpence, including her lunch of bread and
cheese and tea, and more tea with bread and dripping at five
o'clock, before going home. She enjoyed her work greatly.

Mrs. Feeney, having removed black poke bonnet and shawl,
went into the scullery. In that small, dark place, she leaned
towards the sink, held her nose between finger and thumb, and
adroitly cleared her nostrils with an expulsion of air from the
lungs. Then she turned the tap, and found, to her surprise,
that Phillip had been watching her. "Don't you ever do that,
Master Phil, or you'll be getting me into hot water."

Bonnet and shawl being hung behind the scullery door, she
tidied her hair, before going upstairs to see the mis'es, otherwise
mistress. She found Hetty changing the diapers of the baby in
her cot. Mis'es had the fever, and Mrs. Feeney tucked her up in
bed.

"I'll get on all right, mum, you leave it to me, mum."

Hetty told her that Miss Maddison, the master's sister, was
coming at twelve o'clock, and would Mrs. Feeney see about
some macaroni and cheese for her luncheon. And would she
go in next door and tell Mrs. Turney that she would like to see
her? And, of course, to keep an eye on Master Phillip.

Master Phillip meanwhile had gone out of the house, and
was knocking at Mrs. Bigge's front door. He often went in to see
Aunty Bigge, because she gave him cake and comfits. Comfits
were nice to crunch, being little rolypoly white and pink things
with black licorice inside. He liked to strum on Mr. Bigge's harp,
too, and make lovely noises. There were also many fascinating
things to see in Aunty Bigge's house, although he did not like
being kissed by Aunty Bigge, who smelled like some of the cloths
in the cleaning cupboard, or her hair did. Aunty Bigge's hair
had a black bottle smell, a cat's tail smell.

Mrs. Bigge was proud of her hair, which when brushed out
fell nearly to her knees. She had a secret receipt, by which she
maintained what Josiah Bigge called her Woman's Glory. She
used to work a mixture of vinegar, neat's foot oil, and chemist's
civet into her scalp with an old toothbrush. This receipt not
only guarded against any tendency to dandruff, but it gave the
thick tresses a fragrance similar to those of Ayesha, Josiah's

favourite heroine in fiction, by way of Rider Haggard's famous novel. Mrs. Bigge had not the least wish to attract Josiah Bigge, or any other man; she considered that any woman who set out to attract anyone was lacking in self-respect. The hair-treatment receipt was an old one of her grandmother's, and calling herself Ayesha had no more harm in it than Josiah's harp-playing. Good plain cooking was the way to a man's heart.

"Mummy ill in bed, dear? Good little boy to come in and tell Aunty! You shall have a piece of home-made toffee, that you shall!"

Phillip felt disappointment. He had had Aunty Bigge's home-made toffee before. It was not real toffee, being made of dripping and black treacle. He looked round for interesting things when Aunty Bigge was in the kitchen, but saw nothing new.

That day was a strange one for Phillip. He was subdued, rather scared, and unhappy that he was not allowed to see Mummy. Her door was to be kept shut. Mrs. Feeney said "Isolation". It sounded alarming. Grannie said to Aunty Bigge, "Are there any spots on the b-t-m, Mrs. Bigge, with German measles?" He wondered what b-t-m meant.

Mavis was brought down from Mummy's room, and her cot put in the sitting room.

Zippy caught a bird and played with it, and the bird went "Ee-ee". Zippy ran away growling when he tried to take the bird. So he chased Zippy with a cushion and banged him until he let go the bird, which he picked up to stroke, when the bird pecked him hard, hurting his finger before flying away. So Phillip pinched Mavis and made her cry. He took her dolly and gave it first a ride on Daddy's bike, then a swish in the pan by pulling the plug.

Aunty Belle looked round the door and said he was a naughty boy and if he did not behave he would be sent to bed.

"I don't care."

"You cannot love your Mother, if you say such things when she is ill, Phillip."

"I don't love Mummie any more."

Phillip felt like he did when he was chasing Zippy, he did not really mean it, but only half-meant it.

The doctor came and looked down his throat with an ivory thing, not the handle of a spoon as when Mummy used to look down his throat, pressing on his tongue, making him retch. Then he had to take off his jersey and vest.

"No sign of it so far. But the children must remain downstairs in isolation. It's scarlet fever."

When Father came home he was not angry. He said to Aunty Belle, "What rotten luck for you, at the start of your holiday, too! It is very good of you to offer, Belle, and I will send a telegram to Viccy at once."

That night it was strange, sleeping on the floor beside the yellow and brown carpet of the front room, on a big mattress laid there by Father. And the gas lamp went *pop* when it went out, then red, and a little light shone up there all by itself. Phillip lay very still, for Daddy was in his nightshirt getting into another bed on the carpet. And a Nurse was upstairs with Mummy and no one had kissed him goodnight. He hugged Golly beside him.

The darkness seemed to be rushing by all the time. It was thick, and so different from the darkness upstairs in his bedroom. Phillip did not realize that this was due to the curtains being drawn across the poles above the windows. In his own bedroom there was nothing at night over the window.

In the thick dark about him there was a little *pop*, and a little whistle, then some more pops and little whistles.

He wondered why the lamp in the middle of the ceiling was making little pops, now that it was on the by-pass. Then Daddy moved in the dark and sighed and turned over and there were no more pops and whistles. Instead there were slow, soft prods over his feet and beside his legs and he felt very glad, lying open-eyed in the darkness, feeling that Zippy was open-eyed, too. Then Zippy was purring and playing the piano on his body. He could feel Zippy's whiskers near his ears, though they did not touch or tickle him. Zippy's whiskers never did. Then *pop*, and the little whistle again. Zippy was gone. He felt for him, but he was not there.

The cat was creeping, step by step, towards a scent. Then the pop and little whistle stopped and Daddy whispered, "Hullo, Zippy! Where have you been, you naughty boy." Zippy purred loudly as Daddy stroked him. "Where have you been hiding? You naughty boy, Zippy. Ah, you want my warmth, don't you?"

Phillip went to sleep soon afterwards. So did Richard, gently snoring, with the brindled cat against his back, under the bed-clothes.

Isabelle Maddison slept in the sitting room, on an improvised sofa-bed, beside Mavis in her cot.

Upstairs, feeling herself to be swelled red all over, while all her brain and thoughts were a thick brown, Hetty lay unsleeping in her bed.

All the upper windows of the house were open, for the contagious germs of scarlet fever to escape into the air.

Richard was convinced, from an article about Sanatoria in Switzerland he had read recently in *The Daily Trident*, that germs floating in air would follow a warm air-stream, and so find themselves outside. That was why the lower windows of the house were all shut.

The next morning a telegram arrived with the post. It was decided that the two children should be taken to Epsom, where Isabelle Maddison had already arranged to spend the second week of her vacation with her younger sister, Victoria, and her husband George Lemon.

Victoria had replied to the pre-paid telegram, offering to look after the children during Hetty's indisposition, provided that Isabelle would accompany them for the first fortnight. *Please telegraph time of arrival.*

Chapter 11

MAFEKING DAY

THE OUTSIDE porter of Randiswell station had come up with
his trolley, and the black portmanteau, with its thick, cracked
straps, faded white paint lettering, and plaster of old labels,
once Richard's grandfather's, had preceded the travellers by
half an hour. Mrs. Bigge had pushed the mail cart in which
Mavis was strapped. Miss Isabelle Maddison had held the hand
of her nephew. Phillip wore his best suit: white sailor blouse
and skirt, white socks, black shoes with button strap, wide straw
hat with letters in gold on the band, H.M.S. Defiant.

Phillip looked anything but defiant. His face was tearstained.
He had sobbed all the morning at the idea of leaving Mummy.
When the time came to leave, he had clung to the banister rails
half way up the stairs. Mrs. Bigge had finally got him down to the
hall, whereupon he had clung to the post at the bottom. Eventually he was persuaded to abandon the post, vainly admonished
to be a man. Another plea likewise had failed.

"Surely," said a distressed Aunty Belle, "surely, Phillip, you
cannot want to upset your little sister? Look at Mavis, sitting
so still and good in her mail-cart!" Round-eyed, in poke bonnet,
bib, and shoulder-cape, the baby wondered what it was all about.
Soon she, too, was crying. "I want my Mummy, I want my
Mummy."

Phillip's cries were succeeded by deep sobs which stopped
his breathing. Mrs. Bigge was alarmed.

"I've seen a child in that state suck up the contents of his
stomach into his wind-pipe and turn blue in the face and he was
gone before you could say knife," she remarked. "Leave him to
me, Miss Maddison." She lifted up the limp, gibbering creature.
"Would you like to play Uncle Josiah's harp to Mummy, dear?
It's in the front room, and Mummy will hear you through the
open window. Now be an angel boy, and play the harp to
Mummy."

"Yes, play to Mummy," called out the nurse from up above.

Eventually the child grew calmer, with this purpose before him. They went into the drawing room of "Montrose". There he struck a few chords, after nearly toppling the gilt frame into the aspidistra-stand in the bay of the front-room window.

"Mummy will be better now, won't she, Aunty Bigge?"

"Yes, dear."

On this assurance he was led down the road, held by Aunty Belle's hand, and repeating "I made Mummy better, didn't I, Aunty Bigge?"

He cried again when Aunty Bigge said goodbye at the station. She cried too, but only when she was alone once more.

"Now don't cry, Phillip. Aunty Bigge has only gone back to help make your mother better."

"I helped, didn't I, Aunty Belle, by playing the music?"

Phillip soon had other ideas in which he believed. By pushing his hand into the corner, where the cushions of the carriage ended, he could start the train moving. But Aunty Belle would not listen to him. She looked out of the window when he told her what he could do. His faith, however, was not easily abased.

"I can start the train, Aunty Belle! You watch me! Watch me, Aunty Belle! Look, Aunty Belle! I push down here and the train will start!"

"You should not talk so much, Phillip."

Phillip had ridden in a train twice before, and on the second occasion he had made the unique discovery that if he watched when the man with the hat and whistle waved his green flag, and then pushed his own hand down in the corner, the engine whistled and the carriage moved.

"Watch, Aunty Belle, watch me start the train!"

Isabelle Maddison did not look at her nephew. She had for some years past been a governess to a family of gentlefolk, her own class, a minor canon in a cathedral close; and though she tried to make herself believe, in true Christian charity, that Richard's little son was but a child, yet she would be withholding the truth from herself if she did not look the matter square in the face and so conclude—and what her brother had told her confirmed it—that Phillip already revealed some unfortunate characteristics of his Turney blood. Mendacity in a child could not be checked too young; at the same time, it would not be right for her to interfere. Perhaps he would grow out of it.

Isabelle Maddison was thirty-nine years old; she had accepted a life of spinsterhood, but not without certain regrets. It would ill behove her to judge her parents, for after all they *were* her Father and Mother; but she could not help feeling that if she, as the eldest, had not had so many duties put upon her in looking after and tending her younger brothers and sisters—first John, then Richard, then Augusta, then Victoria, then Hilary, and lastly Theodora—and if Father had had more consideration for his family, then she, Isabelle, might have had a better chance of meeting eligible young men in the county, before the break-up of the home. Isabelle felt very nearly bitter about it at times; but always her belief as a Christian made her realize how unworthy were such complaining thoughts, since this life was one of trial and burden to prepare one for the next.

She was a tall woman, with dark brown hair, a big frame and face, and eyes that saw no more within than without. She was not clumsy, but she walked as though uncertain of her own movements. Her father had come to dislike her soon after she had learned to walk, seeing in her some likeness to his wife, with whom he had nothing, psychically speaking, in common. Isabelle had heavy Bavarian, plodding traits. And now at thirty-nine, with thoughts of an approaching change of life—she had observed the difficulties of her late employer, the minor canon's wife—Isabelle felt that she had missed her rightful place as a woman before, it seemed, her life had really started.

"I made the train go, did you see me, Aunty Belle?"

"People who are not truthful do not go to Heaven, Phillip."

The child stared at her face. He was suddenly frightened. Did Aunty Belle mean that Mummy might be going to Heaven?

With several admonitions, earnest and repeated, to be careful and at the same time not to move, as the train rattled over the points for Waterloo Junction, Isabelle waited anxiously by the near side window, ready to attract a porter the very moment the train should stop by the platform. When it did, she let down the window—a matter of some difficulty as a previous occupier of the third class carriage had, for his own purposes, cut off all but two inches of the heavy leather strap. Thereupon her modest black and purple bonnet, the shape of a loganberry, was inserted with the rest of her head into the outside smells of the district.

A porter hurried forward. "Porter!" cried Isabelle, in her rusty voice "Porter!"

The porter led them, carrying two bags, while Isabelle pushed the mail-cart with Mavis strapped in, and Phillip holding part of the handle, down a grimy covered way. Here upon various places of the asphalt floor lay the splattered vomit of volunteer soldiers returning to duty after last furlough before proceeding to South Africa. Phillip pointed one out to his aunt.

"Look, Aunty Belle, some poor little boys have been sick!"

Isabelle hurried him onwards by the hands, saying "You should not take any notice of such things." The boy, who remembered being sick himself after being made to swallow half a cupful of brown licorice powder in water, thought to tell her that some dead birds must have been found by other little boy's daddies in the hissing thing up above the bathroom ceiling trap-door, called the cistern. Mummy had told him about the dead sparrow, and "Just in case, Sonny!" she had induced him to swallow the green-brown *urgh!* licorice powder, and had given him a worn brown penny which tasted cold and thin when he sucked it.

Waterloo Station was crowded with people, all hurrying to look at something. There were lines of cabs, with horses' heads half-hidden in cocoanut nose-bags, and tall soldiers in tight red jackets, white belts, and blue trousers with broad red bands down the outside seams, and pillbox hats on the side of their heads. "Oh Aunty Belle, look Aunty Belle, I am so incited!" for the strains of a band were heard in the distance, with cheers and yes! it was coming nearer. "Ninganing men coming, Aunty Belle!" Aunty Belle was opening her purse and buying a second-class ticket for Epsom at a high-up window, and fearing that she would not let him see the ninganing men, Phillip ran away round the corner, following other children eager for the sights. Soon he was lost among hundreds of people, who began shouting out and cheering so much that he became frightened, but all the noise and the running people took him on.

The band was now very loud, the noise of brass and drums thundering under the roof. And wheels and a pony dashed by, and someone pulled him back just in time, and a roll of news-papers fell with a thump near him, to be pounced upon by a boy with bare feet, to be torn open, and then with a paper apron the boy was shouting out newspapers for pennies, pulling them off under his arm. Lots of men were marching behind the band, carrying what Phillip knew were guns, but what funny men they were, in brown-paper coloured clothes and big, strange hats. And people were laughing and jumping up and down and one funny man with a glass penny in his eye was jumping on his black hat, then picking it up he wiggled it on his walking stick. It was all like a dream, only dreams never were like this one, for he could walk in this dream and he did not have to pull himself along by the banisters and the harder he pulled with his hands the more was the stop-still.

Everybody was cheering and shouting, and taking off their hats, and the strange men in brown-paper clothes were wiggling theirs on their guns. And a man on a horse in red had a black tea-cosy hat and white feathers on it and his horse was dancing clop-clop-clop on the road. And a nice smiling man bent down and said "Hullo, old chap, would you like a tanner for some tucker, eh?" and opening his hand put a new sixpence, with the Queen's head on it, into his hand, and then closed it for him again and was gone.

When he realized he was lost, Phillip began to run everywhere, looking for Aunty Belle. Dream had become nightmare with the shouting and cheering, the white steam of engine whistles and strange, loud hooting noises, like he heard sometimes on the Hill far away where the ships' masts rose above the houses. He began to cry. Where was Aunty Belle? And Mummy's face. He would never see Mummy again. Thereafter his mind was in mad fragments, even when a Mrs. Feeney woman said words and took his hand and then a policeman took his hand and gave him a bun but all he wanted was Mummy. What was his name, where did he live, where was he going to—all was swept away inarticulately under sobs of wanting Mummy.

"Is your Daddy here?"

"I-w-w-w-want-m-m-m-mummy!"

"Have you got a Daddy? What's his name?"

"M-m-m-m-mur-mur-mummy!"

And at last Aunty Belle was filling up to the sky and scolding him and holding his hand tightly and his new sixpence was gone and they were in a train and Aunty Belle counting out pennies for the porter and then the door was shut, both children crying and wanting Mummy.

As he hurried away the porter muttered to himself, "Blimey, the mean old cat, fourpence for minding two bags over 'alf an hour, and Mafeking relieved!" Then, "'Strewth, what a bit o'luck!" For there on the platform before him lay a silver coin. He put it into a flapped waistcoat pocket for his kid at home, a shiny new tanner, his lucky day.

Staring out of the window and everything going backwards, Phillip was soon sick; and when at last they stopped at their station, he was asleep on a seat. Aunty Belle had covered the acid signs of too much excitement with a middle page of *The Church Times*, which she had bought to scan the advertisements of *Governesses Vacant*; for after her holiday with Victoria she must find a new post.

"Do you know Mrs. Lemon's house, The Lindens?"

The driver of the station cab raised his whip; and thither she was driven, sitting opposite her thin, pale-faced nephew with the large blue, almost violet eyes, and—really, whatever was Hetty thinking of?—no knickers or clothes of any kind under his skirt.

"You must be on your best behaviour, Phillip," said Isabelle. "Look at your little sister Mavis, what a good little girl she is to be sure."

Two parlour-maids in black bodices fastened high in the neck, wearing starched, frilly caps on their heads with white tabs behind, and black skirts, were waiting for the sound of hoofs and the jingling of harness upon the carriage sweep of the Lindens. They were glad that children were coming to help liven up the formality of the house.

The door was opened as soon as the four-wheeler stopped. Victoria stood in the hall, just out of the sunlight, waiting to greet her guests.

"Belle, how nice to see you again, dear!"

The sisters kissed.

"Did you have a good journey? And how did you leave Hetty? You must tell me all the news later on. And you are Phillip, are you? How do you do, Phillip."

"Quite well, thank you, Aunt Victoria."

"He has suffered a little from the motions of the train, Viccy. That explains his pallor."

"Dear me, what bad luck! And you are Mavis!" Victoria, liking the child's face, knelt to kiss her.

"You won't kiss me," said Phillip.

"Do you want me to kiss you before you have washed your face, dear?"

"No thank you," said Phillip.

Victoria laughed. "Well, shall I kiss you after you have washed your face, then?"

Phillip, thinking of his mother, shook his head. Then turning away his face, he began to cry.

"Come come, Phillip! That will never do. That is not the way to behave. You must try and be a man, you know."

"I'm a boy!" he cried, between sobs. "Go away, I don't like you! I want my m-m-mummy!"

When the children had been put to bed, to rest before luncheon, the two sisters sat in the hall, where sun-blinds kept carpet and fabrics from fading, and talked. At length Victoria said: "Mavis has a sweet little face, with her long lashes and brown eyes, I suppose she takes after her mother? I have never met her, you know. But what an odd little boy Phillip is, to be sure. He looks so unhappy. Who does he take after? Not the Maddisons, and he is certainly not a von Föhre, our mother's family. No wonder Dickie calls him the donkey boy."

Later Victoria said: when she had seen more of the children, "I wonder if there is anything in what Dickie says, that old Turney is a Jew? I have never met him, of course, and from all I've heard, I don't think I want to. Have you seen him, Belle?"

"He came into the house while I was there, Viccy. He seemed an amiable sort of man, rather like the Prince of Wales in appearance, though I have only seen drawings and photographs of the Prince, of course."

"The Prince of Wales does look a *little* bit Jewish, don't you know, Belle. We have several of the Chosen People who have come recently to live in the neighbourhood. I have not called, of course. Perhaps George will be able to tell us, when he comes home. His head clerk buys their stationery from Mr. Turney's firm, you know."

That evening George Lemon, who had returned from his office in Lincoln's Inn, placed a bottle of champagne in the dining-room bucket, for it was an especial occasion. Not only had Mafeking been relieved, but Hilary was coming to stay, being expected any moment. "That is, if he isn't held up by the celebrations in Town." George Lemon imagined the crowds, the lights, the Regent Street bars, laughing girls' faces, the fun, the fireworks in the Park; and kept his amiable glance away from the face of Isabelle, his sister-in-law, and the pretty, the familiar, the somewhat Burne-Jones, the remotely angelic of Victoria, which before marriage he had found so attractive.

During dinner Victoria brought up the question which had been occupying her mind: for of her brothers Richard was the favourite, and she had always regretted the circumstances of his marriage, believing that he had thrown himself at the first face he had seen after their mother's death.

"Well," said her husband. "The only possible connexion between the Prince of Wales and the Chosen People that I can see is that he seems to prefer bizarre companions, who in the words of Lord Odo Russell the other day 'are not English', being either Jews or Parsees, like Ernest Cassel, or Sassoon, and other rich *arrivistes*. But more particularly to your question, as I've never met Mr. Turney, and am not likely to, I cannot possibly answer. Why do you ask?"

Victoria then mentioned Phillip, and his strange temperament and behaviour.

"He seems to be at cross-purposes with himself," she said. "That is so, in mixed blood, is it not?"

"Well, if you are going into the question of pure blood, who is there in England who could pass the test? They talk about the United States of America being the melting pot, but what about Britain in the past, with all its invasions and foreign settlements? The Lemons are Cornish for a good many generations, most of us have the dark look of Phoenicians, with a few bright exceptions when we cast a fair-haired blue-eyed type like m' sister Beatrice, for example, but we more probably came from the north coast of France, Le Mans may be our derivation. Nobody can be sure. So what does a drop more or less of Jewish blood in the old British bucket matter?" And George Lemon went to the ice bucket, and after the merest token pointing of the napkin-wrapped bottle at Isabelle, who at once put her hand over her glass, filled his own and drank.

George Lemon reflected that the Maddisons fancied themselves too much. That was the trouble with women brought up in the country to believe that their own world of a few square miles was the centre of everything; and where, anyhow, were the Maddisons today? His wife's family had been a branch of the Scottish Maddisons, who coming south of the border, had bought land, acquired more by marriage, and in due course made a fortune out of the coal beneath their properties. There was a baronetcy dating from the seventeenth century. Since the firm of solicitors of which he was a junior partner was one mainly concerned in the conveyancing of land, George Lemon knew many details of landed families which would have shocked most people who believed in their own invincible respectability, were such details made known to them. The entire Victorian idiom was hypocritical, as Theodora, the only decent in-law he possessed, had realised. As for his own dear wife, she would never be able to believe that life should be otherwise than noble and Tennysonian: the penalty of having a dissolute papa!

Thank heaven young Hilary was coming to stay; he had a sense of reality. George Lemon finished the bottle by himself, after the sisters had retired to the drawing-room, and then helped himself to some '64 Cockburn, to celebrate Hilary's inevitable night out, with London gone mad. Why had he not stayed up himself, for such an unique occasion?

Hilary appeared at The Lindens the following afternoon, full of what he had seen. The complete stoppage of traffic, and the vast crowds besieging the West End had prevented him, he said, making his apologies to his sister, from coming down the night before. He had tried to find a place to send a telegram, in vain.

"When eventually I fought my way off the shoulders of those who insisted on carrying me around, I doubt if there was a post office left open in the whole of London. The entire place had run riot. As I've already told George, when I went round to see him in his office this morning, I was coming out of my club, in uniform, for owing to the transport of extra troops to South Africa at Southampton, there has been delay in sending on my boxes, and I had no other kit in town. Well, as I was saying, I was hardly off the steps of m' club, when I was hoisted up on somebody's shoulders. No use me trying to explain that my uniform was not the blue ensign, but the red, I was carried round like a hero."

"Well, you would have been if you had been in Mafeking, wouldn't you?" said Victoria, loyally but inconsequentially.

"I suppose there were some naval gun teams in the column which relieved the place, and that was good enough for the hoi poloi," laughed Hilary. "Lord, what a schemozzle it was! People blowing coaching horns and bugles, waving Chinese lanterns and Union Jacks, carrying portraits of Baden-Powell, men and women of all classes dancing and singing. I got away from my particular idolators outside Swan and Edgar's, and made my way up Regent Street to a bar where one usually sees a friend at any time, it's a great meeting place for sailors. I was having a drink in the long bar with a fellow I know when in came the Prince of Wales with some friends, and would you believe it, he walked the entire length of the bar, sweeping his walking stick along the counter from one end to the other, knocking off every blessed glass! Then in his guttural voice he called out that everyone present must drink the health of the South African Field Force, coupled with the gallant defenders of Mafeking. Lord, you should have seen their faces!"

"I suppose it must have been a shock to them," said Victoria, with her slight smile.

"Shock, Good Lord, no, Viccy! They were delighted! We drank as directed, sang God Save the Queen, and flung our glasses on the floor. Immediately afterwards, H.R.H. went out, everyone standing to attention. Before we knew what happened, he was gone again."

Isabelle looked puzzled. "But surely——?" She looked at her sister. "Would not the proprietor lose all his glasses?"

"Good Lord, he didn't care! It's a custom, you know, to break a glass after an important toast. The Prince of Wales broke them before, as well as after!"

"But who would pay for the—the toast, Hilary?"

"The Prince's equerry, of course, Belle. After all, it was a very special occasion."

"Well, I don't pretend to understand the ways of London Society," said Isabelle. "But it is very nice to see you again, Hilary." She went to give him a kiss, and he turned his smooth, pink cheek to receive the rather thick-lipped pressure of one who had always regarded him as the dearest little brother.

Hilary Maddison was considered to be the fortunate one of the

family. Had he not, at so young an age, travelled around the
world, and being popular, found favour in the eyes of the rich
and important, to the extent of being worth over ten thousand
pounds by his twenty-eighth birthday? Possibly more, for the
value of the farm he had bought in New South Wales had
increased since he had acquired it for a song, when he was twenty-
one. It was worked by a partner, while Hilary continued his
duties as special officer in the *Phasiana*, one of the great white
liners of the famous MacKarness Line. Sir Robert MacKarness,
himself, that tough, blunt Glaswegian ex-shipping clerk, with a
face and physique of Scots granite, had selected him as one of his
particular young men who, he told them, if they could work—
not would work, but *could* work—driving themselves as hard and
as constantly as a yellow-metal screw is driven at the end of its
shaft, then they could not be kept from rising to the high levels of
Britain's major industry, and its only future, upon the sea. And
though Sir Robert MacKarness affected to despise the English
gentleman as effete, yet he knew the value of one who was not
afraid of work, and who would pay the strictest attention to detail
during every hour of the twenty-four, seven days a week, and
fifty-two weeks a year. The future, he said, more than once
to Hilary Maddison, his favourite among his protegés, was
founded in the present; so future and present were coupled as a
universal joint. Experience was everything; let a young man with
ability learn from the bottom upwards, to ground himself in reality,
for the great changes that were coming with the new century.

Hilary had begun work in his Clyde-side office; then he had
accompanied Sir Robert, who had found him to be thorough,
reliable, and with an ease of manner that the older man admired,
as a confidential writer and messenger combined. Pleased with
his work and unfailing grasp of essentials, Sir Robert had used
him on special missions about the routes and ports of the house of
MacKarness—Southampton, Gibraltar, Port Said, Colombo,
Indian Ocean and China Sea, Hong Kong and Sydney, flying
fish and Southern Cross—a pleasant life, with strict attention to
business, with many opportunities in both the world of business
and pleasure. Hilary had many a ship-board romance, discreetly
conducted, of course, and always conscious that the white of
one's uniform was distinct in the nights of phosphorescent waves
under the low blaze of stars. In short, Hilary Maddison, self-

assured by the thought of his ten thousand pounds, every one the product of his intelligence, was extremely pleased with himself and with the prospect of three months' leave before him, after three years' foreign service, in the only place where spring was really spring—England.

When George Lemon came home, talk between the two men was upon another level of living.

"London last night was the strangest experience, George. I suppose it's never happened like that before in all our history. The news of Waterloo, even. Everybody appeared to be in the West End, and the strangest thing was the feeling of friendly unity in the crowds. I should not have believed such a thing possible, if I hadn't experienced it myself. You know Kipling's 'East is East and West is West, and never the twain shall meet', well, they dam' well did, as far as London is concerned. I'm no radical, the idea of men being equal is nonsense—one day at sea in a ship proves that, if proof were required—but I must say it did my eyes good, George, to feel the spirit of unity in the crowds, after seeing so many dagos in the East."

"We've got our little Englanders all the same, Hilary. You've been away, and haven't experienced it. That little Welshman in the House of Commons, whom Lord Lonsdale calls Mr. George, has been standing up for the Boers. The fellow ought to be shot, lettin' the prestige of the country down, giving more powder and shot for the Germans—not your own respected cousins, and their sort, of course, but the commercial gentry around the Kaiser, who have probably fooled and egged on the All Highest to send that dam' sabre-rattlin' telegram to 'Oom Paul'. God, have you seen a photograph of the old blackguard? He's a fool?"

"Kruger? He's something straight out of the Old Testament, by way of an undertaker's shop. The brains behind him are after the goldfields. Barnato, Oppenheim, Wernher, Joel—they are the boys who will eventually matter."

"Of course the Jews are behind everything, but we couldn't do without them. They provide the money for nearly everything, you know."

"Well, now Bobs has gone out with Kitchener—one of our ships had the job of transporting them, by the way—we shall soon settle the Boers' hash. What a word, *Boers*. Rightly named,

if you ask my opinion. I must tell you, George. I saw a curious
sight in Trafalgar Square, of all places. There were a couple of
tommies rogering two tarts up against the wall below the National
Gallery. As bold as brass, and not giving a damn who saw them.
Would you believe it? And in Pall Mall, as I went down to my
club, I saw two fellows turn up a girl, quite young she was, and
smack her bottom in full view, drawers and all, as though it was
part of the festivities. "

"What happened?"

"I didn't wait to see. Besides, there was such a press of
people, all yelling their blasted heads off, squirting water in
people's faces, and waggling ticklers, I was pretty glad to get out
of the scrum and into the comparative quiet of the Voyagers."

Hilary paused—they were sitting in the rose arbour—while he
checked a thought. George had a sharp brain, and would
recognise his train of thought if he didn't go 'possum with another
idea first. Hilary wanted to ask about George's younger sister,
Beatrice, the meltingly beautiful, honey-blonde, blue-eyed Bee,
recently widowed.

"I hear that Dickie's two children are here, George. His
wife's got scarlet fever, Viccy tells me. D'you know, I never
knew Dickie was married until I opened my post bag in Sydney
and heard from John details of my father's death, let me see, it
must be a little more than five years ago. And the next time we
called at Sydney, there was another letter from John, telling me
of his wife Jenny's death in childbirth. I must try and see both
John and Dick this leave."

"Richard's a shy bird," said George.

"He always was. Hullo, here's Belle with his offspring."

Isabelle had appeared round the gravelled path, pushing the
mail cart. Seeing the two men, Phillip hid behind her voluminous
skirts, which stirred some of the yellow pebbles as she advanced
sedately upon her buttoned glacé kid boots.

"Now be a good boy, Phillip, and say 'How do you do'
properly to your Uncles."

Phillip hung back, sucking his thumb, while with the other
hand he held tight to Aunty Belle's skirt.

Hilary tried his charm on the boy. He jingled coins in his
pocket, then withdrew some and made them dance in the palm
of his hand. This not being attractive, he selected a new sixpence

and held it up between finger and thumb. At the sight of the
coin Phillip retired once more behind Aunty Belle's skirts.

"You can't buy him, Hilary," laughed George Lemon.

"Come on, you little rascal!" said Hilary. "Come on, don't
be frightened of me. I'll be jiggered if you don't look just like a
marmoset looking round the trunk of a banyan tree!"

Neither man connected Isabelle with a banyan tree, their
thoughts being with the unusual solemnity in the face of a small
boy. It seemed so funny, the solemn, gazing eyes of the bony,
white face: the mixture of caution, fear, and curiosity.

"He was supposed to have been reared on the milk of a
donkey, but bless my soul, it might very well have been an organ
grinder's guenoy," remarked George Lemon. At the last thought
he had changed the word monkey into its French female equivalent; for in his opinion the boy was exceptionally precocious, and
he did not want to hurt his feelings.

Hilary suddenly darted forward and caught the boy by an arm.
Then holding his wrists, while he faced him, he told him to bend
down his head and Uncle would give him a somersault. The boy
became rigid. "Come on, you young rascal, over with you!"
cried Hilary. "It's very easy, Phillip, why, there's nothing in
it!" As the boy still resisted, he caught him under the arms and
threw him up into the air, laughing as the boy's skirt flew open
on the descent, to reveal above the skinny legs a thin, grey belly.
Hilary threw him up again and again, saying, "There's nothing
to be afraid of! Why are you so scared of me? I won't let you fall!
Come on now, once more, only make yourself less rigid, relax
your muscles, man, relax yourself! Why, you're not half a boy!
You ought to see the little chaps, no older than you, diving in off
the quays of Colombo, a knife between their teeth, and not a
stitch on 'em, not a man jack of 'em over five years of age, and
swimming under the sharks, to rip them up with their knives.
What, don't you want to hear? You little swine you! Did you
see that, George? Look at my hand! The young cuss bit me!"

It had been accidental: Phillip had gasped with fear of being
thrown up, and Hilary's hand had met the little teeth in the
open, rigid mouth.

Chapter 12

GEORGE LEMON HAS AN IDEA

IN THE morning George Lemon, frock-coated, silk-hatted, dog-skin-gloved and carrying a rolled umbrella, left for the station, accompanied by his wife. Victoria, pale of complexion and fair as a Burne-Jones angel, walked with him down the pleasant, secluded road, with its villas standing well back behind cleft-oak paling fences, among trees of lilac, double-flowering Japanese cherry, mimosa and laburnum, all so fair in the sun rising into a clear sky of the south-east, thrushes and blackbirds and chaffinches singing, cuckoos calling from many points of the downs; and immediately and startling near, as though summer shadow itself were vocal, the shaking notes and trills of a nightingale.

Victoria held George's arm tightly in her elation that she was to have his child. She had come with him that morning specially to tell him her secret. Victoria felt unusually free and happy, and this taking of his arm in public, with both hands, was for her almost a defiance of convention. However, they were alone in the road, except for a very fat terrier dog, with grey jowl and teeth protruding with premature senility due to eating too much red meat, who was inspecting the base of one after another of the trees along the sidewalk.

"Hullo, Joey," said George Lemon, whereupon the dog gave one wag of its tail before passing on.

Joey belonged to Sir Alfred Catt, a neighbour. The Lemons held the Catts in some scorn because they were so obviously *arrivistes*, by way of trade and lord-mayoralty of a Midland manufacturing town. Joey, the obese terrier, much larger than any genuine terrier-dog should have been, looked like part of the late Corporation of his master's home-town, its body being encased in blue straps, each one properly saddle-soaped before the morning constitutional, and fastened with German silver buckles. As for the collar, that also was a Birmingham speciality, being of strong leather set with formidable spikes, also of German silver, the points of which had been rounded off, as a concession to canine civility.

The Catts were elderly and childless. Joey (named after the great Chamberlain, of course) along with several blue Persian cats, was privileged to share the bedroom of her Ladyship. The animals were regarded and cared for as a family. Joey, however, contrary to the experience of most eldest sons, had found so much favour in his father's eyes, that he was on the way to a rapid death through kindness. The dog's heavy, studded collar was an armour against having its throat torn out by the savage hairy mongrels of the seasonal gipsies of Epsom; the straps and bands were to protect its heart from excessive exertion when on the leash; but there was no protection for its kidneys, liver, and colon, from overmuch fat, acid, and carbo-hydrate.

Joey, however, all his life had been protected from intercourse with common dogs. Hence, in late middle age, and during walks with his master or his master's valet, Joey's almost feverish interest in the recognition, or perhaps in the collection, of as many visiting cards and calls of his canine neighbours at the bases of trees owned and cared for by the Epsom Rural District Council.

That, at any rate, was Joey seen through the eyes of George Nathaniel Lemon.

Victoria did not really care for her husband's quips and remarks about Joey, the poor old dog. Many of his other ways did, while not exactly shocking her, for she prided herself on her broadmindedness, tend secretly to dismay her sense of propriety. Of course a man's mind was entirely different from a woman's, but even so—— It was somewhat curious, that streak in him, for George was a gentleman, of good family. Victoria could not imagine any of her brothers saying, or even thinking, the things George Lemon said. He was Cornish, of course, that might well be the difference. It certainly accounted for his dark hair and eyes, his brown skin, and a peculiar, almost uncanny, awareness of what she, Victoria, was thinking. How could George then, with all his intelligence, be so, well, crude on occasion? Not that it really mattered in other things, for after all he was her husband; but even so, why did George, so esteemed in his profession, and so popular with people, not realise that it was not very nice to say the things he did at times say?

But that May morning of 1900 as she walked down the avenue of limes, murmurous with bees upon their canopies in the bright morning, Victoria felt free of herself, of her experience, for joy of the new life within her; and she clung to her husband's arm, her somewhat indecorous behaviour happily unobservable by anybody except the snuffling old dog. And Joey, having wagged his tail to greet, on equal term, his friend in the shiner—Joey like all well-brought-up dogs, knew a gent from a common person by his hat, clothes, gait and smell—then trotted on to ascertain what had been doing since his arboreal survey, master's valet waiting at the gate, of the night before.

Victoria (the childish name of Viccy seemed, somehow, to be part of the past) turned back just before the end of the road, not wanting to meet any of George's Town and Golf Club acquaintances who, about that time of a few minutes after nine o'clock, usually passed by on foot or carriage on their way to the railway station. At the parting she hoped that George would kiss her, though she knew the vulgarity of such demonstration in public. George did not; so Victoria returned up the road faster than she had come down it, for the care of the house was her dominant concern in living.

While she walked under the avenue of lime trees, she turned over in her mind what George had said about Dickie's little boy. "A boy needs more affection from his father than from his mother." "Dickie is too self-absorbed, perhaps, ever to share his inner feelings with anyone else." This implied criticism of her favourite brother Richard had somehow prevented her from telling George what she had been rehearsing in her mind to tell him ever since the previous day, when the doctor had confirmed her hopes. George's words had chilled her. Her brother was *not* selfish, and never had been! If Dickie had become more reserved than before who, or what, was to blame? His marriage!

George Lemon, in his first-class carriage, richly upholstered in leather, mahogany, and Liberty fabric, settled back in his corner seat and opened *The Times* in an atmosphere of aromatic, blue Havana cigar smoke. No conversation in the carriage was usual, or conventional, beyond the initial *Good morning* and the briefest impersonal genialities about the weather. He opened the rear pages in order to read the Stock Exchange prices in the lists there, which concerned his holdings; but he thought not of prices but of a case in which he was engaged, of a client who wanted an injunction against a neighbour, alleging that his premises were being used as a disorderly house. The neighbour in question was a peer of the realm, not one of Gladstone's crop of glorified shop-keepers and worthy tradesmen, but one of the oldest families in Surrey.

It was a case of the utmost delicacy, and might, if persisted in, cause a first-class scandal. There had been some investigation by a private enquiry agent, a retired Scotland Yard man whom the partners sometimes employed, and undoubtedly the house in Bryanston Square was a select *bordel*. The point was in the alleged disorder.

With an interior feeling of fascination George Lemon played with the idea of doing some investigation on his own. The enquiry agent had reported that some of the "young ladies" visiting the place were "high class", and from the "theatrical profession". By Jove!

With Isabelle in his house, staying between jobs of work, George Lemon felt more shut-in upon himself than ever. He was glad to have the poor old thing, of course, though by heaven what a frump she was! She couldn't help it, being an effect rather than a cause, a surplus female. To offset Belle's coming, Hilary's visit had been much anticipated. At least he was realistic, having had seen something of the world. Dick and Viccy were very much of a type, thin-blooded people. He hoped his child, of whose coming George Lemon had known without any particular satisfaction, would not take after his wife's family. At least, not the 'Viking' side of it. But you could never tell; it might be like Hilary, who took after his mother, an amiable and easy German woman, whose life had been hell with her husband, from all accounts. Perhaps it might be a daughter, like his sister Bee, a jolly girl with no inhibitions, who was coming to stay.

Beatrice was a young widow: and on previous occasions George Lemon had observed his sister's interest in Hilary; first for the photographs on his chimney-piece while her elderly husband was still alive, and later when she had met him; and the interest was mutual, he had decided. The two, Hilary and Bee, would make a fine pair, he thought.

That afternoon when they returned from a walk, Phillip kept well behind Aunty Belle. To him the new uncle was an object to be avoided, with his pink, roundish face and big white legs wide apart on a chair. With the other new uncle it was different. He was not a great big white man, he was ordinary size brown

face, not ha-ha toothy face like white uncle holding out arms for
him. In dread of this personality, Phillip took a double grip of
the handle of the mail cart.

"I can push, Aunty Belle, you have tired feet, you sit down,
Aunty Belle," he said, and was surprised at the laughter of the
men who, he had been told, were his two uncles. The teeth of
uncle white did not look so much like big-dog-bite after the
laughing. Aunty Belle said, "Now Phillip be a good boy and
say how do you do, to your Uncle Hilary."

"No," said Phillip, meaning that he wanted to go with Aunty
Belle, being afraid of Uncle White. Isabelle misinterpreted the
refusal.

"You must not be rude, Phillip. Now go and shake your
uncle's hand, or you will not have any sop for your supper."

"No, Aunty Belle!" The child clung more tightly to the mail-
cart. Isabelle, embarrassed, unpicked his fingers. The child
clutched her skirts. Hilary laughed. Isabelle became quietly
firmer. The child struggled, and hid his face in her skirts.

"You see," said Isabelle to her brother-in-law George Lemon,
"what Dickie meant by clinging to Hetty's apron-strings? Come,
Phillip, you must not make an exhibition of yourself! There now,
you have made your sister cry! I will not allow such bad manners,
so be a good boy and do as Aunty Belle tells you," she said, her
voice ameliorating.

"No, no, Aunty Belle!"

"Very well, you will have no sop for supper."

"Leave him to me," said George Lemon, gently. He was thinking that if children should be seen and not heard, so should all
governesses, by God. "The boy will be better when he knows us
all more." He turned with a smile to the child staring up at him.
"Now then, Phillip, shall we roll some croquet balls on the grass?
You help me, like a good chap, to get them through the hoops!"

He got up, and rolled a ball for a few feet, then went on his
hands and knees. As soon as the towering size of Uncle Lemon
was gone, and a nice, brown uncle was crawling on the grass, hope
sprang up in Phillip, and he ran forward to play with his new
friend. His eyes lit up and he laughed and cried "Jolly! Jolly!"
as he rolled his ball beside Uncle Brown rolling another ball.
Uncle Brown was a nice man—he was Uncle Lemon.

Phillip's ball was white with blue rings, Uncle's was white with red rings. It was good fun trying to see which ball went through the hoop first. They took turns. Oh, his ball slipped! Uncle Brown let him have another turn. Red ball was near blue ball! "Quick, quick, Uncle Brown!" he cried. Then, "Ha! ha! your ball was too fast; perhaps a daddy-long-legs looked up and pushed it, Uncle Lemon."

"You have a remarkable imagination, my boy!"

The boy was intent on getting the blue ball through the hoop. He rolled it, it slowed, he gave it an extra touch, glanced furtively at the other, and jumped around when Uncle Brown said, "Well, perhaps the daddy-long-legs was pulling your ball back this time, Phil." He added, "Did you see it?"

"No, Uncle Brown Lemon! It was me who pushed it."

"Ha ha!" exclaimed George Lemon, as though to his wife. He put his hand affectionately on the boy's head. "Thank you for telling me the truth. Well done. I must go in now, Phil, and get into some more comfortable clothes. Perhaps if you ask Uncle Hilary, very nicely, to play with you, he will take my place. Don't be afraid of him, he's quite harmless, really. And don't bite him, he's got a horror of hydrophobia! Lives too well on board ship, that's his only trouble. A little too fat. Go and ask him. Say, 'Please, Uncle Hilary, will you play with me?'"

George Lemon went into the house through the open french windows and Phillip went slowly towards Uncle White, looking at him doubtfully. Hilary was sitting in a deck-chair. Summoning up his resistance, Phillip managed to say, "Please, Uncle White, will you play with me?"

"If you shake hands first, and call me Uncle Hilary, that's my name, you know. Then we can be friends, can't we? Shake hands like a little man."

Phillip advanced to hold out his hand. Hilary took it, and pulled the boy to him. He stood him before him, holding him there while he sat himself in the deck-chair, saying, "Let's have a good look at you. I've heard a lot about you, young man. Do you know who I am? We must now get properly acquainted. I am your father's brother. We used to collect butterflies together. You know what they are, don't you? Ha ha! You young rascal, you; I hear you purloined a case of your father's, and took them to bed with you, under your pillow. Didn't you, that? What did Daddy do, tell me? Did he smack your bottom?"

"My farver's stronger than you," said Phillip, not liking this
uncle at all.

"Good for you. So you've got some spunk! Only you should
say 'Father' not 'Farver'. You're too big a boy now to talk
like that. Say it after me—'Far'—go on!"

"Far."

"Now then."

"'Now then'."

"Don't be cheeky, or I'll spifflicate you. Now once more.
'Far—ther'."

"Far—ther."

"Well done! Now you are a big boy, aren't you? Say 'Father'
again."

"Far—ther."

"Splendid!"

Phillip resented the pink face so near his own, the hands holding his ribs. He tried to get away.

"Whoa, young hoss! Answer me, did Daddy smack your
bottom good and hard? You young rip, you! Why should I play
ball with you? Give me a good reason. Come on, don't be
shy! I shan't eat you!"

Phillip began to feel that the Uncle White Hilary might do this
very thing. Hilary was laughing in a way that frightened Phillip.
He struggled harder to get free.

"Do you like stories, Phillip? Shall I tell you about sharks?"

"No, thank you, Uncle White."

"But it's very interesting. What's the matter with you? Other
little boys I know like to be told stories of sharks. Stop wriggling,
or I'll put you in irons, you young cuss, you!"

"I want Aunty Belle!"

"Now now, you must be a man, my boy. Keep still, you little
rip! Very well, into irons you go," and lifting up the awkward
child, Hilary put him between his legs, crossed one ankle over the
other, brought his knees under the white duck trousers together,
and chuckled at the writhings of the skinny creature to escape.

"Don't you want to hear how we catch sharks off the Australian
coast, Phillip?"

"No, you fool!"

"Well, I'm jiggered! You're a caution, and no mistake."

Phillip tried to pull himself out of the locked legs. He clutched the short grass of the lawn, but was pinned between shin bones and ankles. Amusement and dislike possessed Hilary. He would tame the little brute, who had refused his offer of friendship.

"We go out in a boat with lumps of pork and some lengths of stiff bamboo. Then we sharpen the ends of a length of bamboo and push both ends into the meat. Then we tie the ends together lightly, and throw the pork into the water. And then what do you think happens next?"

Phillip was still struggling, his face close to the grass. Only the black-haired back of his head on the thin stalk of neck was visible above the fallen-forward square collar of his sailor blouse. In amusement Hilary lifted up the pleated skirt, and laughed as he saw a small rump sticking up like that of a pale, hairless monkey.

"Well, I'll tell you what happens next. A dead dog is just as good to attract a shark. Or a naughty little devil like you. The shark turns on his back to swallow the meat. Down it goes. But as he digests it in his belly the bamboo bow flies open and rips him up. He leaps out of the water, smacking down to try and get rid of the bamboo spears, but each time he bleeds more, and at the smell of blood all the other sharks come around, and go mad as they lash the water, tearing him to shreds and eating them."

As in a nightmare, Phillip was struggling to get away.

"Let me go, please, Uncle White. I beg your pardon, Uncle White, I beg your pardon," he cried. Hilary was amazed to see that the little fellow was weeping. Immediately he was contrite.

"I say, I'm sorry, young fellow. I thought we were playing a game, Honest Injun, I did! Also, I thought the story would interest you," he said, taking him into his arms, and trying to get Phillip to look at him. "Come now," he said, in his smoothest tones. "Let me dry your tears. Tut tut, this will never do. Anyway, sharks are the most frightful creatures, and deserve no mercy, you know. Have you ever seen pictures of one? Now I wonder what I have got in my pocket. Let's see, shall we? Look, here's a shilling. Don't cry any more. Really, Phil, I intended it only as fun! It was only a game I was playing with you!"

But Phillip would accept neither friendliness nor shilling. What a little freak he was, a proper donkey boy! Hilary let him go, and watched with a feeling of amused contempt his nephew hurrying, head down, towards the house.

As Phillip went through the shadowed room, on the way to

lock himself in the lavatory, he suddenly started, for a voice said, out of nowhere, "Darling, whatever has been happening?"

Phillip looked up, and saw a black shining soft lady, sitting in a chair. She knelt down on one knee and held out black glistening arms to him, and a funny thing like the larder window was over her beautiful face.

"Phillip," said the soft voice. "Oh, you pet! Kiss me, darling!" and the lady lifted back her veil and her smell was lovely. He yielded. Scarcely touching his head with her black fingers she pressed her lips against his cheek, breathing sweetness upon him a moment before she sat back in the chair again; and then leaning forward with one gloved hand upon the handle of her parasol, and her chin supported by a fingertip of the other hand, she said softly, "So you are shy Richard's little boy! And oh dear, there is another tear on your cheek! I tasted one just now with my lips. Are you lonely without your mother? Poor pet, don't feel lonely any more, I will look after you; I am your new Aunty Bee." And over her shoulder she called out, "Hilary, you are a first-class, unimaginative oaf!" She held Phillip close to her, and spoke gently to him, watching the expression of his face, as he regarded her gravely, with his enormous eyes.

Phillip did not realise what she was murmuring to him, so much as he felt what she gave to him of her own feeling; as indeed all the faces he had known had made him, in layer upon layer as a coral reef is built up, in part of their own feelings. This black soft strange lady was not like an aunty.

"You are very sweet, my pet," she said gently. "I would like to steal you, and take you to my home. Would you like that?"

She touched his forehead, and smoothed his dark hair, strangely moved for what she perceived in his face, in the deep perplexity and acceptance of life in his candid eyes, in the sweet mobility and gentleness of his mouth. "Little pet!" she whispered again; and smiling at him with unfirm, quivering lips, she felt the tears coming into her eyes. This child was clear as the Cornish sea of her own childhood; as her own lost innocence, of that time when she saw herself as fair and free as barley in August, waving in the fields of the headland she had known as a child, riding on her pony along the bridle-paths by the cliffs, above a summer sea as deeply blue as the eyes of this most gentle, this most innocent little boy before her.

"How your Mamma must love you," whispered Beatrice.

"Phillip must go to bed now, it is already past his bedtime," said Victoria's voice. She had come silently upon the deep carpet. "Aunty Belle will bathe you, Phillip, and then give you your bowl of sop, if you are a good boy."

"Oh, may he not stay up a little longer, Viccy dear? I have only just made the acquaintance of your enchanting nephew. Viccy, he is fey! Look at his eyes!"

Victoria smiled. She liked Bee; who didn't? The trouble with Bee, she thought, was that, as a successful actress on the stage, she could never know when she was *really* sincere in what she said in ordinary life.

"He *is* fey, you know," said Bee, staring at the boy so tranquil before her. "He is pure Celtic. Look at the shape of his head! Feel this bump at the back. What an imagination must be stored in there—hundreds of years, thousands of years, in that little barrow. The past never dies, you know, Viccy."

"Do you think that accounts for it, then?" asked Victoria, in her thin voice, with an anticipatory smile on her gentle face, as though she would like to believe all that Bee said. The quiet spell was broken by Hilary, magnificent and assured, in his white uniform, stepping up from the garden into the room, and Bee swiftly lowering her veil before turning to meet him. Phillip, feeling blank now that the lady with the yellowy hair and smiling eyes seemed to have forgotten him, as she went away with Uncle White, allowed himself to be led up to his bath, then to his bowl of bread and milk while Aunty Belle told him not to linger as his Aunt Victoria was giving a dinner party that night to many people. He must not forget to clean his teeth thoroughly, to wash out his glass afterwards, to fold up his clothes, to kneel and say his prayers and to ask God to make Mother better soon, then to get into bed—a large, wide bed, like Mummy's bed—and thereafter to make no sound, but to go to sleep.

"You need not be afraid of the dark," she said. "For your Uncle Hilary is going to sleep in your bed beside you. There are six extra people sleeping in the house tonight. So you must be sure to be asleep when your uncle comes up."

"Can I have the door left open, please, Aunty Belle?"

"No, dear, it is not necessary."

"Then can I have the window open?"

Isabelle prided herself that she knew the ways of children. Did she not remember her own childish fears of being left alone, she the eldest who later had the burden of the younger ones?

"Yes, dear, if you are very quiet, and promise not to call out, but to go to sleep immediately, I will leave the door just a little way open. Did you ask God to make you a better boy, dear?"

"Yes, Aunty Belle. And Mummy and Daddy, and Mavis and Mrs. Feeney, and Aunty Bee and Uncle Lemon, and Uncle White and Aunty Victoria and you as well, Aunty Belle."

"Yes, dear, you mentioned them in your prayers, that is right."

"To make them all better, Aunty Belle. Don't forget to leave the door open, will you?"

"No, dear. I'll put the chair here, to stop it from closing. Now go to sleep," she said, as she pushed her wet lips, so much harder than Aunty Bee's, against his cheekbone, "and don't you make a sound, like a good boy."

He made no sound; the tears for Mother fell silently. Later he felt sadly tranquil, as he heard a bird singing *jug-jug-jug*, then *teroo-teroo-teroo*, and watched the sunlight on the tops of trees, then the sounds of people passing in the passages outside, the noises of horses' hoofs and carriage wheels, more voices coming upstairs, doors shutting, and then a lot of talking and laughter from down below. And there were lanterns alight in the garden, and people walking there when it was growing dark—all of it far away from his life, nearly as far away as God, who was waiting a long way away, never to be seen or heard, but just waiting, waiting, waiting, much farther away than Mummie, who was as far away as the world, the world which, however much he tried to make it come nearer to him by thinking it near, always remained far away. Listening and thinking, silently weeping and then singing very quietly to himself about the world—thus the hours passed, and the darkness settled deeper, but still the bird sang *jug-jug-jug*, and then, after waiting, it sang *teroo-teroo-teroo*, and then sad cries came from it. The bird stopped singing at last, and then the horses' hoofs and the carriage wheels were heard again, with voices in the night. The world seemed nearer now, and he felt sleepy, yawned, and thinking of the tree at the bottom of the garden, and the black fence, drifted out of the world.

Chapter 13

PHILLIP ASSERTS HIMSELF

HILARY ROBERT VON FÖHRE MADDISON, going upstairs to bed ten
minutes after one o'clock in the morning, bumped into the white
cane-bottomed chair stuck in the doorway, and muttered a series
of curses *sotto voce*.

Awakened, Phillip lay still with the instinct of self-preservation.
He pretended to be asleep. Uncle lit the gas. But he was no
longer Uncle White; he was black. Phillip, peeping between
half-open lids, thought that this was because it was night. Uncle
sat on the chair and took off his coat, and then he was white on
top again, and creaking. Through narrowed eyes Phillip saw him
take off his shoes, and Uncle was grunting. He watched him take
off his trousers, and his white creaking shirt, then his vest, and
Uncle was big and pink and hairy, like a sort of bear. Uncle put
on a light-blue suit, of coat and trousers, not a nightshirt like
Father wore. And Uncle had a dressing-gown like Daddy's,
only softer and smoother, like it was made of quilt, and a blue
rope to tie it with. Why was Uncle dressing again so soon? Then
Uncle went out and shut the door ever so quietly and the light
was left on, and when he came back Uncle carried a towel. And
then Uncle opened his bag with a snap and closed the bag with
another snap and then he pulled the chain of the gas and it went
out and the mantle was red in the dark like in the front room
sleeping on the floor until it cooled off and a little by-pass light
stayed on. And then the door was opened ever so quietly and
closed again, while he knew Uncle was holding his breath.

When Phillip awakened again he heard the bird singing *jug-
jug-jug*, then *teroo-teroo-teroo* very loudly in the new garden outside.
He lay listening, his eyes wide open and staring round the strange
room. He saw the little light still burning on the by-pass. He
got out of bed and went in the pot under the bed, then got back
into bed again, seeing Uncle White's clothes on the chair. Then
he went to sleep and when he awoke again Uncle was getting into
bed beside him and the springs were sagging and all the bedclothes

were taken, and this made his back cold; so he gripped the bedclothes in a hand over his shoulder, and then rolled over to get them back again, because it was his bed. It was now Uncle's turn to be cold. Uncle laughed and said, "Well, damn my eyes, you little cockerel!" and laughed again as he pulled the top blanket over himself. Phillip was not afraid of Uncle White now, and wanted to kick him for getting into his bed, but instead withdrew as far as he could with the coverlet around him and whispered, his back turned to the intruder, "You fool."

Chapter 14

MANY ADVENTURES

PHILLIP thought it was lovely at Uncle George's house. The sun always shone in the garden. There were lots of strawberries and cream. He was promised a new sailor suit, with *long* trousers. Every night before bed Aunty Bee told him and Mavis about Goldilocks and the Three Bears. Uncle Hilary said that Aunty Bee made everyone feel it was a beautiful world. And Uncle Hilary did not catch him any more, or Aunty Belle tell him he was naughty. And there were lots of wooden boxes and everyone had presents, and there were jars of jelly and nice-to-smell joss-sticks burning in the morning-room on the chimney-piece beside the clock and photographs and little elephants and fat yellow booders.

Uncle Hilary said a booder was a god, but not on this side of the world. And there were little sharks' mouths stretched wide with a stick in them, and one was for Father, with a hammock of sparter grass. Sparter grass was slippery and yellow and heavy and you rolled out easily if you turned over too soon, and Uncle Hilary said it was not sparter grass but es-pa-to grass.

Uncle Hilary gave him the new sailor suit, with *long* trousers, white like Uncle Hilary's, and this made him a big boy, ever so big. "Look, Aunty Viccy, I am as high as this!" and with hand held flat on the top of his head he showed how high he was, much higher than he looked because he was really high up where his head was. Proudly wearing the long trousers, he was like Uncle Hilary, and took Uncle's hand to go for a walk without being asked, while Aunty Bee held Uncle's other hand and swung it as they walked, so he swung Uncle's hand too. And he had a cricket bat from Uncle George and a book of *Just So Stories* from Aunty Viccy; and when Aunty Belle left to be a companion to the Dowager Lady Botesdale she gave him a shilling for his Post Office Savings Book. He loved everyone now, except the gardener, who always said, "Clear off out of it," when he went to watch what the gardener was doing.

Jessie now looked after him when he went for a walk, with Mavis in the mail cart. They went for lovely walks, but he must

hold the mail cart when they crossed the road. His great friend was
an old gentleman dog called Joey who wagged his tail to see him.

One day Phillip took a loaf to have a picnic with Joey. They
ran away together into the woods and saw wonderful birds, and
a big pond where lots of white butterflies were flying up and down
on the water, and huge spotted fishes were splashing with open
mouths to eat the butterflies. They ate some of the loaf, but Joey
took his bits away and scratched earth over them. A man came
up in a brown hat and brown coat and a gun, and tied a string
on Joey's collar and took them back, for they were lost. Jessie
had red eyes, and said, "Oh, Master Phillip, how *could* you!"
And Uncle George said thank you to the man and gave him a
yellow sixpence, and the man touched his brown hat and then
patted him on the head and said, "He's a cute little beggar, sir,
asking me lots o' questions, and all to the point, what's more,"
and Lady Catt cried over Joey and Phillip wondered why she was
not called Lady Dog. Then Uncle George said, "Let me come
on the next picnic with you, Phil old fellow. If I am away, please
wait for me, for I love picnics." Aunt Bee kissed Uncle George and
called him an angel. But Aunty Viccy said he was a naughty boy.

Phillip did not connect the reserve his Aunt Victoria was
beginning to feel for him with the dish of apples on the table of the
morning-room. Every morning one of the apples was being
bitten. The bite was taken, so far as could be decided, before
half-past ten of a morning. At any rate, it was before the children
had their cups of Epp's cocoa at eleven o'clock.

Did both the children go to the dish? The bite was small, and
the skin of the apples being tough and wrinkled—they were
Ribston Pippins from Hilary's farm in New South Wales, brought
home crated in the *Phasiana*—no distinct teeth-marks were visible,
as might have been the case with softer apples. Then there was
the question of the height of the dish from the floor. The dish
could be reached by Mavis alone, only if a stool were put against
the table. There were fingermarks on the table, but whether
they were those of Mavis or of Phillip Victoria could not decide.

So she waited in the hall, where were saddle-bag armchairs
and a chesterfield; jaguar skins on the floor from Malay, and
Hilary; a writing table with blotter set in tooled leather, two
silver inkwells and tray with both quill and steel pens, another
of dark-blue writing paper embossed with the Lemon crest, which

device was also to be discerned upon the envelope flaps. Every morning Victoria sat at her table, attending to her correspondence. Near her was a bowl filled with scores of visiting cards of several sizes; while in the drawer of the Jacobean writing table, with its two latten drops, were hundreds more, all records of the polite rectitude of living.

Victoria wore a white shirt-blouse in the morning, with a high starched linen collar and a thin tie of black velvet, with a grey serge skirt. She called it her housekeeping uniform, since she had no housekeeper. George, a younger son, had yet to make his own way in the world. She must practise economy.

While she attended to her account books and correspondence in the morning, the door leading to the morning-room was left open. Upon the polished parquet flooring beyond the door lay a reflexion of light from the french windows at the farther end of the room. Anyone coming in from the garden would throw a shadow on the dull shine of the floor.

The apple-biting had occurred on the very first morning after the arrival of Dickie's children. Phillip and Mavis were called in from the garden to have their cups of Epps' cocoa at eleven o'clock and put to bed at ten minutes after eleven. At five minutes to one o'clock they were allowed to get up, their faces and hands were washed, their hair brushed, before being bibbed for their midday meal in what was called the schoolroom. The younger of the two maids was appointed to be the temporary nurse, since Isabelle took luncheon with the others in the dining-room.

Victoria, with some reason, suspected Phillip to be the culprit. He had that stealthy look at times, she said; and he appeared in unexpected places about the house, silently staring at her when she came upon him. The gardener, too, sometimes found him in his potting shed, peering and prying, though it was only fair to say that he had done no damage, and in so far as it was known, had removed nothing. Nor did he pick flowers. He did, however, have an unpleasant habit of catching flies and putting them in spiders' webs, then watching the wretched things being eaten by the spiders.

"I hope," she said to him, "that you are not the sort of cruel little boy who pulls the wings off poor little flies, Phillip."

"No, Aunty Viccy. When I am sorry for them, I bash the cruel spiders."

He was inclined to be mischievous, too. One day he went into the kitchen, when no one was there, by the back door, and removed the fly-paper which Cook had hung by her open window. This sticky strip, burdened with the dead and the dying, the frantically buzzing, the coagulated and feebly struggling, had been carried to the potting shed, and placed upon a wide, level web like a blue silken carpet with a tunnel at its dark end where dwelt a particularly big black spider with eight long hairy legs and glistening eyes above the face and inverted horns of a miniature bull. This was Phillip's favourite spider. The gardener, who had just pulled a blackbird's nest with downy young from a bush, to bury in his compost heap, complained to his mistress. It was *his* spider, he said, and he had been watching it for two seasons. He didn't want no one a-messin' about in his shed.

"You must not interfere with the gardener's things, nor must you go into the kitchen, do you understand, Phillip?"

"Yes, Aunty Viccy."

"Did you bite the apples in the dish, Phillip?"

"No, Aunty Viccy."

"It is not a very nice thing to do, you know, when you are a guest in someone else's house, and everyone is being kind to you. You understand what I am saying, don't you, Phillip?"

"Yes, Aunty Viccy."

"Then run along, and be a good boy, and play with your sister in the garden, and don't let her pick the flowers, will you?"

"No, Aunty Viccy."

Mavis did pick flowers, and smacking gently on the hands had not cured her. *Could* it be Mavis, who was biting just one apple every morning—a fresh one every day?

Victoria looked out of the other window. There was the Catt's overfed dog in the front garden, cocking his leg against the cotoneaster, the brute. Opening the window, she shoo'd him away. Joey took not the slightest notice, but deliberately scratched his hind legs on the grass border, then turned over to roll on his back, while gurgling to himself, the fool! Half amused, Victoria watched the old dog laboriously get on his feet again, shake his absurd harness, and then trot down the path round the side of the house to find his playmate Phillip. Well, there was no harm in it; but he was no Fritz: there was no dog like Fritz, and never could be ever again.

Victoria sighed.

There were several photographs of Fritz on the wall, with others hanging there, correctly spaced and aligned. Her favourite photograph was of the family group, on the lawn before the house, the last one taken before the break-up of the family. What a splendid-looking family they were! Father tall and upright, standing between John and Dickie at the back; Mother in the centre, on a chair, Isabelle on her right and Augusta on her left—Mother in her lace cap and bodice button'd to the neck, the elder sisters in white straw hats with flat brims, and print dresses with hooked collars under the chin and sleeves to the wrists. Sitting at their feet was Hilary, in monkey jacket and peaked cap, between Theodora and herself sitting cross-legged and holding lawn-tennis raquettes, their long silky fair hair falling over their shoulders, and such a decent, straight look in their open blue eyes. Just compare that Maddison look with little Phillip's! And there was Fritz sitting at Father's feet, the same challenging look in his eyes as in those of the master he adored! Dogs did take after their masters, she was sure. Where could a finer family be found to-day? If only Father had not been *too good*, he would never have had his heart broken as he did, and so have taken to excess. He was *driven* to it, by those brutes of radicals with the Free Trade!

Victoria, musing with some agitation, as she had mused many times before, saw a shadow on the polished floor by the open door of the morning-room. At last she would catch the thief! She got up and tip-toed across the hall. Peeping round the door, she saw—Joey. His tongue was hanging out as he panted slightly. Joey looked up at her, expectantly, as though saying, "Where's Phillip? Can't he come out to play?"

"Get out, you brute! Get away! Go back to your own garden! Come here, sir! Shoo! Shoo! Be off!"

Victoria followed his tip-tippering feet (for Joey's toe-claws were overgrown) on the parquet floor and out into the garden and round the path and so to the gate. Joey obediently trotted home; while Victoria discovered how he had got in. That beastly butcher's boy had left the tradesmen's gate unfastened again.

The peculiar thing about the incident was that, when she had left the morning-room a moment before, she could have sworn that no apple had been touched in the bowl. But, upon returning there, she saw at once that a bite had been taken out of the apple nearest the edge of the table. Could it have been Joey, fantastic as the idea was? Ah, there was Mavis, sitting on the step, holding a sweet-pea in one hand and her dolly in the other! Mavis was obviously the culprit! So she was put to bed without any Epps' cocoa, it having been impressed upon her that she was a very naughty girl.

The next morning Mavis went cocoa-less to bed again, this time without her doll. As the doll, which Hetty had given Mavis, was the container, preserver, and token of all mummy-feeling for Mavis, she wept. Phillip crept up to see her, and showed her how to catch flies with a scooping hand, in order to make her forget; but Mavis went on crying. Aunty Victoria came in and told him to go downstairs.

During the next seven days one apple on the dish had one bite taken out of it every morning, and as regularly Mavis was taken up to bed without doll or cocoa. Then the dish of apples was removed, without it being known that it was not Mavis who had taken the bite.

Phillip felt no shame that his sister had been punished for what he had done. He was sorry for Mavis being in bed; but it did not occur to him that he was to blame. Being sent to bed, like crying, and being told not to do anything, was just ordinary. There were, however, satisfactions, like presents given to you, and presents you gave to yourself. He had given himself a present of something out of a drawer, which he kept hidden, otherwise it would be taken away from him. It was like a little clock, only it did not tick, and you could not wind it up. When you opened the case you saw

RAT PORTAGE 1896

inside the case. He could read the words and figures to himself, though he had not been able to read words out of books when Mummy had tried to teach him at home.

Then one morning Phillip had seen a tiny little one like his on Uncle Hilary's watch-chain, and learned that it was a compass, and what it was for.

His compass was hidden on a ledge under the morning-room table. He was going to use it, with a slice of the loaf from the picnic, and a packet of Epps' cocoa, when he sailed all by himself away over the seas, on the sledge Father had promised him when he was bigger.

The sledge would be turned into a raft, like the picture Aunty Belle had shown him of a man called Lumber Jack. He had bitten the apples on top of the table because then the people would not think of under the table, where the compass, the bread, and the packet of Epps' cocoa were hidden. In bed at night, thinking of himself sailing away on the raft, he did not cry for Mummy, but saw himself on the gently gliding raft, which had a little sail, and he was safe on it, with his secret food. He sailed from a place called Tilbury, and as he sat by himself on the raft he sang a little song of sadness to the waves and the stars, for he had gone away from everyone he knew for ever and ever; and then remembering where he really was, he was ever so glad that he was lying beside Mavis; and when he put his hand on her soft warm tummy it made him feel very good and kind, for she was soft and warm like Aunty Bee. He loved Aunty Bee, but no one must ever be told.

He was glad when the apples were not there any more, for then Mavis could play with him and have Epps' cocoa. And Uncle Hilary said Aunty Bee was going to be his real aunty, and Aunty Bee wore white like Uncle Hilary, and smelled so nice as she showed him a ring on her hand that went blue and green and red, like the wet grass on the lawn in the morning before his feet made it look broken. Sitting beside Aunty Bee he drove in a carriage, and saw lots of flowers in the fields, and water behind railings, and Uncle Lemon said that the fishes lying in the water clear as gin were trout. It was a lovely drive behind the horse.

One day Father came over on his Starley Rover and sat in the garden, wearing his Norfolk jacket and knickerbockers and new thin cycling shoes without laces or buttons, and a badge in his coat with a wheel on it and C.T.C. He was like a different Father. He said, "Hullo, old chap, how well you look, quite sun-burned," and told him about Mummy, and said she was now in Quarantine, and he thought that must be a very long way away, as far as Uncle Hilary went in his ship. Then Father said, "Mother is going to have a week in Brighton before you return, so that she can pick up," and he saw Mummy as fallen down and unable to get up unless she left Quarantine and reached Brighton.

"Well, goodbye, old chap, keep your pecker up," and Father was going again.

"But, Dick, you have only just come!" said Aunty Viccy. And Uncle George said, "But you will stay for luncheon, surely?" and Father said, "No, thanks, I must get back." When Uncle George said, "I will get you a drink," Father said he would like only a glass of water.

Uncle Hilary said afterwards it was just like Dickie, who liked to wear the hair-shirt. This puzzled Phillip, for Father was wearing his stripey flannel shirt with a collar ending like a butterfly's wings. And when Father was gone, shaking hands with everyone and smiling as he had not often seen him smiling, Phillip went to church wearing the new clothes Aunty Victoria had given him. Church was itchy, as he had to sit so still and not move about, but when the man stopped talking and said, "And now to God the Father, God the Son, and God the Holy Ghost," everyone moved, and he could move too. There were lots of carriages outside the church, and people talking in the sun, ladies with sunshades up. There was red gravy and meat and potatoes and greens for dinner, which was the best part of Sunday, though the afternoon walk with Jessie pushing Mavis in the mail-cart was nice, with lots of things to see. And Jessie talked under a tree to a soldier in a red and yellow coat, and white gloves and belt and a stick called a switch, and the soldier gave him a cigarette card with an old man called Bobs on it. He held the card in his hand and it was crinkly when they got back, and Mavis was asleep in the mail-cart.

Red petals of the hawthorn lay in the dry dust of the road, the lilac began to turn rusty, little green apples with brown bows at their throats were to be seen among the leaves of the apple trees in the garden. There were lots of little shiny green cherries, too, and what Jessie called goosegogs, which were hard and hairy. None of them were nice to eat, so after the first handful hidden on the ledge under the table, with a mince pie taken when no one was looking, Phillip did not collect any more goosegogs.

Uncle Hilary went away and came back wearing clothes not looking like his clothes. Phillip asked him why, and Uncle Hilary said his kit had turned up at the club. Phillip saw the kit as something with a tail and a head like Dick Whittington's

cat in the pantomime Mummy and Aunty Dorrie had taken
them all to, and the club was held over its shoulder with a
bundle of clothes for Uncle.

Phillip did not cry for his mother any more. He was brown of
face and hands. He was more like what a boy ought to be,
thought Victoria. What a change from the wild, staring creature
who had come a fortnight before with Isabelle! As for Mavis,
she was a good little thing, very sweet-tempered now that her
brother was not so selfish with her. At first, he had tended to
push himself before her, as though afraid he might miss something—a tendency that had confirmed Victoria in her belief
that the Turneys were Jews.

Victoria as a young girl had heard her father saying, often
enough, that the Jews were getting more and more a hold on
England, behind the scenes; and everything Father had said was
unquestioned. It was noticeable how, with firm but kind treatment, the boy's trait of selfishness had tended to decrease.

One morning Phillip came to her and said he was "very
incited". She explained that he meant excited. The cause of
excitement was the arrival of the day of which he had heard so
much. Jessie had told him of it, as well as Uncle Hilary and
Aunty Bee. Jessie and her father, the gardener, said it was the
Durby, while Uncle said it was the Darby. Phillip imagined the
gardener's dirty hands, and Jessie's little brother had a dirty face,
so they said Durby. But he was clean, and Master Phillip, so he
would say Darby. He told Jessie that her brother Tom was
"darty". Jessie told him not to be cheeky, or he'd get no more
cigarette cards.

"Fag cards," said Phillip.

"I will tell your Aunty!" said Jessie, stiff white cuff'd and
collar'd over her grey jacket, bought specially for her temporary
duties of afternoon mail-cart pusher.

"You would not dare!"

"Yes, I do dare, then!"

"I'll tell about the soldier!"

"Hur. There's nothing to tell. See?"

"I saw him kiss you."

"That you didn't!"

"That I did! Ugh! he spooned with you."

Spoon was a word learned from Aunt Victoria. Once he had

heard her tell Uncle George that Hilary and Bee were spooning
in the summer-house in the garden, and it was not very nice with
the gardener nearby.

"Well, what of it if he did kiss me? What's wrong with that?"

"Spooning is not very nice."

"Well, it wasn't that kind of spooning, see? I don't come from
a back street, let me tell you, Master Phillip."

"I come from near the Hill. My father is the best man there,
let me tell you."

"Yes, and your ma's coming for you soon, but you'll be sorry
when you leave Jessie, won't you? There now, let's not be cross,
shall us?"

"No," said Phillip. "Let's make it up."

"There's a good boy. Now master and mis'es be getting ready
for the Durby."

Phillip was not allowed to go outside the gate, because there
were lots of bad men about, said Jessie, who would cut your
throat from ear to ear as soon as look at you. And there were the
gipsies who would steal children and dye them dark-brown all
over and take them away in a wooden house on wheels. They
would steal Joey, too, and eat him if they got a chance. Phillip
imagined the gipsies with red faces and jagged teeth and black
hair half over their eyes, like the giant in the story book. So he
carried a switch, taken from the gardener's bundle of faggots, to
fight the gipsies with if they came after him.

Everyone was dressing up. Phillip stared at his aunt's silks
and satins, at the hats with feathers and flowers, the frilly para-
sols, and wondered why Uncle George had a grey hat and Uncle
Hilary a black one. Both uncles had flowers in their button-holes,
and talked about them before taking them out, saying perhaps
they ought not to wear them in wartime. Aunty Bee was more
rustling shiny-black than before, with a big bow across her
throat as she stooped down and put a cornflower in the blouse
of his sailor suit, which had been washed and ironed. He hoped
this might mean that after all they were going to take him. Aunty
Bee said, "I don't know which is the deeper blue, this cornflower
or your eyes, my pet." Oh, if only she would take him where she
was going to the Darby!

Phillip dared to utter his longing to Aunty Bee. Could he
ride just a little way only, on the box of the coach that was coming

to fetch them? Didn't little boys go to the Darby? Only grown-ups were going this time, said Aunty Bee. He might be lost, she said.

"I will be ever so careful, and keep ever so close to you, if you will let me come, Aunty Bee. I will fight the gipsies with my switch!"

Aunt Bee called him her pet and kissed him, saying he must look after Mavis.

"Jessie can do that, Aunty Bee. And the soldier will look after Jessie."

"Oh, Jessie has a soldier, has she? Have you seen him?"

"Only a long way away, Aunty Bee. I didn't see him kiss Jessie, Aunty Bee!"

"You pet," said Bee, laughing, and kissing him again.

"Then can I come, Aunty Bee?"

"I am afraid not, darling. But I will tell you all about it when I come back."

The coach came down the road, and there were smiling people on it, and a coachman in a big coat and shiny hat with a thing like a squashed black beetle on the side of it, and a whip, and another man who had a long bright horn. And he held up the horn and blew it, and the noise was bright like the horn and the grey horses liked it for they jingled away.

The gate was left open, and Joey came in to see him. Phillip told Jessie about the squashed beetle thing and she said, "Fancy thinking Mr. Jones had that on his shiner! Why, it's a cockade, Master Phil! My uncle's a coachman too, and has one like that."

Phillip still thought of it as a beetle, like the one that smelled nasty-sweet when it cocked its tail, and you squashed it.

Left alone with Joey, Phillip thought he would like to run away and be lost. He went round the path, and stood against the brick wall of the house feeling that he would like to be lost in the woods. The robins would cover him with leaves, and Joey would go home alone to his dinner at Lady Catt's, and forget all about him. He would never come back any more, but be dead under the leaves.

Jessie came out to find Phillip a few minutes later, and tell him that his cocoa was waiting for him. She called his name, searched in the garden, then ran back to the kitchen breathlessly crying, "I can't find Master Phillip nowhere, Mrs. Powell. Do you think the gipsies have took him?"

In the midst of the agitation the house-parlourman of Lady Catt's came round, in his yellow-and-black striped vest and white sleeves, to ask if Joey were there, for he must come back for his luncheon.

They came to the conclusion that the boy and the dog had gone on another picnic.

"I'd lay a strap across his backside if I had my way," the servant complained.

Needless to add, he had been often treated that way in his boyhood.

"It's my 'alf-day off, too, and my lady and bloke have gone to the races, and what'll 'appen if Joey don't come back I wouldn't like to say."

Phillip and Joey were in the woods, looking for Goldilocks and the Three Bears. They passed the pond stocked with rainbow trout which had been rolling up after mayflies during their first visit. There were no fish visible now. The sated trout were lying on the bottom of the gravelly shallows, in the shade of waterside trees. Instead of the fish, there was a big grey bird crying *Squar-rk!* Joey said *Wuff!* and Phillip exclaimed *Oh!* as he watched with wonder the bird's yellow beak and black bootlace on its thin head, as it flapped up and beat away over the trees.

Suddenly something very strange and frightful happened. There was a *bang!* The grey bird tumbled and fell down. Phillip half-believed that it was shot by a bad man who would cut his throat, but he thought it was the Keeper who had fired the gun. But it might be gipsies! He ran away with Joey from the place of the bang, in case the Keeper pointed his gun at them and killed them. As he ran he thought that he would never put flies in spider webs again, if only God would save him.

He came from the path to a wider ride. The grass of the ride was marked with hundreds of big nailed boot marks. Joey began to sniff them and to wag his tail. Then Joey turned over and rolled, showing his pink tongue and saying *Huff huff huff*, for known to Joey, but not to Phillip, the golden Labrador bitch had been with the Keeper on his rounds.

Phillip thought that if he went backwards from the boot marks he would be going away from the Keeper with the gun, and so the Keeper would not see him and perhaps shoot him. His one idea now was to get back to Jessie and Mavis. He was lost, but there were men shouting and horns blowing the way he was going, so he ran on. When Joey would not come he stopped and clutched himself with fear, and wanted to go back and whip Joey for being a fool. Then Joey came, sniffing the ground, and Phillip gave him a flick of the switch, but as this made Joey wriggle, and want to roll more, he whipped him. Joey looked sad, so he stroked him, and told Joey he was sorry, and afterwards Joey followed him properly down the path.

A bird like a hen's husband flew up with a long tail saying *Kock-koch-karr!* and its wings hit the twigs and the leaves. This was probably a rich stockbroker bird, who owned the wood. He remembered Uncle George saying to Uncle Hilary, *A queer bird has taken the shooting, a stockbroker, I hear.*

Phillip and Joey got safely out of the wood. There were a lot of people, hundreds and hundreds and *hundreds* of people, over the grass where the wood ended. There was a hard-wire fence, with sharp, grey spidery spikes on the wire. Phillip lay down and wriggled under the lowest wire, slowly because of the spikes, and triumphantly reached the grass. There was a rope fence over the grass, and pieces of wood with rope loops over their squashed tops, and this fence was easy.

Beyond were wooden houses on wheels. An old woman smoking a little black pipe upside down sat on the steps of one house. She had a brown face and dark hair like Uncle George's. There were lots more people. Several thin dogs with tails curving under them ran at Joey. Joey stood still wagging his tail and saying *ee-ee-ee* as the thin dogs sniffed him. One big dog pulled the fur on Joey's neck with his teeth. Joey lay down and held up his bent legs. When the dogs had sniffed and wee-ee'd on Joey they ran away. Joey stood up again and came beside Phillip and stayed close to him until they were under the other rope.

And there were hundreds and hundreds and *hundreds* of peoples, men shouting, with paper boards on them, men with pearly buttons on their coats and trousers, and hundreds more. The grass was trodden flat like on the Hill on Band Night when all the poor people came there to hear the band playing and Mummy told him not to speak to the poor children. Poor children were rude and nasty, and now Phillip did not speak to them. An old woman with a basket gave him a toffee apple on a stick and he said "Thank you" before she could say "What do you say?", and the old woman said, "What a dear little gentleman you are, and what blue eyes you have. What's your name, dearie?"

She had a brown wrinkled face, so she might be a gipsy. Frightened, Phillip replied, "I'm Mr. Cornflower."

"Well well, fancy that now. Are you with anyone? Where's your mummy?"

Phillip did not know what to say, so he said, "My mummy is dead," and when she looked at him sadly and said "O-oh!" he believed that Mummy *was* dead after all.

"Are you all alone, ducks?" she said, holding his hand, which made him very afraid, for now he was sure she was a gipsy to steal him.

"My mummy isn't in heaven really, she's only in Quarantine."

"And where's that, ducks?"

"Near Brighton next week, I think." Then raising his cap he said "Good-bye" to the old woman, and hurried away, before she could find out he was not Mr. Cornflower at all, but Phillip Maddison.

When he looked back, she and two other ladies were looking at him. He hurried on, to hide behind peoples. When he looked back again, the first old woman waved her hand. He waved back. She thought he was Mr. Cornflower, ha ha!

No one would know his real name was Sonny, no one could steal him now he was Mr. Cornflower! He found a piece of string, and to make himself look not like a boy who had run away, he tied it to Joey's collar, then he could say he had come to get back Joey who had run away from Lady Catt.

Hardly had Phillip devised the excuse when Joey was pulling him on the string, as though he, Joey, had come to get back Phillip. The reason was soon apparent. There by a big yellow, red, and black coach was Lady Catt, smiling. Joey wagged his tail and Phillip raised his sailor cap, the new black round one with H.M.S. *Brittania* on the band. He said, "I found Joey, Lady Catt." Lady Catt smiled, and her teeth looked like Joey's teeth, yellow.

So Phillip's day at the races turned out to be a good one, after all. Lady Catt let him stand on the box with Mr. Lady Catt who was called Sir Alfred, and he saw very thin horses running all together, their hoofs thundering. There were men in caps and coloured clothes, leaning on the horses, as though they were talking to the horses' ears, but they could not hear if they were, as everyone was shouting. Then the horses were gone and a lot of bits of earth were in the air behind the horses. And men spying with telescopes.

Phillip remembered best the lovely sandwiches to eat, and the sweet cold lemonade to drink. Mr. Lady Catt Sir Alfred took him to a place behind a big sack on sticks and there was an ever so big hole in the grass full of yellow wee-wees and he widdled into the hole and did not wet his trousers. When they got back to the coach Lady Catt said, "Haven't you got a whistle? I will buy you a whistle, and a lanyard, to wear with your sailor suit." When he said "Thank you, Lady Catt," she kissed him and said he was the best-mannered boy she had ever known, a perfect little gentleman, and he felt very good and quiet.

Aunt Victoria shook her head when he was taken home, and Lady Catt had said good-bye. Aunt Victoria said he was nothing but an anxiety, and no wonder his father was unable to do anything with him. And when next day Lady Catt called to give him a whistle Aunty was very nice and smiling to Lady Catt; but afterwards she said he did not really deserve it, for worrying everybody so.

"I shall not tell your mother this time," she said, sitting at the table in the hall, her eyes wide, "but really, you know, you must try not to be so tiresome. It is perfectly plain to me that you have been indulged, given your head too much, and that is not good for either young horses or children, Phillip. Do you do as you please when you are with your mother? Do you take advantage of her kindness to you? If so, it is not playing the game, you know, old chap. Do you understand what I am saying, Phillip?"

"No, Aunt Victoria," said Phillip, staring at her.

"No, I do not suppose you do, you funny boy," said Aunt Victoria, with a faraway laugh. "And what's more, if you did understand, I do not suppose it would make any difference to you, would it?"

Phillip did not know what Aunt Victoria meant, but her tone of voice indicated that he must say No, so he said "No, Aunt," and continued to look up into her face in such a way that she smiled, in spite of herself. And she said, as she stroked his hair, "You're a pickle, Phillip, that's what you are. Now run along and have your cocoa, and for heaven's sake, boy——" But Victoria by this time had forgotten, if she had ever known, what she was going to say. On impulse she kissed him; which perhaps was the best thing to do. He was much nicer a little boy after that, and came and told her things; but, oh Lord, he did not seem to have the slightest idea what was fact and what was fiction.

Chapter 15

HETTY MEETS HER IN-LAWS

When she was out of quarantine, Hetty and her mother had a week together by the sea at Brighton. Hetty felt better than she had done for a long time. She loved Brighton, having spent several holidays there as a child. The fishermen, the cobs with their brown sails, the capstans by which they were hauled up the shingle out of the battering waves, the brown nets hanging out to dry, and the dim green Aquarium, with fishes swimming in the tanks; the strange Pavilion, with its domes and Eastern-looking architecture, the sea-front and the groins, the spray shooting up and falling over the road in a gale; the electric railway by the sea, the piers, and the theatres! Doctor Brighton was the best doctor of all.

The day approached when she would be returning home, and fetching the children from their aunt at Epsom. Hetty was a little apprehensive whenever she thought of her husband's relations. After some discussion on the subject of Etiquette with her mother, she wrote a letter to her sister-in-law, fully conscious that she had never met her. She hesitated many times over the question of whether to begin *Dear Victoria*, or *Dear Mrs. Lemon*, and after spoiling three sheets of writing paper, finally got something finished.

17 Rawley Square,
Kemp Town, Brighton.

My Dear Mrs. Lemon,

I do not feel that I know you well enough to call you by the name my husband has always used when he has spoken to me of you, but I do want you to know that I am ever so grateful for your great kindness in looking after my little children during my recent illness. Dickie told me that Phillip looked as though he were having the time of his life, the country air must suit him, after the fogs and cold winds we have had in the late winter.

Here it is very nice by the sea, the weather has been perfect, men having been fishing day after day on the Chain Pier and

Mamma and I have had several rides on Volks' electric railway along the front.

I do hope the children have behaved themselves and given no trouble whatsoever. It is so very very kind of you, and Isabelle, to have had them to visit you, and next Thursday if all goes well I hope to come by an early train, arriving at Epsom some time in the a.m., and bring them home again. I am now completely restored to health, the period of quarantine being over before I came here with Mamma.

With kind regards, and renewed thanks for all you have done,

I remain,

Yours very truly,

HENRIETTA MADDISON.

"I expect," said Victoria, in the garden on the Thursday morning, "Hetty did not have a time-table to hand, for she has not said what time her train will arrive. Otherwise I could have sent down word to the station fly to bring her here."

"Perhaps she would rather find her own way, and walk up," said Beatrice.

Victoria did not reply at once. Her *idée fixe* was bothering her; she was thinking of her brother, and what a pity it was. But then, she told herself, everyone had to make his or her own life.

"Anyway, I expect she will be here sometime. I have arranged for a cold luncheon. I hope she can eat salmon, there's a ham, and a tongue, as well. I thought it would be nice to have a simple meal out here. What do you think, Hilary?"

"Oh yes, it is a very pleasant place, Viccy."

The three were sitting in the arbour, an affair of rustic poles and palings, overgrown with rambler roses and honeysuckle. It was built in the Black Forest style. It occupied one flank of the lawn, which was also a tennis-court. Hilary was lounging in the hammock. He had brought three hammocks home from the tropics, one for Dickie, another for George, and the third for himself.

Bee and Viccy were sitting on cushions laid under the rustic seat. It was a pleasant retreat, half in sun and half in shade. A goldfinch had a nest in an adjacent apple tree. The twitterings of the fledglings was audible every few minutes, when the parent birds flew, quite fearlessly, to their young. Victoria was fond of goldfinches, and could not bear to see them or any wild birds, in cages.

They were talking about the theatre. Recently Hilary and Bee had been together in London, and had seen several shows, including *Messenger Boy* and *Floradora* at the Lyric. Victoria listened to their conversation, while wondering if Bee would be able to settle down with Hilary, after the excitement of her life on the stage. And why had she, suddenly, married a man so much older than herself, and a woolmaster from Bradford, of all things? He had been a worthy man, in his way, but he had been nearly thirty years her senior. Bee could have married almost anyone she had liked: then why John Murgatroyd? Could it have been for his money, or because her own father had deserted his family when Bee was only three years old, and so had lacked all her life a father's affection?

Victoria's fingers were busy at her crochet-work, as she half-listened to the twitter of the goldfinches and the inconsequential talk of Bee. She was now speaking about a friend of hers who had been the centre of a ridiculous case about a year previously, when the landlady of a public house, or an hotel, appropriately named "The Hautboy", had had the sense to refuse refreshment to that friend of Bee's, who certainly should have known better, for appearing in what she had the effrontery to call "rational cycling dress". It had been quite a *cause célèbre*, and George's firm had briefed counsel. She had told George at the time that no action for damages could possibly succeed, and events had proved her right. Lady Harberton had lost the case. Victoria recalled the unhappy argument with George, after the verdict, George declaring that it was bad law, that the Judge had misdirected the Jury. How *could* he have been so obdurate as to miss the *obvious* rightness of the verdict?

What Victoria had deplored was the lack of responsibility shown to society by one who should have known better. A woman, particularly a titled woman, should set the best example to others, in all things. She must uphold the traditions of her class, not debase them. Lady Harberton had revealed her lack of the sense of responsibility in other ways. She had started what she called *A Sanitary Congress*, and had demanded that women should all wear short skirts!

George had declared that it was a hoax, but she had not believed it. It was a craving for sensationalism in a thoroughly vulgar age! The idiotic song people were singing, it rang through her head at times, and now Phillip had got hold of it, through Jessie, she supposed—a perfectly absurd little jingle, *Daisy, Daisy, give me your answer do . . . stylish marriage . . . can't afford a carriage . . . only a bicycle made for two!*

How splendid was the spirit of the old Queen, by contrast! Victoria recalled the remark the Queen had made during the last Christmas, at the time of the black news after the lost battles in South Africa—*No one is depressed in this House. We are not interested in the possibility of defeat.* But at the same time it really had been an eye-opener to read that, of the first hundred thousand recruits for the new army, two thirds had been pronounced to be unfit. Now *that* was something that *did* need rectification!

"What do you think, Viccy? Shall I, or shall I not?"

"I am afraid I was day dreaming, Hilary——"

"I was asking Bee if she would like me to buy a self-propelled carriage."

"A self-propelled carriage? You're not serious, surely, Hilary?"

"Why not? We have self-propelled ships, so why not such vehicles on the road?"

"But if they are not stopped, they will spoil the countryside, Hilary! Look at the dust they kick up, apart from the noise! Do you like the beastly things, Bee?" she asked, expecting to be supported.

"I think they are great fun, Viccy! Four of us had a wonderful run down to Henley last year. I nearly eloped with the driver, only he, dear boy, was already bespoke by Rosie Shoon."

"Rosie Shoon?"

"A very good friend of mine, at the Gaiety."

"Oh."

"And who was the driver. Come on, tell us," said Hilary.

"A Cornet of Horse named Footeweke."

"The Marquis of Footeweke? So that's the sort of gal you are, is it? 'Stage-door Johnnies.' I thought you'd given up your fast living!"

"Well, you may as well know the sort of person you're marrying! Anyway, I was the chaperon, you see. J. M. was alive and kicking then, and he made no objections."

Victoria thought that this was hardly the way to refer to one's late husband, even if he had been a woolmaster; but she said nothing.

"And did you get so far as Henley?" asked Hilary. "I'm interested in the internal-combustion engine. So is my chief, Robert MacKarness."

"But they make such a foul noise, and kick up such a dust!"

"The dust will abate quite a lot, Viccy, now that there's a law passed saying that only smooth tyres may be used."

"Well, I cannot say I approve the idea, anyway! You asked my opinion, and there it is."

Victoria felt that the two together, Hilary and Bee, were, in a way, in league against her. Beatrice realised this and said, "You must see *Floradora*, Viccy! I am sure it would delight you. We must take her to a matinee, Hilary." Beatrice sang softly,

> *O my Dolores,*
> *Queen of the Western Sea,*

and then hearing, during a pause, a movement on her right hand —Victoria was on her left—she glanced slowly sideways and saw, through a gap in the light green leaves of the rose briars, a little face watching her.

It vanished. She smiled to herself, but said nothing. The watch hanging on her bodice by its golden bow told that it was eleven o'clock, the boy's bedtime; he would be so excited that his mother was coming, that enforced rest would do more harm than good. She thought of her own two little tots, at home in Tenterden in Kent, in the care of their nannie, and her mother. She was taking Hilary there to see Mamma shortly. At the end of her year of (official) mourning they were to be married.

There was the ring of a bell in the house. Beatrice saw, through the gap in the pergola, the boy running tiptoe over the lawn towards a clump of snowberry bushes.

"I wonder if that can be Henrietta?" said Victoria, getting up, and going towards the french windows. Left with Hilary, Beatrice said:

"I wonder what she's like, darling?"

"We'll soon see, won't we? I don't suppose my brother Dick had any reason for hiding her. I'm just going upstairs, Honey Bee; I'll be down again in a minute." And kissing Honey Bee, Hilary went into the house by another way.

Left alone, Beatrice arranged the shoulder frills of her black silk muslin blouse. She was entirely self-assured in what she called to herself her war-paint. Her *ensemble* had been carefully chosen. Yoke and neck-band were of black silk net, transparent to the top of her collar bones; below was finely pleated muslin, crossed by bands of black velvet sewn with sequins, a black silk stomacher for her twenty-one-inch waist, and a velvet hip-band lying close upon her black silk skirt. Her figure had hardly suffered from child-bearing; and on seeing her clad in this Parisian creation by Worth et Cie of New Bond Street, Hilary had risen, and so had come to the gaff. Thus Beatrice thought of it, lightly within herself.

Hilary, self-assured, and with a fine conceit of himself, had seen it another way: that his own splendid life could be made finally perfect by having the Honey Bee always to return to, in a home of his own. Were they not, in every way, and particularly in the basic way from which life flowed, perfectly matched? So, almost casually, these two experienced people had come mutually to the idea of marriage.

Beatrice's hat had been chosen to set off her fair hair and blue eyes. It was of black scalloped straw, with a cluster of small black aigrettes rising from a jet paste buckle on the crown of the hat. It was a hat smaller than the current fashion, an affair of *chic* and lightness of heart. From the brim in front hung a fine-gauze veil, which when tied under her chin added lure and mystery to her oval face, which had a kind of glow about it, a softness due to washing only in cow's milk, she believed. Beatrice also liked to believe that the colour of her eyes was of that uncommon china-blue tint which had characterised the great courtesans of history. She regretted only one thing about her person: that her hair was not raven-black, but of a commonplace honey-paleness. To be sure, it was soft as silk—and since it pleased the men she liked, it did not worry her unduly.

"After all, life is short," said Beatrice to herself, as she got up to shake out her fine feathers, "and if one has got to be sad, one may as well be sad with a certain gaiety." And in this mood, carrying her parasol, she walked to the clump of snowberry bushes where Phillip had hidden himself in sudden agitated inability to face his mother.

"Phillip," she said, "your Mummy has come."

There was no answer.

Beatrice parted the bushes, and saw him sitting there, unmoving. She thought to herself, Stage fright!

"Come on, darling, Mummy will be simply longing to see her little boy again."

"No, no," he said, "I do not want to see her."

From the house, from a bedroom with all the windows open, could be heard the joyful cries of Mavis.

"There, you see, my pet? Let's go together and say 'How d'you do', shall we?"

Phillip crawled further into the bushes. Beatrice thought she understood his feeling, that it would be best to leave him alone. Poor little fellow, he had missed her so much, and now his feelings were carrying him in the opposite direction.

"I know, you're an Indian! You're going to give Mummy a surprise! My little boy hides, too, when I go home, at first." She went back to the arbour, feeling within herself some of the mixed emotions of the boy.

Hetty, too, was experiencing mixed feelings. She had prepared herself for the visit to her younger sister-in-law with some trepidation. She had a feeling that her husband's relations did not approve of her. Sarah had understood her apprehension, and to help dispel it she had made Hetty a present of a new frock from Peter Robinson's in Oxford Street, which had been altered by a "little woman" in Randiswell.

As soon as Beatrice saw Hetty, coming with Victoria through the open french windows, she liked her. She understood her nervousness. Immediately she sought to put her at ease.

"My dear, what a beautiful frock you are wearing! Oh, where *did you* find such a treasure? And *how* are you? May I call you Hetty? I have heard *so* much about you, I feel I know you as an old friend." Impulsively she kissed the smiling, child-like face before her, moved by the innocence and candour of the countenance.

Hetty's frock was of silk taffeta in black and white stripes, with a bow at the throat, tucks on the shoulders, black lace on the bodice, braid on the skirt, a frill around the hem. White lace on her cuffs half concealed her small slim hands, one of which held the skirt up just above her ankles, exposing the frill of a petticoat, and *glacé* kid slippers with beads on the pointed toes, flat heels, and one-button strap. She was a picture! The bodice was boned, seamed, tucked, darted, and built up to give a high, full bustline, accentuating her small waist without the use of corsets. A sweet child-mother, with Mavis holding her other hand, determined not to lose her again. She would melt a heart of stone, thought Beatrice—and Victoria could see in her only a misfortune for her brother!

"My dear, you look the picture of health and happiness!"

"Oh yes!" said Hetty, with her gay little laugh. "Doctor Brighton! The sea breezes were so health-giving."

"Where is Phillip?" enquired Victoria. "Surely he cannot have run away again?"

"Oh, I do hope Sonny has not been giving any trouble?"

"Oh no, of course not, Hetty. He is a bit of a mixture, all the same, you know!" with a smile. "A pickle, I should call him."

"Oh dear," said Hetty, not quite knowing how to take this.

"The spirit of adventure is strong in him, the pet!" exclaimed Beatrice. "Have you told Hetty, Viccy, how he went to the Derby, all by himself, except for an old dog living down the road, belonging to 'Mr. Lady Catt Sir Alfred', as he calls our worthy ex-Lord Mayor of Birmingham?"

Seeing Hetty's face, she took her arm, and giving forth all her charm, said smilingly, "Phillip has quite won our hearts, the *dearest* little pet! I would steal him if I could! I am sure he is most intelligent. What eyes he has, full of what the French call *sensibilité*."

"Where can he have got to?" said Victoria. "He cannot be far away."

When they discovered Phillip concealed in the snowberry bushes, it looked as though Beatrice's remark about wanting to steal him had already suggested a fact. He refused to come out, after repeated cajolery on the part of his aunts, and was eventually left to himself.

Hilary joined them in the arbour, where Mavis sat beside Hetty, clinging to her mother's skirt. While they were talking there, the boy appeared in the opening, a woeful look upon his face. When Hetty said, holding out her arms, "Aren't you coming to me, Sonny?" he turned and ran away.

"We're not taking enough notice of him," laughed Hilary.

"I should have thought we were taking too much notice of him," remarked Victoria.

"Perhaps he will settle down if we leave him alone," said Hetty.

"He's a naughty boy, isn't he, Mummy? He bited the apples." At Mavis's unexpected statement, Victoria cried, while a faint pink came upon her cheeks. "So that's who it was! And you were punished for it! Oh, you poor little girl!"

Explanations followed. Hilary chuckled. Hetty felt upset, wanting to explain that she was sure Sonny had not known what he was doing; she had never known him to do that sort of thing before.

"Small boys are little devils, you know, they grow out of it," said Hilary, and Beatrice gave him a grateful glance.

Phillip refused to leave the snowberry bushes. In the end Hilary had to lug him, protesting and weeping, to the arbour. Phillip refused to go near his mother, pulling against his uncle's hand and finally sitting down. Hilary dragged him before Hetty.

"He needs a strong hand," he declared, slightly out of breath. "He's remarkably strong, despite his skinny appearance."

Beatrice noticed that Hetty had gone pale. Poor little mother, how sensitive she was! Why could not they leave the boy alone? She felt a momentary hardness against Hilary, and had to resist an impulse to give him a kick. As for Victoria, that woman was cold as a fish.

At this point a maid came out, bearing a silver tray with glasses, a bowl of cracked Wenham ice, and a jug of lemon squash.

"I think we'll have it in the hall, shall we? It's cooler indoors," said Victoria, and the maid, with a bob, took the tray back again into the house.

They got up, and Beatrice, shaking her skirt with her black gloved hand, said that she would speak to Phillip and follow them into the house.

"First nights are always the most difficult." She smiled at Hetty, who gave her such a sad little glance of gratitude that Beatrice felt momentarily near to tears.

A couple of minutes later she was leading by the hand across the lawn a docile small boy, green marks on his white sailor suit, his tear-stained face set with an expression of desperate acquiescence. They sat down together in the arbour.

"Tell me why you don't want to see Mummy, Phil?"

He shook his head.

"Never again?"

"No, Aunty Bee," and then he broke down and sobbed. Beatrice, who had hoped he would say that he wanted her, and was prepared, thereafter, to plead for Hetty, to her surprise found she was crying too. With tears running down his cheeks he stared at her tears, before pulling his handkerchief from his pocket so that she could wipe her eyes. The compass fell out, and she saw it. She recognised it as belonging to Hilary, but said nothing for the moment. The business of wiping tears away must be gone through first. Afterwards:

"That's a nice compass, dear," she said, opening the case. "Where did you get it? Did Uncle Hilary give it to you?" She felt mean, asking a question of which she knew already the answer.

He stared at her, his eyes wide open.

"I expect you borrowed it, for a long long journey, didn't you, dear?"

"Yes, Aunty Bee."

"But now you are going home again with Mummy, you won't need it, will you, dear?"

"No, Aunty Bee."

"Then shall we put it back?"

"Yes, Aunty Bee. And the cocoa, too. And the bread."

Beatrice laughed. Light came in the boy's face again. "I was naughty, wasn't I, Aunt Bee?"

"Aunty Bee doesn't think so. But some people might call it stealing, so perhaps it is best not to take any more things, don't you think?"

"Yes, Aunty Bee."

"Well, I'll put the compass back. Look, RAT PORTAGE is scratched on it. I wonder what it means. 'Portage' means travelling in the backwoods, while 'Rat' may be the name of a river. I think Uncle went on a fishing adventure once, in Canada, where he saw lots of Indians, with canoes, who lived in painted tents called wigwams. And just think, this little compass showed him all the way there, and all the way back again! Perhaps he will take you one day, when you are bigger. Won't that be fun?"

"Yes, Aunty Bee! And per'aps I'll see the Three Bears!"

"You pet! You'll find a Goldilocks one day, but she will never never *never* love you so much as I do!" and Beatrice picked him up and, to his embarrassment, kissed him in a way he had never been kissed before.

"All gone tears, my pet?"

"Yes, thank you, Aunty Bee!"

They went into the house. Phillip went upstairs, and put the compass back where he had found it. Aunty Bee washed his face. He sat next to her at the table, while Mummie sat on the other side with Mavis.

It was lovely, with nice pink fish and cucumber with yellow sauce, and strawberries and cream.

When they were leaving, Aunty Viccy gave him the biggest money he had ever seen for his moneybox, a yellow one with a man on a horse killing a dragon, a new one, said Aunty, with the year 1900 underneath. The cab was waiting; he did not want to leave, but hid his face in Aunty Bee's shirt, and Uncle Hilary laughed and tickled the back of his neck. He cried as they drove away. In the train he was sick, and lost all his strawberries on the floor. Mummy took them into another carriage where he lay down and went to sleep, thinking of Indians and fishing, and clutching the big money, tied in a corner of his handkerchief, in his hand.

Chapter 16

DAME SCHOOL

THERE WAS a dame's school near the end of Charlotte Road,
run by two sisters named Miss Fanny and Miss May Whittaker.
To this school one September morning came Hetty, dressed in
her Sunday best, holding Phillip by one hand and Mavis by the
other. The boy had the fixed anxiety of the unknown in his
face. He wore a new suit, which his mother had bought him from
the new big shop in the High Street, Rindman's of the Arcade.
She had been saving up all the spring and summer for his
first boy's suit. It had a little jacket with a belt, in the Norfolk
style, with knickerbockers buttoning below the knee. She had
waited for the end-of-summer sales, when it had been marked
down from twelve and eleven three to seven and eleven three.
She had tendered four florins in payment, and the farthing change
had been given to Phillip. With this coin he purchased an
ounce of aniseed balls, which Hetty told him he must not bite
with his teeth, in case he broke them. He had already broken
a molar trying to crack a brazil nut.

To make the entry into school easier for the children, Hetty
took them first to the end of Charlotte Road, pointing out the
house which was St. Catherine's Kindergarten as they passed,
and declaring that it was just the same as any other house. She
was going to take the children first to the Bon Bon, a sweet-
stuff shop round the corner in the High Road. Hetty hoped that
the familiar scene would be reassuring to Sonny, who had
hardly spoken since leaving the house. He held her hand tightly.

The Bon Bon was one of a row of little shops comprising a
greengrocer's, a haberdasher's, a corn chandler's, a furniture
shop, and Leo the chemist's, whose front held two big bulbous
glass jars containing respectively red and blue liquids. A ha'penny
stick of Fry's chocolate purchased at the Bon Bon and divided
between them was to be the reward for being good children.

Having watched that his sister did not have more chocolate
than he received, Phillip walked back past the other shops

holding his mother's hand, while clasping in the other two and
a half inches of chocolate bar half an inch thick. If he sucked
it slowly, then he would be with Mummy longer. He was
frightened of going into the house Mummy had shown him, behind
the shut door. Father had told him of how little boys who were
not truthful often grew up to be bad men, who were put into
prison behind big iron bars. Father had said, "You do not want
that to happen to you, do you? Then be a good boy, and do
not tell any more fibs." Cousin Ralph had told him, when he
and Jerry and Ralph had galloped over the Hill on their steeds,
using their switches to make them gallop, that at school if you
didn't do your lessons properly you had to hold out your hand
and swoosh! didn't the master cut down the cane, and didn't
it hurt. But, said Cousin Ralph, if you get a black horsehair and
put it in your hand, when they give you the whack, it will split
the cane right up to the top and sting the master's hand. Also
your knuckles were rapped on the lid of a desk, or they copped
you one with a round black ruler. In school they gave you lines
to write out while the other boys played in the playground after
school, and they stood you in the corner if you talked or laughed
in the classroom.

"Come on, Sonny, eat up your chocolate, there's a good
boy," said Hetty. "Look, Mavis has eaten hers up already."

"Father said to suck sweets, not to bite them, Mummy."

"Now, Sonny, don't be merely annoying, dear. Miss Fanny
Whittaker will expect us to be punctual. I loved going to school
when I was your age, it was the happiest time of my life."

Hetty was talking out of her own nervousness. The children
had been with her, except for the period of scarlet fever, since
they were babies, and she grieved secretly that already they were
old enough for school. She felt the coming separation more than
she dared admit to herself, and certainly could not reveal to
Richard. The old days were already gone, when Sonny, with
his curls on his shoulders, would run to her with such keen delight
and cry "Ning-a-ning man, Mummy, ning-a-ning man come!"
and wait so eagerly for the penny from her purse, to run and give
it to Carlo. What had happened to Carlo and his little girl
with the tambourine? The monkey had died long ago of
pneumonia. One Thursday Carlo had not come; nor the next.
No longer was the barrel organ to be seen, hauled up the road

in a series of zigzags from curb to curb, Carlo with his rounded bowler hat straining between the shafts, and all for Sonny's weekly penny; nobody else in Hillside Road had ever given the Italian anything. "Gone! Gone!" Sonny had cried, when the ning-a-ning man had come no more.

Yes, she would miss Sonny in the house, helping her to dry the spoons and knives and plates after washing up, bringing in the bread from the baker, and opening the door to the tradesmen who called for orders from Randiswell. She would miss, too, his strange and sudden statements. Hetty had recorded some in her leather-bound *Log Book*, which she had used for her Diary when she had gone to Canada, nearly ten years before, with Papa to visit Charley learning to farm in Manitoba. She had been looking at the book before she left with the children for the Kindergarten that morning.

I must be quick and put this bottle's head (cork) on, it may catch cold.
How does God put our skins on? Does he sew them on with needle and cotton?
Do tell Mavis to be quiet, she keeps interrubbering me so.
Does God keep our skins in a box? He does our toe-nails, because I have seen them.

After the Epsom visit she had noticed a change in the boy; at times he did not appear to be the little son she had known. She had taught him the elements of writing, he could copy letters and figures in his spidery hand, with pothooks and strokes; but he had actively disliked his lessons. She thought perhaps it was because his brain worked too quickly. He could not sit still or concentrate for more than a few moments. She did so hope he was not going to grow up to be a difficult boy.

Hetty's mind was set on getting her son a presentation to Christ's Hospital, popularly known as the Bluecoat School. She had learned that the Canon of Westminster Abbey, who had a presentation in his gift, was an uncle of Roland Tofield, with whom, before her marriage, she had made friends on the French Riviera at Hyères, and who later had been instrumental in getting Dickie a billet in the Moon Fire Office. She had not spoken to Dickie of this future plan of hers, nor had she ever told him of her part in his appointment, because he was of such a jealous disposition.

One of Hetty's secret griefs was that her husband persisted in believing that she cared more for the children than for him. It was not true, but he often behaved, and indeed spoke, as though it was. And now Sonny had got the idea from what his father had once said. She had not written Sonny's remark in her *Log Book*, for very shame, and also because, should Dickie see it, he would very likely regard it as confirmation of his thoughts. But Hetty remembered the exact words of Sonny on that occasion.

"S'posin' you had to choose between me dying, or Father dying, who would you choose, Mummy?"

"You should not think, or even say, such things, Sonny. I love your father and my children equally, you see."

"But s'posin' you *had* to choose, who would you choose? S'posin' there was a red-hot fire everywhere, who would you save?"

"I would save you all, Sonny, if I could, with God's help."

"But Mummy, s'posin' God had set the fire alight, as a trial and tribulation, who would you save first?"

"I will not answer such a question, Sonny. Of course I love your father just as much as I do my children. Now be a good boy, and polish the fire-irons with emery paper for me, and I will give you two jamjars to take in the basket down to Hern's and you shall have the penny from them for your money box."

If the mother, always so aware of the fleetingness of life and the moment's impermanence, concealed her sadness that her little ones were partly to be lost to her now they were about to enter another world, there was no such reticence in the demeanour of Phillip. He stared with wide eyes and pale face at the black board on the post with its lettering in gold-leaf.

ST. CATHERINE'S SCHOOL FOR BOYS AND GIRLS

WITH KINDERGARTEN

Miss Frances Whittaker, Honours Diploma,
University of London,
Headmistress.

Miss May Whittaker, L.R.C.M.,
Assistant Mistress.

There was a snail stuck on the lower edge of the black board, which had a thin greenish mould growing on it, as had the post.

The house faced north, with the usual thin hedge of privet rising above the cast-iron railings on top of the wall. Phillip pointed to the thin silver trail, by which the snail had travelled upwards at the end of summer, and exclaimed "Ugh! It's a snaily old place!", and nothing would induce him to enter the gate. His mother had to leave him there.

When Miss Fanny Whittaker came out, a tall, spare woman with grey hair, sad brown eyes, a little beard, and a silver cross on a chain round her neck, to speak kindly to him, Phillip gripped the cast-iron railings and refused to budge. Hetty pleaded with him, but he would not let go his grip.

Miss May Whittaker came out, while the Headmistress went back into the house to look after the class. Miss May was short, with a round dimpled face, her chin was covered with thinner, softer hairs, and her eyes had a less faraway look in them. She spoke to Phillip, inviting him to have a ride on the rocking horse, Dobbin, inside; but no, he held on to the railings. When his mother said she would have to go away, he began to cry. This made Mavis cry. She hid her face in her mother's skirts, while Hetty tried to soothe her in vain.

Appeals to Phillip to set a good example, endearments and promises of reward, exhortations about his manhood by Miss Fanny, coupled with a plea from Hetty for him to be a good boy and think of his little sister, were all unavailing. So Hetty took Mavis in, as there was nothing else to be done.

Inside the school, Miss Fanny suggested to Hetty that she should pretend to take him home, and see what happened. This she did; and fifty yards or so up the road he stopped crying, and said, "Why isn't Mavis coming, Mummy?"

"Because she is happy with the other little boys and girls, Sonny."

"But they will beat her, Mummy."

"No dear, of course they won't. She is going to play with beads, and learn to draw with crayons all sorts of lovely things. Then she will have a nice dinner, and I shall bring her home in time for tea, with dripping toast. And she will learn to play the piano."

"But they will hit her, Mummy, I know they will. I saw them hitting other little boys and girls."

"You imagined it, Sonny."

"They will hit me, I know they will. Ralph said they would."

"He has been frightening you, the silly boy. He likes to frighten others, I know. He is very naughty. I have half a mind to tell his mother."

A few minutes later, Phillip returned to St. Catherine's School. Hetty knew by the way he held her hand that it was an ordeal for him, but once started, he went into the house, and sat down beside some other boys of his own age on a bench before a table, and appeared not to mind when she left.

Paper, pens, inkwells were familiar things, and he could write his name in capital letters on the top of the foolscap like the boy on his left side had done. There was a blackboard and they had to copy figures from it, two rows of them, and then draw a line under them with a thin yellow ruler. Miss Fanny said, "Add them together and write your result below the line. And when you have done that sum, copy the figures again, and subtract the bottom row of figures from the top row, again writing down your answer under a ruled line."

Not knowing what Miss Fanny meant, Phillip looked at the next boy's paper. The boy had written the word EXAMEN on his paper, so Phillip wrote EXAMEN on his. Then he copied the figures from the blackboard, and drew a line with the ruler. But a blob came out of the inkwell on his nib, and before he could stop drawing the line the blob had made it very thick with ink. So he blotted the ink with a piece of blotting paper which already had a lot of upside-down writing on it, and so did not suck up the ink, but squashed it everywhere. He dipped his pen again in the inkwell and a drowned black fly came out. An inspection of its corpse gave him an interest for a while, before he blotted it to see what would happen. It looked so thin then that he put it back in the inkwell, after which he jabbed about with the nib to see if there was anything else interesting inside it. By this time sundry smears had somehow surrounded the sum to be done on the paper. So he returned to the puzzle, finding it instantly insoluble.

He copied, for his answer, the top row of figures in reverse, under the line. By the same method the subtraction sum was decided by copying the lower row of figures backwards, under the new line he had drawn, bloblessly, with the ruler. It was a nice line, with only a little smudge at one end, like Zippy's fur when he had had a cold bath.

Father still had cold baths, so did he, in the mornings. Only he never got in the water, but waggled his hands about, as though splashing, then wetted the towel to make it look as though he had got in, and wetted his feet to make marks on the cork mat.

After the exam, he learnt that he was in Form Two. This was higher than Mavis, who was in Form I, which was indistinguishable from the kindergarten.

At the end of the week Phillip was used to going to school in the morning, eating his sandwiches in the other room for dinner with a glass of milk poured out by Miss May, and returning with Mummy and Mavis in the afternoon. He liked school, chiefly because of the play in the back garden. He had learned, among other things, that by holding up his hand, and saying "Please Miss Fanny, may I leave the room", that he could stay in the lavatory and look at a comic for as much as five minutes before pulling the plug, as though he had done something, before going back again. Nobody could find out, after he had pulled the plug.

One morning, when he had put up his hand to go to the lavatory, he went round all the pockets of the coats in the cloak-room to find out what was in them. With excitement he found quite a lot of pennies. What a wonderful discovery! He put them all in a glove, and the glove in his pocket; and after waiting in the lavatory to pull the plug, he returned to the classroom, where Miss May was telling how William Rufus was hunting deer and was shot by an arrow and a charcoal burner took him on a sledge in the New Forest in eleven hundred. He was writing down the letters 1100 when Miss Fanny came into the room and spoke to Miss May and by the awful feeling he had in his stomach he knew it was about the pennies. So he thought he would get the glove out of his pocket at once.

His desk was near the stone slab of the fireplace. The fire was not lit; the stone was clean, its hearth-stoned surface untouched by foot and unsoiled by cinder. Paper, wood, and coal lay within the iron grate, ready for a match on the first cold morning of autumn.

Miss Fanny Whittaker said, "Pay attention, children."

They all looked up.

"Now I have something very important to say to you all. Has anyone lost any money this morning?"

She had got so far when Phillip, having pulled the glove from his pocket, threw it under the grate, and hardly had the coins jingled on the stone when he called out, "Look, I have found this!" and getting off his chair, picked up the glove, and carried it to Miss Fanny.

Miss Fanny Whittaker looked at Phillip. He held out the glove heavy with pennies. She took it without a word, exchanged a look of her dark eyes, which seemed set in some remote, far-off pain, with her sister May, standing by the blackboard with the names of the Norman Kings of England and the dates of their succession chalked upon it; and went out of the door.

The lesson was resumed. Phillip forgot about the pennies soon afterwards, which meant that no one mentioned the matter again. He never felt in the pockets for pennies again. Nor did he ever cry again, while at the school. The personalities of the Misses Whittaker were such that not one of their pupils was ever in distress. He liked painting pictures and drawing, and sums about apples and horses galloping and history where cakes were burned and Hereward the Wake had a secret path through a swamp, and Robin Hood and his Merry Men.

Richard remarked the change for the better in Phillip, and said to Hetty: "You see, I told you he needed proper discipline," and Hetty said: "Yes, dear." She did not show her husband the children's reports for she did not want him to know that in the exams at the end of term Phillip had come bottom in his class in every subject. There was one consolation, in his Conduct report, which was *Good*.

Christmas brought great excitement. Two rows of Japanese lanterns were hung across the sitting-room ceiling from corner to corner on Christmas Eve; while after lots of brown paper parcels of presents had been carried into the front room, the door was locked, and the key hidden in Daddy's pocket. Then Daddy dressed up as a detective. He wore a funny hat and had a bulls-eye lantern shining in the dark of the coal-cellar. He told them a wonderful story of nearly catching a butterfly with the lantern and a net, on the Hill, only bad men attacked him and he fought them and knocked them over and they all ran away, but when he went to look for the butterfly it was gone, and it was ever so rare, called a Camberwell Beauty. It was a wonderful lantern, and you could hide the light by turning the shutter, and no one could see you in the dark.

O, if only he could have a lantern like that for a present, to put on his raft when he went down the Thames, wearing a hat just like Daddy's. Daddy said that one day if he was a very good boy he might give him the hat and the lantern too, to look for butter-flies and moths with. In bed that night Phillip tossed and turned, thinking of having a hat to go over the ears in snow and a dark lantern, and of what Father Christmas had brought him, and if he would see Father Christmas when he filled his stocking hung on the rail at the bottom of the bed.

O, he could never, never go to sleep! His mind raced and raced over hundreds of things and places, far away over the sea where sharks jumped with spikes of bamboo cutting their stomachs and black men and esparto grass hammocks and lions and temples with priests burning joss sticks and Joey the old dog and the gipsy woman who might have stolen him and turned him brown all over if he had not hidden his name from her, and said he was Mr. Cornflower.

Then Phillip heard Father Christmas coming, so he closed his eyes in terrible excitement and hardly dared to breathe and he was frightened to open his eyes for Father Christmas would be sure to see, for like God he knew everything, being up in the sky and able to look down always.

There were sounds in the room and rustlings and the noise of things going into a stocking like when a stocking was pulled over a shoe in hide-and-seek in Aunty Dorrie's house with Jerry and Ralph and when Father Christmas was gone he got out of bed to look and Mummy came into the room and said, "Oh Sonny, why are you not asleep?" and he said: "Mummy, I heard Father Christmas come just now, quick, quick, pull back the curtain and you will see him on the roof, for I heard his sleigh-bells when he came down the chimney!" And Mummy said: "Wait till the morning, dear, to look in your stocking, for you must get some sleep, you are so very very excitable, and you must rest your brain, dear." Mummy kissed him, and he kissed Mummy, and when she was gone he looked in the stocking, smelling the orange and the apple; licking the whip-top to taste the wood and to try and find out the colour; sucking the sugar mouse, and biting just a teeny-weeny bit off its nose; counting the nuts; feeling a box of marbles and a big glass blood-ally. There were biscuits; a sherbert bag; a licorice boot-lace; a wooden pencil box with pencils and pens in it, rubbers, and nibs; a rubber ball; and a banana. He put them all back, with a feeling that hundreds of starling birds were running up and down inside him all singing and whistling and trying to fly out of his throat.

After breakfast they all went into the front room, and unpacked the parcels. He had a brown football from Uncle Hilary with black stitches in the leather, which was hard and greasy like a real one; a bird-book with lovely photos from Aunt Viccy; a penknife with two blades, one big and the other small, from Aunty Bee; a disappointing prayerbook from Aunty Belle; a red book for collecting stamps and a big boy's white jersey from Mummy; a walking stick with a silver band and a real gunmetal watch from Father; a box of chocolates from Aunty Bigge; a lovely box of Nürnberg gingerbread from Minnie; a pocket book with words printed on it in gold and *Mallard, Carter, & Turney, Ltd.* from Grandpa and a five shilling piece; a dozen handkerchiefs and half-a-crown from Grannie, and lots of Christmas cards, including one from Mona Monk who Mummy said was in an Institution. Phillip asked what this was and Mummy said he would not know if she told him, and after thinking about this Phillip thought that if he would not know if Mummy told him, would he know if Mummy did not tell him. So he asked Mummy to explain, and she said it was a sort of school, and he must write a nice letter of thanks to Mona, and she would also send her a parcel of clothes which Mavis had done with.

Phillip had given Daddy a box of matches, a toffee apple, and a packet of pipe-cleaners; and for Mummy some curling pins and a reel of strong thread to sew boot buttons on with, from a poor man who had come to the door one day. They were very pleased with their presents, saying they were just what they wanted, and he felt he was a good boy.

Then Daddy opened his surprise, in a big wooden case. It was a musical box, that played big thorny round tin pieces of music which clanged when you shook them. He said it was a German Polyphone. It was lovely music, like the bells of St. Simon's when you were walking over the Hill to hear Mr. Mundy preach and the anthem afterwards, but the Polyphone was much nicer.

The Polyphone played during dinner of turkey, Christmas pudding, and mince pies. Afterwards Daddy carried it and put it on a table in the corner of the front room, and then went back to the sitting room to read a book called *Lorna Doone*. Mother said he might want to go to sleep, so they must creep upstairs when they went out of the front room. It was lovely in the front room, with Mummy and Mavis, with a blazing fire and lots of nuts and figs and tangerines and preserved fruits to eat. Mrs. Feeney washed up in the scullery, to give Mother a rest. Mrs. Feeney had come to cook the turkey, and was having hers in the kitchen when Father got up and said: "Please do come and join us at Table, Mrs. Feeney, it is Christmas when all old friends come together," and Mrs. Feeney said: "Oh, I can't do that, sir, thank you all the same, for I know my station," and Father said: "Your place is with those who owe you so much for your good service, Mrs. Feeney," and so Mrs. Feeney had had dinner with them. Mother said that Mr. Feeney had gone into the hospital for incurables in London and she was all alone in the world now. So Phillip gave her his sugar mouse for a Christmas present.

Chapter 17

RETURN OF THEODORA

THEODORA MADDISON, after several weeks of sailing along the south and west coast of France, in a Greek schooner carrying a cargo of Turkish tobacco, arrived at the port of Bristol with the mixed feelings of one who had been abroad nearly six years. After saying goodbye to the companions of her voyage she walked to the dock gates and feeling extremely thin and emptied out, a hollow woman, took a fly to the heights of Clifton, overlooking the city, where lived a woman friend of Cambridge days, with whom she had corresponded during her sojourn abroad. It was the last year of the century, and her arrival in the land of her birth left her tremulous and exposed in isolation. She stopped her cab on Clifton Down, after the long pull up from the docks and river below, to give the horse a rest, and also to assemble her thoughts.

It was chilly in England, after the hazy blue heats of the Mediterranean Sea. And the faces of the people, so white, so shut-in upon themselves; the raggedness of the poor so pallid and dour: so unlike the brown-limbed, merry poverty of the Aegean. Theodora wept a little in her loneliness, as she walked across the grass of the common, where sheep grazed amidst thorns and holly trees. This was her country, which had driven out Byron and Shelley; this was her own, her native land; and engaged in an unjust war against a valiant minority of Dutch colonists in South Africa. Such an unpropitious start for the new century, which was to purge so much of gross materialism of the old century which had just passed away! In some disappointment she returned to the fly, and got in, the horse reluctantly leaving its unexpected feed of grass, to be jogged to Cabot Crescent, where her friend lived.

The two young women (who nevertheless thought of themselves as matured and staid, being twenty-six years of age) were of like mind, both classical scholars; and so neither felt an uneasiness at the meeting, only restrained joy that the other showed a splendid happiness in her face. Both were full of the project that had been discussed during many letters, to start a school for young gentlewomen that would be based upon the truths of nature, as revealed by the great philosophers and artists of all known civilisations.

That evening, after a vegetarian supper, the two friends, wearing white hats of Bedfordshire straw with wide brims, starched linen collars with pale blue ties, white blouses, and simple dark blue skirts whose ends were a sensible two inches off the ground, to leave the dust where it belonged—Rechenda had insisted on lending her great friend a set of her clothes from Cambridge days—went for a stroll upon the Clifton Downs. It was a fine evening, and they made their way down to Brunel's suspension bridge, which spanned the deep gorge over the estuarial curve of the Avon. Theodora still had her sea-legs; the bridge seemed to be swaying, the rocky cliff face opposite suddenly to be lurching. They were approaching, arm in arm, the centre of the bridge, when she said that she felt giddy. They had been walking in the middle of the roadway, but now the passage of several carriages, containing people out for an airing in the warm summer weather, made them seek the sidewalk. Theodora clung more nervously to her friend's arm, as over the painted steel parapet the tiny ribbon of road beside the river became visible. But she controlled herself; and forcing her gaze upon the shining and steep mudbanks of the river below, said: "I wonder how true the story is, that a young woman fell from here soon after the opening of the bridge twenty-five years ago, and was saved by her crinoline and the soft mud below?"

"I do not believe it, Theodora. It is apocryphal. Why, surely the passage through the air would either force up the frame of the crinoline, distorting it out of its bell-like shape; or more likely the poor woman would have been turned over by the rush of air, and fallen head first. Like most stories told or opinions held by the majority, it has no basis in fact."

They followed the last of the carriages coming in from the Somerset side, and reached *terra firma* with its green grass once more. Theodora's spirits lightened.

"I am sure, Rechenda, that once our school is known, it cannot fail to be but a success. We are on the verge of a wide and deep spiritual awakening, not only in this country, but throughout Europe. It is to the younger generation of women, the mothers to be, that we must look, to receive the new ideas. I will not say our ideas, for that would surely be to show an arrogance based on a mere revulsion from the modern scene; for the old poets, visionaries, and artists knew it long ago. Our principles must be based upon a synthesis of all that is clear and noble in the past. We are the heirs of their wisdom."

"I was much impressed by the teachings of Johann Heinrich Pestalozzi you sent me, Theodora. Oh, he is so clear, so true, so divinely right!"

"Is it not curious, Rechenda, that though Pestalozzi was famous in his day, a hundred years and more ago, his ideas should still be, in Keats' phrase, 'caviare to the general'. Look at the smoke from the factories of Bristol down in the hollow there—what truth can prevail in the wretched conditions of the slums, in the competition of the counting houses, in all the material wealth being created in such sunless places? And how strange to think that Napoleon fought, in part at least, and caused such human suffering, for much the same ideals as Pestalozzi. You know, after Napoleon was taken to St. Helena, he said that if his system could have prevailed, the 'canaille' of the big cities would have become the best-educated in Europe."

"But he took to the sword to clear the way for his ideals, and so his ideals perished by the sword."

"Yes, history reveals that there is no hope in political revolution. The Chinese have a saying, 'He who slays the dragon, becomes in turn the dragon'."

Rechenda could not resist retorting, "And they have another saying, 'A dragon in shallow waters shall be eaten alive by shrimps'."

They both laughed. "Well, we are agreed that our ideals must not in any sense be political. Oh, the dear man Pestalozzi in his castle at Yverdon in Switzerland—I can see him now, among his waifs and orphans, or the flowery slopes under the peaks of the eagles, giving his children—they all called him 'Father', you know —the love and tenderness that their very souls cried out for. Now just look at those children, by contrast, over there!"

Two bands of boys were shouting, taunting, and fighting with sticks around an overturned perambulator. Some had helmets, made of newspapers, on their heads. One boy was crying, holding a bloody nose. Some had button-hole badges in the lapels of their coats, little discs of celluloid imprinted with photographic heads of Baden-Powell, Lord Roberts and Kitchener. They were playing a war-game; but both sides having declined to be Boers, they had combined to set upon a third group of three more ragged children, about an old perambulator filled with sticks for firing, which they had decided was a Boer läger. The boy with the bloody nose had been pushing the perambulator with his smaller friends; now it was wrecked, its contents scattered.

"You see," said Theodora. "They have no idea what they have done. They are only reproducing the minds of their parents. The truth is not in any political action, which must always be based on material expediency."

She spoke to the injured boy, after the others had run away, and did her best to comfort him. His smaller brother and sister stood by, looking wan. Theodora and her friend set about collecting the scattered sticks, and lifted the perambulator on its high wheels again, to fill it. Afterwards she gave each of them a penny, and the three children went away more hopefully.

"I have often thought, Rechenda, that I might perhaps serve the better if I went among the poor; but it is the ruling classes that need to know the true way, just as much as the poor. And do you know, I think I have the motto that shall express our ideal; it is one of Pestalozzi's remarks that he made most often to his children. 'Without love, a man is without God; and without both God and love, what is man?'"

So it was determined; and the next day the two friends, feeling that they were doing something enormously risky, went to an estate agent to make enquiries about the lease of a country house, where they would found their new school. The curriculum would include riding and callisthenics; spinning and weaving; singing and drawing; reading, writing, and arithmetic, with classics and mathematics for those who showed an aptitude; botany and natural science, cooking and gardening, should go with music, swimming and dancing.

At the end of a week the house was found, in the Quantock hills of Somerset, and near the sea. They considered taking it on a twenty-one-year lease, after an architect had been called in to advise about the practicability of certain alterations necessary for a girls' school. They went into the details of capital expenditure, and had a deed of partnership drawn up. But before the final settlement, and to allow both of them time for reflection, Theodora, who had written in the meantime to her brothers John and Richard telling them of her return, left Clifton for a round of visits.

The first was to be a sad one; for her eldest brother John, whom she had seen last in Devon with Jenny his wife, together with Dickie and Hetty and her baby godson Phillip, was now a widower, his wife having died in giving birth to a son, William.

So Theodora was going first to her old home at Rookhurst, to see John and his boy, who now would be five years old. Then on to London, to stay with Dickie and Hetty, and see her godson, who must be in his seventh year! It was hardly to be believed that the baby she had held on her lap, on the grey bouldered shore of Lynmouth in that remote summer of a vanished century, would now be running about, talking, and perhaps be going to school. She wondered what sort of a boy he had grown into. How she and Hetty, before he was born, had hoped that he would be a poet! Theodora felt a quickening excitement as the train took her south-eastwards, to the town of Colham, to stay a week with John; after which she was going to London, to see her nephew and godson, the little "donkey boy", who had so very nearly died at birth, and his mother with him.

As the engine smoked through the countryside, the corn harvest already cut and stooked in field after field, and cattle lying contented in meadows that, despite the prolonged summer weather, still looked so very green after the harsh lands of the Aegean—but how she would miss the flowers in the rocks!—Theodora felt her heart renewing itself with the thoughts of England rushing upon her eyes through the open carriage window.

She sat alone in a carriage; and without reserve, she found herself speaking with the tongues of the poets—Francis Thompson, Keats, Shelley, and Shakespeare. After a time her exuberance settled to a more concrete contemplation, and with that mood many memories reappeared with startling clearness before the eye of her mind.

She thought of Sidney Cakebread with whom her youthful self had fallen so helplessly, so agonisingly in love, a condition which had impelled her to leave England. She had heard not one word of him during the years of wandering abroad: never once had Hetty mentioned him. His children must be growing up now, three boys and a little daughter. How had his marriage with

Dorrie Turney fared? They had been ill-matched. Dorrie, sweet and gentle as she was by nature, knew little of the empire of the mind.

Would Dorrie have been different if she had had, say, an education at the sort of school she and Rechenda were going to build? Surely she would! The future of the world lay in the full and proper education of women. Western civilisation had fallen out of balance since the time when women had been subjugated, stultified, and treated as chattels by men who had ceased to use their bodies in natural actions, but become soft and cunning in trade, in the acquisition of property through stock markets and the counting house. And having perceived the problems of the nineteenth century in the spirit of truth, Theodora felt an immense optimism for the future.

Her visit to Rookhurst was not what she had imagined it to be. She was, indeed, shocked by the appearance of her brother John. Already his face was lined, his beard was streaked with grey, and the hair above his temples was grey, too. He appeared to have let himself go, and was by that so much a stranger to her. He lived in his library, while the house was run by an odd little housekeeper-cook, with the help of daily women coming in from the village. As for her nephew William, he was a dear little fellow, but obviously had been allowed to run far too wild, in the sense of growing up apart from his father. Obviously John had never recovered from the death of Jenny.

Theodora, after some hesitation, made suggestions to her brother, who appeared to have decided that his life was over. The house was neglected; some of the rooms had been closed, the furniture covered with sheets, the shutters barred upon the windows. They had been shut up for some years now. The outer woodwork of the house needed painting. So did the gutters, which were choked with leaves. Some of them had grass sprouting out of them a foot high. Down one wall the water from a choked lead spout, cracked by frost, had spread in a green delta, the damp blackening the plaster of the rooms within. As for the gardens, they were a wilderness. They had been bad enough during Mother's last years, since Father had gone away, but now they were choked with thorns, unbelliferous plants, and nettles.

A feeling of helplessness gradually overcame Theodora; the spirit of the place was affecting her as it had affected her brother.

Poor man, what could she say, what could she do to help him to
find himself again?

Theodora thought of telegraphing to her friend Rechenda to
come and stay, as her guest, in Colham. There she would
discuss the matter with her; for it seemed to Theodora that her
duty lay in looking after her brother, and in particular of that
nephew of hers. Obviously something was wrong in his upbringing. John said he was deceitful, and already showing some
of the traits of their Father which had ruined the family. How
could John misinterpret his own condition so? Had he lost all
sense of cause and effect, of objectivity?

Theodora did not like to tell her brother that he was making the
memory of Father into a scapegoat for his own defects; at the
same time it was remarkable how, now that he had let his beard
grow, he resembled Father. Father had tried to find the ideal,
and had never succeeded; while John, having found it, was
denying all further growth by living solely in the past. So Theodora concluded, before she wired for her friend, who was a
woman of exceptional beauty of both mind and body, and not
unlike Jenny. Perhaps John would find in Rechenda a comple-
ment to what he had lost. For so young a man ought to marry
again, if only for the sake of his little boy!

As she waited for a reply, Theodora began to plan the school
in Ravenscombe Park by herself, for, she thought, she would
never dare to take a partner to replace Rechenda; but the reply
when it arrived by a boy on a pony cantering up the weedy
drive stopped further ideas. Rechenda had gone to look after an
ailing sister, and a letter was following. This letter contained the
grave news that the sister had had an unexpected haemorrhage,
and upon examination, was found to be suffering from phthisis.
Poor girl, consumption of the lungs!

So at the end of her week's stay Theodora left her old home
somewhat sadly, feeling the inadequacy of herself. Brother John
got up from his cracked leather armchair, Isaak Walton's
Compleat Angler before him on the reading stand, and in carpet
slippers, came to the door to bid her goodbye. So did Biddy,
the cook-housekeeper, a chubby little woman in elastic-sided
boots which Theodora recognised as once belonging to her own
mother. As for her nephew Willie, he had disappeared after
breakfast that morning, to go fishing in the Longpond with

another little boy, the son of Frank Temperley, the farmer who had been the close boyhood friend of Richard.

Theodora left for Colham station in a seedy brougham driven by the local grocer, a new man, taking with her a couple of pounds of fresh salted butter, a small crate of farm eggs, and John's kindest regards to Dickie and Hetty.

"I haven't seen either of them since Lynmouth, Dora, it must be all of six years ago. Well, that is our fate, I suppose. Come again sometime if you do not mind taking us as you find us. My very best wishes for the success of your school. Now remember, don't lay out all your capital at the start, or you may find yourself with that toppling thing, an inverted pyramid. Goodbye, goodbye!"

Theodora's last view of him was as he waved from under the gothic arch, while the swallows dived past the familiar figure and rose without fear to their nest on the beam above the porch enclosing the massive oak door. She thought of Homer, the most homeless of poets; and then of Virgil, and could scarce repress her feelings for "the tears of things".

A somewhat disturbing journey followed; and the arrival at Waterloo was like a personal reproach, with views of squalor and poverty increasing as the city was reached. Why, why had she left the Isles of Greece? What could one woman do, however dedicated, to alter the static?

However, she must not allow her feelings to take charge of her. She recalled how bleak had been her emotions when first she had arrived in Athens, after the long and enchanting approach through the islands. Sursam corda!

At Randiswell station Theodora left instructions with the outside porter to take up her box to the address she gave him, at six o'clock, it now being just before three in the afternoon. She wanted to walk and collect her thoughts before arriving at Richard's new house, the site of which she remembered from the day of the picnic when Mr. Turney, Dickie, and herself had driven on to Vicar's Hill, after the birth of Phillip. There was a direct way to the eastern side of the Hill from the station, and thither she went, glad that the day was fine and sunny.

It was a steep approach, past a row of houses, at the end of which began a line of spiked green railings, and then an iron gate opening upon a wide gravel path. She saw a notice board on a freshly-painted green post, on which was pasted a notice of several thousand words in close type, divided into sections and numbered paragraphs, of rules, regulations and by-laws of the Open Spaces Committee of the London County Council. So the Hill had been civilised, the Kentish district had been absorbed by London! She recalled that Dickie had hoped that would never happen.

She walked on up the very steep path, and when she was upon the summit her spirits rose with the view. Here at least were light and air, and a feeling of spaciousness. It being a Saturday afternoon, the green fields were in movement with many children, whose shrill cries made her happy, as she saw them as coils and twists of repressive homes and schoolrooms being thrown off under the sky. They were returning to nature, they were happy.

Upon the summit of the hill, where gravel paths led off in several directions, what a transformation! Here were tennis courts marked off, trees planted, and seats erected at intervals. She sat down near a small hut with pointed roof, surrounded by railings. Soon a keeper in brown uniform, leggings, and bowler hat came out, with a canvas bag in one hand and a thin steel rod, long as a walking stick, in the other. Theodora watched him lock the door of the hut, walking over the grass and stabbing pieces of paper with the steel rod, then transferring them to his bag.

To Theodora this was a pleasing sight; but on reflection, she decided that tidiness must begin at the other end, in the enlightenment of children. Children were flying kites, bowling hoops of wood and iron—boys preferred the iron hoops, she noticed—and others were playing leapfrog. She looked eagerly, wondering if one of them was her nephew. A haze hung over the horizon to the south and east. There seemed to be ever so many more rows of houses than when she was last upon the crest. And walking onwards, she passed by the square brick bulk of the grammar school, and moving out of its northern shadow, saw upon the distant ridge the familiar grey tower-flanked length of the Crystal Palace.

The sight renewed particular memories; for over the ridge, seen vividly in her mind, lay the red-bricked villages amidst the herb farms of Surrey, and Cross Aulton in particular. Ah, those radiant days of flowers and cool flowing water, of music in the Turneys' house, before the tragedy of male possessiveness, and domination over the lives of wife and daughter, had occurred.

Were the Turneys still at Maybury Lodge? And how was Hugh, who had fancied himself to be in love with her? Perhaps he was happily married by now. And Joseph, the youngest boy, as dull as Hugh was vivid, he must be grown up. He was a schoolboy then. It was almost frightening, to think of how people and places changed: how they were changing every moment of the night and the day.

How remote already seemed her arrival at Bristol in the schooner *Myonides*! And even her visit to Fawley. She saw John waving from the porch: the moment of departure from her brother that morning was for ever gone. Never again would it be the same arrival at the little wooden station of Randiswell under the humped-back brick bridge, or the whistle sound the same note of departure. Theodora sat down on a seat, momentarily overcome by the fearful feeling of having been suspended, for an instant, on the perimeter of Time's wheel.

She wandered northwards to the remembered slope leading down to what Hetty had called the Warm Kitchen. Here Dickie and Sidney Cakebread had tobogganned during the hard winter, soon after Dickie and Hetty had set up their little household in Comfort Road. How much smaller the warm kitchen looked now!

Below on the level sward a cricket match was in progress; while beside her was a new circular bandstand. In the cage-like centre of its white-boarded ceiling, under the iron roof, was a sparrow's nest, with long grasses hanging between the spaces of the bars. A London sparrow had set up home there. The mother bird flew out as she watched; while on the roof, in his sombre uniform of chestnut, black, and fawn, chirped father sparrow, entirely content with the home found for him by the London County Council. The sight released Theodora's spirits; suddenly she felt free and gay, light-hearted. Happy little fellow, with wife and bairns under the Band Stand! She said to herself, "There is nothing good or bad, but thinking makes it so!" and glancing at her watch, saw the time was only a few minutes short of four o'clock, and now she must descend to find the house in Hillside Road.

Theodora found it without any difficulty, although the Hill had been thoroughly civilised. A wide gravelled gulley led down the southern slope of the hill, and beyond open park gates stood the houses of Hillside Road. The first house had a little turret at its end. A pleasant looking man in Norfolk jacket and cloth cap was standing on the pavement, clipping a privet hedge. As Theodora went through the green iron gates a young woman of extraordinary beauty came out of the house, a small girl beside her. Theodora was struck by the happiness on all three faces. She found herself smiling, the woman smiling at her. The man, who was tall and upright, with a large fair moustache, raised his cap.

"What a beautiful day," said Theodora. "What a pretty little girl you have. I hope you will forgive my speaking to you, but I find it so strange to revisit this place after six years abroad. My brother and his wife live here somewhere—I wonder if you would be so good as to direct me—their name is Maddison."

"They live three doors down," said the woman. "If you had arrived five minutes earlier, you would have seen Mr. Maddison leaving for a ride on his bicycle."

"Oh, thank you," replied Theodora. "I will find Hetty in, perhaps. It is so kind of you to help me," and she walked down the asphalt pavement, noticing that it was already cracked in places, and the flowers of pink convolvulus were looking out. Nature, she thought, will not be denied.

She stopped at the gate on which was painted the word *Lindenheim*. It gave her a start, for it was the name of her mother's old home in Germany. So this was Dickie's little house. She stopped by the gate, to get herself together, for so much had happened during the six years, and she was suddenly overcome. And while she stood there, preparing herself to lift the latch of the gate, she heard the sound of a child sobbing.

The top of the square-cut privet hedge was about six feet above the level of the asphalt pavement, and two feet thick behind an oak fence, so from where she stood by the step Theodora could not see that the middle window of the front room of the house was open wide. She thought the sounds came from the little lawn behind the hedge; and lifting the latch gently, she opened the gate and went inside, peering round the hedge. A rag doll lay on the grass, beside a book, a shawl, and a cane-bottom rocking chair. She saw the open window, and stepping over the bordering rockery of the path, went to it, to peer over the cream-painted sill.

She saw a small boy with dark hair sitting on a chair before a table in the centre of the room. There was a blotting pad, an inkwell, and a sheet of paper on the table before him. The pen was stuck in the inkwell. The boy's back was towards her. His arms were laid on the tablecloth, his face was buried in them. As Theodora stared at his back the boy lifted up his head, got off the chair, and cried in piteous tones, "O! O! O!" and taking the pen, stabbed the paper with it, then uttered a low wail of despair.

He saw the face looking in the open window, and stopped still, staring at her.

"Hullo, Boy," said Theodora. "Are you Phillip?"

"Yes," he said, almost inaudibly.

"Do you know who I am?" she asked, ignoring his tear-stained face.

"Yes, Aunt Theodora, on a sailing ship."

"How very clever of you to know that so quickly. How do you do?"

"Very well thank you, Aunt Theodora."

"That's right. Now tell me what's the trouble, Phillip."

Theodora had to ask again, to draw out of him the surprising confession, "I have been mischiev-i-ous."

"Oh," she said, and asked what he was writing. He brought a foolscap sheet. He brought it to her. On the top, in her brother's meticulous handwriting, was the phrase, *I must not tell lies.*

Underneath, the boy had made some sort of attempt to copy the letters and words, accompanied by several inky blots and smears. In the margin she noticed a picture. Judging by the outline it was a sparrow sitting on the roof of the bandstand on the Hill. There were the straws, hanging from its nest. The drawing had been scratched out. Theodora could scarcely refrain from smiling, as she divined what had been Phillip's thoughts as his task grew the more wearisome to him. He had copied only four rows before the lettering became grotesque and ragged, ending in a splutter and two wider inkless lines where the nib had broken off.

"Oh dear, the nib wasn't very strong, was it, Phillip?"

"No, Aunt." Sniff-sniff. "And when I have done all my lines I must go to bed, and not go to the party next door, and"—the voice became as though strangled—"have—have—have bread and water for my tea."

Theodora stared at her nephew. Never had she seen a child looking so unhappy.

"But there will be other parties, won't there?"

"Un-Un-Uncle H-H-Hugh is g-g-go-going away to the war, and m-m-may never come back any-any-any more."

"Uncle Hugh? Uncle Hugh Turney?" asked Theodora, after a pause.

Phillip nodded his head. "Yes, Aunt."

"Will you tell your Mother that I am here? Is she about?"

"She's gone to see G-G-Gran'ma."

"Are you all alone in the house, then?"

"Yes, I am. But Mummy won't be a minute."

Theodora was puzzled. "Where does your Grannie live, Phillip?"

"Next door."

"Next door? Then has she moved from Cross Aulton?"

"Yes, Aunt. Long ago, before Mummie had scarlet fever."

Theodora was so surprised that she did not know what to think. Could there be some connexion between the boy's unhappy condition, and the Turneys living so close to her brother and his wife?

"I hear Mummy!" cried Phillip. "She's come by the back gate which Grandpa had made in the fence by the back door! Shall I open the front door for you, Aunt Theodora?"

"Thank you, Boy, that would be so kind," said Theodora.

When she saw Hetty she felt that six years had made no difference. Smiling, and clasping hands, both women declared that the other had not changed in the very least; but when they were having tea in the garden, sitting on the lawn under the elm tree now eight or nine feet high, with Mavis quietly eating her bread and butter and drinking milk from her Jubilee mug between them, Theodora could see that Hetty was not really happy.

"Isn't Phillip having any tea, Hetty? What has happened, or should I not ask?"

"He took some sherry of Dickie's this morning, Dora, and upset the decanter, after drinking some."

"Just a boyish prank, Hetty, surely nothing more?"

"He is rather troublesome, in other ways, I'm afraid, and it worries Dickie very much. Phillip is going to a new school next term, perhaps that will give him the necessary discipline."

Theodora said nothing.

"Donkey Boy's gone to bed," said Mavis, suddenly. "He was a naughty boy, wasn't he, Mummy? He will be like Daddy's farver, won't he, Mummy, when he's a man?"

Theodora was startled. John had made a similar accusation

against his small son. Could the war mentality have affected both men, with its partisan distortions?

"Be quiet, Mavis, I will not have you say such things! Oh, I haven't shown you your room, Dora. It's the end one, up there, and gets all the morning sun. There's a thrush that sings on the top of the elm tree."

Looking up, Theodora saw Phillip's face at the window. It disappeared immediately.

"How very peaceful you are here, Hetty," remarked Theodora, sad at her own unconscious irony. "Some neighbours in the top house, as I passed by, told me that Dickie had just gone out on his bicycle. Is he as keen as ever on his butterflies?"

"He spends a lot of time in the country, I am so glad he has kept up with his cycling. I think he expected you later on, Dora, or he would have stayed in. I am afraid he has given up his butterflies."

"Donkey Boy took Daddy's bufflies," Mavis said.

"He seems to be a regular pickle, doesn't he, Mavis? Are you ever naughty, too?"

"Donkey Boy makes me naughty, doesn't he, Mummy?"

"No Mavis, you really must not say such things! And you must not call your brother, 'Donkey Boy'."

"Daddy does," said Mavis, looking unhappy because Mummy was cross with her.

"What your Father does is nothing to do with you, dear. You see, Dora," she went on hurriedly, "I can seldom find time to take them for walks, and since Dickie was so upset by the behaviour of a little maid I had, he does not like the idea of having another in the house."

"It must be very difficult for you, Hetty, I can see that."

Theodora was struggling against the prevailing unhappy feeling about her. What had happened to her old friend, to change her so? Hetty always had been a nervous little person, but she had always had an outlet to her personality. Now she seemed to have lost her resilience, to be shut away inside herself. And what, in heaven's name, were these two parents doing to that unhappy little boy? Would she be showing an unpardonable interference if she enquired? Or worse, might not Hetty break down, and this condition lead to a worse one with Dickie?

Perhaps she was exaggerating within herself a small incident? Phillip taking sherry, and drinking it? She was sure no small boy would mean harm by it: it must have been a childish prank! Small children drank wine with their meals abroad, it was a normal thing. And all children showed a natural curiosity, which too often was misinterpreted as mischievousness. As though having divined her thoughts, Hetty said, "You see, Dora, Phillip is so very, very mischievous." She pronounced the word as though it had four syllables, as Phillip had done.

"Surely all small boys are by nature—mischievous, Hetty?" Dora, after hesitation, whether to pronounce it with three syllables or four, pronounced the word correctly. "What is this I hear about the sherry?"

"He found his father's key in a drawer of his desk, and opened the cupboard below the bookcase, and helped Mavis and himself, Dora, while I was upstairs doing the bedrooms."

"Perhaps he had seen Dickie doing just that, Hetty, and wanted to be like him."

"Yes, he did see Dickie giving a glass of sherry to Sidney Cakebread, when he called in the other evening."

Sidney Cakebread! Theodora's heart beat in her ears. She made herself speak equably when she had recovered her balance.

"Children are imitative, you know, Hetty."

"Yes, of course, naturally."

Theodora felt the matter was distressful to Hetty, so she changed the subject.

"How is Sidney?" she asked, with a smile. She added with a laugh, "Do not be anxious on my behalf, Hetty. I am now fully the mistress of my feelings."

"Of course, Dora. Sidney is very well. He and Dorrie live in Charlotte Road, now, you know, just round the corner. Oh yes, there have been many changes since you went away! Sidney and Hughie are in the C.I.V.'s, and sailing for South Africa in a day or two. Papa is giving a little party this evening, for the grandchildren as well, and Mamma expects us all. Would you like to see her after tea, Dora, or will you wait till we go in to supper? I am afraid Phillip won't be going, he has to stay in bed."

"May I decide a little later, Hetty? I have something of a headache, and think I shall lie down for a while."

"Yes, of course, Dora. Do please do just what you want to do. Shall I show you your room?"

What Hetty had not dared to tell Theodora was the incident that had made Richard so angry with the boy, before he had learned of the sherry incident. Letting himself into the house with his latchkey, quietly, he had heard the children playing in the front room; and looking round the half-open door, to give them a surprise, he had been shocked by what he had seen. There was Phillip under the table, struggling with Mavis and interfering with her clothes. Dickie heard Phillip saying, "Come on, be fair, I have shown you mine, now you must show me yours!" Hauling him in a rage from under the table by a leg, Richard had set the boy on his feet, and demanded to know what he meant by it.

"Nothing, Father."

"I'll teach you to behave like that, you disgusting little beast! How dare you?" He had shaken Phillip, hit him with his flat hand on the side of the head, then put him across his knee, and holding him with one hand by the neck, beaten him as hard as he could with his other hand.

Afterwards, Phillip had been sent upstairs to bed. It was then that Hetty had summoned her courage to tell Richard about the accident with the decanter.

"Accident, you say? But how did he get to the cupboard in the first place."

"I think he must have found the key somewhere, Dickie."

"And opened the cupboard by accident, too, I expect you want me to believe?"

"No, Dickie, I think he did it more out of curiosity than anything else."

"Well, that is an admission anyway! And to what do you attribute his behaviour towards his sister just now? At any rate it shall not be said of me that as a father I failed in my duty to try and check his badness! If I did what I ought to do, I would give him a thrashing, at this very moment, that he would not forget in a hurry! Do you want him to turn out to be like one of those blackguards on the Hill, who have no respect at all for women?"

Hetty could not bring herself to tell Theodora all that had happened. She showed her to her room, saying that she hoped her headache would go after a quiet rest.

She said nothing about her own headache.

Chapter 18

RICHARD'S SATURDAY EVENING

DURING A recent Saturday afternoon cycling expedition Richard
had come upon a house being built in a clearing of a wood, a
hundred yards or so off a lane, in a secluded spot near Reynard's
Common. There amidst the stack of bricks and timber, the white
square of putty lime beside heaps of sand, scaffolding, tiles, a
bath had stood, filled to the brim with clear greenish water. It
was to this secret place that Richard had set out, watched from
in front of Turret House by Mr. and Mrs. Gerard Rolls, a few
minutes before the arrival of Theodora. The Maddisons and the
Rollses had what was called a bowing acquaintance. Hetty had
left cards at Turret House when the Rollses had come to live there,
after their marriage, and had had cards duly left with her. There
the matter rested, for neither man wanted his leisure after the
day's work to be violated.

No one was to be seen in the clearing within the wood. Richard
was hot and dusty, the grit of the white glaring road was upon his
face and in his ears. The green-tinted, slightly shivering clear
water looked cool and inviting.

On impulse he took off his shoes and stockings; then off came
his coat, followed by collar, tie, shirt and vest; and thrilling with
adventurousness, his knickerbockers. Now was the critical
moment. Supposing someone came! His name taken: a prosecu-
tion for indecency! He stood white in the sunlit silence a moment
before stepping into the water and sliding under to his neck.
Up and out again, greatly exhilarated and refreshed, but an
underlying sense of anxiety; a quick smoothing away with his
hands of water from hair of legs, arms, and chest, and so into
knickerbockers and safety! What an adventure! He felt a new
man afterwards; and pedalling away down the lane, with its
turtle doves and yellowhammers dusting themselves upon its
forsaken length, sang a few snatches of the song of his youth,
The Arab's Farewell to his Steed.

He arrived back at his house, feeling pleased with life and the prospect of seeing his favourite sister again after so long a time. He had forgotten all about Phillip, towards whom his attitude— apart from the periodical exasperations of the boy's mischievousness—was that he dash well wished that the little cuss would not be so meddlesome, inquisitive, and show so persistently a lack of respect for the law of *meum et tuum*. He did not want continually to be upbraiding him, exhorting him, and, in the last instance, punishing him. But why would he not see reason, why was he not amenable to decent behaviour? Failing that, he was compelled, in his duty as a father, to punish him—the silly little donkey boy.

In this mood, having greeted Theodora, he went upstairs, saw the boy in bed, gave him a talk to show the unreason of interfering with another's belongings—"Hang it all, Phillip, I don't take your toys, do I?"—and then told him he could get up and go to the party next door, provided, of course, that he saw to it that he behaved himself properly.

"Thank you, Father," said Phillip. When he was alone again, the boy's mouth became dry with his haste to dress himself, in his anxiety not to miss a moment of it.

Richard had made an excuse for not going to the party by saying to Hetty that he had a long-standing engagement on the Hill, for a kite-match in the evening of the second Saturday in August. It was true that he flew his kite in friendly rivalry against that of Mr. Muggeridge whenever he met him up there; and that he had recently built a new model of a kite, as had Mr. Muggeridge, and the last time they had flown, they had agreed to meet on the following Saturday, if fine, and try them one against the other; but the real reason for not going to the party was Richard's dislike of his wife's family.

This dislike was not exactly reciprocated; for the Turneys were, without exception now that Thomas Turney had shown signs of mellowing, easier people. The hasty temper of the menfolk— the Old Man himself had Irish blood mixed with his heavy-clay yeoman stock—went with a generosity of nature that had not been spoiled by, because not confined to, pavement living. Thomas Turney had been brought up the hard way, working on his father's farm with his brothers and sisters from the age of five onwards; but though his father had been stern, he had never been unjust. When he had punished he had done so in anger; and then forgotten the petty incident; while the culprit, so-called, had gone back among his brothers and found there a rough but instant sympathy.

Thomas Turney was sitting, in the mellow-bright harvest sun above the south-west, on the balcony outside his open bedroom door. The opposite door of Hetty's bedroom was also open; and Thomas Turney had heard, with satisfaction, his son-in-law telling little Phillip that he could get up and go to the party. The voice had come down the corridor along the southern upper wall of the house, with its varnished wallpaper and polished linoleum, to the older man on the balcony.

Tom Turney was now sixty years old, and the second senior partner in Mallard, Carter and Turney Ltd. of Sparhawk Street, High Holborn. His business affairs had gone well since he had helped to establish the firm of printers, account-book makers, lithographers, and stationers thirty years before. His interior problems had settled themselves, too; his children were grown up, and partly off his mind. His eldest daughter Dorothy, with her four boys and small daughter, had moved into the neighbourhood, where he and Sarah were able to keep an eye on them. Hubert, his eldest grandson, was a promising boy at his father's old school, Dulwich College. He was intended for the Firm.

Hubert was a compensation for the earlier disappointment of Charley, Thomas Turney's eldest son; though to be sure, Charley was no longer the ne'er-do-well, being safely married, and in the import business at Durban. Hugh, poor silly fellow, was the only child that now remained a worry. Tom Turney still felt discomfort whenever he remembered that occasion of showers of pennies upon the stage when, ridiculously overdressed, poor fellow, as Chittybucktoo, the Japanese Gipsy with his Violin, Hughie had appeared, for the first and final time, at the New Cross Empire, and got the bird of many whistles.

Hugh Turney now had, in his father's eyes, committed the crowning folly of joining the City Imperial Volunteers Mounted Infantry, and, much more a matter of disturbance, Sidney Cakebread had joined with him.

Tom tried to convince himself that it might be the making of Hugh. As for Sidney, his house of long-established City wine merchants had been very generous in the matter of paying his salary while he was away: but supposing his son-in-law did not come back, what would become of Dorrie? And Tom Turney,

to his hasty shame and immediate elimination of the idea, thought
that if it were the case that Hugh—— No, he must not allow
such thoughts. They came from long-seated worry, for Hugh
had been a trouble to his mother and a burden on himself ever
since he had made the mistake of sending the boy to the university.
It had been a waste of time and money, and had only unsettled
Hugh for a commercial career, spending two years with young
rips and wasters, and giving him airs and ideas beyond his
station. Well, let him go out on the veldt, and become a hero
if he could! As much chance of that as the sparrow had, chirping
on the gabled roof above him!

Tom Turney readjusted the position of his right leg cocked
over the other, looked at his watch on the gold chain across
his blue serge waistcoat, with its hanging albert seal, and settled
back in the cane-bottomed chair for ten minutes' cat nap.

Richard saw him sitting there a few minutes later, when he
tip-toed across the carpet for the very purpose of finding out if
Mr. Turney was still *in situ*. He had spotted the figure of his
father-in-law in the chair as he pushed his cycle up the road, and
had pretended not to see him; even as Tom Turney had pretended
to be asleep, in order to avoid calling out to his son-in-law. The
older man was quite ready to call down a greeting, but he knew
Dick's aversion to himself. A pity he had been so hasty years ago
when the young fellow had come to ask him for Hetty's hand.
But there, if Dick still bore him ill-will, he couldn't do anything
about it.

Richard crept out of Hetty's bedroom, and tip-toed down the
stairs to the sitting room, to his tea alone with Dora, for Hetty had
made an excuse to leave the two together. He had already
changed from his cycling suit to an old tweed jacket and white
flannel trousers with brown stripes, in anticipation of a pleasant
evening on the Hill. He was now perturbed about the problem
of passing Mr. Turney's house after tea; for he did not want to
be seen carrying his kite and reel of twine by the figure on the
balcony. The alternative was to walk downhill to Randiswell
and all the way up beyond the eastern boundary of the Hill.
Why the deuce should he, a grown man, have to do that? How
long was Mr. Turney going to monopolise the balcony?

The opportunity to slip past was provided by the arrival of
Dorrie, and the four Cakebread children walking proudly up

Hillside Road with their father and uncle in khaki uniforms, jingling spurs strapped to brown boots, bandoliers across tunics, and felt wide-awake hats with the left side pinned up. Richard, who had retreated from his porch, heard his father-in-law calling down a greeting. "How are ye, come along in!" He heard him pushing himself out of his chair, and going away into the bedroom. Quickly Richard seized his winder of twine and the new five-foot kite.

Phillip, his hair plastered flat with water, ran before him, nearly slipping in his eagerness upon the curving, sloping path to open the gate for Father.

"Thanks, old chap," whispered Richard. "Now behave yourself, won't you?"

"Yes, Father."

"Keep your sailor suit clean!"

"Yes, Father," and Phillip ran back into the house, terribly excited. His secret hope was that Uncle Hugh would have his gun with him, and he would be allowed to hold it.

Safely past Mr. Turney's house, Richard began to feel keen anticipation of the meeting with Mr. Muggeridge.

This acquaintance was in his usual place, on the grassy area beyond the eastern edge of the gulley. Richard had to walk to the top, and then return parallel to the gulley and above it; for the sloping sides above the wide gravel way, planted with white-thorns, were forbidden to the public. The area was railed off below, with wooden seats at intervals, and fenced with hurdles of hazel wood above, of the kind used for folding sheep. One of the many rules and regulations forbade entry among the thorns, which thereby had become the hunting ground of small boys, including Phillip, who had hidden a candle-end and a penny packet of Epps' cocoa in a tin box down a crack in the clay, under a bush, and covered it with grass.

Mr. Muggeridge's kite was already high in the northern sky. He stood gently pulling the string to and fro, as though he were soothing his white captive, urging it to rise higher on its dancing tail of newspaper wads. Mr. Muggeridge, when Richard approached, raised his bowler hat and bade him good-evening. Not to be outdone in courtesy, Richard raised his straw boater and said, "Good evening, Mr. Muggeridge. A nice southerly breeze after the heats of the day."

"Yes, Mr. Maddison. So you brought your new model, I perceive. Bit light in the frame, isn't she? And I fancy the loop is fixed rather low."

"Ah, the proof of the pudding is in the eating, Mr. Muggeridge!"

"Time will tell," remarked Mr. Muggeridge, solemnly.

Richard's friend was a thin man with a pale determined face, whose eyes, hair, and profuse side-whiskers were of deepest black. Mr. Muggeridge worked in the counting house of a Bermondsey potted meat factory; and although he was twenty years older than Richard, he had no grey hairs. This condition he ascribed to the healthy atmosphere of cooking mutton which pervaded the building where he had spent most of the last forty years of his living: mutton being the basis of the various potted meats. Mr. Muggeridge's reasoning was simple. It was well-known, he said, that sheep had the largest amount of hair of any animal, and since the hair grew out of the resources of the body, so these resources, released into the atmosphere like the scent of hay, or the odour of flowers, most contain much essential virtue, which, breathed into human lungs, would enter the system and assure a good growth of hair, provided of course, that the roots were of good stock.

Mr. Muggeridge had expounded this theory to Richard, who had kept a straight face while with contented puffs of his meerschaum pipe, and rhythmic pulls on his string, the senior kite-flier had proved his point with a little tug of his flowing whiskers.

A queer old codger, thought Richard, with his frock coat, bowler hat, fancy waistcoat of cream cloth with faded red squares and brass buttons, green trousers, and brown boots. Mr. Muggeridge knew a little about butterflies, and had a smattering of knowledge about many subjects which made the desultory talk between them pass the time pleasantly enough. The real tie, however, was that both men had taken *The Daily Trident* from its first number, and swore by it.

The evening breeze freshened, and up went Richard's kite. It had a bamboo frame tied in a cross, kept in position by taut string connecting the four bamboo ends. Upon this framework had been pasted, with a mixture of flour and water, several sheets of newspaper. The tail was made of wads of newspaper, graduated in size, strung upon fifteen yards of string.

Up went the kite, composed mainly of a score of issues of the *Trident*. It rose straight up in the wind, like a white serpent with a hooded head, its long white tail following it. Richard let the twine slip through his hands from the coils already laid upon the grass, the white serpent sank upon its skeleton tail again: but before it could touch earth he tautened the line, up it shot again. Richard wound the twine round his hand, for the pull was surprisingly heavy in the increasing wind; the kite rose up and then, without warning, described a semi-circle, and followed by its segmented tail, dived head-first to the ground.

"There you are, you see!" said Mr. Muggeridge, removing his meershaum pipe, "what did I tell you?"

Running forward, while trying to unwind the coils round his hand, Richard let go the cord. Too late! The kite plunged into the middle of a game of tennis near the hut of the park-keeper. "Oh Lor'," he cried, fancying the work of several hours to be shattered.

The resilience of bamboo, and the strength of American wheat flour combined with the newsprint of *The Daily Trident*, however, had saved his kite. Apologising for having disturbed the game, Richard withdrew, followed by a band of small boys, who were inevitably attracted to anything out of the usual. Of course they wanted to help, and to ask questions. Richard did not reply, wary of making himself a mark on any future occasion when he should appear with his kite. He had learned his lesson during sledging on the Hill during the hard winter of '95; he had given some boys a "go", as they called it, on his sledge, and for months afterwards some urchin or other was liable to recognise and make for his presence. Too much of a good thing, by half!

"I told you so," remarked Mr. Muggeridge, with satisfaction: "Your loop was tied too low."

Richard did not reply to this implied censure. The slip-knot on the twine had obviously slipped down the suspending loops, so that the pressure of air had been too heavy on the top section. It was easily adjusted; up the serpent rose again, to rise and fall, climb and drop away farther each slipping of the twine through his fingers, until it was beyond the tennis court, high over the building of the Lavatory with its bushes and flower beds, and away towards Pit Vale and the Heath beyond. Not that it could get so far, but that was the fancy of the flier, and the ambition, too: for Richard intended to have, one day, one of the new box kites, perhaps two in tandem, held by fine steel wire on a windlass, to fly out of sight over the Thames. At night he would run up an Aeolian harp on the wire, by means of pulleys, and fill the air with mysterious music.

"That's better, Mr. Maddison. You've got the loop attachment right now."

"I think it was right before, you know, only it slipped down, Mr. Muggeridge."

"I pointed it out, if you remember, Mr. Maddison."

Richard, the argumentative and stickler for details, was the first to resent what he called hair-splitting in others. He made no reply. He had four hundred yards of cord on his winder, and as that was the competition length possessed by Mr. Muggeridge, and it had been agreed that the kites must fly in the same air-stream, the two men stood side by side, yellow straw boater and black bowler, brown beard and black whiskers, brown tweed and black melton, white flannel and green flannel (*could* those unusual trousers of Mr. Muggeridge's have been made out of the old cloth of a billiard table?), two stalwarts of fresh air and *The Daily Trident*; while their kites, equally adherents of the most successful journalistic venture of modern times, rode upon the summer winds of Kent.

In the midst of the sunlit evening scene there was a sensation on the Hill. It stopped even the tennis (some of it two-handed, since the local standards were hardly those of Wimbledon, or the brothers Renshaw) and set everyone, old and young, peering upwards. For, drifting over from the direction of the Crystal Palace, the sun glinting on the spheroidal grey of its serene approach, was a balloon, looking, Richard remarked to Mr. Muggeridge, as though St. Paul's Cathedral, in the great heat of the day, had blown a leaden bubble.

"Stunning, isn't it, Mr. Maddison, when you think of the wonders of science? Silk of the worm, gas out of the bowels of the earth, a basket made of willows by the river, and Man's ingenuity takes him right up there."

"I wonder where he'll be by nightfall—over Hertfordshire, I expect. He'll have to get down, before he can get back."

"You're postulating a hypothesis, Mr. Maddison. How d'you know he don't live in Herts?" Puff puff, of the curved yellow meerschaum, with its dark-brown spreading stain below the wide bowl, the much-desired "colouring" of the meerschaum devotee.

Inwardly nominating Mr. Muggeridge to be an argumentative old ass, Richard replied after a pause, "Well, supposing he lives in Surrey, Mr. Muggeridge?"

"I see no objection to that contention, Mr. Maddison. None at all. The answer is equally simple—he may have friends in Herts, expecting him. He may even have telephoned from the Crystal Palace, before he cast off. Endless possibilities." Puff puff of Hignett's *Cavalier* tobacco.

Endless for you perhaps; but you won't draw me, thought Richard.

The balloon moved over them, far above the kites. A drift of dust seemed to fall away behind it.

"My word, the fellow's possessed of intrepidity, Mr. Maddison! He's released sand, to rise higher! Perhaps he's out for a record, and is off to Scotland for the Twelfth. Did you read the article on grouse shooting in the *Trident* today? First class, I call it."

"I haven't come to that page yet, Mr. Muggeridge. I leave it for the late evening, when the children are asleep. Well, how goes the time?" He opened his watch. "Twenty-five-minutes after eight. I shall haul in in another twenty minutes."

Shortly after nine o'clock Richard walked down the gulley again. The seats were all occupied by couples, two to a seat, unspeaking as they sat close together with their arms around one another. Others, less conventional, were strolling over the grassy spaces, seeking places where they might lie down upon the earth and find a greater relaxation after the constrictions of the working week. Since it had become a London recreation ground, the Hill had lost its former evil reputation; it was now part of a police beat. A certain area had been set apart for Free Speech; other places for the playing of games. Richard preferred it in the old days, for then it was, to some extent, wild; he had to admit, however, that it was pleasant to have an hour or two now and again with a respectable fellow like Muggeridge.

Chapter 19

PARTY AT GRANDPA'S

STILL IN the mood of the fine weather, and the success of his new, narrower design of paper kite, Richard changed his trousers to a pair of dark material, washed his hands, brushed and combed his beard and hair, suddenly having decided to go into Mr. Turney's to wish the two men in khaki good luck before they left for South Africa.

He was delighted, and surprised, by the welcome given by the several children opening the door for him. The food had been cleared away, the table was in process of having all its removable leaves lifted out and the frame screwed back, to provide more room for the guests.

There had been sixteen faces round the table: Sarah and Tom at top and bottom, each in their high-backed chairs, and next to Sarah the chief guest, an old gentleman, with flowing side-whiskers, who lived in a terrace cottage in Randiswell named Mr. Harcourt Newman.

Grace before meals, of course; and when dutifully bowed heads were lifted, young eyes surveyed the feast. The meal was of the simplest for the time of year: tongue, chicken, pressed beef, with hot new potatoes and a salad, followed by trifle, mince pies, plum cake, and ice-cream brought by Sidney from Buszard's in Oxford Street; Barsac or Medoc to drink, with lemonade for the children. Then bon-bons to pull, with toys, paper caps, and mottos, while nuts, raisins, figs, and preserved fruits were consumed. Afterwards the younger ones had to help carry the plates and dishes into the kitchen, cook having had the evening off. Cries, shouts, whistles came from them, released by the occasion of new and abounding life.

"Now," said Thomas Turney, "the children can go into the back room, he-he, for I'd like to read ye something out of Shakespeare."

So the children were sent to play in the end room, Sidney warning his wild boys, whose energy had released an equal

wildness in their cousin Phillip, "No hooliganism, mind!" The
children departed with enthusiastic swiftness. The two elder
boys, racing to be first, leapt down the three stairs and landed
on the slippery oil-cloth below, to fall and slide into the closed
door feet-first with a decided bang. This brought an immediate
return of their father, clinking with burnished steel metal about
the feet, to reinforce his warning about hooliganism; unfortunately
for Sidney the rowels of his spurs, their swan-necks worn low
down and loose upon the heel as was the regulation, clashed upon
the second stair and he too fell, while his three sons, all wearing
Eton jackets and trousers, fell upon him, while Phillip shouted
out, "No hooliganism, mind!"

Sidney laughed, and ruffled the boy's hair, when the scrum was
over. Then came a discreet knock on the front door; the boys
raced to open it, scrambling upon the stairs. Phillip was pushed
back and Gerry trod on his fingers. "You fool!" he shouted after
his scampering cousin. "Oh—oh!"

Sidney tried to pick him up, but with face held in his arm the
boy lay across the stairs, giving way to the pain. Meanwhile
the door had been opened, and when the caller was recognised,
he was invited in by three voices.

"Come in, Uncle Richard, come in do! I saw your socking
great kite going past! Grandpa, it's Uncle Richard!"

"Oh, come in, Dick, come in!" said Tom Turney. "Glad
to see ye, glad ye could come. Have ye had any supper? Did
ye win your kite-flying contest? Dick, help yourself to a glass
of port. Are ye sure ye wouldn't like a sandwich?"

"No thank you, Mr. Turney, really, thank you. I have only
called in to pay my respects to the occasion."

Richard helped Hugh to carry the leaves of the table outside,
while the Cakebread boys helped. Soon it was done, and the
door closed.

"Now find yourself a place, and sit down, boys. I am going
to read some passages from Shakespeare. Fill your glass and
find yourself a chair, Dick."

Thomas Turney held an old duo-decimo volume, bound in
leather and tooled in gold-leaf, one of a set which was reputed
to be the first of its format, and printed during the active career
of the actor-playwright. Tom had a habit of reading from this
poet, on occasion after an evening meal; and the passages he

had chosen for this night were from *The Life of King Henry the Fifth*. He thought this appropriate, since the two soldiers were about to depart for the Field. Richard's unexpected arrival had set him back a little.

There was further delay while Richard went to greet his mother-in-law; thereafter to be introduced to Mr. Newman, a courteous old-world figure in thin grey serge frock coat, high-cravat and tall collar, who enquired after Richard's success with the new kite in a quavery tenor voice; and after shaking hands punctiliously, as befitted one born while the late Queen was but a girl, Mr. Newman sat down again. The newcomer, or latecomer as the host considered him to be, then made the round of greetings and hand-shakings all in turn—"How do you do" to Mr. and Mrs. Bigge, Mrs. Cakebread, Sidney Cakebread, Hugh and Joseph Turney, all in turn. At last it was over; and Tom Turney assembled himself to read from his chosen passage, the Chorus before Act IV.

He cleared his throat. But where was Hetty? Had she not returned? And where was Phillip?

"Hasn't Hetty come back? She must listen to this, it's too good to be missed." Tom got up from his chair, opened the door, "Hetty! Are ye there?"

"I shan't be a moment, Papa," came a voice from the kitchen. Tom went to investigate.

"What's the matter? Is the boy hurt?"

"No, Papa, it will soon be all right. He fell over, that is all. Please go on with your reading, Papa."

"No, I'll wait. Plenty of time. We'll wait for ye, Hetty."

"Oh Papa, please don't!" thinking of Richard. "I'll be along presently."

"What's the matter with Phillip, eh?"

The boy was snivelling as his hand was being bathed in warm water and borax powder. "How did it happen?"

"That fool Gerry," said Phillip. "Oh, it hurts!"

"Come come, my boy, be a man! Bring the boy in, Hetty. Would you like to hear the scene before a battle, Phillip, what say?"

"Yes, please, Gran'pa."

"That's better. Now be a hero. Nelson didn't cry when he lost his arm, you know. Many a soldier in South Africa has a worse hurt than you. Think how much more it would have been if a cannonball had struck your whole arm off."

These words, meant to comfort by contrast, had the effect of quietening the boy.

"Now come in, and sit still beside your mother, Phillip, and don't crack any nuts while I'm reading, will ye?"

"No, Gran'pa." Tom had seen that the pockets of the boy's long white trousers were wedged tight with brazil nuts, almonds, and raisins.

"That's right, come along in, then."

At last, gold spectacle frame on the end of his bulbous nose, book open on cocked knee, Tom Turney prepared to read. First, he must acquaint the company with some details of the poet's life.

"As ye know, the identity of William Shakespeare is a mystery. Some say he was Francis Bacon. Others claim that the Earl of Oxford wrote, or rewrote, the plays already in existence, and hid his identity behind an actor of the name of Shakespeare. Others, including his contemporary Kit Marlowe, who was stabbed hard by here, in Greenwich during a brawl, have left evidence that Shakespeare, the actor, possessed in his person the genius of the supreme poet. However, be that as it may——" Tom peered benevolently over his spectacles at Phillip sitting cross-legged on the floor near him—"Shakespeare was a man who had the spirit of England in himself, in all its forms and fancies. As a little tot he must have been as sharp as a needle, listening to other men, observing their ways and their speech, taking it all in, whether they were farmers speaking, or great lords, or kings, or queens, or sailors, or huntsmen—Shakespeare had the ear for truth, my boy. He-he-he, what say?"

"Phillip didn't say anything, Papa," said Hetty.

"I didn't say he did, my girl. How's your hand, better, my boy?"

"Yes, thank you, Gran'pa."

"That's right. Let him answer for himself, Hetty. Now what's the matter, hey?"

"Please, we want to come!"

There was the noise of snuffling and tapping on the door. Two little girls, both wanting Mummy, disconsolately waited to come in. The boys were rough, they said. There was further disturbance among the seated; spurs clanked on oilcloth and clinked gingerly down the stairs this time. Three brothers, in the back room, wrestling on the floor and banging about with cushions were cuffed lightly on cropped heads and nominated little devils. One gilt-framed picture, a steel-engraving of Gainsborough's portrait of David Garrick by the bust of Shakespeare, was hanging awry.

"Tell them to come in and listen, Sidney," the voice of Grandfather called from the front-room.

"And you damn well sit still while the Old Man elocutes, or I'll know the reason why!" whispered the father.

At last, before the assembled and heterogeneous company, Tom Turney took up the little faded duodecimo again, its pages yellowed by acid and impressed by irregular type, and glancing through the ground pebbles in their thin gold casing astride his nose variously coloured by toddy, port wine, and Hollands gin, all taken in moderation, prepared himself to read.

Theodora, whose eyes had not so far met those of Sidney, sat with her hands upon her lap, feeling that she did not belong to anybody any more. She was suffering from the reaction of so many people's feelings since her departure from her friend in Clifton. A line of Browning's ran through her head, *Never the place, and the time, and the loved-one altogether again.*

"This is the night before the battle of Agincourt, nearly five hundred years ago," said grandfather, looking around over his spectacles. "And it might be today, in South Africa at this very moment, since the sun rises upon almost the same line of longitude. Before I begin, boys, just think that, five hundred years ago, Englishmen who were a-bed in England then, are, through the children of their children's children, acting much to-day as they were then. The Turneys," he said, taking off his glasses, "were yeomen farming land then, as they are farming land to-day, some of it the same land."

"Surely, sir," interrupted Hubert Cakebread, who resembled his father in some ways, "a generation of farmers who farm their land while lying in bed, do not last for so long, as farmers I mean?"

Everybody laughed at the courteous gravity of the question, including Tom Turney.

"How right you are, m'boy! I was thinking of another speech of King Harry's, about gentlemen lying a-bed in England on St. Crispin's day. However, this is before the battle. Imagine the scene: the dark night, the camp-fires winking in the valley, the horses at the picket lines, the sentries moving up and down. But listen to Shakespeare——

> *Now entertain conjecture of a time*
> *When creeping murmur and the poring dark——*

Sarah, I think it would be better by candlelight, let's turn the gas out, shall we? Sit still everyone. Have you a candle handy?"

"There's one on the kitchen chimney-piece, Tom."

"Fetch it, will ye, Hetty, like a good girl."

Hugh got up off the floor, and opened the door for his sister.

"All these interruptions are bad for your aesthetic nerve, sir," his voice said gravely. "Besides, the form of the entertainment is not classical."

"What do you mean by that expression, m'boy?"

"The best turns go on last, not first, sir," replied Hugh. "The incomparable beauty and precision of the passage you are to read us, to our lasting benefit no doubt, should follow, not precede, the rougher, rowdier elements of any show. So with your permission, while footlights are being arranged, I will entertain the company on the banjo. Then your lines, sir, with their sublimity and appositeness, will suitably crown the evening."

The Cakebread boys approved this. "Good old Uncle Hugh!"

They could now wriggle, and talk freely. They had heard Uncle play and sing often enough, and always with the keenest delight. Hugh Turney, had his anxiety and versatility not over-borne him, might have been a success on the halls in the character of his simple self, with banjo or violin. He had a dry wit, and his manner of speaking was in the nature of parody of himself in the character of a gentleman of culture and education. He enjoyed making his gravely humorous, slightly pedantic little speeches; and his audience, including his father and brothers-in-law, enjoyed the fun with him. Richard was surprised at this aspect of Hugh Turney.

"My respected parent, and pater of paters, happily fondling his duodecimo, to the consternation of the worm that channels in the binding, having agreed to assume his rightful place in the programme, the top of the bill, I will now proceed to tell you, in music, how I came to take the Queen's shilling and to wear the Widow of Windsor's uniform, in conjunction with my respected colleague and brother-in-law, Sidney Puddingtart, Esquire——"

They all laughed, and seeing Father laugh, Phillip wanted to show him how he could make him laugh too, at jokes, and jumping up, he shouted, "Sidney Baconfish!" and bobbing down, promptly disappeared under the table, overcome by the enormity of what he had done.

Encouraged by the laughter, he tried again. "Sidney Cheese-bone!" And withdrew once more to think out more funny names.

"No more, Sonny, that's enough!" said Hetty, not wanting him to excite himself too much. Besides, he might very well use some of the crude expressions he had picked up from boys on the Hill lately.

However, once started, Phillip was not to be restrained. Jerking up head and shoulders, he shouted, "Sidney Sherrysoup." Announcing to all and sundry, "I *love* jokes!" he vanished but to reappear with "Sidney Sugarsalt!" and going back to his retreat, bumped his head on the edge of the table and collapsed for the second time that evening with the tears of pain.

"There, you see," remarked Richard, with a glance at Hetty, as though it were her fault because she had not spoken sternly enough to the boy.

Hughie had his banjo, and was testing the pitch of the strings. Mrs. Bigge leaned over and said something to Richard, but he did not catch what it was. Hughie struck a chord.

"I beg your pardon?" said Richard.

"I said, 'Boys will be boys', Mr. Maddison."

"Oh, yes," he replied, airily. Mrs. Bigge nodded her head several times, glancing around to indicate sympathy for all concerned.

The room, with its undrawn plum-coloured curtains hanging on brass rings from poles above the windows was filled with the throb of the banjo. Hughie struck an attitude as he put on a straw hat, and began the song which had swept all London.

" *When you've shouted 'Rule Brittania'—when you've sung 'God Save the Queen'—*

When you've finished killing Kruger with your mouth—
Will you kindly drop a shilling in my little tambourine
For a gentleman in khaki ordered south?
He's an absent-minded beggar and his weaknesses are great—
But we and Paul must take him as we find him—
He is out on active service, wiping something off a slate—
And he's left a lot o' little things behind him!

"Now chorus—you all know it, ladies and gentlemen!"

Duke's son—cook's son—son of a hundred kings—
(Fifty thousand horse and foot going to Table Bay!)
Each of 'em doing his country's work (and who's to look after their
things?)
Pass the hat for your credit's sake, and pay—pay—pay!"

Phillip was enthralled. He had forgotten the crushed finger
nail turning red, and the bump on his head. He did not know
what all the words meant, but one here and another there, in the
throbbing pulse of Uncle Hugh's music, gave him pictures.
Horses, men marching, bands playing, people cheering; wonderful!

" There are families by thousands, far too proud to beg or speak—
And they'll put their sticks and bedding up the spout——"

Phillip saw silent women pushing hundreds of sticks and pillows
and bedclothes ever so quickly up all the pipes of houses to stop
the water from coming down.

" And they'll live on half o' nothing paid 'em punctual once a week
'Cause the man that earned the wage is ordered out.
He's an absent-minded beggar, but he heard his country's call
And his reg'ment didn't need to send to find him:
He chucked his job and joined it—so the job before us all
Is to help the home that Tommy's left behind him."

People coming down the Hill were stopping outside the gate,
listening. When Hugh had finished, and the last chorus was sung,
Sidney said,

"Now's the time to pass round the hat, and give the collection to the local fund," but at once he saw that it was impracticable.

Hetty and Sarah had brought back two candles, for Tom's sight was not what it was.

"One more song," said Hughie, strumming the guitar. With the straw hat on the back of his head, he sang:

> "*Goodbye my Bluebell, farewell to you,*
> *I shall be dreaming of your eyes so blue,*
> *'Mid camp fires gleaming, 'mid shot and shell,*
> *I shall be thinking of my own Bluebell.*"

Phillip thought this was sad and lovely. He wanted Uncle Hugh to go on singing and playing for ever. Theodora watched the intense eagerness in his face, the boy's complete absorption, and thought that he might have a musical talent. And during the last verse of the song, which Hugh sang with a wistful melancholy, she glanced at Sidney, and knew that his feelings were as her own. The shock made her neck and forehead flush hotly. She lowered her gaze. The years between had made no change.

At last Mr. Turney, with two candles alight at his elbow, began reading.

> " *Now entertain conjecture of a time*
> *When creeping murmur and the poring dark*
> *Fills the wide vessel of the universe.*
> *From camp to camp, through the foul womb of night,*
> *The hum of either army stilly sounds.*"

Tom peered over his spectacles at the faces, and went on slowly and impressively.

> " *That the fix'd sentinels almost receive*
> *The secret whispers of each other's watch;*
> *Fire answers fire, and through their paly flames*
> *Each battle sees the other's umber'd face;*
> *Steed threatens steed, in high and boastful neighs*
> *Piercing the night's dull ear; and from the tents*
> *The armourers, accomplishing the knights,*
> *With busy hammers closing rivets up,*
> *Give dreadful note of preparation.*"

At this point the speaker blew out one of the candles, and went on in slow, sonorous tones.

> " *The country cocks do crow, the clocks do toll,*
> *And the third hour of drowsy morning name.*
> *Proud of their numbers, and secure in soul,*
> *The confident and over-lusty French*
> *Do the low-rated English play at dice,*
> *And chide the cripple tardy-gaited night*
> *Who, like a foul and ugly witch, doth limp*
> *So tediously away. The poor condemned English,*
> *Like sacrifices, by their watchful fires*
> *Sit patiently, and inly ruminate*
> *The morning's danger, and their gesture sad*
> *Investing lank-lean cheeks and war-worn coats*
> *Presenteth them unto the gazing moon*
> *So many horrid ghosts. O! now, who will behold*
> *The royal captain of this ruined band*
> *Walking from watch to watch, from tent to tent,*
> *Let him cry 'Praise and glory on his head'*
> *For forth he goes and visits all his host,*
> *Bids them good-morrow with a modest smile,*
> *And calls them brothers, friends and countrymen.*
> *Upon his royal face there is no note*
> *How dread an army hath enrounded him;*
> *Nor doth he dedicate one jot of colour*
> *Unto the weary and all-watched night;*
> *But freshly looks and overbears attaint*
> *With cheerful semblance and sweet majesty;*
> *That every wretch, pining and pale before,*
> *Behold him, plucks comfort from his looks.*
> *A largess universal like the sun*
> *His liberal eye doth give to every one,*
> *Thawing cold fear. Then mean and gentle all,*
> *Behold, as may unworthiness define.*
> *A little touch of Harry in the night.*
> *And so our scene must to the battle fly;*
> *Where, O for pity! we shall much disgrace*
> *With four or five most vile and ragged foils,*
> *Right ill-disposed in brawl ridiculous,*

The name of Agincourt. Yet sit and see;
Minding true things by what their mockeries be."

Tom Turney laid down the book, and relit the other candle at the flame of its fellow.

"Well, my children," he said, "that is William Shakespeare. And it is true to-day as it was in the times of which he wrote."

"Thank you, sir, for reading the passage," said Sidney.

"It was most impressive, Mr. Turney," quavered old Mr. Newman.

"Yes, yes," murmured Mr. Bigge.

"There'll never be another like him," remarked Hugh.

"Beautiful language, beautiful!" cried Hetty.

Sarah wiped away a tear; and held her daughter Dorrie's hand.

"Well, boys, what did ye think of it, eh?"

"Oh, we learn it at school, Gran'pa," said Hubert. "But it sounds better in the dark from you, sir."

"The Elizabethan spirit, will it ever visit England again, Mr. Turney?" said Theodora.

Richard was thinking, not of the scene Mr. Turney had read, but of the hypocrisy of the old man: that he could not, being what he was, possibly understand the passage. He was bogus, a sentimentalist, enjoying the sound of his own voice, and extracting the feelings of Shakespeare, as though they were his own. Even so, he could not altogether spoil the beauty of the phrases, which were a revelation. Richard had never seen a Shakespearean play, and had only dull memories of trying to learn by heart certain passages in his private school at Slough.

All parties have to end, to the grief of little children dazed in enchantment. Up Hillside Road came the steady pecking of a horse's hoofs; the crunching of iron wheel-rims on granite kerb-stones, the cry of "Whoa!", the jingle of reins, a momentary silence in the night as the cabman descended.

His round face peered in the open window, to vanish again as Tom invited him in for a glass of punch. He came in, watery-eyed, hoarse-voiced, tarred bowler hat on his head. Cracked and thickened fingers enclosed the glass, and with a "Best respects",

the liquid went down his throat. A toast; and glasses refilled.
Might the children have just a little sip? There was no harm in
it; wait a minute, add more sugar and lemon and hot water to
their glasses.

"The Queen, God bless her!"

They stood in the light of seven candles now burning on the
chimney-piece. Then they held crossed hands, swung arms as
they sang *Should Auld Acquaintance be forgot.*

Sarah was crying silently; so was Dorrie, and her sister Hetty.
Tears filled old Mr. Newman's eyes; the dead glimmered there.
Mrs. Bigge smiled as her tears fell; even the cabby brushed the
back of his hand across lashless lids. Richard, despite himself,
moved to his sister Theodora and took her hand; for he could see
how she was affected, and he admired Sidney Cakebread. The
small boys were silent as bandoliers and slouch hats were put on,
straps fastened under chins. The party was breaking up, the
party was broken, it was night, the horse was turning round, the
candles smoking in the carriage lamps, sparks arose from braked
wheels sliding over flints of the road. The shoes of the horse
struck sparks, too. Then down from the zenith of the sky slid a
shooting star, towards the mass of the grammar school dark
against the curious and pale horizon of the north-west.

And Phillip cried in his bed, because Uncle Hugh and Uncle
Sidney had gone away and might never come back again. In
the next room, equally silent upon her pillow, Theodora was
weeping, too. There were other tears in the night; and when
summer was gone, and leaves were fallen, and winter was come
again with fogs and frost, Thomas Turney came in one morning,
after Richard had left for the City, and said to his daughter, "I
have bad news, a cable from Hugh. Sidney Cakebread has died
of enteric fever. Will ye come with me, Hetty, and break the
news to Dorrie?"

Chapter 20

COUNTRY COUSINS

"AUNTY BIGGE, Aunty Bigge, I am going holiday-making to my cousins at Beau Brickhill, before I go to the new school after Easter! The outside porter is coming up for our portmanteaux soon. And Grannie has given me a shilling; look, Aunty Bigge!"

Phillip was looking over the garden fence, which was low, since the Bigges' gravelled back way was nearly two feet below the Maddisons' back way. The six-foot fence was therefore only four feet high where Phillip was looking over.

Mrs. Bigge was watering some flower-pots on the shelves of her greenhouse, which enclosed an area from her back door. Spring was in the air, rooks in the row of elms beyond the bottom line of garden fences were cawing at their nests. This was, however, not entirely the spring the Bigges had looked forward to. A row of scaffolding had recently arisen beyond the rookery. It looked as though bricks and mortar were about to creep across the lower levels of the Backfield, that waste of long grass and wilding thorns, which had been one of the attractions before the Bigges had moved to the desired solitude of Hillside Road.

"What, are you going all the way up to Scotland, dear?" Mrs. Bigge's question was asked humorously, for Phillip's face was almost entirely enclosed by a deerstalker hat.

"Oh no, Aunty Bigge. We are going to Cousin Percy's."

"Where did you get that wonderful hat, Phil? Did your father give it to you, dear?"

"No, Father didn't give it to me. I found it. How are your ferns to-day?"

"There's a nice boy to ask! They are very glad to be seeing the sun, dear."

"I expect everything is, too. Isn't it nice and warm to-day?"

"Yes. How long are you and your mummy and sisters going to be away in the country?"

"A fortnight, Aunty Bigge. Would you like me to send you a new picture post-card from Beau Brickhill? I have lots of money."

"Now that would be very kind of you, dear. But you mustn't waste your pennies on an old woman like me, you know."

"But I like you, Aunty Bigge, and you do not look like an old woman at all."

"You little dear!" cried Mrs. Bigge. "I believe you mean it, too! Do you?"

"Yes, Mrs. Bigge."

"Then give us a kiss, ducks—or are you too big to be kissed, eh?"

By standing on his toes he could just reach the top of the fence with his chin; and as Mrs. Bigge's side was so low, she had to fetch a box to stand on. She gave him three good kisses on his cheek. "You're growing quite a big boy, aren't you, dear?"

"Yes, Aunty Bigge, I am an inch higher on the door since I was eight. So I have grown an inch in one year!"

Hetty measured her children's heights on the jamb of the sitting-room door, once a year on Phillip's birthday, marking the lines with a knife.

"Well, you are big enough to look after your Mother and Mavis and Doris on the journey."

"Yes, Aunty Bigge. I have some money, and I am going to buy a Pluck library, and if you promise not to tell Father, also a Union Jack library, and the Boy's Friend."

"I won't tell him, dear. But ought you to go against your father's wishes, if he doesn't want you to read such things?"

"I don't care."

Mrs. Bigge looked at the boy. More than once on hearing his cries as he was being caned Mrs. Bigge had had to go away to another part of her house and try and think about other things. Mr. Maddison, she knew, considered that the reading of "bloods" inspired his son to mischief.

"But you ought to care, dear, for your mother's sake. You must try and be a good boy, now that you are growing up. There now, you think Aunty Bigge is preaching, don't you, eh?"

"I don't mind."

"Well, do try, dear. You see, if you are disobedient it worries your mother, and then Father is angry with her for not being sterner with you, and so your mother is made very unhappy. But you know that, don't you, dear?"

Only the ear-flaps of the deerstalker, tied across the crown, were visible now from the lower side of the fence.

"There now, I've made you close up. How nice it will be with your cousins, won't it?"

After a pause the boy said:

"Percy has a gun, and he can shoot bats."

"Are you going to shoot bats, too? Is that why you're wearing that hat?"

"Yes, Aunty Bigge. It is a bat-stalking hat. You see, I want to stuff a bat and put it in a glass case, in my museum."

There was the sound of a window opening high up in the wall of the house. Immediately the boy flitted round the corner, out of sight. Hetty looked down upon the scene below from the yellow brick cliff.

"Oh, good morning, Mrs. Bigge!"

Phillip reappeared, without the hat.

"Ah, there you are, there's a good boy! I was afraid Sonny had run away again," she said, with an apologetic laugh. "Come along, dear, and help me bring the bags downstairs. The outside porter will be here soon, and we must catch our train, mustn't we, Mrs. Bigge?"

"That's right, dear. Sonny has been saying good-bye to me, like the little gentleman he is. Now run along, dear, and help your mother."

Phillip ran off, feeling good that Mrs. Bigge had called him a little gentleman.

Ten minutes later the outside porter from Randiswell Station was wheeling his iron-wheeled trolley down the steep asphalt pavement of Hillside Road. There were three bags, two of white rush secured with brown straps, and a larger portmanteau of leather and brown canvas.

Richard was going to look after himself during the fortnight his family would be away. He did not want Mrs. Feeney to come during that time, and had declined Mrs. Bigge's invitation to have his meals with them. He was looking forward to a spell of quiet by himself.

Grannie Turney went with them to the station, pushing the go-cart in which sat the youngest, Doris. Wanting to be apart, Phillip walked in front. Across his shoulder was slung his new satchel, in which were his own particular treasures, and a special packet of banana sandwiches. He had planned to ride in a carriage by himself, and to climb up into the rack. There he saw himself reading the new Pluck Library with the dark lantern beside him, the Sherlock Holmes hat on his head, the blinds down.

The hat and lantern were packed in his satchel. He had discovered them in the tin trunk in the attic above the bathroom ceiling. He had explored all the attic, from the gable in front where there were chinks of light, the chirp of nesting sparrows, and dim remote street noises, to the water-tank in the middle, and the joists at the other end over his bedroom. There were many interesting things hidden in the attic, among them a very heavy and old round leather case with red silk inside, and an old top hat fitted into it. There was a long narrow wooden case with fishing rods in it, and leather pocket-books of fish-hooks with flies on them. There were small boxes filled with brass gimp with swivels and treble hooks fixed to them. There were little painted fish above the treble hooks, made of fish-skin. There was a pile of yellow butterfly boxes. And in the long japanned tin trunk were some clothes, a soldier's uniform, red jacket with things like gold shell-fish on the shoulder straps, and a funny pair of boots. At the other end of the trunk he had come across the deerstalker hat and the bull's-eye lantern. In the tin trunk was a big violin bow, three black leather books with writing in them, and some photographs. The photographs were of no interest: but the detective's hat and lantern were a wonderful find. He was taking them to show Cousin Percy, who had a real gun with which to shoot birds, bats and rabbits.

Led by Phillip, the procession went down Charlotte Road, where the black branches of the horse-chestnuts were glistening with big buds brown as toffee apples. Phillip had discovered that they were no good to eat. He and Gerry had climbed up one tree and picked some, finding them sticky and nasty. Gerry had spoken of a fortune by using the gum for flypapers. Perhaps they could sell the discovery to Grandpa? Meanwhile some of the collected samples had been fitted as heads of arrows, to be shot at other boys with their string-and-bamboo bows. A window had been broken in Charlotte Road. Running into Gerry's house, the cousins had hastened upstairs, to climb through an upper window and so to hide on the high brick wall dividing the lean-to sculleries of the paired houses.

Now, as he passed by the house, Phillip looked up and saw that the window was still broken. He looked the other way, in case someone was spying.

Sarah Turney, now sixty-two years old, left Hetty at the bottom of Charlotte Road, kissing her and the little girls good-bye—Phillip would not come to be kissed—went into No. 202, to visit her eldest daughter Dorothy. She had two sovereigns in her purse to give to Dorrie. Unknown to Tom, who already made his daughter a monthly allowance, to augment the very small pension she received as the widow of a trooper, Sarah gave her something extra every month. Sidney Cakebread's firm had been generous when he had died in the South African war; they had paid his widow two years' salary in monthly instalments: but this money was now spent.

Hubert, the eldest boy, had left school and was working in the Firm, living at home; while the second boy, Ralph, considered by his grandfather to be a poor specimen, was being educated at the West Kent Grammar School on the Hill. Gerry, the youngest boy, had been sent to the council school in Wakenham Road, to win a scholarship to a secondary school. Phillip was to join him after the Easter holidays.

The decision to send Phillip to an elementary school had been taken by Richard and Hetty only after some perturbation and argument, following on Hetty's failure to get a presentation for the school on which she had set her heart since before he was born—Christ's Hospital, in Charterhouse Square. However, things would not be so bad when Sonny had won a scholarship: perhaps the two years among the very poor children who went to the council school would not, as she dreaded, turn him into an unruly boy, with bad habits of speech and behaviour.

"Well," Richard had said, "all schools were free schools, in the old days. I have done my best with the boy, to give him an idea of how to conduct himself; but your leniency towards him has countered all my efforts. Taking sides with him as you have done, exonerating his bad behaviour, only makes matters worse. Well, if his behaviour gets worse at the school, I cannot help it. I have done my best, and have apparently failed, as far as Phillip is concerned. And while you continue to side with him against me, I cannot see how things can ever improve."

"Oh, Dickie, how can you say I go against your wishes? I am always telling Sonny to be good, and not to touch your things."

The fact was the boy listened neither to his father, nor to his mother. Once, and once only, had Hetty caned him. She was looking out of her bedroom window while she was making the bed one morning when she saw, to her horror, Phillip across the road, with Mavis, behaving in a most shocking manner against the park railings. In shame, anger, and desperation she had run downstairs and across the road, to grip their arms and drag them into the house. Phillip had never seen his mother so angry before, and was for the first time in his life scared by her: by the look on her face, especially at the way she showed her teeth.

"You bad, *bad* boy, you! I sometimes wonder if you are not my son after all! How *dare* you behave like that, for all the neighbours to see!"

Phillip was too over-awed to say that they had only been pretending to be dogs, and that Father had told him liquid manure was good for grass. To Phillip's dismay and incredulity his mother had taken him upstairs, got the long thin cane from the wardrobe in the front bedroom, and chased him into his bedroom. There he had gone to ground under the bed, where she had swished the cane to get him out. He had held on to the end, saying, "I'll tell Father of you, using his cane without permission!"

When he had seen she was serious, he had ceased to evade her. He had done what he was told: taken down his trousers, and lain on the bed. He looked at her with a puzzled look as she stood above him, the cane raised.

Hetty gave him one cut. She had not struck hard, for when he was half-naked, remorse for the utter perplexity in his face had overcome her. She felt she was betraying him. But she must not weaken now, for his sake. She had compromised with one cut. As the cane came down he put his hand over his bottom, and it struck him across the back of the fingers. He buried his face in the bedclothes, all resistance gone.

"There now, Sonny, I did not mean to hurt you, dear, but you *must* be a good boy; you are driving your father and me to distraction. Please try and be a good boy in future, won't you?"

Seeing her distress, his emotion set upon its course: he would hide himself away, and not eat any more food until he died. He got over the other side of the bed and under it again, to lie still on the floor. Hetty had left him, and gone to speak to Mavis, who was boo-hoo'ing in her bedroom.

When she had returned to Phillip, after half an hour, during which no sound had come from upstairs, she had found the door locked. She asked him to open the door and to come down and be a good boy again. Silence. Surely he had not become ill? She was always afraid that, with his highly strung nature, coupled with the fact that before his birth Papa had knocked her down and she had remained unconscious for several hours, any sudden shock might injure his brain. Supposing he was lying in a fit, and it was all her fault? Oh, why had she used the cane?

Hetty knew in her heart that it was wrong to punish young children. Theodora, who had started her school in Somerset, had written in a letter, received three months ago, that many of the ills in life, a waywardness and tendency to wrong-doing and violence, were in many cases to be attributed to severities in childhood, imposed upon tender minds by unknowing parents. It had been a bewildering, disturbing letter. Could such a thing be happening to her little boy, already so afraid of his father, to make him estranged from his mother, the one who loved him more than anyone else in the world! And worse, he might be lying there, behind the locked door, unconscious!

Hetty tapped on the door again. She listened. There was no sound inside the bedroom. The key was not even in the lock. Perhaps he had swallowed it, in his frenzy! Sonny, Sonny, open the door at once! No reply.

Hetty had run next door to confide her fears to Mamma. The first thing she saw there, to her surprise and joy which showed itself in laughter, was Sonny, talking to Hugh in his room, which was next to the garden. Hugh was about to play on a violin which he had made out of a cigar-box.

"How did you get here, Sonny?"

With a glance at Hugh, the boy had replied, "A little bird brought me, Mummy."

"That's right, Hetty," said Hugh. "The stork was that little bird. Well, sister, we are about to have a lesson in the art of producing sounds of beauty from the gut of a cat and the tail of a horse."

Hugh had not long returned from South Africa. He was brown of face and lean of body, noticeably bow-legged after much horse-riding. On his bedroom wall, framed, was a certificate of thanks for his services to King and Country signed, in print by the block process, by the Lord Mayor on behalf of the City of London.

Phillip had been forbidden by his father to go into Hugh Turney's room; but the boy went there whenever he thought he would, to see the one who was not like an uncle at all, but a nice person to be with. Hugh told Phillip stories of the war which were not like the stories he had read in a book sent him by Uncle John in the country, called *For Valour and Victory*. Uncle Hugh said that at the battle of the Modder River all the soldiers ran away so fast that more were trodden underfoot in the rush to the rear than were hit by Boer bullets. Most of them had been Scotsmen in kilts, the Highland Brigade. Uncle Hugh told Phillip how the Boer women and children had been put in big lägers, or cages, many thousands of them, where ever so many had died of fever.

"War's a swindle, my boy, and anyone who believes in the glory of war is a first-class bloody fool. Only jackals profit from war—the contractors, the arms manufacturers, together with the gold-fields capitalists—Midas & Co. Listen to this——" and the sardonic voice chanted:

> " *Where those three hundred fought with Beit*
> *And fair young Wernher died?*
> *The little mound where Eckstein stood*
> *And gallant Albu fell*
> *And Oppenheim, half-blind with blood*
> *Went fording through the rising flood—*
> *My Lord, we know them well.*

"Those lines, my boy, come from a satirical poem by Hilaire Belloc, called 'Verses to a Lord who in the House of Lords said that those who opposed the South African Adventure confused soldiers with money-grubbers'. Hello, here's your mamma coming. What have you been up to now, eh," and he winked at Phillip.

Phillip winked back. Uncle Hugh was a wonderful man, a soldier of the Queen. He said "bloody"; Phillip would say it, too, when he was by himself.

Hetty wondered how Phillip had got out of his bedroom. Had he slipped out, locked the door behind him and, creeping downstairs, got into the next garden by way of the kitchen steps, or perhaps by the french windows, in the sitting-room and over the garden fence? He would not say; nor did Hugh Turney know.

Phillip had discovered, in his exploration of the attic, that he could crawl on hands and knees over the joists to the water tank, and, squeezing past it, continue over the front bedroom ceiling, through a small opening at the apex of the common wall between the two houses, and so, by way of Grandpa's bedroom ceiling, joists, and water tank, to the trapdoor in Grandpa's bathroom. Opening this, he had slipped through, after arranging that the trap should shut as he let go with his hands. If detected, he would pretend to have come upstairs to the lavatory.

Phillip told Cousin Percy Pickering of this secret place while the two were lying in bed, a bolster between them until Percy's mother could know how harmoniously or otherwise the two would fit into the same bed. It was Phillip's first visit to Beau Brickhill.

"Does your father use that bloody cane I saw hanging on the back of his chair at supper, Percy?"

"No fear! Dad don't beat me."

"Has he ever, Percy?"

"No. Nor does Mum, or Granpa, or Gran."

"Then why does it hang there, Percy?"

"I dunno. It always has."

"This is a lovely house, isn't it? I like being here. Will you be my great friend, Percy?"

"Well, I've got a great friend already. His name is Fred. You'll see him tomorrow when we go nesting."

Phillip was silent for a while. Then he said:

"Couldn't I be your other great friend, Percy?"

"'Course you can. You can join our football team if you like. That's a spiffing lantern you've got. Did your Dad lend it to you?"

"Yes, only don't tell my Mother. She isn't supposed to know. It's a secret."

"Between you and your Dad?"

"Yes, sort of. I say, Percy!"

"What say?"

"I will give you some of my sweets when I buy them. I've got lots of tin to spend."

"I'll let you shoot with my saloon gun if you like."

"Oh, spiffing!"

Uncle Jim called up the stairs: "Stop talking you two, and go to sleep. Good night!"

"Good night, Uncle Jim."

"Good night, Dad."

It was wonderful to lie in bed, talking in whispers . . . whispers . . . whispers . . . while the mice in the old house ran over the thick uneven slabs of the chestnut floor unheard, for the boys were asleep.

Downstairs in the kitchen parlour, by the coal fire, Hetty and Eliza, her cousin and childhood friend, were talking over a cup of tea before going to bed.

In another room, where the half-sized billiard table stood, Eliza's husband, James Pickering, partner in a firm of corn and seed merchants, was sitting at his desk, entering the day's orders in a book.

"Well, Hetty," said Eliza Pickering, "here you are at last! I can hardly believe it is really you."

She was a dark, small-headed woman, of Brythonic or ancient British type; she was dressed in black, with dark hair parted in the middle and drawn back plainly over her head. "I cannot tell you how nice it is, after all these years, to see you again. It's just like old times, and with all the children about it makes me feel young again."

"Yes, Liz," smiled Hetty. "Everything is just as it used to be!"

She glanced round the room, at the tall grandfather clock with the flowers painted round its face, and the pheasant across the yellow-white dial; the wooden salt-box on its nail above the long-handled basting ladle and the two-pronged meat-fork hanging beside the hearth; the copper pans on the chimney shelf; the pictures on the wall; the long farmhouse table and the high-backed chairs at either end, their woollen antimacassars on the tops, and the old yellow cane hanging by its curved handle.

"Even the cane is still there, I see! It quite used to frighten me when I was a child."

"I remember my father saying that he bought it at the Michaelmas Goose Fair for a penny during the Crimea war. He brought it home and hung it there, and there it has remained ever since. I have never known it to be used. Now tell me, dear, how is your husband?"

"Oh, Dickie is very well, thank you. He's very keen on flying box kites now, from the Hill with a friend. I am so glad he has taken it up as a hobby."

"Of course, he always disliked the City life, and wanted to be a farmer, didn't he? Well, I am glad he's settling down. It's a very hard life, farming, you know."

"Yes, I know. Papa says it is a thing of the past nowadays."

"Jim feels the depression quite a lot. Farmers are not growing so much corn as they did, they say they can buy feeding stuffs cheaper. However, we mustn't grumble. How is Dorrie nowadays?"

"She isn't very well, I'm afraid. Her heart you know. Sidney's death was a great shock."

"Yes, it was to us all, Hetty. How are her children? She has three boys and a girl, has she not?"

When Hetty had told Liz of Dorrie's family, Liz asked about her Aunt Sarah.

"Mamma is growing very old, I am afraid, Liz. But she is cheerful, as always."

"And how is Hugh? He had rheumatism very badly, didn't he?"

"He is better now, he has treatment from the doctor, still," said Hetty, and changed the subject. She told her cousin about the decision to send Phillip to Wakenham Road School.

"Of course both Dickie and I have discussed it all ways, but it seems the only thing to do, to work for a scholarship. I did so want him to go to the Bluecoat School. It would have been so very good for him. But I am afraid it is out of the question now."

"He seems a nice boy, Hetty; very quick, isn't he?"

"Yes, sometimes I think he is too quick. He can't be taught, I'm afraid, his lessons upset him."

"In what way, Hetty?"

"He doesn't seem able to learn at all. Even Dora, who is very good with children as a rule, found it next to impossible to get him to understand what she was trying to show him. He just cries, and says he cannot. His head seems filled with the papers he reads; though Dickie has forbidden them, it makes no difference."

"Poor little fellow. But he is a good boy, by his face, Hetty."

"Oh yes, I am sure he would be all right, with the right example before him. But there, it is too late for the Bluecoat School now. Ah well!"

"Who is this Sir Roland Tofield you mentioned in your letter, Hetty?"

Hetty told her cousin about her romance on the Riviera long ago, while omitting the part her friend of those wonderful three weeks had later played in getting Richard an introduction to the Moon Fire Office. Nor did she confide in Eliza that her recent letter to her old acquaintance had been replied to by a secretary, who had written that as Sir Roland had been called unexpectedly abroad he was replying for him. Sir Roland had asked him to say at once that as he had no presentation for Christ's Hospital in his own gift, it might perhaps be more effective if Mrs. Maddison made direct application in those quarters where such applications would, he felt sure, receive all due consideration.

Hetty felt shame whenever she recalled the letter. Obviously Sir Roland Tofield must have considered her request to be presumption on her part. And worse, could he have thought that she—— Hetty baulked at the thought. She had seen a photograph of him with his wife and two children in an illustrated weekly paper in her father's house.

"Haven't you a sister-in-law who started a school, Hetty?"

"Yes, Theodora took a lovely old house in Somerset, with a friend of hers in partnership. She has rather spoiled her chances, Dickie says, by embracing Women's Suffrage."

"Oh, so she is one of these Suffragettes, is she? What a pity. We have two in the parish, madcap creatures they are, too, riding about in a motorcar, and without hats, no sense of modesty, making fools of themselves, for all to see."

"Dora is not that sort, of course——"

"No dear, of course not. She is probably deluded by some unscrupulous companions."

Hetty felt she had given a wrong impression of her great friend.

"Oh, Dora is a wonderfully clever person, Liz, and writes such interesting letters. She knows so much about all kinds of things. What induced her to join the movement for Women's Suffrage was hearing Mrs. Pankhurst tell of a little girl of only thirteen having an illegitimate baby." Hetty's voice showed her embarrassment at mentioning such a thing. "Poor girl, I am sure it was not her fault in the first place." Hetty was thinking of Mona Monk. "She exposed the baby when it was only a day old, and was hanged, poor thing."

Eliza Pickering made a double clucking noise with her tongue, a bird-like sound, between that of a partridge talking to chicks and a hedge wren as cat or weasel passes underneath. She shook her head slowly. She sighed.

"That was wrong, Hetty, that was wrong. We need a change of heart in this country, it has never been the same since Gladstone died. The Tories are hard men, and dead set against all progress."

Hetty agreed with this, though not without a qualm of disloyalty to Richard, who was against Liberals and Free Trade. Boldly she said, "I was about to say, Liz, that Dora wrote in her letter something I have remembered ever since. 'The vote is denied to children, idiots—and women.'"

"What's this I hear about the Tories?" said an amiable voice. James Pickering, smoking a pipe with curved amber mouthpiece, and yellow bowl carved in the shape of a negro's head, had come quietly in his carpet slippers through the other door. He was a Saxon of middle height, with yellow fuzzy hair, pale eyes that seemed to be a mixture of blue and amber, and a large yellow moustache dyed brown below the nostrils by the smoke of many hundreds of packets of Westward Ho! tobacco.

"I was just saying how the Tories keep back progress, Jim," said his little black-bodiced wife, nursing a cup of tea between her hands on her lap.

"I should just about think so too!" exclaimed Jim Pickering, removing his calabash pipe. His yellow eyes glared at imaginary wickedness in space, and from his nostrils issued a double jet of tobacco smoke. "Why, look how the Duke here, owning tens of thousands of acres in the county, and other large estates in

Devon, Scotland, and all those streets and squares in London ...",
and for the next three minutes he expatiated upon the evils of
great landlords.

"If a man wants to build his own house, can he get a bit of
land to build it on? Will the Duke's Steward sell? And look at the
parsons he puts in his livings! Look at the trouble we had to get
the Gas Company established!"

James Pickering was a radical indeed, and while he held forth,
match after match was needed to keep alight the fuming head of
the negro. Finally he started a new pipe, a rustic-looking affair
of cherry-wood, which being properly packed, burned fragrantly.
It may have been mere coincidence, but at once his indignation
abated; and with his usual mild demeanour he settled in the
armchair his wife dutifully had vacated. With a cup of strong
tea well-stirred with sugar, James enquired how his uncle by
marriage, Tom Turney, was getting along in his business.

Hetty gave him all the news about Papa and Mamma,
Charley, Hughie, Dorrie, and Joseph.

"And how is your husband, Hetty? How does he like in-
surance after banking?"

"It is more interesting work, Dickie says. The people there are
easier to get on with than was the case at Doggett's."

"Look who bank at Doggett's!" exclaimed James, removing
the cherry-wood, and appearing to glare. "All the rich Tories,
the great landlords! Your husband is well out of such an
atmosphere, I should say." His pipe glowed, smoke issued from
his nostrils in two streams. "The Duke banks there, of course,
all the landlords stick together! Give me a local bank anytime,
though more and more are being swallowed up by the big ones
with headquarters in London, more's the pity."

"Still, they can't do that with gas, thank goodness, Jim,"
declared Eliza; and Hetty had to restrain herself from laughing
as Jim blew another cloud of indignant smoke from his nostrils.
James Pickering was secretary of the local gas company, whose
ironwork adjoined the railway station.

In the morning all were assembled for breakfast in the parlour
of Beau Brickhill, as they called the house among themselves. It
had been built on a field of that name, the copyhold of which had
been held by a branch of the yeoman Turneys since the sixteenth

century. Brickhill House had been built from the profits of a brick-making business on the site. The underlying blue clay of the ten acres of Beau Brickhill had been dug out, in a series of flat terraced pits, to be moulded, dried, and finally baked in stacks of heavy flat bricks which had been of the first quality for building. The layers of blue lias, or gault, had lain upon gravel, under which in turn lay a yellow clay, holding water, so that when brick-making had been discontinued, with the working-out of the stratum of blue lias, deep ponds had formed in the eight acres to a depth of twenty-five feet. These ponds lay behind the gardens of the house. Reeds had sprung up in them and sallows upon the banks; fish had appeared, said to have been brought there as spawn upon the legs of mollerns, dipchicks, and other wildfowl.

Phillip thought it was a wonderful house, the best in the world. There was a Grandpa and Grandma in it, and their name was Thacker. Looking at Grannie Thacker at the end of the breakfast table (for Brickhill belonged to her), and at the cane hanging upon the back of her chair, Phillip thought that her name must have something to do with the cane. It was like the word in the Pluck Library when Tom Valiant, with a club made of rolled-up examination papers, and disguised in a white sheet to be a ghost, went *thwack-thwack* on the bald square head of the German master, who was a spy in disguise. Percy's grandmother was very thin, so her name was thin, not thwacker, ther-wacker, but thin, thacker. Thin Thacker, Tin Tacker, like the long blue hair-pins Mummy wore in her hat.

"Do you know who I am, Phillip?" asked Mrs. Thacker. She was dressed in black, and sat thin and upright in a wooden corset. She smiled and said, swaying stiffly, "Do I remind you of anyone?"

Why was Mummy smiling at him, and Aunt Eliza, too, and Uncle Jim? Phillip shook his head.

"I am your grandfather's sister, Phillip. Your grandfather Turney!"

Phillip could not understand it. The idea of Gran'pa Turney having a sister was outside his world. "Oh," he said.

Grandpa Thacker sat at the other end of the table. He had a thin red face and a long beard down to the mother-of-pearl buttons of his black-braided waistcoat. He wore black mittens

on his hands; his fingers were pink and nobbly. He had a big
red handkerchief with white spots on it. Before saying grace he
blew his nose like a trumpet and then folded the handkerchief up
carefully before putting it in the pocket of his dark-brown velvet
coat. During grace everyone bent their heads but only Grannie
Thacker really shut her eyes, Phillip noticed, peeping from face
to face.

"For what we are about to receive the Lord make us truly
thankful" said Grandpa Thacker, and everyone said "Amen".
Phillip was thinking of how soon after breakfast would he be
able to go to the Pits and catch perch and pike there. He had
read all Father's books in the bookcase about fishing, and knew
about paternoster tackle, live bait, spinning for pike, and brandling worms for perch.

During breakfast he was so excited that he wanted to leave
after the porridge; but when Martha, an old woman, appeared
from the kitchen with a plateful of hot sausage rolls and he had
tasted one, he forgot about the pressing need to dig brandling
worms in what Percy called the trash heap up the garden.

The sausage rolls were very tasty, the meat being of a pig
recently killed, minced in the hand-machine and flavoured with
oatmeal and herbs. A corm of cut garlic smeared around the
mixing bowl had given a hungry flavour. The rolls were followed
by strawberry jam on home-made bread, with pats of butter,
not spread thin on slices as at home.

At last he could eat no more.

"Have you filled your belly, little fellow?" asked Grandpa
Thacker, looking down from the end of the table.

"Yes, thank you, Grandpa Thwacker," replied Phillip.
Everyone laughed, and Phillip wondered why.

"Theodore Thacker is my name, little fellow. Can you say
that, eh?"

"Yes, I think so."

"Can you say it six times over without fault, little fellow?
I'll gi'ee a ha'penny if you can."

Phillip remained silent.

"Go on, earn the money, Phillip. I would if I were you,"
Aunty Eliza urged him, across the table.

As he did not speak, Uncle Jim said: "And I'll give you a penny
if you can say 'Theodore Thacker threshed a stack on Saturday

and thickly thatched the stack with straw' six times without fault, my boy."

"I'm not so clever as you are, Uncle Whipper," said Phillip, and this time he knew why everyone laughed.

Uncle Jim said: "He's sharp as a needle, your lad, Hetty."

"Go on, try it," said Aunt Liz, but still Phillip did not attempt it. He wondered where the catch was. Grandpa Thresher gave the cane to Grandma Thacker-Thicker-Thocker-Thugger-B— but he must not think the word Cousin Ralph used, for it was a very bad word and meant something awful, like its sound.

If he said the bad word suddenly by mistake it would be terrible, nobody would think he was a good boy anymore, but find out what he really was, a bad boy all through. He was not *really* a bad boy, like Cousin Ralph, because he never really meant to be naughty, but always *pretended* to be naughty when the feeling like wire in him made him do the opposite. Mummy said Ralph was really naughty because Uncle Sidney had died, and Aunt Dorrie could not control him, his elder brother Hubert being away at boarding school.

The fishing was almost as wonderful as the books Phillip had read. Richard had allowed him to look at the fishing books in the glass bookcase, on condition that the boy washed his hands first, and put the books back in their places afterwards. Phillip thought that the Brickhill Pits were like the Longpond Father had told Mavis and him about during Sunday morning walks to Cutler's Pond at home. When he got his first bite Phillip was so excited that he gave such a big jerk, when his quill float rose up and then dived under, that the silvery fish went right over his head. It was a fish with red fins, gold eyes, silver-green scales and dark bars down its sides, while its back fin was like the top of a Roman's helmet, and spiky. He recognised it for a perch from the plate in Payne-Galways' book on Coarse Fishing. Percy told him to be careful of the spines, which could draw blood.

With trembling fingers Phillip put his fish in the pail half full of water, then threaded a fresh brandling on the hook as Percy had shown him. Very soon the float dipped under again, and he gave a flip with the end of the bamboo pole, and then cried out to Percy that he had hooked a big one. Percy came and showed him how to play it, holding the pole so that the strain was off the thin top and the fish tired itself out before you drew it in slowly to the side. Then telling Phillip to hold the pole, Percy stood on the plank laid on the reeds, stooped to hook his finger in the red gills, and lifted the perch out.

"That's a half pound if it's an ounce," said Percy. The perch splattered about, raising its back fin in agony; but Percy said it was done to stab his hand as he worked the hook with a thin wooden degorger out of its throat. Into the pail it went, with the other one.

Soon afterwards the fish ceased to bite. Percy said they had gone down into a deep hole to lie up. So the anglers moved to another pit. Little birds with yellow streaks behind their eyes were chattering and making skrittchering noises in the reeds. Percy said they were reed warblers. They made nests of spear-leaves plaited round stems of bullrushes. There were sand-martins flitting over the water. It was all marvellous and strange to Phillip. Best of all was the flashing sight of a greeny-blue kingfisher flying so straight and fast that he could only just see its wings beating. Percy said you could easily shoot one. They came up from the Satchville brook to fish in the pits, and always perched on the same places on the low willow branches. Phillip asked if he might shoot with his gun, and was overjoyed when Percy said he would let him.

"Pray don't say a word to a soul, for the Duke won't have kingfishers shot. He will find out if you do, for he has a hundred game-keepers. The Duke's park has a wall twelve miles round it, and there is every kind of pheasant in the world inside, besides ostriches, emus, bison, and hundreds of other animals."

Phillip thought the Duke must be a very big person, and with a very dark black beard, a sort of giant, or even ogre.

The next day was Sunday. Everyone put on best clothes. Phillip and Percy were told to keep in until they went to church, for they must not get their boots or their collars dirty.

Shortly after half past ten the party left for church, Gran'pa and Grannie, Uncle Jim, Aunt Liza, Percy, Polly, and Phillip. Doris had been left behind, for she had caught a cold. Her puckered face, mouthing "Mummy!" behind glass, appeared at an upper window, as the party walked down the village street. She had escaped from Martha, who picked her up a moment later, and took her back to bed, where she cried herself to sleep.

Phillip looked up at the great holly hedges they passed by. They were dark green, and tall and as smooth as the side of a house. When they left the village, and had passed other hedges and walls, they came to a stile, which led along a footpath to the church seen among trees. The bells were ringing out, and it seemed to Phillip that the swallows were the sound, blue steel clanging over the buttercups in the grass.

By the lych-gate leading into the churchyard stood an ugly old blob-nosed red-faced man in a red and blue uniform with silver buttons, and a cocked hat. He wore white gloves and had a smooth black stick with a silver knob on it. He touched his hat to all the men going in who wore tophats, Phillip noticed. Grandpa Thacker and Uncle Jim wore tophats, and they nodded to the old man and said: "Good morning, Beadle."

It was suddenly cold inside the church, where the ropes went up and down quickly as men pulled them. The bells stopped when the Beadle came in, and behind him were a lady and gentleman with some children wearing gloves. "That's the Squire," whispered Percy.

The Beadle opened the gate of what Uncle Jim had already told Phillip was the Lady Chapel.

Then a single bell tolled and the parson came in in white, and prayed.

The organ was like a piano, only it was squeaky and wheezy. The man playing it made his feet go up and down underneath and they stopped when the music stopped with a kind of gasp, followed by a muffled thump, and then a noise like a football bladder suddenly being untied. Phillip realized that the man's feet had been pumping air into it all the time. It wasn't really an organ after all, it was only a hurdy-gurdy! What a swindle!

Impressed by the importance of his discovery, he turned to Percy and whispered:

"Our church at home has a real organ, a hundred times as big as that little thing, which I wouldn't give a penny for."

A moment later he started, for the silver knob of the black stick had tapped him on the shoulder. Turning round, Phillip saw the Beadle looking at him.

"Sss-sh!" said the Beadle, as though some of the air of the hurdy-gurdy had escaped from him. Phillip sat as still as he could after that.

After singing and prayers, the Squire read the lesson, in a throaty voice. He had a lot of lines on his face, and white whiskers, and blew his nose on a red silk handkerchief before he started to read. He looked cleaner than the churchwarden at St. Cyprian's, the new church in red-brick in Charlotte Road, where sometimes he had to go on Sundays when Father was not taking him and Mavis for a walk.

The Squire looked like Mr. Newman, Grandpa Turney's friend who lived in a little house opposite the Randiswell Baths, with a house-keeper to look after him. Phillip called in to see Mr. Newman occasionally, because Mr. Newman always offered him a slice of cake and half a glass of port. Mr. Newman was a funny sort of man, for he treated him as though he were a grown up gentleman, instead of a boy, so Phillip thought there was something a little daft about Mr. Newman, who bowed to him when he shook hands. Mr. Newman called his house the Ginger Bread House, it certainly was very small compared with his own house. Though Beau Brickhill House was ever so much bigger than his own house.

Phillip thought of Mr. Newman as the Squire read from the Bible on a big brass stand with eagle's wings open on top of it. He was sorry when he said "Here endeth the first lesson", for now it was dull singing, with the foot-flapping man working away at the hurdy-gurdy.

The rector's voice was just like a rook's cawing in the trees of the Backfield. The Devil, my friends, is waiting to *Caw! Caw!* We may deceive ourselves, my friends, but we do not *Caw! Caw!* For what shall it profit a man if he *Caw! Caw!* Phillip remembered going to the theatre to see Uncle Hugh play his violin. Aunt Dorrie, with Bertie, Ralph, and Jerry, and Mummy and Grandpa and Grandma all sat in a row in red seats. Mummy said Uncle Hugh was nervous and not a bit like himself, oh what a pity, what a pity, after the people high up in the gallery above had whistled and thrown pennies on the stage. Mummy said "Clap hard! Clap hard!" and they had all clapped, and he had cried out "Caw on! Caw on!" after, but the curtain had come down, and everyone had laughed. He had not known why, until Mummy said it should have been "On Caw!" the other way round. Grandpa Turney had said to Mummy as they were riding home in the tram, "Poor silly fellow, will my son's conceit never let him learn?" That had been a long time ago, at the New Cross Empire.

Caw caw! my friends. It was like waiting for an egg to boil, for there was an hour glass on an iron bracket fixed to the wall beside the pulpit. It made Phillip think of the ostrich's egg on the table in the front room at home, brought back by Uncle Hugh from South Africa as a present to Mummy. He tried to see the sand falling from the top shiny glass to the bottom one, but it was too dark in the church, as the windows were stained glass with pictures of the disciples and Christ in blue, red, green and yellow.

After looking at these, Phillip searched through the prayer-book for interesting bits, a fruitless task on previous occasions, but one nevertheless hopefully undertaken. There were only Collects, one of which he had to learn for Mummy every Sunday afternoon; Psalms with strange names and unreal words to God; Burial at Sea; Baptism of Infants; The Marriage Service; and that "final refuge of the destitute", as Uncle Hugh called it, to read people a man or woman may not marry.

A man may not marry his grandmother.

At long last came the noise of people stirring as the parson turned and said: "And now to God the Father, God the Son and God the Holy Ghost", the most welcome moment in church, except the start of the going-out music. How bright was the sun outside, how blue the sky, how green the grass among the grave stones. Everybody was raising hats and curtsying to the Squire and his wife, and the coachman and a footman in tall hats and white breeches with shiny black boots stood by the shiny carriage.

Phillip thought the Beadle was just like a blue-and-red beetle fly climbing up the grasses in the Backfield in summer.

When the people were gone, Mother said she wanted to look at the tombstones in the churchyard. "Look, Sonny, at all your Turney ancestors, they go back hundreds of years." But Phillip slipped away with Percy, because he wanted to see a jackdaw who could talk, after its tongue had been slit, said Percy.

On the way back they stopped to look at the wicker cage hanging on a cottage wall, beside a damson tree. Phillip hoped it would say something, perhaps swear, like a parrot, but the bird only looked anxiously at them. It seemed to be huddled, Phillip thought. They left it, and arrived home first, to see the chicken for dinner turning on the jack-spit before the parlour fire. It turned first one way, then the other, slowly, while the clockwork in the brass case went *click* before every turn. Martha poured spoonfuls of fat from the tray below over it, to baste it, she said. Phillip wondered what it did with the lump on its behind, which Percy said was the parson's nose. It looked a funny thing.

The day before Phillip had seen a big white cockerel hanging head downwards inside a cupboard in the kitchen. Its legs were tied together with string, which was looped over a nail. Upon asking Martha why it was like that, its comb so red and its eye flicking, he had been told that the blood must all run to its head before it was killed, to make the flesh white. Phillip had wanted to let it go, it looked so unhappy, but Percy had said: "Pray don't, for Grannie likes white meat", and then Percy had closed the cupboard door again.

Was this the cockerel, on the spit, he enquired; and on being told yes, remarked that it had shrunk a lot.

In the afternoon the five children went into the garden, for the grown-ups wished to be quiet. They were not allowed to play croquet, as it was Sunday, but otherwise they might do as they liked, provided they made not a sound. Phillip wanted to explore the loft over the stables, where were wonderful things to be seen, all piled and standing about there, and covered with dust and cobwebs. Percy had taken him up there once, and he had seen a stuffed fox, birds in glass cases, a pair of riding boots with wood inside them, piles of old books and magazines, an Aunt Sally dummy for making clothes on, besides other things in drawers and cupboards.

Percy said they could not go. "Dad says the stable loft is out of bounds on Sundays."

"But he won't know, doesn't he go to sleep in his armchair on Sundays, in his sanctum?"

"He hasn't got a sanctum, he sleeps in the billiard room, Phil. All the same, I ain't going to go in the loft if my Dad says No."

This puzzled Phillip. Why did Percy always do as he was told? He went to the stable door, but Percy said, "Pray don't, pray don't!", so Phillip went into the garden. Percy said the trees along the walls were peach, greengage, and quince. There were box-hedge borders to the paths, lots of paths. One led to the Maze, where there was a seat with a sundial before it.

Here the girls went to sit, in the sun and out of the wind, playing mothers with their dolls. Mavis was now seven, and the eldest of the three. Her cousin Polly was Doris's age, five. Polly Pickering was stronger, lither, more direct, merrier than the round-faced, white-skinned Doris, who, her father declared, took after her German grandmother. Polly had the Irish colouring of her great-grandmother, who had been Thomas Turney's mother: red cheeks, dark curly hair, grey eyes. Polly had a definite will of her own, where her parents were concerned. Polly would do only what Polly would do.

On the lawn, Phillip and Percy, both nine years of age, were playing at Public Speaking. Phillip had suggested the game, after the manner of the various Sunday afternoon addresses to be heard on the Hill, near what was called the Socialist Oak. Standing on a rustic-work table, Phillip wearing deerstalker harangued his audience of Percy, sitting on the iron seat under the cherry tree. When Percy's turn came he was allowed to wear the cap, while Phillip was the audience. Phillip was thinking of the gun when he lent the cap to his cousin.

The game was to see who could make the funniest speech. Inevitably the tone, or quality, fell off. At last, so amused were the boys at their own competitive wit that while Phillip stood on the table Percy stood on the seat, both speechifying anti-phonally, one replying to the other, and each trying to cause the most laughter. The three girls came out of the Maze to listen. Wilder, more outrageous, became the repartee.

"I am speaking to dogs, whose hind legs go up like railway signals as they run on the pavement and——"

"I am talking to cows, who never wipe their——"

"My friends, have you ever tasted soup made of——"

"What does the Beadle feed on? If you turn up a cow's pancake you will see lots of little beadles underneath——"

The three girls shrieked with laughter. Thus excited, Phillip became more outrageous. He was about to imitate a dog on the table top, when to his dismay and immediate deflation he saw the face of Grandpa Thacker looking at him from in front of the summer house. Oh lor', would he be sent to bed, for rudeness, and on Sunday, too?

"Oh my sainted aunt," he said. "Percy, quick, did he hear what I said just now? Anyhow, swear I said only 'pancake', not 'pat', won't you?"

"It's all right, Phil," called out Polly. "Grandpa's deaf, and can't hear a word."

Immediately Phillip's spirits were inflated. "Well, my friends," he concluded, "you have heard my policy for thatching Theodore Thacker's trousers with tar, tintacks, and—cow-shakes." He waggled a fore-finger at them, in the manner of old Mr. Chivers, the thin, blue-faced, gentle Altruist, by the Socialist Oak. "I will now give you, if you will be so good as to accept it, a tract dealing with my little address." And lifting Mr. Chivers's imaginary, faded yellow straw hat, with its threadbare black band around it, Phillip jumped down from the table.

The septuagenarian Theodore Thacker, who had watched "the little fellow's" antics with keen amusement, went back to the house to report that the children were playing quietly on the lawn and not making a sound, bless their little hearts.

Chapter 21

TABLE FOR A PARROT

RICHARD was content during the two weeks his family was away. A man of precision and regular habit, he found the time passed pleasantly enough. His breakfast was simple: shredded wheat with milk, an Empire apple with brown bread and butter, two cups of tea. Since the family was away, he had used the portion of the housekeeping money for himself, by agreement with Hetty; and so he had given himself a treat of having a light luncheon at an A.B.C. in the middle of the day, instead of taking his usual tin box of sandwiches.

He continued to spend as little as possible on himself, deeming it his first duty to think of the family, to provide for his wife should anything happen to him. His life was assured for five hundred pounds under an endowment policy maturing in his sixtieth year, with accrued bonuses every year; if he died meanwhile the capital sum would be available for Hetty and her children.

Richard did not think of them as his children; they were Hetty's children.

While the family was away, he thought much of Hetty, Phillip, Mavis, and baby Doris. In physical absence a happy sense of their existence pervaded the quiet regularity of the house, to which he returned between half-past six and seven o'clock of an evening, in daylight. After grilling his two kippers under the gas, while the kettle heated on the top of the grill—or toast under the grill if it were to be boiled eggs—he sat down at the kitchen table, to enjoy his meal, with *The Daily Trident*, that infallible companion of his spiritual life, propped up against the milk jug before him. Immediately after the meal, he washed up, leaving sink and scullery table clean, cloth rinsed and wrung out to dry, everything in its place. The next operation was the cleaning and polishing of his black boots for the morrow morning. The Japanese blacking was in a deep and narrow earthenware jar, a black liquid which had to be applied with a stick, after stirring.

275

Applied evenly by a brush, the boots were left to dry; later they were polished, and put in their place in the row under the kitchen dresser.

There were three tasks he had set himself to accomplish while the family was away. First, to hang the pictures which brother John had sent him from Rookhurst. John had written to ask if Richard would care to have them, they were of little or no value, apart from a sentimental one. They were a series of steel engravings of naval battles in the Napoleonic wars. There was also the meeting of Wellington and Blücher on the field of Waterloo. They had hung in the schoolroom during Richard's childhood, and as a link with the past were dear to him.

The steel engravings, in their clouded brownish-yellow frames of the hue of malacca cane, arrived by Carter Paterson. The crate was standing in the lower passage to the sitting-room, waiting to be opened when he had purchased the necessary hanging fasteners.

The second task was to rig up an electrical timing device, by which he hoped to be awakened at twenty minutes after seven of a morning.

The third was to make a small table to hold a very special object that he was expecting in the middle of the second week. It was to be a surprise for the children on their arrival home. It was an African parrot, which his brother Hilary was bringing back in the *Phasiana*.

Richard set about hanging the engravings first, to get them out of the way. When he took them out of their case, many memories came upon him. For a moment the impact of old time was so great that he sat down on the stairs to try and recapture the life gone by; but always such attempts were vain; after the first poignant glimpse, they were gone the instant he tried to find them in the camera obscura of the mind. It was as though one almost got outside of Time, in a terrifying instant, in the opening and closing of a shutter. Indeed, life was a series of pictures, altering every instant of Time; a flow like a river, always going on, but never the same at any given moment. And when a man or an animal died, that series of records perished with the individual. How could memory have any validity, since it was entirely personal?

It was never any good to think like that. It was weakness, a

sort of sickness. He might be a weakling, as Father had more
than once declared, but at least he had tried always to face up to
life as it was.

Richard stared at the engravings, his sight unfocus'd. He was
lost in poignant feeling. He was overcome, and went into the
front garden, to feel the sun on his face. Its touch restored him,
and he returned indoors to consider where the half-dozen faded
and varnished engravings should hang, and in what order. He
lined them up against the wall, and stood back to survey them.

There was really little difference between them. All were
crowded with detail of sail, cannon, struggling men in disastrous
attitudes—Copenhagen, Nile, Toulon, Cadiz, Teneriffe, Trafalgar—Battle, Murder, and Sudden Death—horrible pictures
really! No wonder John wanted to get rid of the beastly things.
To think that these pictures had fired his imagination as a small
boy! How much more pleasant would be pastoral scenes, water-
colours of the downs, the meadows, the beech hangers and the
thorn-grown tumuli.

However, up they should go, hanging on their copper gimp,
seedy relics of the past, the cobwebs black with old dust still on
their backs. As for Wellington and Blücher, and the butchery of
Waterloo, that could be got rid of in Hetty's front room. There
was a space over the sideboard.

The hanging of the pictures, after careful brushing and cleaning of the frames, left enough time to go upon the Hill for a walk.
It was a fine evening, the sun going down in a clear sky. Several
kites were waggling their paper tails in the evening breeze, but
Mr. Muggeridge's was not among them. He had stolen a march
on him, having taken to box kites in series, and his were the
champions so far; but let him wait! Richard had a surprise in
store for Mr. Muggeridge. He intended to appear one day with
the new pattern of double-box kites. He had seen and ordered
at the Civil Service Stores in Queen Victoria Street, a kite six
feet wide and another, the pilot, four feet wide, of the new design.

Next evening, after two ounces of pressed beef and a lettuce,
followed by a slice of Dundee cake, Richard tackled the second
job. He had invented an electric alarm to be worked by the big
wall clock at the head of the stairs. This involved a certain length
of thin copper wire, enwound with green silk for insulation,
being taken along the picture-hanging cornice above the stairs,

and led down the frame of the bedroom door, and through a hole
in the frame to the bedroom within. The wire was then led down
the inner frame to a small switch conveniently placed by his side
of the double bed.

At the clock end, another wire was attached to the pivot of the
hour hand, while its twin, to complete the circuit, was secured to
a thin strip of brass foil a third of the way between the black
Roman numerals VII and VIII on the enamelled face. When
the tip of the lower hand met the brass strip, it made contact;
the circuit was closed between the motor of the alarum bell and
the wet cells on a shelf above the coal-cellar; and when he switched
on beside the bed, the bell should ring.

It was finished at ten minutes after seven. The clock ticked on.
Richard sat on the stairs, and read *The Daily Trident*, waiting for
the little lilac spark to leap, like a kiss, between the short steel
hour-hand of his clock and the thin brass strip on the rim. At
twenty past seven, exactly, the *liaison* was made: the alarm rang.

There is no satisfaction like that of creative achievement.
Richard went for a walk on the Hill, remaining to see the golden
showers, the silver plumes and coloured balls arising from the
Sydenham ridge in the first Brock's Firework Display of the
season at the Crystal Palace. Somehow the scene had lost its
former glamour; the shrill cries of children sitting on the grass,
were infinitely pathetic to his way of thinking. What were they
born for, but to whiten with marble greater areas of the ossuaries
in London's yellow clay? Conscious of his extreme loneliness,
Richard returned down the broad gully, hearing with some comfort the bells of the wethers in the fold beside the grammar
school. Sheep still grazed on the Hill in spring and early summer.

He was not entirely alone, however: the inside pages of *The
Daily Trident* remained to be read. His newspaper, folded, awaited
him upon the inner ledge of the window by the front door, held
there by the brass arm of the extension fastening. The arm was
never moved, for the window was never opened, to be a tempta-
tion to thieves. There the *Trident* waited for him, beside the
clothes brush, companion of the armchair.

That evening he sat in the front room for a change, and played
several discs of the Polyphone. His favourites were *Over the Waves*,
the Radezsky March, the Austrian National Anthem, and the
Witches' Dance from "Macbeth".

After his *soirée musicale* he went down to the sitting-room, and smoked a pipe. While he was reading the *Trident* he heard, faint and far away, the sounds of a violin. Hugh Turney was playing in the corresponding room next door. Later, when he went into the dewy garden to look for slugs and snails on his new lettuces, Richard heard the remote throb of a harp from the house below, where Mr. Bigge was dreaming that he dwelt in marble halls.

Richard thought, with a tinge of self-scorn, that once he, too, had had musical ambitions. The violoncello now stood against the brick wall under the sitting-room floor, lowered there through the trap-door in the floor of the lavatory. And there it would lie for ever, so far as he was concerned, a thing of the past.

He longed for his family to be home again; but as he longed, his heart also was heavy. It would have to remain so, he reflected, until things changed in his home.

The next evening he set about his third task, that of making the table for the parrot cage. His tool chest and bench were in the workroom next the bathroom; and here he worked during the succeeding nights, happy in his creation. The exercise was beneficial; life glowed in his whole body, revealing his true self in the gentle, kindly expression of the face. He was thinking of the pleasure the parrot would give to the children. There was nothing to disturb him as he cogitated, measured, marked, sawed, gouged, tapped, and fitted. The act of planing seasoned oak brought a pleasant sweat upon the pores of his skin, releasing nicotine and salts which had been burdening the stream of blood within, and thereby his mind.

When the table was finished he took it out in the garden to rub it with sandpaper before feeding the wood with linseed oil. He stood it near the elm tree, which as a sucker had arisen in four twigs from the ground, and now grew four-boled like two interlocked heads of an Exmoor stag, one trunk higher and straighter than the rest. It was strong enough to support one end of the hammock.

The wooden fence shutting off Mr. Bigge's garden was low from the prospect of the upper garden; since all the gardens, and indeed the foundations of the houses, of Hillside Road were made in a series of terraces. Mr. Bigge's Virginia creeper covered his side of the fence, including the posts and wires of the extension.

Behind his lattice of green and ruddy leaves he worked in his garden without being overlooked.

Josiah Bigge was glazing a small greenhouse at the bottom of his garden. He had recently bought it second-hand from a shop in Randiswell, which had an outside stall covered by a tattered awning. The shop was kept by a gipsy named Nightingale, a sweep by trade and a general dealer of old things, which he collected, and delivered after re-sale, in a shallow drawn by a donkey. Usually his trade was done in the lesser streets of the district.

Mr. Bigge, as he passed by the shop one day, had stopped to examine a notice on a sooty dog-eared card stuck in the window.

SMALL

GLAS SOUSE

FOR SALE

AST WITHN

CHEAP

Mr. Bigge had asked within, or rather, since he had a dread of fleas, upon the threshold. Mrs. Nightingale, feather-hatted, and clad in purple, green, and black silks, had taken him to the garden of an old wooden cottage, standing at the corner of a new row of brick houses. The weatherboard cottage was to be pulled down, the old couple owning it having died. Already the damson trees had been cut down; they had been the last of their kind to be seen from Randiswell Road.

Mr. Bigge had bought the glass-house for five shillings, on condition that the sweep took it carefully to pieces, and re-erected the frame in his garden for a further half-crown. Mr. Bigge made a further condition of sale. It was not to be delivered in the donkey shallow. Mrs. Nightingale had quite understood; a donkey shallow was not respectable in a high-class road like Hillside. She said that her old man would borrow a coal cart and 'oss, the same cart what took coals up Hillside, and deliver the glas souse on Sa'erday ar'ernoon.

Politely concurring, with little incipient sucking and bee-like noises coming from his bearded lips, Josiah Bigge, in frock coat and top hat, had gone on his way to his business in the High Street, his eyes shining with thoughts of the potted plants he would grow in his new conservatory. There would be *philodendron cordatum*, the house vine; *sansevieria*, the bow-string hemp, called vulgarly mother-in-law's tongue; *tradescantia*, the wandering Jew; the rubber plants, *ficus decora*, and its sister *benjamina; cissus rhombifolia*, the grape-vine ivy; and best of all, the Lilies— *arum, ricardia*, and *callas*.

The following Saturday afternoon a coal cart had crunched up the flinty surface of Hillside Road, driven by the well-soaped sweep, a clean bandanna round his neck, in his best suit of whipcord, flap pockets to jacket, stove-pipe trousers crenellated from knee to heel. By tea-time the little framework had been erected at the bottom of the garden of "Montrose"; by six o'clock Josiah Bigge, green baize apron round his waist and gardening hat, a varnished straw with turned-down brim, upon his head, was busy with the putty knife. He had beside him, in addition to the boxes of clear glass panes cut to measure, a smaller box in which were a number of blue and red lengths of glass, thin slips of waste from the stained glass windows of the new brick church which had been built in Charlotte Road, on ground that had been allotment holdings for half a century. With these lengths of coloured glass, Mr. Bigge intended to adorn the lower borders of what he called his Plantarium.

On the higher side of the fence Richard was busy, that Saturday evening, with sandpaper and linseed oil rag. Mrs. Bigge, looking down from the window of an upper room, watched the two men busily at work. Like two boys, she thought approvingly. A hobby kept a hubby out of mischief. Now would it not be a neighbourly thing to invite Mr. Maddison in for a cup of tea or cocoa after his labours? And might it not lead to a more neighbourly relationship? Mr. Maddison was, she considered, a man who kept himself far too much to himself. Every man needed the company of other men at times, to keep him from brooding.

Mrs. Bigge's motive did not, she told herself, arise out of mere curiosity, but from consideration for Hetty who, poor little woman, had much to put up with. Had Hetty not told her how she dreaded the nightly games of chess her husband expected of her—games that she could never win, to Mr. Maddison's exasperation? Josiah, on the other hand, was a good player of chess, one usually forced to play against himself, since he had no one else to play with. Again, Mr. Maddison had a fine tenor voice—she had heard Hetty accompanying him for *The Arab's Farewell to his Steed*—and St. Mary's Church in the High Street needed new men in the choir.

Mrs. Bigge had a natural inclination towards benevolence; she tried to make the world a little better than she found it. If the two men could be friends, she was sure it would help matters for Hetty. Josiah needed taking out of himself in some ways; he felt he had missed some things in life. Only the other day Josie was saying he had never learned to fly a kite, and now he feared it might be too late to learn.

Animated by good intentions, Amelia Bigge arranged her hair in the spotted Chippendale looking-glass standing on her chest of drawers. By the looking-glass stood a Chelsea china ring-stand, a long thin hand-painted porcelain box for hat-pins, her mother's two vinaigrettes, and a pin-cushion. Having tidied up, Mrs. Bigge went downstairs, and out into the garden to the steps, made of old railway sleepers, under the arch of entwined honeysuckle and yellow ivy, which led down to the path at the end of which her hubby was working, quiet as a solitary bee. Whisperings ensued.

Josiah's gentle "Yes my love," and frequent noddings, indicated that he agreed with everything Amelia suggested. If ever two minds thought as one, they did between this husband and wife. Nevertheless a problem was presented: who was to ask Mr. Maddison in? And what would be the most suitable time to ask him? And should the invitation be spoken directly over the garden fence, thus revealing that they had known he was on the other side of the screen of Virginia creeper? If that were to be done, might it not be an affront to privacy, the purpose for which the creeper was planted in the first place? Perhaps Mr. Maddison would not like to be addressed in that manner? Would it be more fitting to write him a little note, and slip it through the letter box? And supposing, my love, that Mr. Maddison does not really want to know us? Yes yes, yes yes, we must not be too precipitant.

Four years before, when Mr. Maddison's little wife had had scarlet fever, Mr. Maddison had shown a distinct friendly side, and Mrs. Bigge had spontaneously been able to suggest to Mr. Maddison that she would be only too pleased to hand him two meals a day over the garden fence; but since that time, Mr.

Maddison had gradually closed up, and there had been nothing beyond a bow, a "How d'you do" and the weather.

The whispering and bee-sipping noises ended in Amelia Bigge's plan to wait by the fence up above, by the back door of the conservatory, and from there to pop up, or rather out, and, as Mr. Maddison was walking up with his table to the open french windows, she would invite him in.

There she waited, and thence she popped a few minutes later. Richard bowed, and agreed that it was a fine evening, before modestly qualifying Mrs. Bigge's remark that he had made a very nice table.

"Oh, it will be sufficient for the purpose, Mrs. Bigge."

Mrs. Bigge restrained herself from asking what was the purpose; instead she said, "I have some cocoa on the stove to heat, Mr. Maddison, and Josiah and I were wondering if you would care to come in and have a cup with us, and perhaps a game of chess with my husband afterwards, or are you too busy?"

"Thank you, Mrs. Bigge, I shall be delighted to come. I will just wash my hands, and shall be ready in say, ten minutes, if that is convenient?"

"That will do very nicely, Mr. Maddison!"

Richard was feeling content with life. He had made his table without committing a single mistake, and the wastage of wood had been of the minimum. The sawdust had been carefully swept up and put in a paper bag, for use on the bottom of the cage when the parrot should arrive. He put his tools back in the chest, after smearing the steel parts with a thin film of oil to preserve them against rust. He was pleased that he had done what he had planned to do. The varnished steel-engravings on the wall above the stairs had settled down against the varnished wallpaper; old and new together giving a feeling which each, by themselves, had lacked before. His patent electric clock alarum operated without fault.

He had been up in the attic earlier that evening, carrying a candle; he had thought to unpack the bull's-eye lantern from its place in the Japanned uniform case, but his hands had been dusty from his work, and he had not wanted to spoil the uniform within. This, since Richard had come to know his dead father through his journals, had become almost sacred to him. He now had a sympathy denied to him during his father's life. He realised now, through his own experience of being married, that his father had had quite a lot to put up with from a wife who had not really been able to share his life, but had thought only of the children. Why, if his own Mother had not shown such a preference for himself, had not wanted to shelter him so obviously from Father, he might have been able to give Father the affection he needed!

This change of view, or emotion, had affected other earlier feelings. Nowadays Richard, seeing himself as hopelessly middle-aged and done for in life—he would be forty in two years' time—often felt himself critical of his mother. Her presence in his mind was a dissolving figment, somewhere near Hetty.

The visit to No. 10 was at first pleasant to Richard. Everything in the room looked new and alive to him, after the energetic use of his body in the polishing of the table. He thought that Mrs. Bigge's daughter was a jolly young woman, and when it was suggested that he should sing a song—"You have such a nice voice, you know, Mr. Maddison"—he returned with alacrity, after only the least protest, back to his house to get the sheet-music from on top of the piano in the front room. An impulse to carry in the Polyphone as well came upon him; he hesitated between the wish and the thought that they might consider him to be taking advantage of their kindness. Besides, the weight of the thing, together with the steel discs, was too much to carry. Anyway, he must not stay long, as tonight there was an evening newspaper, *The Pall Mall Gazette*, to be read as well as the *Trident*, before going to bed.

As on previous occasions, the Arab said farewell to his Steed in a wave-like series of throaty tenor sounds, to the piano accompaniment of Miss Bigge's licenciate (Royal College of Music) playing. The Steed in Richard's mind was not wholly equine; it was a mixture of horse, old Starley Rover, and new, magnificent, all-black, gold-lined Sunbeam with Little Oil Bath, which he had admired and desired at the Stanley Cycle Show in the Agricultural Hall of Islington the previous November. He had half a mind to buy one next year. It would last a lifetime. Farewell to the Starley Rover!

Afterwards, Mr. and Mrs. Bigge sang their favourite duet, *O that we two were Maying*, by Gounod. They stood behind their daughter, the Long and the Short of it, thought Richard. He did not know the feeling that they felt to flow between them, as it had flowed steadily, almost sedately in its own assurance, since the first meeting at the Band of Hope garden party in St. Mary's vicarage grounds in the golden days of the Rev. the Hon. Legge, who had been the first to congratulate Josiah Bigge and Amelia Tidy on their betrothal.

After the singing, Norah Bigge played *The Lost Chord*, followed by her best test-piece, Chopin's *Polonaise Militaire*, concluding, as was suitable on Saturday night, on a quieter note, *Beethoven's Farewell to the Piano*.

As the lid was quietly closed Mrs. Bigge beamed with pride at her accomplished daughter, remarking that the world would be a happier place if all children could learn the pianoforte when they were young. This remark put Richard on his guard, lest it lead to a more direct suggestion in regard to Phillip and Mavis.

But nothing of that nature was to follow. Chess was suggested, and the well-brought-up Miss Bigge murmured about some letters to be written, as an excuse to retire to her own room. The chess-board was set out, and Mrs. Bigge prepared to follow her daughter upstairs, with a more direct "I'll leave the gentlemen to their game now, and may the best man win!" At the door she said,

"I do hope that Mrs. Maddison and the children are well, Mr. Maddison, and enjoying themselves? Oh dear, I quite forgot to enquire before. How are the little dears?"

Richard replied that Hetty was well, and had written that they were enjoying themselves.

"That's right! They will be coming back soon, I expect."

"Yes," said Richard, "they are to return at the end of next week."

"The country air will do them all so much good, Mr. Maddison. I was telling my hubby here the other day, that I thought at first they were off to Scotland, little Phil wearing that old deerstalker hat," went on Mrs. Bigge, happily. "He was so excited at the prospect of getting a bat to stuff, for his museum, he said. He looked rather like a bat himself, his little face over the fence, with those big flaps tied over the crown of the hat."

Then observing Mr. Maddison's face, she realised that perhaps Phillip had taken the hat without his father knowing anything about it; and with a discreet loud cough she left the room, to hurry upstairs to Norah and confide in her daughter the fears that possessed her.

Mr. Bigge won the game easily. Soon afterwards, having thanked Mrs. Bigge for a most pleasant evening, Richard left the house and returned to his own. He locked the music of his song in his desk in the sitting-room, feeling that he wanted never to sing it again. Then he climbed through the trap-door in the bathroom ceiling and, finding that neither the hat nor the lantern were in the uniform trunk, his face became set in a reserve of suffering, that he could never, never, never trust anyone in his family.

Chapter 22

RICHARD'S RIDE

On the following Monday Hilary Maddison arrived before the sign of the silver moon hanging over the doorway in Haybundle Street and, entering through the massive mahagony double swing doors, found himself in the Town Department, with its long mahogany desk curving round the corner. He saw Richard immediately, working with others at a long double desk with its ground-glass screen between the two rows of writing figures.

Richard saw his younger brother at the same time, and getting down from his stool, walked over to Hilary with a slight smile upon his face. After greetings, Hilary realised that Dick would not want to be kept very long from his work, and so suggested he should come back for him at his lunch hour, and take him out. Richard demurred; he was not used to such an irruption in his life. Hilary saw this, and as he had plenty of people he wanted to see, he did not press his older brother, but suggested he should call for him at six o'clock, and take him out to dinner at his club. This invitation likewise disturbed Richard, because he had no evening clothes, and furthermore, he knew that Hilary was a member of the Voyagers, to which some of the directors of the office belonged. It was not a place, he considered, where he should show himself.

"Well, anyway," said Hilary, observing his brother's hesitation, "I'll call for you at six o'clock, old man, and we'll go somewhere quiet. Then I'll run you home afterwards with the parrot. Six o'clock then. Au revoir!"

At six o'clock there was a surprise for Richard. A motor car stood outside the Moon Fire Office, shaking with metallic heart-beats. It was painted blue, and lined-out in red, the colour of the russian leather upholstery of the high padded seats. A crowd was collected about it. Two polished brass oil-lamps gave the panting monster a look of the East. Richard thought of Aladdin's lamp. Hilary was to him a sort of wonder boy, visitant from an Eldorado of open skies and deep blue water, coral isle and pagoda, gold and lapis lazuli. By contrast, he himself was an automaton of sooty air, imprisoning railway carriage, a failure of drab suburban existence.

"Jump in, Dick, she's a good ride. An improved model of Panhard et Levassor, with poppet valve, *and* a grilled-tube radiator! She's a continental, of course, and absolutely reliable."

"Wherever did you get her, Hilary?"

"In Marseilles, on the way home. She was a present from a Nabob. Pretty, isn't she?"

"A *present*, Hilary? It must be worth a small fortune!"

"A mere flea-bite to a Bombay merchant nowadays. I did him a small service, and he was duly grateful," Hilary laughed.

"Am I expected to ride in this?" asked Richard next. He was considerably disturbed, and a little afraid. What would happen to the family if he were killed?

"Yes, safe as houses."

"But do you understand the London traffic, Hilary?" Richard had always imagined his brother travelling by rickshaw in the East. "What about the horses, Hilary?"

"Horses never so much as looked at me, coming here from the Voyagers Club in Pall Mall."

This was true. The cab and bus and dray horses were more used to the new style of horseless vehicles upon the cobbles and wood-blocks of the twentieth-century street surfaces of London than was Richard, who, so far, had not trusted himself to a steam-driven omnibus.

It was therefore with some trepidation that he climbed up and into the lobster-blue unfamiliarity and, feeling much as a lobster with human mentality might have felt before entering hot water, seated himself upon the crimson leather. Once there, his fears lessened. It had such a wealthy feel and look about it, a solid assured feel, a Board Room atmosphere of Directors, famous and noble names signing policies placed, with silent respect, before them on the big Board Room table, swiftly to be blotted, removed, and replaced. After twenty years of sedentary life Richard felt a slight sense of importance, mingled with guilt, finding himself seated in such a thing of wealth and distinction, and before the very entrance to the Head Office in Haybundle Street, not a stone's throw from the Royal Exchange and the Bank of England.

Such constrictions of behaviour in the mind would have been unintelligible to Hilary. His mind had been formed upon the reflections of another world altogether. Aboard ship he had made many friends among the temporary inhabitants of state-room and promenade deck, one or two of whom had taken to the handsome young officer for his gaiety of spirit combined with a sense of propriety and unfailing good manners, which never for a moment permitted the ships' officer to presume upon an accidental acquaintanceship. The world upon a great liner of the Merchant Navy of the most powerful nation ruling the seven seas, carrying members of the richest country upon earth, was one of relief and stimulation for the passengers. They lived a fabulous existence after the first few days of every voyage. Freed from terrestrial perplexity, freed from contact with the world of business, from the complications of ordinary human relationships, the healthy among the voyagers were translated to another plane. They were guests of sempiternal sun, sea and air. Wireless telegraphy had not yet been installed in the "floating white cities" of the MacKarness Line. Prices of bourse and stock exchange had not yet come through the ether, to extrude from ticking machines in worms of tape, to become parasitical upon the mind, to rugate the brow, to cause fingernails to drum on state-room tables in indecision. The seas of China, India, and vast Pacific Ocean were still remote and paradisal.

Hilary Maddison was always easily conscious that he was armigerous, that he was the son of a gentleman, a landed proprietor; and any defects in his own education due to later impoverishment of the family had been made good, in his own estimation, by the proper use of the faculty of imitation. The great ones of the earth, ambassadors, viceroys, and governors-general, walking the promenade deck of the *Phasiana*, had been his models. His ambition was to be recognised and accepted as one of themselves. This had been achieved in sufficient manner. Standing invitations to houses in London and the country had followed; a noble marquis had put him up for the Voyagers; Sir Robert MacKarness himself had proposed him for the Oriental. And Hilary had his own home in Hampshire, conveniently near the Solent, where Bee, his beautiful wife, welcomed him after his voyages to the Far East. Profiting from advice given by the more communicative among the passengers,

Hilary had seen his investments more than trebled since the turn of the century; and that was only the beginning, in his own estimation.

Beside him in the Panhard et Lavassor sat Richard, clutching the edge of the seat, his mind between anxiety and pleasure, and with memory of that horseless carriage of long ago, bombarded by the filth of the streets—nearly ten years, a whole decade, previously. It really was a pleasant experience to be passing the Royal Exchange in such elevation. What would the fellows at the office think, who had seen him in such splendid state? It was remarkably smooth to ride in, quite different from what he had imagined; the propulsive noises of the engine did not disturb one, as he had thought, nor were they at all vibratory in the frame. The feeling of speed was very great; it was advisable to hold to the brim of one's hat; the thing simply sped past cabs and carts and omnibuses, doing at times nearly twenty miles an hour. In a moment they were under St. Paul's, and hardly had one time to say Jack Robinson when there was Ludgate Circus, and the vista of Fleet Street before one. Here they had to wait, for the cross traffic over Blackfriars Bridge, while the brass lamps jigged up and down. Hilary pulled on the long handle of the hand-brake.

"Nice little motor, isn't she, Dick?"

"Well, I certainly see it from a different angle now, Hilary, though there is comparatively no dust in the London streets, I'll admit. In Kent nowadays, when one is out for a cycle ride . . ."

"Ha ha, the thing is to leave your dust behind for others, Dick!"

That is all very well, thought Richard, who more than once had been one of the others to be half-suffocated in white dust kicked up by the beastly things on country roads. Road hogs, he called them.

Hilary drove up Fleet Street, and along the Strand, turning down a side-street in order to leave his Panhard in a space beside the new gardens on the Embankment. He intended to take Dick into the Hotel Cecil. They alighted. He mentioned it to his brother, who showed reluctance.

"I'm not used to such places, Hilary, old chap."

"As you like, Dick. There's a comfortable little place in the Strand, Simpson's, where the saddle of mutton is good. Or

Rule's, if you like, there's more life there, theatrical people, you know, only they come in later. How about Romano's?"

"Will your motor car be all right? Won't anyone steal it?"

"Good Lord, no. There's only four like it in England. No thief would be able to dispose of a Panhard et Lavassor! Hi, there! Keep an eye on my motor, will you?"

The cab-runner sprang forward. Hilary had selected him from others waiting at the back of the hotel because his boots were polished and his clothes brushed.

"Keep an eye on her, will you? Keep the boys away, and don't let anyone go near her." Hilary jerked his head towards a subdued queue of poor children lined up along a wall for the kitchen waste that would be available round about midnight.

"Leave it to me, sir. Thank you, sir," said the man, eager gratitude in his face.

Simpson's it was. A sherry before the soup, another glass with it, to prepare the stomach for the roast. And what mutton it was, brought on a wheeled trolley, under a German silver cover, a flame of alcohol licking the chafing dish below. Generous thick slices, carved by the under-chef. As the trolley moved on, a waiter discreetly dobbed two tablespoons of redcurrent jelly upon each plate; another followed with baked potatoes, floury under their crisp brown crusts, breaking at a touch; and a braised onion as large as a *boule* used in play on the Mediterranean coast where the onions had been grown.

For wine, Hilary chose a claret, which was carried to the table horizontally in a wicker basket, for the dark-red crust to remain unbroken upon the inner glass. The cork being drawn, it was regarded by the host before the wine was poured, in small measure, into a glass. Hilary sniffed it, sipped it, rolled it round his mouth, and looking up at the wine-waiter, gave a nod of approval. The wine-waiter, subdued pleasure on his face, bowed to Hilary, and poured a little wine into a fresh glass placed before the host; and the honours being done, he proceeded to the guest, to fill his glass three parts full. Then Hilary's glass was filled. With a slight bow the wine-waiter retired, leaving the bottle in the basket by Hilary's hand, which had slipped half-a-crown into his palm.

Food and drink soon released their generosity of life in Richard.

"Viccy's little girl must be three years old now. The last time I saw her, she was crawling all over the garden. Have you been to see them recently, Dick?"

"I don't think I've been there since Hetty had scarlet fever, Hilary. One gets out of touch, you know, in my sort of life, more's the pity."

"That's some time back, isn't it—let me see, it was before the old Queen died. Yes, my god-daughter Virginia Lemon must be three now." Hilary took out his note-book. "How old are your children now, Dick? When are their birthdays?"

"You really should not bother about them, Hilary. You must be a very busy man——"

"Not too busy to take an interest in my nephew and nieces, Dick. Phillip was born in April, eighteen ninety-five, I know that. Mavis?"

Richard told him the date in June 1897; and Doris's birthday in 1901; and protested once more what was, in effect, a disturbance of his own life. He was outside the rest of the family now; he was a failure.

"I'm told John has changed a lot since Jenny's death, Dick. Let himself go completely. William, his son, was born after Phillip, wasn't he, in the winter of 'ninety-six? I must go and look him up. How about coming down with me one week-end? I could run you over, you know, and back again, without any trouble."

"I hope that isn't too literal an offer!" and Richard laughed at his joke, hoping thereby to divert his brother's intention. He could not bear the idea of seeing his old home again.

"Why are you laughing? Oh, I see! No fear of that! The Panhard's as safe as houses. You must also come with me to the Lemons. You're Viccy's favourite brother, you know. In fact, to all us three younger ones you were our hero."

"Oh come, my dear fellow! I?"

"It's a fact, all the same, Dick. You were the big brother, helping Father to keep the old place together."

It was eight o'clock when they left. The sky beyond Nelson's column was nearly drained of colour. Spots of yellow light were dancing with the jingle of hansom cabs in the street. Shops were being shuttered, with clank of iron bar, and roll of iron wheel. They walked down to the Embankment, seeing the river gleaming on the flood. The faithful runner stood by the mechanical horses. He too received half-a-crown, rare receipt equal to a day's pay for a labouring man. The runner added God's blessing to his thanks, declaring that he knew a real gentleman the moment he saw him. With the greatest eagerness he leaned forward to give unspoken sympathy to his benefactor heaving at the handle cranked to shaft and massive flywheel.

"Stand back, you boys!" he cried, glaring around. "Can I help, sir?"

"It might break your wrist if the engine fires on the wrong stroke." Hilary tugged again. Suddenly he fell back as the thing spat, hissed, and clattered at him.

He tried again, after retarding the spark. An enormous bang followed. This, he said, was due to the spark being too retarded. Adjustments were made. Once again he turned, licking his lower lip. With a soft connecting sound the engine set its super-structure dancing; power thumped confidently. Hilary lit the oil lamps. The brothers Maddison climbed up. A scraping of cogs followed; a heartier thumping; and then four thin grey rubber tyres, taking the weight of successive vertical spokes of ash upon the lowest section of their containing rim, rolled in the direction of the Houses of Parliament, dark against the lowering west. The parrot in its cylindrical cage, covered with green baize secured with string, was waiting with the porter in his lodge within the wide doors of the Voyagers. Held on Richard's lap, it travelled upright in the Panhard steering for Westminster Bridge. River lights were left behind, to be succeeded by a far converging avenue of yellow twinkles remote and brown in the dim dark distance of the Old Kent Road.

The Daily Trident had from the first sponsored the new motoring. The "craze" had been one of the things Richard had never been able to understand in an otherwise sensible newspaper with its feet properly on the ground. During his ride through the dusk, in the cool air of the streets, with the feeling of being remote from the squalor and thus able to enjoy its picturesqueness, he had, as he told Hilary while crossing Randisbourne Bridge, to revise his opinion. He had had a wonderful experience.

"Will it be able to get up Hillside Road?"

"Well, a model has crossed the Alpes Maritimes and then the

Massif Central, so we shall probably manage to get there without the need to shove."

As they turned the corner and chugged up Hillside Road, a surprise met Richard. The bedroom window of his house was lit up. Burglars? Hetty was not expected home until the morrow. Then her figure was seen in the window, looking at the approaching noise. What could have happened?

Mrs. Bigge came to the gate as he got down from the Panhard, the cage in his arms.

"My," she said, "I wondered whatever it could be coming up our quiet little road! Surprise on surprise, Mr. Maddison! First Mrs. Maddison returned a day early, owing to whooping cough in the country, now a motor coming up! Why, whatever have you got there, Mr. Maddison, a parrot?"

"Yes," said Richard. "You must come in and see it one day soon. I think it is asleep now."

A wild scream came from the cage. "Oh, my!" said Mrs. Bigge. "Polly's woken up. Well, I think you'll find all all right, Mr. Maddison, so good-night!" and Mrs. Bigge tactfully retired.

Richard put the cage upon the lawn behind the privet hedge, as Phillip ran down the porch and to the gate. He stared at his father and uncle, and at the motor car.

"Coo, I say, look at that!"

"Hullo, young fellow," said Hilary. "D'you remember me, eh?"

"Yes, Uncle Hilary. Is it yours?"

"Say 'How do you do' properly to your Uncle, Phillip," said Richard, annoyed by the boy's gaucherie.

"How do you do, Uncle Hilary?"

"Well?" said Richard. "What else?"

The boy did not speak.

"Aren't you going to say anything to me?"

"Yes, Father." He remained silent.

"Have you lost your tongue while you've been away?"·

"I don't know, Father," he said, twisting his hands before him.

"Well, open the gate, my boy."

Phillip held back the gate. Richard waited for his brother to enter first.

"Aren't you pleased to see your father?" asked Hilary, ruffling the boy's hair as he passed.

"Yes, Uncle Hilary."

"Well then, say 'How do you do, Father' to him."

"How do you do, Father."

"That's better. And how are you, Phillip?"

"Quite all right, thank you, Father."

Richard stepped back and lifted up the cage. He carried it past a wide-eyed Phillip. Many times he had imagined Hetty and the three children coming into the sitting-room and seeing the parrot in its cage on the table in the corner beside the fireplace, and visualised the surprise and pleasure on their faces. The picture was shattered.

Sarah Turney was in the kitchen, giving the little girls their bread and milk. Richard went into the front room, and lit the gas.

"Sit down, Hilary," he said. "I'll be back soon. Would you like to see the paper?" He put *The Daily Trident* on the table. "Now, if you will forgive me, I'll go and find out what's happened."

"I'll just check that the Panhard is all right, Dick."

Hardly had he gone outside, when Hetty came into the room. She looked well and smiling, to Richard's relief, for that aspect of her homecoming fitted into his mental picture. Polly Pickering, it appeared, had developed signs of whooping cough, so they had all left Beau Brickhill a day early.

"I did not send a telegram, Dickie, not wishing to alarm you. I do hope our coming will not put you out in any way."

Mavis and Doris ran into the room, with glad cries of "Daddy!" Richard knelt down and kissed Mavis; he loved his elder daughter. Doris' head was patted.

"May I come in?" It was Sarah at the door. Then Hilary reappeared. He showed his charm to the old woman, treating her as if she were an Indian princess. Sarah responded to this consideration shown to her by a young man, and so Hilary was able to continue with his best manner. Mrs. Turney, he thought, was much nicer than he had imagined from what his sister Victoria had led him to believe. But then, no woman's judgment was to be taken seriously, particularly about another of her sex, whatever her age: an aboard-ship philosophy.

Phillip was by the green-covered cage, peering and listening. Was it a jackdaw? Or a parrot? If only Father would say! A raucous shriek made Sarah jump. "Goodness gracious, children dear, what a surprise!"

This was Richard's opportunity. Carefully he unknotted the string, while the children waited with part-suppressed excitement.

"Quick, Daddy! Oh please be quick!"

"Patience, Mavis. Curiosity killed the cat, remember."

"What is it, Daddy? I know it can't be a cat, for cats don't have cages."

"All in good time, young woman."

"*I* know what it is!" cried Phillip.

"Ss'sh, Sonny!" warned Hetty.

Father took so long, Phillip suffered for the delay. He wanted to offer his penknife, but Father always unpicked string. At last the baize was removed, with warnings of the bite that could be given by a fearful beak. As an added precaution, the cage was put on the table. There, walking sideways on its perch, was a grey and pink bird.

"You must thank Uncle Hilary nicely for the present, children."

"Thank you, Uncle Hilary. Does it speak, Uncle Hilary?"

"I don't think it is the kind that talks."

"It might talk if you slit its tongue, Uncle Hilary."

"What a ferocious thing to suggest! Where did you get that idea?"

"They slit jackdaws' tongues, then they can talk, Uncle Hilary."

"Good lord, whoever told you that?"

"Grandpa Thacker did, also Cousin Percy."

"Really? You surprise me, young man. How would you like your tongue slit, eh?"

Phillip did not know what to say.

"Now, Hetty, I think it is time for the children to go to bed, what do you say?"

"Yes, dear. I'll take them up immediately."

"Oh, Mummy, can't I stay up a little longer, and see the parrot?"

"You heard what your father said, Mavis. Run along up. Say 'Good-night' to Grannie, and Uncle Hilary, and your Father, dear."

"Oh, Mummy—— Is Polly her name, Father?"

"We'll see, later on. Now up you go. That includes you, Phillip. You can see the bird tomorrow."

Reluctantly they left the room. Grannie said she would take up the little girls.

"Good-night, Mummie; good-night, Uncle Hilary; good-night, Father. Mummy, you won't forget to tuck me up, will you?"

"Good-night, Polly!" cried out Phillip, showing his face round the door.

When they were gone, Richard led his brother down to the sitting-room. Hilary thought he would leave as soon as he politely could, and be in time for a game of billiards at the club.

Richard drew the curtains. He unlocked the cupboard under the bookcase, and took out the decanter of sherry, nearly empty. He had no whisky or soda.

"I'm afraid I've only got sherry, old chap."

"Oh, I don't need anything, Dick. I ought to be getting back soon. If the plugs oil up, or I get a puncture——"

"Well, stay just a little while. May I offer you a cigar? Hetty will be down shortly. I'm sure she would like to talk with you."

"Yes, of course. She looks very well, Dick. The holiday has done her good. So you've got your father-in-law next door?"

"Yes, Hilary. I am away all day, of course, and it is nice for Hetty to have her people so near."

Bravo, thought Hilary; old Dick always did bite on the bullet.

"Well, it's been a great pleasure to see you again, Dick. I've bought a place in Hampshire, you know; you must come down and visit us for a week-end. That reminds me, I must make an early start, and get down there to-morrow. I want to run over and see John shortly. Can I give him any particular message from you, Dick?"

"Oh, give him my very kind regards, Hilary."

Hilary looked round the room, which he found depressing. Dick was a stick-in-the-mud, all right. "Very comfortable little room this, isn't it? Is it warm in winter?"

"Oh yes, I can't find much fault with it."

"Being up a bit, I suppose you get less fog than in London itself?"

"Yes, but when it's a proper pea-souper we get it everywhere, you know, much the same."

"I think I'll just see that my lights are all right, Dick. Don't disturb yourself, I can find my own way."

Out of consideration Richard insisted on going with his brother, explaining that the path through the rockery by the gate was treacherous. So, apparently, was the surface of Hillside Road, for one of the front Dunlops of the Panhard was flat.

"Damn!" said Hilary, under his breath, as the bright lights of London faded. There a flake of flint was, sharp to the hand, sticking out of the rubber tread. It was not possible to repair it in the dark. There was only one thing to do: to return to Town by train, and come down and repair it in the morning.

"We can put you up, if you would care to stay, Hilary."

Hilary said it was most kind of his brother, but he had arranged to meet a man at the club at ten o'clock. Would he mind if the Panhard remained there all night? He would come down first thing in the morning.

While they discussed it, a policeman walked up the road, and stopped to admire the vehicle. Hilary explained the dilemma; the policeman replied that it would be quite in order to leave it for the night where it was. He would ask his relief to keep an eye on it. A shilling went into his pocket.

"If you'll excuse my saying so, but I shouldn't leave the hammercloth out."

This was the chequered rug, with its backing of plain melton cloth. So Hilary, after a few more minutes with Hetty and Richard, and the hammercloth folded and stored in the front room, took his leave.

"Well," said Richard, in the Sportsman armchair just before Hetty went upstairs for bed, "I think I might be of service to my brother Hilary. I will get up early and mend the puncture. I would have suggested mending it for him while he was here, but it was a question of the light. My bull's-eye lantern is missing from where I put it in the trunk in the attic. I have an idea how it came to leave the trunk. Perhaps you have, too?"

While he was speaking, Hetty thought that one of the lamps of the motor car, removed, would have given at least as much light as the dark lantern: and that the idea of mending the puncture had come to Dickie as an afterthought. Could Phillip have got up into the attic and taken it?

"Are you sure it isn't there, Dickie? I don't think Phillip knows about the attic at all, when I come to think about it, dear."

"Obviously the boy knows more about it than you do, then. I'll go up right away and find out." Richard got up from his chair.

"Oh, Dickie, please! Sonny will be asleep now. If he has taken your lantern, I am sure it is only because he likes to think of you, dear."

Richard stared at his wife. "Can I really believe my ears? Are you seriously suggesting that a thief robs somebody also because he thinks he is like his victim? If that is your idea of morality, then it is not mine! But then I well remember how you got rid of my only pair of walking boots for me, when first we set up in Comfort House, or have you forgotten?"

"Yes. Dickie, I was very sorry about that, and have said so, many times."

"Oh, well." Richard settled back in the armchair, to read *The Daily Trident*. But concentration was impossible. Was Hetty incurably foolish? Did she really mean what she said? A boy stole from his father because he liked to think he was his father. Yes, yes, certainly! The thief stole from the rich man because he liked the idea of being like him, with his money! Let Hetty put that in her pipe and smoke it.

There was the sound of a chamber pot being moved above the ceiling.

"Phillip is awake. I shall go up and ask him."

"Oh, please, Dickie, if he has taken it, do not punish him to-night. He was sick in the train, and now is so very very excited about the motor car, and the parrot——"

Richard went out of the room. Hetty heard him walking softly upstairs. She listened to the dull sound of his voice above.

He returned. "'No, Father', 'No, Father', 'No, Father'. As I expected."

"Are you sure, dear, you looked properly? He's so very small to be able to climb up into the attic alone."

"Very well, we will settle this matter once and for all! Come with me upstairs, this very moment, and see for yourself! Come along! I insist on fair treatment!"

Hetty followed Richard upstairs. He fetched the portable

steps from the carpentry room. He climbed up into the attic, and brought down the long, narrow tin trunk. Laying it upon the bathroom floor, he invited Hetty to open it, repeating that she could see for herself, and be satisfied.

Hetty slid back the lid fasteners. Within lay the scarlet uniform.

"The lantern was in that corner when I saw it last. Underneath the trousers, there!"

Hetty felt something hard. She drew forth the dark lantern.

"Obviously the boy has put it back since coming home!"

Downstairs in the sitting-room, *The Daily Trident* had no savour. Richard put it down for the second time. Surely she had seen or heard the steps being moved? Well then, had she seen or known what the boy had been doing since her return?

Hetty replied that she was sure Phillip had not been upstairs for more than a minute. He had been next door most of the time, with his grandparents. They had asked him to supper, and he had stayed with them until a few minutes before Dickie's return.

"If I can believe what you say, then I must also believe that I am in process of losing my sanity. For I will stake my oath that the lantern was not in the trunk yesterday!"

Richard slept in his dressing-room that night. He lay withdrawn from himself, sleepless until the early hours, by which time his entire life had been reviewed in terms of mortification and despair. He put part of his condition down to the unaccustomed heaviness of the food and the wine. With immense relief he woke to see daylight, and got up to mend the puncture. Taking the tube to the water-butt to detect air-bubbles, he saw two dead fish lying, belly up, just under the surface. They were perch.

So Phillip had done some fishing. If the boy had confided in him about the fish, he would have told him to put them in the bath, with cold running water to make the oxygen necessary to keep them alive. Then he could have taken his perch in a pail in the morning to the Randisbourne, and released them in the river. There they would have had at least a sporting chance of living. No fish could possibly survive in stagnant water in the butt. The water was dead, void of oxygen.

He lifted the fish out. They were covered with mucus, having died of asphyxiation. They might almost be a symbol of his own life, of his own home, where truth did not live. His own son, secretive and untruthful; a coward; and his mother largely to blame for helping to estrange him, in his early years, from his father.

Looking up suddenly, Richard saw Phillip staring down at him from the open bedroom window above the water butt. The head was instantly withdrawn. He took the fish and buried them under the elm-tree in the garden. Then went to look at the motor car.

Having already levered up the front axle, and put bricks under it, he set about examining the outer cover. There was a dun sharp edge of flint through the rubber and canvas, obviously picked up in Hillside Road. He worked it out, and put a canvas patch under the cut in the tyre. He pumped up the tube.

The air was still holding after his cold bath. He put the repaired tube back, pumped it hard, levered up the front axle and kicked the bricks away, let the wheel take the weight again. The Panhard et Lavassor was now ready for its journey down into Hampshire.

Chapter 23

PHILLIP'S RIDE

AT BREAKFAST Richard said, "Phillip, I strictly forbid you, under pain of a thrashing, to go anywhere near your Uncle's motor-car, both before he arrives, and after he arrives, except, of course, by his invitation. Is that quite clear?"

"Yes, Father."

"And you, Hetty, are a witness to what I am saying!"

Richard had had visions that morning, while dressing after his cold tub, of Phillip clambering upon the seat, letting off the handbrake . . . the motor-car running down the road to crash into the houses below.

"Yes, Dickie, of course. I am sure he won't disobey you."

"Well, I am not so sure! I have found you out!"

In agitation Richard shook a warning finger over the breakfast table at Phillip, while the two girls and their mother sat silent upon their chairs. "You are a deceitful little beast, and I shall never believe a word of what you tell me in future. Now, if you please, Hetty, I will not have any interference!"—for Hetty had given him an appealing look, as much as to say, Let the children eat their breakfast in peace, dear, and you too; I am sure there is some mistake about the lantern and the hat— "You are always ready to side with the boy!"

Leaving half his rasher of bacon on his plate, Richard got up from the breakfast table in the kitchen, and taking down the lantern from the top shelf of the dresser, stood it on the table. His eyes fixed upon his son's face, with its downcast look, he cried:

"Do you see that? Look at it closely! That small silvery speck, there! I found that just as it is now, stuck to the cowl. What is it? You may well ask! You——" turning to Phillip—"you know what it is, do you not?"

"No, Father," Phillip replied miserably.

"What is it, Dickie?" asked Hetty, staring at the silvery mark.

"Better ask the boy—your best boy."

"Do you know what it is, Phillip?"

302

"No, Mother."

"Very well, then I will tell you, since Phillip has not the courage to own up! It is the scale of a fish. Moreover, it is the scale of a perch. I found two dead perch in the water-butt this morning. Need I say any more?"

Phillip had gone grey in the face.

"Did you take the lantern, Sonny?" asked Hetty.

Phillip hung his head lower.

"Yes, he did! I saw him lighting it, with Percy," said Mavis, suddenly. "He stole it from the loft, to look for bats with, in the summerhouse at Aunty Liz's!"

"I didn't!" muttered Phillip, beginning to cry. "That was another one, belonging to Percy's friend."

"I am of a good mind to write to Mr. Pickering, and find out how far that statement is true! Now listen to me! I will give you until I come home this evening to make up your mind in the matter! If you admit your fault, then I shall give you a caning; if you persist in your underhand and dishonourable persistence, and your Uncle does not substantiate your statement, then I shall wash my hands of you altogether, and take steps to get you sent to a Reformatory! I'm sick and tired of your underhand, creepy-crawly ways!"

"Oh, Sonny, you naughty boy to worry your Father so! How dare you do such wicked things?"

"It is all very well to talk like that now!" cried Richard, his voice raised with his distress. "You should have been firmer with the boy before, not condone his every whim and fancy as soon as my back is turned! Well, you have heard my last word!"

Richard rolled his table napkin, thrust it into the ring, and went upstairs to clean his teeth, preparatory for departing to the station.

"You naughty, *naughty* boy!" said Hetty, knowing that Papa in the bathroom next door had been listening to Dickie's raised voice. "I shall never trust you again!" to the boy now sobbing with convulsive gulps.

"He *did* take it, *and* Daddy's hat!" said Mavis, pointing her finger at Phillip's downheld face. "And Mummy's blamed for it!"

"Shut up, you fool!" he moaned.

"He *did* take it, *and* Daddy's hat," echoed Doris, solemnly.

"I don't know what I shall do," cried Hetty, in despair. She got up trembling from the table. "I have given up all my life to you children, I have done everything I could to please your Father, and now you, Sonny, have broken my heart!" and her face puckering as the tears fell, she went out to hide herself in the front room.

The two little girls were now sobbing unrestrainedly. A series of raucous shrieks came up the passage, from the parrot in the sitting-room. "Sah lah! Sah lah!" it shieked, in Hindustani.

"I shall go mad," moaned Phillip. "I shall kill myself," and he got up and went down to the lower lavatory and bolted himself in. Should he put his head in the pan and pull the plug with a piece of string first tied to the chain? Or open the trap door and jump down under the house and bash his head against the brick wall where the 'cello stood, until his neck was broken? Lying on the floor, he moaned in helpless abandon for a few moments, then an idea came to him.

Unbolting the door, he went up to the broom cupboard under the stairs, and took out the box of cleaning materials. Wiping his tears on a rag, he opened the front door and set about cleaning the brass. He would make it shine so bright that perhaps Father would forgive him, and not thrash him with the cane with his trousers down and lying on the bed. Oh, if Father was going to thrash him, he must kill himself.

He was rubbing the dull, sulphurous brass surface with all his energy when Richard came downstairs, and went to the coat-hanger to get his straw hat. Phillip stood back. He wanted to beg Father's pardon, but the words would not form themselves.

At such times of emotion Phillip could not speak properly. When he tried, it was as though an extra hole had opened in his throat and his tongue had dissolved. He made clucking noises, and when words did come, they were clipped, half swallowed, and hopelessly jumbled. He wanted to tell Father that he was very sorry, to beg his pardon, to say he would never touch any of his things again; but the words would not come. He stood still as Father walked down the porch, and a choked cry broke from him as he disappeared.

Phillip thought he would run after Father and tell him he had put the lantern back by climbing up through Grandpa's bath-room trap door. He must say he was sorry before it was too late, and he was taken away to the Reformatory. He had seen the Reformatory boys playing football on the Hill, while a master ran among them, blowing a whistle and pointing. The boys never laughed. They wore black jerseys and black trousers to below the knee. All their heads were clipped short, so that they would be recognised as convicts, Cousin Ralph had said, if they ran away. They were thrashed a terrific lot, said Ralph, and had been sent to the East London Industrial School for stealing, setting fire to things, smashing windows, and acting like the roughs they were. They were awful-looking boys, like Flashman in *Tom Brown's Schooldays*, and would torture a new boy, especially if he could not fight, Ralph had said. And he would never never see Mummy anymore.

The tears running down his cheeks, he went on with his chores. After the knocker, the rim of the bell push, after the bell push the letter box, after the letter box the round handle. He would put his penny that week in the collection bag for Mr. Mundy. He cleaned and polished the handle of the garden door, which was unlocked only on Tuesdays, when the dustman came to empty the dustbin. After the brass-work, there were the fire-irons to rub with emery paper, and the steel shutter over the fire-place, which took a lot of doing as there were holes all over it, like acorn-cups, as well as lines, in the pattern.

Down in the sitting-room he watched the parrot for a while, giving it a pencil to bite; but the parrot dropped the pencil and continued to climb about inside the cage and would not speak when spoken to. He grew tired of watching it, and thought to dig up the perch from where he had watched Father burying them, from the back bedroom window, and see if the parrot would eat them; but perhaps it would be better not to do so. Or he might go in and see Uncle Hugh, who was always a nice person to see and talk to. He wasn't like an uncle at all. Mummy said he was very ill, with something that sounded like part of a train accident, words like "locomotive and tax here". Uncle Hugh had to be careful how he walked, with his two walking sticks with rubber on the bottom, as his legs were sort of wobbly sometimes. Through the high-up open window, with the stained-glass, in the wall above the passage fence, Phillip listened and heard Uncle Hugh groaning in his bed. It was no good going to see him when he groaned, for then he would never play his violin.

He washed his face to get rid of the tear-stains, and having brushed his hair, went out to look at the motor-car. He was careful to stand well away from it, looking at it from a distance only. He would keep always a long way away from it. While he was guarding it, the gate of the top house clicked, and people came out.

They were Mr. and Mrs. Rolls of Turret House. They were very nice, always smiling at him when he said, "Good Morning", as he passed. Phillip was afraid of them, because Mummy said that they did not want to know her children. They never invited him or Mavis or Doris to their parties. They did other people further down the road, called Wood, although the Woods were not so high up the road as the Maddisons.

Phillip felt proud that his uncle had a motor-car. He thought it a wonderful fine thing. Uncle Hilary was richer than anyone else in Hillside Road.

"Wait for me, Dads dear, wait for me!"

Phillip looked up the road and saw Mr. and Mrs. Rolls waiting, and then their little girl ran out of the gate, and held their hands, and they were walking down the road. When they came nearer all his thoughts about the motor-car went from him, as he looked into the little girl's face. She had wide blue eyes and fair curls falling down under a white sailor hat with a black bow. She wore a white sailor blouse and skirt. When she looked at him and smiled his heart beat wildly, he dared not look at her again.

When the beautiful people were gone round the corner, he imagined himself driving the motor-car full speed down the road, and winning all the races with it like Jack Valiant in the *Pluck Library*, while the face looked at him, smiling because he was a hero. The fancy faded, leaving a deep ache.

In a few moments there was something to think about, for from down Randiswell way he heard the rapid ringing of the fire-engine bell, and then the clashing hoofs and trundling of wheels as the four grey horses of the Fire Engine dashed at the gallop up Charlotte Road. Men in bright brass helmets stood on the red engine by the smoking funnel. *A Fire! Fire!* Boys were running out from the houses in Charlotte Road below, and also across the grass of the Hill. Could he be in time if he ran, and perhaps save a child's life?

Phillip had soon climbed over the railings in the gulley. He ran up the steep slope among the thorn bushes to the hurdle fence above, and was crossing the grass, fists clenched and elbows into sides to run the better, when he turned his head and saw Uncle Hilary walking up Hillside Road. He stopped, and returned.

"Hullo, young fellow, where are you off to? There's no fire, it's a practice. They told me at the railway station. So I've saved you a run. Well, how about one in the Panhard? What, your Father has already mended my puncture? That was very civil of him!"

Phillip remembered the ride in the blue and red motor-car all his life, the chequered hammercloth round his knees like a real coachman. Uncle Hilary took him down through Randiswell, where he dared to wave as he passed Helena Rolls, feeling a wonderful happiness as she waved back, and on to the High Street. Turning south, they were soon out of the area of streets and houses, and on the grey road to Cutler's Pond. It was like a story. On they went past the Pond, round the bend by the water-cress beds, where a big cedar was growing by another pond, near an ivy-grown wooden mill called Perry's. After that everything was strange and new.

They went up a hill and to Phillip's surprise came to a town. He had imagined that all beyond Perry's Mill was fields and country. They went down a lane beyond a railway station and along by other fields, coming at last to what a finger-post said was Reynard's Common. Trees and bushes grew here, with gorse and broom, and lots of pebbles, where were only blackened stems of burnt trees.

"Work of naughty boys, I'll be bound," said Uncle Hilary.

Beyond the burnt places were silver birch trees, and two deep ponds with firs and pines on their banks held together by brown roots on top of the pine-needle slippery ground.

Here Uncle Hilary stopped the motor-car by tripping the switch, he said. They got down by the ponds. The sun shone slantingly on the bigger pond and many fish were to be seen lying just under the surface of the water. They had red fins.

"I expect they are either rudd or roach, Uncle Hilary."

"And those very big brown fellows, see them in the middle? They're carp."

The carp, said Uncle Hilary, was the fox of the waters, it was so cunning and hard to catch. Phillip thought it was as wonderful a place as Brickhill. Uncle was a very nice man, not a bit like the White Uncle who had squeezed him between his legs and not let him go until Aunty Bee came, when he had been only a little boy.

"Well, Phillip, we must think of getting back."

Back in the town, Uncle stopped before a shop and said: "What would you like for a birthday present, eh, Phillip? Your Mother tells me you will be nine next week. Is that right?"

"Yes, Uncle Hilary."

"Well, let's see what they have got here, shall we? How about this, eh? An electric torch. Ever had one?"

"Oh, no, Uncle Hilary!"

"Well, we'll have that one. Only don't waste the battery flashing it on in the daytime. How about a football? Oh, I gave you one, did I? A magic lantern, how about that?"

"Oh, thank you, Uncle Hilary!" Phillip clasped his hands as hard as he could in his excitement, in case Uncle might change his mind. But no, Uncle was going to buy it!

They went into a tea-shop. Phillip ate three cream buns, a doughnut, and a macaroon, followed by an ice-cream.

"We'll take some back for your sisters, shall we? How do you get on with them. Do you like your sisters?"

"Oh, yes. I get on very well with them, thank you, Uncle Hilary."

"That's right. I remember how we, in our family, that is, your Uncle John, your Father, and the Aunts—my sisters—were all thick as thieves. Yes, we were a jolly family. You've never met your cousin Willie, Uncle John's boy? I suppose you've not been to Rookhurst?"

"No, Uncle."

"Well, I'm going to pay them a visit shortly. Shall I give Willie your love. He's rather like you. You two ought to get on. What do you want to be when you grow up? An open-air life, I hope. How about being a farmer?"

"Yes, please, Uncle Hilary."

"Good. Now your mother tells me you're in trouble with your father, Phillip. Is that right?"

The boy stared with frightened look at the man. The remaining part of the doughnut, oozing strawberry jam, remained in his paw.

"Tell me, Phillip. I've been a naughty boy myself, you know."
The boy remained silent.

"Don't want to say anything against your father, is that it?"

Phillip thought he was expected to say yes, and with hope in his voice, he replied, "Yes, Uncle Hilary."

"H'm. Eat your doughnut up, boy. We must be getting back. I've got to go all the way down to the coast, right through the New Forest. Ever been there?"

"No, Uncle Hilary."

"Lovely place. You must come down one day, and see Aunt Bee. She's a particular friend of yours, you know. Remember her?"

"Yes, Uncle Hilary," he smiled.

"Well now, tell me what went wrong between you and your father. Took his dark lantern, didn't you, without asking? Come on, you can tell me: I shan't split on you."

"Yes, I did, Uncle Hilary. But I didn't break it."

"Why did you take it in the first place?"

"Because I wanted it so much, to get a bat with, because I like bats better'n butterflies."

"Do you, b'jabers. Well then, why didn't you ask your father?"

"He would have said 'No', Uncle Hilary."

"How d'you know, if you didn't ask him?"

"Father always says 'No', Uncle Hilary. He doesn't like anyone touching any of his things, Uncle Hilary."

"H'm! I don't blame him. Why should his things be taken specially when they get spoiled. I shouldn't like you if you took my motor-car without permission, and smashed it up."

"I wouldn't ever take it, Uncle Hilary."

"Well, thanks for the reassurance! Why wouldn't you take it, tell me that?"

"My legs aren't long enough to touch the pedals, Uncle Hilary."

Hilary roared with laughter. Then he looked seriously at his nephew.

"You're a funny fellow, you know, Phil. You've got plenty of intelligence, really. And it's the kind of mind that sees clearly. Every answer you've given me is logical, and factual. In other words, you have in every instance spoken the truth. Then why in heaven's name, does your father firmly believe that you are incapable of telling the truth? Can you answer me that one, now? If you can, you're more clever than I am. Well, what do you say?"

Phillip said nothing. He did not understand what Uncle meant. He thought of Uncle going away for ever, like Uncle Sidney, and never coming back. And Father was going to thrash him if he told him he had taken the lantern, and send him away to the Reformatory if he didn't say he had taken it. Terror in both directions closed upon his mind, obliterating the cakes, the birthday presents, the motor-car ride home.

"Why, what's the matter now? Come, come, you mustn't cry! You're a big boy now. Think of when you went to the Derby with the old dog, d'you remember? That was a pretty plucky thing to do, the spirit of your Viking ancestors coming out, if you like. Don't cry, Phillip. Here, take my handkerchief to dry your tears with."

Phillip's mind had broken down under the dilemma. In the motor-car, on the way home, he was sick. Hilary stopped, helping the boy to clean himself up. Afterwards Phillip sat beside the driver, "very white about the gills", his uncle remarked. Phillip thought of the time coming nearer and nearer when Father would come home. Turning up Hillside Road, they passed Mr. and Mrs. Rolls and Helena Rolls on the pavement. Mrs. Rolls waved to him, and he waved back, but with face turned away, as tears were falling again. He hurried into his house before Mr. and Mrs. Rolls and Helena Rolls could catch up with him and see his face. He ran to the downstairs lavatory, and bolted himself in.

Hilary explained to Hetty that it was, perhaps, the motion of the vehicle, or the fumes of the engine. It took some people like that at first, he said.

"Do you mind," said Hetty, nervously, "if I say something to you in confidence, Hilary? You don't mind me calling you Hilary, do you?"

"My dear Hetty! I am honoured. Please believe that anything you tell me will be in the strictest confidence."

Hetty did not know precisely how to express what was weighing on her. She could not say anything against her husband for she could not even think anything against him, such was the loyalty of her nature.

"It's about Dickie and your son, isn't it, Hetty?"

"Yes, Hilary. I wonder if you saw Dickie, you could say a word for Phillip? You see, he is a strange little boy, and intensely susceptible. Dickie tells him things, and shows him his butterflies, or he used to at any rate, and once he showed him the lantern, which I know means so much to Dickie because it was his grandfather's, as was the deerstalker hat he treasures equally —well, I am afraid it will all sound rather peculiar, but you see, Phillip seems to have the same feelings for Dickie's things, and I am sure he gets them from his father. I expect what I am trying to say sounds very silly."

"Not in the least, Hetty. But if I may say so, I can't quite see the connection between what you say, and Phillip taking his father's things behind his father's back. Out in the world, you know, that sort of thing is called stealing. And you know what small boys are, they break things. It's a mistake to let them have them too young. I had a telescope when I was only about ten. Of course I pulled it to bits, and lost one of the lenses. It was too good for me."

"Yes, Phillip soon picked to bits the watch Dickie gave him, too young, for a Christmas present."

"Exactly! Now tell me if I can help you in any way."

"I was wondering if it would not be bothering you too much, if, when you return to London, you might have a word with Dickie about Phillip being more adventurous than really bad, Hilary."

"Well, I shall have to leave it for a week or so as I'm due to return direct to Hampshire. In fact I ought to be on my way there now, by way of Mitcham and Hampton Court."

Hetty tried to conceal her despair. "Oh yes, well, please think no more of it. I expect things will come all right in the end." She gave a little hopeful laugh.

"I'll write a line to my brother, if you like."

"Oh no, Hilary, please don't! I think he would know I have been speaking to you about Phillip."

Feminine "logic", thought Hilary: his brother would know

whether he spoke of the matter direct or wrote about it, for how
else could he, Hilary, have got his information?

"School may make all the difference, I expect. Cricket, and
football, sweat the vice out of 'em. Boys are inquisitive little
brutes, anyway, by nature." For a moment Hilary had an idea of
offering to pay the fees of a decent school for Phillip, but he
dismissed the idea. Let the boy find his own level. "Well, it has
been so nice seeing you, Hetty, and don't let these trifles worry
you. Dick's a bit of a worry-guts, you know, as we used to tell
him. Your boy's got plenty of ability, Hetty. He's a cute little
beggar in many ways. Well, I must be on my way. I've brought
a few things for the nieces. Will you let them have 'em? Good
bye, Hetty, and don't worry—life's too short, I find."

Phillip came out of his hide, farewells were said. The Panhard
et Lavassor drove away up Charlotte Road, turning south for the
Crystal Palace and beyond into Surrey and the road to the West.
Hilary arrived at his house at a quarter-past seven in the evening,
happy and pleased with his day's run.

At a quarter-past seven Richard returned from London.
Phillip was waiting for him. Phillip, weeping, confessed. He was
ordered upstairs to prepare himself to receive his punishment.

Afterwards Phillip lay in bed, his head on a damp pillow,
listening to a thrush singing on the chimney-pot of Grandpa's
house. The starling no longer sang there, since Phillip had shot
it, for skinning and stuffing behind glass, with his father's air-gun.
The skin was hidden on top of the cupboard, where he had thrown
his gollywog and forgotten it.

When the thrush had gone, Phillip heard Uncle Hugh playing
his violin. When that stopped, and Uncle Hugh had clumped
away on two sticks to supper in the front room, Phillip sang his
song to himself. It was in the usual minor key, but the notes did
not run into one another as in ordinary songs. The notes were
lonely notes, like the wind in a keyhole or telegraph wires. They
rose and fell, and were his secret music of beyond the sunset, and
among the stars. He sang them quietly to himself, for no one
must hear.

The music gave way to interest in the state of his behind.
Creeping out of bed in his nightshirt, he took down the looking
glass from the chest of drawers, and, baring his rump, examined

in the light of his new flash-lamp the long blue-red weals across the torn skin. They stung like billy-o, and were sticky with a sort of water. He counted ten, and then went back to bed again, crying to himself. Later Mummie came up with a glass of water and slice of bread. He shook his head. "No thank you." She put them beside his bed. They were untouched when later she came up to say good-night. He would not kiss her, though she came back three times to ask him.

"No thank you," he said each time. When she had gone downstairs, the pillow received more tears. The sad song consoled him, as with open eyes he thought of Helena Rolls, of her golden curls and wide blue eyes, and her smiling, and it all seemed to be up in the sky.

Chapter 24

PARROT MULTIPLICATION

"Now just look and see what a nice little gentleman Phillip Maddison is, sitting so still in the back row and never giving any trouble," said Miss Norton, and the Third Standard obediently turned round to look. Phillip, dressed in blue jersey, navy-blue knickers, black stockings and button shoes, had been sitting without movement for the past five minutes, his hands folded behind him to draw back his shoulders in the approved manner, and his eyes looking straight ahead.

The tribute came as a complete surprise to Phillip. Miss Norton had been giving a geography lesson, with coloured chalks on the blackboard, and he had not listened to a word of what she was saying.

"He pays perfect attention, children," went on Miss Norton. She was a pupil teacher under the new School Board of Education, and received a salary of forty-five pounds a year, "an articled forty-fiver", as it was called.

"Now everyone turn to their front, hands behind heads, and try to be like Phillip."

Phillip felt a nice feeling. He stared straight to his front, hands clutching elbows behind him, and breathing as slightly as possible to keep his jersey from rising and falling. He would always be very good now.

"Hands behind head, now, Phillip," said Miss Norton gently. With a start the dreamer realised what was said. He disentangled his aching arms, and clasped his hands behind his head.

"We will have five minutes' rest, children, before continuing."

When he had to copy the figures on the board on to his slate, with the grey slate pencil, he did his very best. Later he stopped himself from drawing a whale and a shark on the clear spaces on the other sides of Ireland and Great Britain.

It was the summer term at Wakenham Road School. Phillip liked Miss Norton, who was a quiet-spoken young woman wearing black boots hidden under a black skirt, a white blouse with a high starched linen collar with a black bow, while her mousey-coloured hair bulged out flatly on top of her head with the aid of a concealed padded wire frame.

"Now pay attention, children. We will go through the multiplication tables again. Now all together when I drop the pointer!"

Miss Norton raised a ground ash stick, tapering gradually to its point, like half a billiard cue.

"Wait till I drop the point! Are you all ready? 'Twice one are two', and so on until you reach twelve. Then pause while I raise my pointer, and when I drop it, begin 'Three ones are three', and so on, up to ten times table." A gasp of awe greeted this adventurous height. "And to the one who keeps on longest I shall give two good marks to add to the total for the week. The one who wins the most for this week shall be the one to clean the blackboard for me all next week, and, as you know, the three highest totals at the end of term are to have each a prize. Ready, everyone?"

"Yes, Miss Norton!" came with shrill massed expectancy.

The pointer dropped. The multiplication race began. A little girl with honey-coloured hair over part of her eyes stayed the course the longest—she fell at seven nines—and with excited laughter was given the two marks.

"Well done, Dorothy!"

Dorothy gave a quick glance at Phillip, who was sitting, still and rigid, with arms folded behind him, hoping that Miss Norton would give him at least one mark for the best behaviour. He had followed along as far as six eights, and thereafter had sung a chanting song of his own, without any actual words. Numeration did not interest him.

During play-time massed cries, considerably shriller in pitch above the classroom chanting, came from the two asphalt paved spaces enclosed within high brick walls, the Boys' and Girls' playgrounds of Wakenham Road School. Richard never went near the place. He had known green fields there before the building had been put up. It seemed to him that universal education for the factory civilisation of the times was somehow directly linked to the mass graveyard on the other side of the road, where heaps of yellow clay and wilted flowers were ever increasing. He did not express this thought; it was inherent in his increasing retirement from those about him. He knew that he was becoming an embittered man.

On the south side of the main school buildings was the Boys' playground. On the north was the Girls' and Infants'. Hither every morning Hetty walked with her three children, under the line of polled elms on the cemetery side of the High Road. Phillip disappeared into the Boys' playground, Mavis and Doris into the Girls'. The entrance to the Girls' was past a lodge occupied by an old man with a rutty face, named Mr. Scrivener. He was the janitor, an old man so gentle and unspeaking that no new child was afraid of him after a day or two; and thereafter did not even notice him about the place, except that a kind face sometimes moved past in a vivid world.

At the end of the term, Miss Norton gave three prizes to her best pupils, who would be moving up after the holidays. The third prize was given to Phillip, a little yellow book called *How Arthur Won the Day*. It was the story of a boy who went with bad companions, and did bad things, such as roasting stolen pheasants' eggs in the embers of a fire beside the hedgerow, and being found out by the keeper. Stealing eggs led to stealing money and that was the end of Arthur's friend, as far as Arthur was concerned, for he turned back and won the day just in time. Phillip hastened home to show his prize proudly to Mother.

"Look, Mum, I've won a prize!"

Miss Norton had written his name on the flyleaf, *Phillip Maddison*. Phillip added underneath, in his spidery school-writing *First Prize for Coming in Third*.

At the beginning of the second term, after the summer holidays, it was decided that the three children might go to school by themselves. Phillip was put in charge of his sisters, but very soon he left them to get to school by themselves, preferring to walk with his cousin Gerry. One day, to liven up the walk, he and Gerry wore their overcoats back to front, and an errand boy on a bicycle with a basket threw eggs at them. This involved a chase of the boy whenever he was seen again; and as the errand boy's friends came to his help, a feud grew between Gerry and Phillip on one side, and the roughs from Comfort Road and the streets beyond.

One of the roughs had a younger brother in the school, a

heavy boy with a big face called Mildenhall. This boy remained
in the Third Standard, to which Phillip had been moved up
from Miss Norton's classroom. Phillip had not been in his
new desk more than a week, when, looking up from the brown-
backed *Pluck Library* he was reading under the desk, he saw
Mildenhall looking across at him. At the time Mrs. Wilkins, the
new mistress, small and dark with pale serious face, was writing
sums upon the blackboard. Her back being turned to the class,
Mildenhall slowly raised his fist, with his thumb, sticking out
between the first and second closed fingers, and shook it
menacingly at Phillip. Phillip's stomach immediately flunked.
Mildenhall's meaning was clear. Phillip thought of the big boy's
thumb jabbing into his eye innumerable times during the lesson,
in which he got all his sums wrong.

"Come, come," said Mrs. Wilkins, looking at his slate, as she
paused between desks. "What's the matter with you today,
Phillip? You'll have to stay in after prayers and get these right."

Mrs. Wilkins had started her teaching career in the old
century, when pupil teachers had received twelve pounds per
annum.

"Yes, M'am," said Phillip, with some relief, because then
Mildenhall might forget to wait for him.

At four o'clock the bell rang for the classes to file into the hall.
All the rooms, built centrally around the main assembly place,
had a wall, or partition, of varnished pitch-pine, with glass
panes in the upper half, looking into the hall, which had big sky-
lights in its roof. The school was thereby much enlightened.

The hall itself faced a raised rostrum built above its west end.
The rostrum was reached by two wide stairways leading up to it,
one on either side of the hall. Here stood the dreaded figure of
Mr. Garstang, the Head Master, every nine o'clock when the
classes filed out for prayers in the morning, and again at four
o'clock in the afternoon before going home.

The Head Master, Mr. Alfred Garstang, or Gussy, was a figure
of near-terror to Phillip. Not that Mr. Garstang had ever
spoken severely—and he could be very severe—to Phillip, or
that he had shown towards Phillip any voice or manner other
than one of kindliness. Phillip was afraid of him, because of
what he had been told about Gussy by other boys as soon as he
had come to the school. Whenever Mr. Garstang came near him,

Phillip felt that Mr. Garside's eyes might, at any moment, pierce his pocket and see the *Pluck Library* folded inside.

Mr. Garstang was a short man in a tail coat, with a slightly curved front behind the lower buttons of his waistcoat, and wide pointed wings to his collar, which looked very sharp. He was partly bald in the front of his round head, and the hair remaining to him was always pressed down in straight flat black lengths across the pink and polished skin of his skull. Gussy looked straight at the boys, quelling them without intention. His brown moustaches were twisted at the ends to long points which drooped downwards. It was this moustache which was so alarming, in front of the deep, quiet voice which was inseparable in Phillip's mind with the cane.

Sometimes on the rostrum above the hall before afternoon prayers were to be seen the backs of boys' heads and their shoulders by the remote wall. The boys were behind the big desk in the centre of the rostrum where Mr. Garstang stood, revealing partly bald head, round pink face with great moustache, and length of gold chain passing through a button-hole in rotund black waistcoat. The desk, level with the top of the pitch-pine banisters, cut off all view below the gold chain.

The sight of boys facing the wall at the back of the rostrum made Phillip stand stilly quiet when he toed, with other children, the white line of the Third Standard. There were many such white lines ranged in parallel down the hall, with an interval in the centre. The white lines ranged downwards from the Infants in front to the biggest boys and girls of Standard Seven in the rear.

There was only one Black Line in the hall. It was a terrible place, by the stairs up and down which Mr. Garstang moved to his study. The boys at the back of the rostrum were those who had been sent to stand on the Black Line during the afternoon. When the bell rang for afternoon prayers, the boys on the Black Line had to go up the stairs to stand behind Mr. Garstang's desk.

The Head Master dealt with them promptly before prayers. When all the classes were in the hall, standing to attention on the white lines, Mr. Garstang would pause, looking, it seemed, at every child staring up at his face. Suddenly the part of Mr. Garstang above the desk would turn sideways and the voice would boom, "Well, my friends! And what are you doing here?"

No boy ever made reply. Sometimes the row of cropped heads would make a sort of tentative movement, half turning before, overcome by the gaze of Mr. Garstang, they found safety in facing the wall again. Then with a hissing sound, which seemed to echo in the breath of the children in the hall below, a cane would be drawn from the bundle standing in the upright glazed drainpipe beside the desk. With his left hand Mr. Garstang would haul a boy, sometimes wriggling, across the desk, and holding him by the neck, would strike him again and again with the his cane, black coat-tails visibly dancing about during the sudden animation.

Sometimes a boy cried out while he was being lugged across the desk. It made no difference. He was swiftly beaten, and as swiftly discarded for another to be hauled up for the same whirlwind swishing, and so on to the last boy. There were never more than four, and the beatings were only occasional; but the bristle of canes rising over the top of the desk, the drooping points of Mr. Garstang's moustache, almost wider than his jowl, made an impression on the children of the awe-ful results of being sent to stand on the Black Line.

The white lines down each side of the hall were subduing in themselves; they were of silence, looking straight to the front, and stillness, and, being lines, were connected with the Black Line, the terror of all Wakenham Road School terrors in Phillip's mind. Such was juvenile superstition, and imperfected love, in the winter of 1904.

Mr. Garstang lived on the south side of Charlotte Road. On occasional and startling moments he was to be seen, a quiet human figure wearing square-crowned black hat and tail-coat, swinging an unrolled umbrella as he walked sedately to school. Whenever Phillip passed Mr. Garstang's house he looked straight ahead, unspeaking as he hurried onwards. Mr. Garstang sometimes wondered why; for he was interested in the little boy, knowing something of his history from his friend and fellow antiquarian, the vicar of St. Simon Wakenham.

As he stood on the white line of Standard Three, Phillip wondered if he would be sent to the Black Line if he could not do his sums after school. At the same time he wondered, if he did them quickly, Mildenhall would be waiting to fight him. Phillip was terrified of the idea of fighting. He was no good at fighting. Whenever anyone hit him, or even pretended to, he shut his eyes. And even if he tried to keep them open, and to dodge, Mildenhall was a much bigger boy. Mildenhall might do to him what he had seen him do to another boy, give him a nose-bleeder and then sit him on the hard playground. He had seen Mildenhall sit on other boys, saying they had sauced him, when they hadn't. Mildenhall had poked Phillip in the ribs as they had filed out of the classroom, and whispered to him, "Donkey Boy! Yer farder's Ole Tin Wills! I'll l'arn yer!"

When, having done the sums for Mrs. Wilkins, Phillip left the classroom, lots of boys were sliding on the playground. Snow had fallen. Thankfully he slipped out of the gate and along the road home. At tea, with fried sprats, he told his mother what Mildenhall had called him. She said, "Oh dear! Do they still remember your father?"

"Remember what, Mum?"

"Oh, nothing, dear. You would not understand," a remark which made Phillip determined to understand. On Saturday morning he asked Mrs. Feeney what "Tin Wills" meant.

"They called the first bicycles that, Master Phil. It was a low expression. Your father would not like to hear it from you, so be a good boy and forget it."

This reply made Phillip think more about it. Thinking about it made him remember it. Later in the morning, when he and his cousins Ralph and Gerry, and other of the Band, were around the camp-fire hidden in a cleft of the slopes of the Backfield, he asked about it.

"'Jesus Christ on Tin Wheels' was how they used to sauce your Old Man," said Ralph.

Phillip was shocked at this use of the name of Jesus, and subdued because Father had been sauced like that. His father was the best man in Hillside Road. He was the best cyclist, too, with the only Sunbeam with Little Oil Bath and Three-speed Sturmey-Archer gear to be seen anywhere.

Chapter 25

BIG TREES AND BIG KITES

ONE afternoon on coming home from school Phillip climbed up the elm tree and saw something in the Backfield which made him most curious. It was a sort of very long cart, with two pairs of stubby wheels each end. They were far apart and connected by a thick piece of wood. Soon he had hopped over the fence, startling a blackbird who was scratching in the heaps of rotting lawn-mower grass thrown over from Mr. Bigge's garden, and had crept along a dog path under the thicket of elm suckers. This brushwood surrounded the row of tall trees in whose tops the rooks were cawing at their nests.

He stared at the strange cart. The letters *FITCHYSON, Timber Merchant, Pit Vale Sawmills*, were painted on a board nailed to the left side of the front carriage. Whatever was it there for?

There was a new notice board put up at the far lower end of the Backfield, and he ran over to have a look at that. It was a notice that *Desirable Residences* were to be erected. He ran back through the grass, thinking himself to be Umslopagaas in *Nada the Lily* running with his assagai to warn Allan Quatermain that strange scouts were tracking over the veldt. On return he hid in the thicket, and was wondering where he could get a real assagai, when fear that Father might be coming home early to fly his big double-box kite, nearly a man-lifter, on the Hill that evening, as there was a fine breeze, made him get up. The Backfield was forbidden, therefore the more exciting a place to hunt in, to stalk birds and cats, and other boys, and bake potatoes in the embers of a fire like Arthur who won the day.

Safely over the fence, he climbed the tree again. This was not forbidden, though Father said he must always hold tight with at least one hand when he was up there, as broken limbs would mean a heavy doctor's bill, as well as goodbye to his chance of winning a scholarship.

Making sure that the strange new cart could be seen from the tree, so that he could not be caught out in a lie and sent to bed,

Phillip went indoors again, to try and learn Kings, Queens and Dates for Mr. Groat. Mr. Groat, who lived in No. 9, called "Chatsworth", coached him twice a week for an hour on Mondays and Fridays. Mr. Groat was like Mr. Garstang, a Head Master, but as he lived in Hillside Road, there was no cane with the coaching.

When Father came home, Phillip told him about the cart he had seen. Father went down to have a look. Then Father got over the fence, and said Phillip could come with him for just that once. Phillip pretended to get over clumsily, as though it was the first time; but Father said, "Come on, old chap, by the clay marks on that board you usually do it in one hop, sole of right boot there, and down. Don't you think I know? I've been a boy myself, you know."

Father was not angry, and he did not know what to say.

"Bless my soul, it's a timber waggon. They are going to cut down our elms! Well, there you are, my boy! Progress. What a shame! Money, money, money, that's all some people think about. Goodbye to the rooks."

"I saw a notice board down over there, Father. I walked down and back. It said houses."

"Well, I suppose it had to come sooner or later. We must make the best of it, that's all. There's some wonderful leaf mould under here, you know. It's the very thing for the garden. Better get it while we can. Would you like to collect some of it in a pail for me, or as much as you can get up, and just tip it over the fence at the bottom, where it is low?"

"Yes, Father. Now, Father?"

"Oh no, we are just going to have tea. I have brought something home for tea. We must wash now, to be ready in time. How are you getting on at school, old chap?"

"Very well, thank you, Father. I can do woodwork now, under Mr. Mansard in the Woodwork Shop. Satinwood is very nice, my favourite wood, I think."

"Yes, it is a good working wood, though your tools have to be sharp to cross the grains properly. I don't suppose you are allowed very sharp tools, though. A chisel can give you a very nasty cut if it slips. Shall I give you a leg up?"

"No thank you, Father, I can get over easily." And placing his hands on the fence the boy sprang up, his two toecaps bumped the wood, he swung his right boot lightly on the top, and vaulted over, with a quick glance at Father to see if he saw how well he could do it.

The something extra for tea was scotch shortbreads. After bread and butter, they melted sweetly in the mouth, and took away hunger.

"The Scots work on oatmeal," said Father, "so do horses."

After tea Phillip went into the front room with a list of Kings, Queens, and Dates to be learned. He was busily frowning when Father looked round the door.

"Hullo," said Father. "Would you like to come for a walk with me, and see if we can spot that big chub that is supposed to be lingering on in the Randisbourne? Or are you too busy?"

"No, Father," said Phillip, looking up from the page.

"He is very good, he has already been learning his dates before tea," said Hetty, peering round beside her husband.

"There you go," Richard remarked, half playfully. "I cannot have a word with the boy on my own, but you have to come and prompt him. I have not the least intention of taking him from his work," and putting on his tweed cap, and taking his walking stick, Richard went out of the house.

"What have you been doing to annoy your father, Phillip?"

"Nothing, Mother!" He scowled. "Father and I understand each other." Hetty had to go away into the kitchen, to hide laughter, which was near to tears.

The trees in the Backfield were soon down. Phillip watched, after running all the way home from school at midday, the last of the elms tottering after a great creak, then a sort of shriek and a swishing noise as down it went, and *thump*, it seemed to bounce before getting small all at once and lying still. Men with axes lopped and topped it; then when he came home in the afternoon the trunk had been sawn into sections with two-handled cross-cuts with teeth like the huge pike in the Brickhill pits. At the end of the week only the branches were left; but the rooks still cawed high in the sky.

Hundreds of navvies appeared early one morning. They had leather straps holding up their corduroy trousers below the knee, and with little wooden scrapers thrust in the straps, to clean their spades as they dug away the grass for a road. Carts took the sods and made a huge heap in the middle of the level place below the slopes of the Backfield. Then the carts took all the sections of branches which had been cut up with axes, and men built a great bonfire of them, but without setting it alight. Next they covered the bonfire with an enormous amount of clay, all the carts taking it up. Only then did they set light to the bonfire.

While the heap was burning, day after day, other men were building foundations and walls of houses, in two rows down the new road where many smaller branches had been laid for a foundation. A steam-roller went over the branches and crushed them flat. The enormous heap of yellow clay went on burning day after day, and at night there were little flames over the heap, which Father said was a miniature Etna. After a fortnight the heap had turned red.

This was ballast, said Father, to lay on the new road; but the builder had changed his mind, and had put down gravel and flint instead, from the pit near the poplars where the kites sailed over. This was harder and better altogether for road metalling, said Father.

So the red ballast heap remained after the houses were built; and so did the marn ponds just behind the garden. The builder was an ass, said Father, and was asking to be made bankrupt, to go to all the trouble of mixing and pouring the marn, to make bricks with, and then to swop horses in midstream and decide to buy bricks instead.

Phillip was forbidden to go anywhere near the ballast heap, which was still burning. Steam and smoke sometimes issued from the cracks in the mass of several hundred tons. If he fell in, said Father, only his white bones would be found in many years' time.

The bricklayers departed. The windows of the houses were glazed, each pane of glass bearing its warning nebula of white-wash, as a warning to painters with ladders, said Father.

One morning a frightful smell was wafted into all the houses of Hillside Road. It came as the shelter of the workmen's privy was being pulled down, fifty yards beyond the row of garden fences. Gran'pa, after making everyone gargle with Sanitas, went down to Randiswell Police Station about it, to learn that Mr. Bigge had already called to complain. The pit was strewn with lime and filled in.

In addition to gargling, Hetty had made the children wear

handkerchiefs soaked in Dodder's disinfectant over their noses, and sent them on the Hill. Mildenhall was there with some of his gang. They threw stones at Phillip as he ran away, and shouted out, "Laugh at 'im! Laugh at 'im! Frightened of a little ——," a very rude word. The Lanky Keeper chased the boys for using the word which, he said, "was not even in the Bible, and that's sayin' a lot!"

The marn pits remained in Phillip's mind as things of terror, worse than quagmires, worse than the Exmoor bog which had sucked down Carver Doone after Jan Ridd had torn out the muscles in Carver's arm like the string out of an orange. Gerry said that even frogs were drowned in the yellow marn. But Phillip had seen something much worse than frogs drowning. He was looking over the fence one Saturday morning when he saw a dog chase a cat into the marn, and the dog jumped in after the cat. Phillip cried out to Mrs. Bigge, to Grannie, to Mummy, to anyone to come quick, for all their fur was gone and their heads and tails were hidden, too, in thick yellow marn. As he watched they became shapes hardly moving; and only little bumps showed day after day where they had drowned.

When the wood of the stinking shed had been removed, and the houses were all finished, men came and cut channels in the sides of the marn pits, so that the water underneath the yellow pug trickled out; and the following Saturday morning when Phillip climbed over the fence, and laid a flat board on the marn and slowly walked out, in terror lest suddenly yellow squeeze up and suck him down, he discovered that there was no more danger.

The marn was firm; cracks were opening across it everywhere; soon he was stepping upon it without fear. There was the cat's skull. Its skin easily came off, with the whiskers; and near it the dog's white teeth seemed to be wanting to bite it. With Father's fork he dug both skeletons out, washed them in a pail of water drawn from the butt, and reburied them in Grandpa's garden, for the time when he should make his underground museum, like the one made by the mad genius whose inventions Jack Joker saved for England from the spies of Germany, in the new *Emerald Library*.

Richard looked forward to his kite-flying in the fine summer evenings. One late July evening was a special occasion, for he had a new pilot box kite, and hoped it would go so high as to be almost out of sight. Phillip was asked to go upon the Hill after his homework was done, and take turns with cousin Gerry at holding the heavy winder.

As soon as Father was gone, Phillip closed the book and decided to have some music. He played the Polyphone for a couple of tunes, and then decided to go and see Gerry.

This cousin was a tall, blue-eyed boy who liked "young Phillip" as much as Phillip admired "old Gerry". Gerry knew lots of nice things to talk about, and was never sarcastic like Ralph. Gerry was as tall as Ralph, who had rabbit teeth and cold sort of eyes, like a cod's on the fishmonger's slab. Ralph went to the West Kent Grammar School. He was one of the Yah Boo Boys, who had a feud with the prefects. The boots of the Yah Boo Boys often thumped on the tricky asphalt paths of Hillside Road, as they ran past, shouting and laughing, their books in straps over their shoulders, to be thrown down when they stopped and shouted up the gulley to their pursuers, "Yah Boo! Yah Boo!" The Yah Boo Boys cheeked the keepers on the Hill, too, particularly the Lanky Keeper, who was very thin and tall, with a gruff voice and a huge brown bushy moustache. The other keepers were fat and round, with the exception of Skullface, who was always trying to catch you among the forbidden bushes, or hiding while you tried to get sparrows' nests up the trees or under the eaves of the lavatory. To do this you had to climb the spiked railings, and tread among the flowers, which was strictly forbidden. The eggs therefore were more valuable.

Phillip did not care for cousin Ralph. He thought he was a fool, ever since the day when some of the Yah Boo Boys, dashing down through the bushes, had settled in the grassy corner where the hurdle fence met the spiked railings, opposite Grandpa's house across the road. They had begun to light Ogden's Tabs. Ralph had called Phillip over, and said,

"Would you like to see smoke coming out of my eyes?"

Phillip said smoke couldn't do it.

"You watch steadily, and see, if you don't believe me," replied Ralph. "Hold my hand to see there is no deception. Hold it tight."

Phillip did so.

"Now look hard at my eyes."

The other Yah Boo Boys were grinning. Ralph drew a lot of

smoke from his Tab, so that it glowed bright red, and then drew it into his lungs, while staring at Phillip's eyes. Suddenly Phillip cried "Oh!" then "B—— you!" for the end of the cigarette had been put on his wrist. Ralph's toothy grin came through the green bars of the railings.

"I suppose you think you are funny, don't you?" shouted Phillip, after looking at the little white blister on his skin.

"I do," grinned Ralph.

"You are, you know, too! You look exactly like a monkey in the Zoo, behind bars!" and so saying, Phillip had gone in to see Uncle Hugh, pleased that the other boys had laughed at Ralph, who had said, "You young s——," another very bad word.

But that was long ago, at the beginning of Standard Three, and since then Phillip had had nothing more to do with his cousin Ralph. Gerry was the one he liked.

Hastening up the gully, that fine July night, he found Gerry holding the winder, while the kites were ever so high in the sky.

Winking an eye, Gerry beckoned Phillip; then transferring the handles to Phillip, he said "So long, old man, see you later. I'm meeting my Dinah by the Refreshment House." Phillip thought Gerry was a wonderful grown-up person to be able to speak of a girl like that, much less to *dare* to meet one.

Certainly Phillip did not dare to think of—he dared not even formulate in his mind the name of Helena Rolls. She was too far above him, she was remote as the high blue of the sky.

The summer wind, blowing from over the distant downs and the fields of Kent, coming from the high chalk cliffs above the fretted edge of ocean, passed over the streets and houses, the open spaces and the diminishing trees south of the river; and streaming up from the heated slopes of the Hill, ascended in flowing strata under remote cloudlets which lay at the zenith seemingly without movement. Under the speckled white flitch of cirrus the small speck of the pilot kite was trying ever to rise higher against the weight of the twine holding it to the wooden backbone of its big brother below, the broad double-box with wings giving it a bat-like appearance; or an Emperor Moth, thought Richard, with its hues of purple, brown, and black. He thought of his splendid kite as alive above the earth, a thing inanimate but with a soul, as it strove to break away, as it hummed its plaint, moth-like, upon the ascending cord curved by wind and terrestrial gravity in tension from himself. He imagined the kite looking down upon the scene below, wanting freedom, but attached to its master. Unaware of the thoughts of the small boy behind him, the human captive holding with tired arms the ends of the horizontal rod that supported the winder, Richard felt glad to be alive.

Two hundred yards away, aloof, lest his home-made newspaper kite foul those of the dogmatic Mr. Maddison—for the two had by now exhausted all conversational possibilities—stood Mr. Muggeridge, wondering by the feel in his abdominal scar if the weather was about to change.

Phillip looked about him to try and find interest in something. There was only the usual sight of people standing still, looking up at Father's kites for a while before moving on. The pilot on top was lifting the double-box. Father wore his two thick leather gloves, and had to hold on as hard as he could. The cuttyhunk line scorched the flesh if it slipped, said Father. Looking across the grass, Phillip saw Mr. Muggeridge holding his silly old paper kite with one hand, while it swung to and fro and wiggled its tail like a lamb when it punched the ewe for milk. Mr. Muggeridge's kite was a soppy newspaper one, its tail in curl-rags. Huh! Any fool could make a kite like that; he had made one himself earlier in the summer, and given it away for nothing.

Father was hauling in now, hand over hand, slowly, and he had to ask someone to wind the slack on to the winder. A smaller boy obliged. The double-box that Father called the Emperor Moth was slowly moving from left to right against the grey clouds which had half covered the white flossy ones up above. Then the cuttyhunk jerked on the winder, and nearly pulled it out of his hands. The wind was gusty.

"I can't hold it, I daren't take a turn round my hand," Father was saying to another man. "It would cut my hand in two." Others were waiting now, ready to help. Someone said a storm was coming up.

"Take the boy's winder, do you mind?" Father said. A man took the winder and Phillip, happy to be free, ran forward to watch. It was like a tug of war! Father was saying that he would try and go forward to fasten the line to a seat; that would hold it.

Mr. Muggeridge's paper kite was now weaving like a mongoose before a snake. Suddenly it turned right over and plunged down

with a flapping noise. Hurray, thought Phillip, that would teach
the old fool a lesson for daring to argue with his father! He
hoped it would hit the keeper's hut and stick in the roof like a
harpoon. The wind was now very cold under his jersey. A
grumble of thunder came from behind the Crystal Palace. A
storm was coming, hurray! The pilot kite, very high up in the
sky, was swinging from side to side. Father and the man helping
to hold the cord by the winder were now being pulled over the
grass.

"I ought to warn you!" cried Father: "If the seat won't hold
it, you must watch that the line doesn't foul you anywhere."

Many people were now hurrying up. When Father got to
the seat, he shouted to the man to lower the winder, so that he
could pass the line under the top bar of the seat, at the side.
The line hummed a dangerous high note as it was held taut on
the wood. Father took a turn round the top bar, and once again,
and then again, and tied a knot, saying: "By Jove, my palm felt
on fire", and shaking off his leather glove, there was a blue line
right across like a cane mark where the cord had cut his skin.

Several people pressed to see, and Father cried: "Stand back,
please! If this powerful cuttyhunk breaks it will crack like a
whip-lash, and may take an eye out!"

Then the seat began to tilt back on the grey galvanised loops
of its legs and several men tried to grab it, but it fell over backwards, and so did they, and, Oh glory, on the strong wind that
turned the trees grey the seat was bouncing and sliding over the
empty tennis court. It hooked up the net and went on dragging
and tearing it.

People were shouting, "Billo! Billo there! Look out! Hi!" but
the seat caught in the big thorn tree and started to climb up it,
then it went right through the branches and over the grass where
the East London Industrial boys played football in the winter.
A lot of boys were running after the seat, and hanging on to it.
It was terribly exciting!

Phillip ran after them with the others, shouting out "Let it go!
Let it go!" for he wanted to see the seat rise up into the air and
go on forever, like Johnny-head-in-air in *Struvelpeter*. But the
seat was held at last, and then to Phillip's utter disappointment,
Father took out his ivory penknife and cut the line. At once the
kites dropped away, waggling slowly, falling about limply and

growing smaller and smaller, shaking their heads as though
sadly as they went far over the poplar trees at the end of the
Hill and at last were lost to sight.

Thunder was rolling nearer with livid flashes of lightning.
They all hurried away off the Hill, while Father said he would
see the keeper later, measly Skullface who tried to catch boys,
about the damage to the seat. The trees all had a pale, grey look
in their twirling leaves.

"You see, old chap," he said to Phillip, as they hastened down
the gully, the winder with only a little line left on it under his
arm, "wet cord is a conductor of electricity, and we all might
have been struck dead if lightning had taken it into its head to
travel down from those nimbus clouds overhead. I wonder if I
shall see the kites again? I marked my name and address in
indelible pencil on the struts, with promise of a reward."

Later that evening, when Phillip was in bed, there came a
knock on the front door. He heard the bell ring as well. He
hopped out of bed and crept along the passage. Three rough
voices spoke at once when Father opened the front door on the
chain. Then there was talking, the men calling Father "Guv'nor".
Phillip heard the chain go off, and then the chink of money.
A voice said, nastily, "Blimey, what's this?" Father said, "That
is one-tenth of the value to which you are entitled by law. You
can take it or leave it."

"It's not worth the tram ride up from Vilo Dogs! What you
fink we are, 'king kids?"

"That's all you'll get, the kites aren't worth very much, you
know."

"Come on, leav'r old Jew, mates, an' next time let 'im climb
on the roof and get 'is 'king kites by is 'king self!"

Phillip crept back to bed, thinking of the awful swearing at
Father. Mum came up later, and told him that the men had
been very rude when Father had given them ninepence each.
Phillip immediately felt ashamed because Father had not given
them more.

Father put the kites in his workroom, and then Phillip fell asleep.
At breakfast Father talked about a windlass and piano wire,
which was beyond him, he said. When Phillip went on the Hill
to look at the seat, it was cemented back in its place.

Chapter 26

HAYLING ISLAND

PHILLIP made friends with a dog on the Hill. They used to go hunting deer together, and Rover, as Phillip called him, kept the wolves at bay when they attacked his herds in his domain. He was Sir Phillip now, as Cousin Gerry had knighted him one Saturday morning, saying: "Those are your lands, Sir Phillip", and pointed with his switch before galloping away. But Father saw him with Rover one afternoon and said he must not consort with strange dogs, in case they bit him. If a dog had hydrophobia, said Father, it would go mad if you gave it a saucer of water to drink. Everyone it bit would foam at the mouth and scream at the sight of water.

Phillip listened, and that was all: for he was beginning to see and feel Father as something that was always trying to stop him doing what other boys did, and besides, he was always grumbling and so the only thing to do was to keep out of his way as much as possible and not let him find out anything.

There had been a glut of cherries earlier that year. Masses of cherries were for sale in barrows in the street outside the school for a halfpenny a pound, black ones and red ones. The black ones were sweeter. Father had objected to him buying cherries in the gutter, saying they had been handled by dirty paws with no idea of sanitation. They must be washed first, before being eaten. As far as Phillip was concerned, they were washed in his mouth; the daily after-school bag was empty long before he reached even Charlotte Road. He bought some for the other boys, out of his fretwork money from Grannie. He made all his fretwork things for Grannie, who gave him a shilling an object. After selling her the seventh pipe-rack, Grannie said gently that she did not smoke, and would Phillip think of something else for the next time? So with pattern pasted on thin sycamore wood clamped to the vice on the edge of the kitchen table, Phillip began an entire piano front, to be completed in sections of twelve. He grew tired of fretwork after the second section, and asked Grannie if she would mind if he did not do the rest. After all, he pointed out, she had not got a piano.

"No, dear," said Grannie. "But it is very good of you to think of me. Perhaps I shall have a piano one day, and then you can finish the screen for me."

In compensation Phillip brought her a chaffinch's nest, from which the young birds had flown. They were not fleas in the bottom of it, among the horsehair and the feathers, he said, but only tiny beetles which did not bite you.

Cherry hogs were the rage at school that summer. All along the walls of the playground boys crouched behind their wooden frames made in the workshop, inviting all comers with bags of dried stones to try and win lucky shots. You knelt down at a chalk line and flipped or rolled your hog towards the satinwood frames, which had square holes in them along one edge, like the holes of a mouth-organ. If you got a hog in the smallest hole, you got ten hogs back, but the largest hole at the other end was worth only two. Mother made him a little linen bag to keep his hogs in; but Father saw them, and saying they were stones harbouring germs, sent him to wash his hands—he was an hour late for tea—and confiscated the hogs.

Phillip swopped the rest of his cherry hogs for five-stones. A boy had got five knuckle-bones of a sheep from a butcher, and boiled them to get the shreds of meat off them. You threw them up, while crouching down, and tried to catch them on the back of your hand. Then on your fist at the side, and other places in succession. Some boys bought five-stones at the shop, five for a ha'penny, but real bones were best, for then you could think of cannibals in canoes in the South Seas, like in Father's book, which had been his prize at school by what was printed inside the cover.

Meanwhile Richard had thrown the grubby cherry stones one and two at a time among the thorns of the gully, hoping the seeds would sprout and take root. He had never forgotten what he had heard, as a boy, of the effects of cholera sweeping through the East End of London, killing hundreds of men, women and children. It had been said at the time that the germs had been brought on a ship arriving at the East India Docks, with a Lascar crew, and that they had spread by way of an infected hawker with a fruit barrow.

Having got rid of the cherry-stones, Richard felt that he ought to make it up to Phillip with some marbles. So he bought him a box from the newspaper shop by the station, and a big blood alley with green, red, and yellow stripes inside it. Germs were less likely to live on stone or glass.

When Phillip took the blood alley to school, Mildenhall took it from him and put it in his pocket, saying, with thumb showing through clenched fist, that Phillip would get that in his eye if he told his cousin Gerry. A score of times as he lay in bed at night Phillip saw himself, stripped to the waist, rippling with muscles, weaving around Mildenhall and then with a tremendous straight left, knocking him backwards off his feet, while boys cheered and in the distance Helena Rolls smiled at him, and giving him a bow off her plait, asked him to wear it for her sake.

Now it was time to go away for the summer holidays. With some of the money Grannie had given him for the pipe-racks Phillip was going to buy some fishing tackle, hire a boat, and get *Pluck Library* as well as the *Union Jack*, for holiday reading. Father had forbidden this literature, saying it gave a boy entirely wrong ideas about life, and tended to make him wild and in some cases encouraged possible criminal tendencies. Father had no objection to him reading the *Strand Magazines*, in their thin pale-blue covers, which filled an entire drawer below the clothes cupboard in his bedroom. Phillip had read every Adventure of Sherlock Holmes during the past winter and spring, and had been horrified to learn that in the end Sherlock Holmes had fallen in a death clutch with the terrible Professor Moriarty over a precipice.

Yet, despite exercises with his father's dumb-bells and Indian clubs, Phillip remained a thin, pale little boy, frightened of Mildenhall; until the summer holidays came, with fresh and sunlit prospect. They were going to the seaside, to a faraway place called Hayling Island.

Phillip duly bought his *Plucks* and *Union Jacks* at the bookstall at Waterloo, and put them to mark his ownership of a corner seat facing the engine. This time he was determined to be strong, and not to be sick. His sisters also had their special holiday papers: Mavis had *Comic Cuts* and Doris had *Little Folks*.

"Now I must sit here, by myself, at this end," said Phillip. "Please tell Mavis to get in the other corner, Mummy. I may

want to change my seat at any moment. Also, her face opposite
always worries me." So far the family had the carriage to themselves.

"I like this end best, too," said Mavis. "And your face not
only worries me, it makes me laugh, the way you look when you
are reading."

"Come along to this end, Mavis, it is just as good, dear."

"Oh, you always put him first, Mummy! It isn't fair!"

"Go on, Mavis, obey your mother, this is my end!"

"I don't see why I should, just because you say so, so there!"

"Mother said so, too. Wash your ears out."

"It's going to be a lovely day, and so don't let's start bickering,
there's good children."

"I like that! Why, you *never* wash. Who pretends to have a cold
bath, when he swishes the water with his hands, I'd like to know."

"Who puts powder on her face—to cover grime with chalk
dust?"

"What about the dust in your ears! You *never* wash them."

"Children, don't bicker so!"

"I wasn't bickering, Mum, I was just asking Mavis to move in
case I want to be sick."

"I know, dear."

"You favour Phillip, just as Daddy says!" cried Mavis, from
the opposite corner.

"You silly fool, shut up!" said Phillip. "If I have to put up
with that from Father, there's no reason why I should have to
put up with it from a bit of a girl like you."

"Bit of a boy yourself! You aren't very strong, are you?
Anything makes you sick."

"Your ugly mug does, certainly."

"Phillip, I won't have you speaking to your sister like that!
I've told you before. I shall tell your father if you are not a good
boy."

"I don't care. You can't frighten me! All right, if I spew right
over you, Mavis, it will be entirely your own fault."

"Have this orange," said Hetty. "It will settle your stomach,
dear. And I won't have you using such an expression. Where
you pick up such things from I do not know."

"I heard it from your brother Hugh."

"Phillip, how dare you speak so familiarly of your uncle! I

am not concerned with what Uncle Hugh or anyone else does, I will not have you speaking like a common little boy."

At this point an elderly woman got in. She was dressed all in black, and conveyed such an atmosphere of lugubrity that the conversation closed. Phillip had his stories folded beside him; he was putting off the wonderful moment of beginning to read, pretending to himself that he did not know they were there, so that he might pretend suddenly to have discovered them. Then Mavis was on her feet, to look out of his window as the whistle blew. Phillip got up and elbowed her away, while Hetty told him not to put his head out, in case it struck a signal. She worried in case the door had not been closed properly after the lady had got in, and was in apprehension until the lady said, "There is a distinct draught, I think I must ask you to let me put the window up half-way", as she rose to do it.

"Sit down now, Sonny," Hetty said politely, "and read your papers, like a good boy."

The elderly woman put on a pair of steel-framed spectacles and took a Bible out of her rush bag, watched by Phillip during intervals of looking intently out of the window. When she got out at Clapham Junction he said, "Phew! What a niff! I bet she don't use Pears soap." There were many enamel advertisements for this luxury fixed to the sooted yellow-brick walls beside the railway lines. "It's enough to make anybody sick."

"Phillip, how dare you!"

Despite herself, Hetty could not help smiling.

"There you go again, encouraging Phillip!" said Mavis, watching her from the opposite corner. "You pander to him."

"Hush, Mavis; you should not say such things."

"Father says them, so they must be true, so there!" and Mavis wrinkled her nose at Phillip.

"Now who would like a nice banana?" asked Hetty, taking up her bag, in an attempt to restore harmony.

"I would like a nasty one for a change," said Phillip.

"You won't get one at all, Sonny, if you talk like that! There's a black one here, I've a good mind to take you at your word. Now be a good boy, and don't annoy. We are all going to have a lovely holiday."

Doris sat beside her mother, holding tight to a wooden spade and a little painted bucket.

"Give Phil the black banana, Mum, just to show him!" said
Mavis.

"I'll put it in my pipe and smoke it, like the mat in the hall!"
retorted Phillip.

"Isn't he barmy, Mum?"

"Then Father is barmy too, for he said it first!"

"Hush, Sonny, you should not say such things about your
father."

"Well, you tell Father not to say such silly things to me. Putting
the hall mat in my pipe to smoke! Poof!"

The incident of the mat had happened when, after a raining
day, Phillip had come home with muddy boots and forgotten to
wipe them on the mat. Father had been home, and sending him
back, had told him to come in the front door quietly, close it, wipe
his boots thoroughly, go out again and repeat the same actions
six times running, to teach him to remember.

"Don't let me or anyone else have to remind you about the
mat in the hall again, young man. Now put that in your pipe
and smoke it."

Phillip had imagined a huge bowl, stuffed with the coconut
mat, and thick blue smoke rising out of a pipe with a stem as thick
as a cricket-bat handle. Recalling the pipe, the thought of it
made his head ache, and nearly broke his neck, to have such a
monstrous thing in his mouth. It made him feel sick, too. He
closed his eyes and tried to sleep; but opening them again,
there was Mavis staring at him with a grin. She was hoping he
would be sick, he thought. He closed his eyes again, but now the
smell of the mat being smoked in that pipe made him feel sick.
He kept very still.

It was only lately that the antagonism between Phillip and
Mavis had become sharpened. They had never really been
friends, and now their worlds did not even touch. Phillip was in
Gerry's Band; Mavis had two particular friends in the school,
who absorbed her emotions and feelings. Both her girl friends
lived in Charlotte Road. The trio usually walked to and from
school together, in a world of their own.

Little notes passed between them occasionally; sometimes two
were not speaking to the third; the quarrel was made up. Arm-
in-arm three loving girls, oblivious of boys, walked together on

the pavement; then another remark—it is always what was said by the third girl—would cause a different coalition of Mavis and Violet against Marjorie, or Marjorie and Violet were not speaking to Mavis. In times of harmony they exchanged Confession Books, where heart-burning statements about best friends were recorded, sometimes to be scratched out with ink or smothered by wetted indelible pencil, substitutions made, later to be cancelled. Once Phillip had written sarcastic remarks about Violet's thin legs and Marjorie's calves like table-legs, in Mavis's book, an action that caused protest from Mavis, a reprimand not to spoil other people's things from Hetty, and "I don't care, I'll do what I like" from the culprit.

These sarcasms and antagonisms between the children were hurtful to both Richard and Hetty, in their separate worlds or provinces of thought. Richard could not understand it; he and his brothers and sisters had not been like that. He had long decided that it was through Turney traits that such things occurred. As for Hetty, she looked back on the life of her old home with Charley, Dorry, Hughie, and little Joe as one of merriment and accord. Why could not Phillip and his sisters be as they had been, in the old days? So while Richard withdrew into himself more and more—while continuing to like Mavis, because obviously she liked him, whereas Doris showed no desire to be other than her mother's child—Hetty strove, by acting always as peacemaker and ameliorator, to avoid the discord which was wearing her out.

The train was now running rapidly. In an effort to not think of being sick, Phillip began counting the telegraph posts as they blackly hurtled past. His eye rose and fell with the curve of the massed wires. He turned for relief from the rising and falling blows on his eyes to contemplation of green fields and ripening corn. A motor-car travelling along a road trailed half-a-mile of dust behind it, and though it was far away, and easily raced by the train, somehow the dust made him feel as though it were in his own throat. Then the trees in the fields and the hedges, that Father had called hedgerow timber on the Sunday-morning walks to Cutler's Pond while Mother cooked the Sunday dinner —all the hedgerow timber got in the way, and to remove it he had to imagine he was driving a huge chariot like Boadicea's, with scythes on the hubs, cutting down the beastly trees. Now the smoke was coming in the open window. He left it, to sit in his corner, while Mavis opposite was combing her doll's hair with a horrid comb. Ugh! he could see *glue* on the doll's skull! He could *smell* the glue——

"Go away from looking at me! Stop her, Mummie. She taunts me!" he cried feebly.

"Ha ha, you're green about the gills! Mummy, quick, Phillip's going to be sick!"

"Oh, Sonny dear, do you feel all right?"

"Tell Mavis not to grin at me," he mumbled, as his mouth filled with water. "Oh!" and he lay back, his hand over his eyes, while the beastly train shook and made horrible grinding noises in his ears.

He staggered to his feet. Mavis now retreated to the far corner, clutching her doll, its blanket, and its home-made underclothes.

"All right, Sonny, come with me to the lavatory. Open the door, Mavis," as the victim, staring eyes circular with shame and fear, tottered out of the carriage and away to sanctuary just in time.

He returned five minutes later with pale face, tears of exhaustion after retching still on his cheeks.

"Look, I can see tears! Cry baby!" said Mavis.

"Cry baby," repeated Doris.

Hetty smacked Mavis, who thereupon began to cry.

"You should not taunt your brother when he is ill, Mavis!"

Hetty was thinking of Sonny when, for weeks after his birth, he had not been able to keep down any food, and she had feared for days and nights that she would lose him. If old Mr. Pooley had not brought the jug of ass's milk when he did, at the crisis, her baby would have died. Poor Mr. Pooley, he and his dear little mother donkey had been dead three years now. Mr. Pooley had lived to be one hundred and five years old.

"Mavis does not really mean what she says, Sonny."

Indifferent to words, the invalid desired only to lie down on the seat, a rug over him, and to forget everything. He went to sleep, and awoke, aware of the world once more, as the train slowed up before Havant.

Here they had to change, and await the local train to Hayling Island. There were twenty minutes to spare before that was due to depart, and so Hetty began to think about getting a cup of hot beef tea for Sonny. There was a lady waiting for the same train, and approaching her, she asked if she would mind keeping an eye on her two little girls while she left the station; only for a few minutes, since her little boy had not been very well. Mavis and Doris, the luggage piled before them, were in the open shelter on the platform, playing Neighbours with their dolls on the seat. With a smile the traveller said she would remain with them, and after thanking her Hetty, holding the boy by the hand, went out into the High Street.

Beef tea was the best restorative for Sonny, as for herself after a bilious attack, when the period of nausea had passed; so the thing to do was to look for a tea-shop. After walking down a hundred yards or so, and not finding one, anxiety about the train—the need to be not too long away—made her go into a grocer's shop and enquire. There was a tea-shop at the end of the High Street, she learned, five minutes walk away; but on leaving the shop, two short blasts on the whistle of an engine made her wonder if after all she or the porter had made a mistake in the number of minutes to wait—perhaps he had said ten, and not twenty. There was a public house opposite; and remembering how once in her girlhood, after a bad crossing from Ostend to Harwich, Papa had given her some brandy and how much better she had felt, Hetty crossed the road and after some hesitation went through the door marked Private.

"I have a little boy who has been sick in the train from London. Might I have a little brandy, medicinal of course, to help restore him?" she asked the man behind the counter, who had two waxed spikes to his black moustache.

He gave a glance at Phillip's thin pale face, and said, "A glass of hot milk with an egg in it, and a lacing of three-star's the thing to put that rooky right. Plenty o' time for the Hayling train, m'am, and I've got the milk already warm on the hob. Ada!" he barked to someone behind a curtain, "whip up an egg and milk, not too hot, and put a jerk into it." A deep voice behind the curtain said, "I 'eard, and you ain't got a squad on the square."

Enlarged photographs on the wall revealed the landlord's military past. He took up a glass, and polished it.

Hetty had not long to wait. Sounds of swizzling in a glass came through the curtain; then a stout woman with a big toothy face and motherly smile appeared with the glass on a tray.

"It's not too hot, m'am," she smiled, "and I put a little sugar in it, that will do as much good as the brandy, before the egg can get to work in the little lad's stomach."

Phillip had a picture of the egg, a sort of Uncle Hilary Humpty Dumpty, getting to work with mallet and chisel, shavings all about its feet in a cavernous workshop of his stomach. Shavings, ugh! He did not want to put the glass to his lips, the smell of the milk in his nostrils made him feel sick; but after the first sip all reluctance instantly went, and he swallowed it in eager sips, exclaiming, "It's lovely! Brandy, is it? It must be lovely to be a drunkard."

"Hush, Sonny!"

"How old is your little boy?" asked the woman.

"He is nine and four months," said Hetty.

"I didn't think he was so old as that. Has he been very ill?"

"Only when he was a baby. We could not find the right food for him, and after two months he weighed a pound less than he did at birth. Yes!" exclaimed Hetty, "I very nearly lost him."

Phillip, as he sipped the hot drink, wished that she would not talk about him before strangers. He dreaded people to know that he had been fed on donkey's milk. It was a disgrace. Some of the Mildenhall gang knew it, but if decent people ever knew it, and told Mr. or Mrs. Rolls, he would run away to sea and become a cabin boy, never to return.

Both the landlord and his wife seemed to take a personal pleasure in watching the life come back into the boy's face. And because the little mother seemed hardly to be grown up, to be scarcely more than a child herself, they refused to charge her anything for the drink. Hetty thanked them, but said she must insist on paying.

"It's a pleasure, m'am. You see, we had a little boy once, only he was taken from us," said the woman, softly, and so Hetty said no more. She smiled at the woman, a tear in her eye; and offering her hand to both of them, thanked them again, while Phillip did likewise, and raised his cap on leaving.

"People when you get to know them are so very very kind," said Hetty, as they hurried back to the station, "so very very kind, once they understand one another."

More warm feelings were to come; for the woman who had promised to look after Mavis and Doris turned out to be someone Hetty had known at the Ursulines' Convent at Thildonck. The children rejoiced in their mother looking so gay as she talked with the new lady, Mrs. Robartes. The train went over the sea, and they saw ships and boats and seagulls. Mrs. Robartes told Phillip that at low tide the harbour was all mud, and many of the boats lying there were old hulks, and would never go to sea again, being abandoned. Then after crossing the black bridge they were on Hayling Island, passing cornfields and haystacks, and far away could be seen the Isle of Wight.

From the station, where they said goodbye to the lady, they rode in a cab through the village and came among trees to a lane behind a common. The sea, the sea! There beyond gorse and brambles among patches of brown shingle could be seen a blue-grey placid level. Phillip was wildly excited. He kept jumping up and down; and out, as soon as the cab stopped at Sea View Terrace.

Sea View Terrace consisted of a row of half-a-dozen cottages, with plastered outer walls dark grey with the blown spume of many winters, and yellow-brown in patches with orange lichen. The terrace was built opposite the Lifeboat House, about a minute's walk from the shingle slope to the sea. The Maddison lodgings were in No. 2, kept by an old spinster of the name of Barber. Miss Barber was plump, with no eyebrows; she wore a lace cap pinned to her wig, while her body was enclosed within a boned black bodice and black skirt dating from about the time of the Franco-Prussian war. Phillip hoped she would not want to kiss him. Off the children ran, to see the sea, having promised to be back in time for tea at half-past four.

At half-past four Miss Barber brought in the tray of boiled eggs, cottage loaf, butter, and cake, with the tea-pot under a thick woollen tea-cosy looking like herself. Phillip ran in, just in time. Miss Barber told him that he must always be punctual for his meals if he did not want to miss them. He waited until she had gone, then breathlessly told his mother that it was a wonderful place, with fishing boats, anchors, bathing tents, a life-saving apparatus, a real lifeboat in the house, and, most wonderful of all, porpoises coming up black out of the waves quite near the shore.

"They come in after the shoals of mackerel," said Miss Barber, reappearing with a bowl of raspberries. "They look fearsome creatures, but they won't hurt you if you meet them bathing."

Phillip had no wish to read now. Here was everything just like a book, except that he had to share a bed with Mavis. Mummy came up to put a bolster between them, to stop kicking matches. The very first morning the postman brought him a postcard, a funny picture of lots of men playing conkers, who had come over with William the Conqueror. It was from Father. It was the sort of thing Father thought funny, but he could see no point in it. Father's writing on the other side hoped he and Mummy and Mavis and Doris had had a pleasant journey, and that Hayling was as nice as he had hoped it would be. It ended *Yours affectionately, Daddy*; but it was Father writing, not the ever-so-long-ago Daddy who had taken him to the Jubilee Bonfire.

On the following Sunday, Father arrived at dinner-time on his new black Sunbeam with the Little Oil Bath. He wore his dark-brown cycling suit and cap, and said he had averaged eleven miles an hour, having started soon after five that morning. Phillip shook hands with Father, and felt that it would not be so nice now that he had come, even though he was not stopping, being on his way down to Dartmoor, which he said he wanted to explore.

Sunday at Hayling Island was not so dull a day as at home. You could take off your starched collar after going to church in the morning, and put on your jersey. There was no Collect to learn, but no shops were open, or boats allowed on the sea. Church was not so bad, you could see the sunshine inside this church, not like church at all.

Richard's two-day stay had been prearranged; Hetty had packed for him a spare flannel shirt, bathing dress, and a pair of brown-striped flannel trousers which, after many washings, had shrunk and become of yellowish hue; still, with the ends let down, soap rubbed on the creases, and then pressed with a hot iron on a damp cloth, they were presentable. So, when Mrs. Robartes drove to Sea View Terrace to call on Hetty on the Monday afternoon, and was introduced to Richard, they could accept an invitation to go on the following afternoon to the Robartes' tennis party.

Phillip was glad to see Father and Mother so well-dressed and happy. He promised to take his two sisters back to tea at Miss Barber's between four o'clock and a quarter past, to be in time for half-past. He was put in charge, said Father; he was head boy now. He promised not to bathe, as the tide would be high, and there was a back-drag on the shingle. With sunshade up, and long skirt held out of the dust, Mother left with Father, and above the sky seemed wider and clearer.

While Phillip and his sisters were playing on the shingle an exciting thing happened. A boat rowed up with a net on the back. One man in big leather boots jumped out, to hold a rope on shore. The other two men sat in the boat, each holding an oar. They dipped their oars occasionally to keep the boat beyond the breaking waves. Then the man on shore pointed out to sea. Phillip looked, but could see nothing. Then looking at the man's big leather boots, which the sea wetted each time a wave ran up, Phillip saw a tiny fish, then another—there were hundreds of tiny fish. He pointed to them, and the fisherman said "Brit".

He suddenly shouted, his arm pointing. At once the men lay on the oars, and the boat moved out to sea, the net dropping over the back. The men rowed hard, the oars seemed to bend. They turned the boat, and rowed in a wide loop, then came toward the shore, by the lifeboat house. The man on shore was pulling in the dark-brown rope. Then putting it over his shoulder he trudged step by step toward the boathouse. The boat grated into the shingle, the two men scrambled out, and began pulling in the other end of the rope. Corks floated in the loop out to sea. Phillip took the rope behind the skipper and helped him haul in.

As they pulled in, the men drew nearer to one another. Phillip pulled with all his might. The arc of corks came nearer; then he stopped pulling, to watch the men hauling in the net. They left it in little heaps, which the waves rushed over, and sucked back from, with glinting brit on their sides. The water inside the corks was dark blue, and the little brit were jumping out like drops of rain coming out of the sea. The men bent low, you could see the darns in their jerseys. They hauled faster as the corks came nearer shore.

"Look at the fish!" cried Phillip, jumping away from the rope. Hundreds of fish were moving about, making the water dark. Soon the net came in like a big stocking and there were thousands of fish threshing about under the string squares, green fish with blue bars on them and curved thin tails. Mackerel!

They flapped on the pebbles, twisting and jumping, so many mackerel that the net could not be pulled in, but lay where the waves were breaking. One of the men waded in and began to throw them on the shingle, saying, "I reckon there's two hundred stone here, Dad."

Many people were now watching. Phillip saw one man who was watching with hands in pockets suddenly bend down and pick up a fish. He put it head first into his inside pocket, beside an envelope. Then he stood as though nothing had happened, his hands in his pockets again. He had on dirty white tennis shoes, with his big-toe toenails sticking out.

At last the mackerel were all in a big heap. The skipper said to one of the younger men, "Go after the cart, Bob." Then he said to the people, "I'm selling eight a penny! Fine fresh mackerel!"

After hesitation, Phillip pulled from his trousers pocket, with some difficulty, for his hands and clothes were wet, the two pennies he had been fingering there all the afternoon, for a ride on the Life Saving Apparatus. But he had been too afraid to go up so high. Now he went to stand by the fisherman.

"Right you are, sonny," said the man, taking his twopence. Then with a knife he cut a piece of twine, and threaded sixteen fish on it, through their red gills. The bundle was very heavy, so the man cut another piece of string, took eight off the bundle, and threaded them on the new string. Feeling important, Phillip asked the man the time.

"Five after four, turn o' tide," said the man, without looking at a watch.

Proudly lifting his two shiny wet bundles, Phillip said to his sisters, "Come on, children, we must go to tea now, I promised Miss Barber we wouldn't be late. Half a mo', I must count my fish. No one's going to cheat me." He counted sixteen. "That's right. Come on, children." He gave the fish to Miss Barber.

"I'll grill four for supper, and souse the other four right away, dear," said Miss Barber, in reply to his request that she see to it that they were cooked before they went bad. Eight, he said, were for Dr. and Mrs. Robartes.

He had an idea that after tea he would take them to the house, which would give him a good excuse for calling.

"I'll leave you in charge of Doris, Mavis," he said. "I shall have to run most of the way, else these mackerel might go bad in the sun."

"Mummy said you must remain with us, and you promised," protested Mavis. "Anyway, if you go, I don't see why I shouldn't."

"But I don't want you. They are my fish, not yours."

After more bickering, he set out with the fishes. To his exasperation he was followed by his sisters. He ran to the village, looking back at the turn. He heard Mavis shout "It's all right, I know the way", so he took this to be a good excuse to go on by himself. It was not far. Mummy had pointed out the house, behind tall hedges, when she had taken him to the shop to buy a new pair of plimsolls, and white cricketing hat to stop sunstroke.

He went in through the gate, and rang the bell of the front door. A maid came. He said, "Please, I've brought these for your master and mistress. My father and mother know them very well, and came to the tennis to-day."

Mrs. Robartes appeared. "Come along in, my dear, how very kind of you to bring us some fish."

"They are quite safe to eat, Mrs. Robartes, and very fresh. You can grill them or souse them."

"How clever of you to know, dear. Now come in and join us. You are just in time for tea. Where are your sisters?"

"I think they are coming, Mrs. Robartes. I could not control them."

He knew it was all right when Mrs. Robartes smiled. Father smiled, and so did Mummy.

"Your little boy has brought us some fresh mackerel, Hetty. How extremely thoughtful and kind of him, to be sure. Ah, there's the bell, that must be your daughters! How your children must love you, dear!"

It was wonderful in the big room with the soft chairs and pictures of the sea and cornfield on the wall, much nicer than his house. It was funny bread and butter, all tiny rolled pieces with green crunch stuff inside. There were all sorts of little sandwiches, cakes, chocolates and marzipans. Afterwards Father played tennis and hit the ball ever so fast over the net, and when he served he won his service almost at once. He was the best player. There was another man who tried to copy him. This man played Father a single afterwards, while Dr. Robartes, who was short and rather fat, sat in a deck-chair and watched with the other old man.

Father and the copy-cat man played crouched down. They hit every ball hard and only sometimes into the net. Often they hit the ball before it bounced, slamming away, this side and that side, ever so quickly. Phillip wished Father would play on the Hill, just to show everyone. Then Mildenhall would not call him Tin Wheels any more.

Father did not say "Van in" and then "Van out" as the players on the Hill did, but "Vantage in" and "Vantage out". They banged away. It was over! "Well played, sir. I think that's Game and Set." Who had won? Father had! And the other man was a captain, too!

On the way home, Father said, "Captain Spalding has some big guns, Phillip, up in the red-brick forts on the mainland, on top of the downs. They are to keep any invaders away from our country. I shall be cycling past them to-morrow, on my way to the West. Now tell me about the fish." He laughed. "Did you buy them at the fishmonger's? Or catch them yourself? Which is it, eh?"

"I bought them from the man with the net."

"Phillip did buy them, Daddy," said Mavis. "I saw him buy them. There were hundreds and hundreds and hundreds on the beach. If I had had my purse with me, I would have bought some, too."

"Copy-cat!" said Phillip. "Anyway, I thought of it first. Now we are going to have a surprise for supper. Please don't tell what it is, Mavis, or you, Doris, will you?"

"I don't know what it is," said Doris.

"I simply cannot think what it is," said Father.

"I can!" cried Mavis.

"Then don't tell, dear," said Hetty. "Let it be a surprise."

"Poof!" replied Mavis. "Anyone can guess."

"Be quiet, Mavis!" hissed Phillip, in agony in case she told.

"Oh, tell me!" cried Doris.

"Anyway, Phillip didn't catch them himself, he only bought them!"

"I believe it's only fish!" exclaimed Doris. "I don't call that a surprise!"

Phillip abruptly took to his heels. He ran with all his speed back to No. 2 Sea View Terrace. He leapt upstairs to get two pennies out of his purse hidden under the grate in the bedroom fireplace. With the coins in his hand he ran to the Life Saving Apparatus. He must show Daddy that he was not always a funk: if he held tight to the two handles on the pulley wheel, he would not fall and break his legs on the shingle so far down underneath the cable.

Phillip paid the twopence to the old boatman, who gave him a pulley; and with throat suddenly dry, he reached the platform and adjusted the rusty wheel of the block over the cable.

When the others got to Sea View Terrace, they saw him launching himself off the high platform against the sky, hanging to the block as it went faster and faster, then at the end of the eighty-yard cable he hit the end buffer with his feet and dropped down.

He returned at once to the house, to sit and look at a book of uninteresting picture postcards, feeling a strange satisfaction that Father had seen him do a thing that, only that morning, Father had said looked to be far too dangerous for any small boy to risk his neck on.

Chapter 27

TWINEY'S

"IT's no good trying to make me win a scholarship! I'm an old hulk, an old hulk, quite worn out!" shouted Phillip. The lace of his boot broke. He took off the boot and flung it into the space above the pot-board below the kitchen dresser. "I can't learn at all! I can't! I can't, I tell you!" and the other boot followed the first.

He sat on a chair, completely dejected. "I am an old hulk! I shall never go to sea again!"

"Sonny, it is not fair for you to talk to your mother like that! I am only trying to help you. You must work harder, dear, and so win a scholarship, to fit you for a good position in after-life. You will thank me afterwards that I tried to make you work."

"Which after-life do you mean?"

"Hush, Sonny, hush! You must not say such things! You must do your work, dear."

"But my brain is worn out, quite useless, I tell you! Oh, I shall be late for school, and perhaps go on the Black Line! Where are the new laces? Quick, I tell you!"

"I shouldn't help him, Mummy, if he speaks to you like that! He wouldn't dare to do it if Father hadn't gone to the station!"

"You shut up, you fool, Mavis! Get out! Get out!! Get out!!! I'll slosh you, you beast!" He chased her out of the kitchen, and slipped in his black-stockinged feet on the oilcloth. The front door banged.

"Have you hurt yourself, Sonny?"

"Oh, I'll be late for school! Quick, quick, take this lace out of Father's boot. I'll pay him back. You owe me two jam-jars! Quick, do as I say! Where's my homework? Where did I leave it? Who's hidden it? I bet Mavis has!" and he stood in the kitchen, near to tears.

Hetty got him off to school at last, the borrowed lace in his boot. From her bedroom window she watched him running over the grass below the sheep-fold, a short cut. She could imagine his desperate face, fearful of being late, of being sent to stand on the Black Line. Why was there this difficulty in getting him off to school, morning after morning?

It was a scene that nowadays Hetty was becoming accustomed to. Phillip was always in trouble: he never seemed to do things the proper way, but gave himself, and her, continual cause for worry. The moment Dickie's back was turned he went his own way entirely. She was always dreading what he would do next, and so cause Dickie's anger when it was found out, with inevitable punishment to follow.

He did such inexplicable things. When they had come back from the seaside, having nothing better to do, Phillip had spent much of his time in the Backfield. One day towards the end of August, in the very hot weather, he had set fire to the long yellow grass deliberately, in several places at once; and then had run home in terror and hidden himself under his bed, too frightened to come out.

There were about eight acres of waste land left after the building, most of them on the slope below the distant railings of the Hill. The slope was covered with yellow, brittle grass. Fanned by the breeze, the flames spread rapidly in the long grasses. A high pall of yellow smoke drifted over Hillside Road. The noise of crackling flames increased, a wind swept the fires towards the wooden fences. Then the sound of the fire-engine bell sounded.

Soon Hetty, standing talking to Mrs. Bigge, with Mrs. Groat looking over her fence below, and Hugh in the garden above, heard the noise of galloping hoofs, the bell clanging nearer.

"I saw Phillip climbing over his fence in a great hurry ten minutes ago, Mrs. Maddison," remarked Mrs. Groat.

"I cannot say whether or not Sonny had anything to do with it, I am sure," replied Hetty.

The noise of fierce crackling now came from all across the field. White and yellow smoke rolled in coiling drifts over the gardens.

"I am going to fill all my pots and pans and pails with water." Mrs. Bigge went into her house, and closed the door behind her. She was deeply hurt, for another reason, which Hetty knew only too well. Hetty was living in dread of her husband finding out what Sonny had done to Mr. Bigge's little greenhouse recently. She went upstairs.

"Oh dear, what shall I do, Mummy?" the voice came from under the bed. "Will they take me to prison?" He lay huddled against the wall, in the farthest corner away from the door. Suddenly exhausted, Hetty cried:

"Oh, why do you do such things, you foolish, foolish boy?"

"I don't know, Mummy."

"Was anyone else with you?"

"No, Mummy."

"Did you do it all alone, then?"

"Yes, Mummy."

"I can only pray that it will not cause all the new houses to be burned down. Really, Sonny, you are a trial and a tribulation, you know. Sometimes I think you are not my little boy any more."

"If I pray hard enough, perhaps God will forgive me. I have prayed, Mummy. Do you think God will answer my prayer?"

At this point Mavis came upstairs to say that there were some policemen in the Backfield, with the firemen in helmets. They were beating the fires with sticks.

"Oh, oh," wailed Phillip. Then, "Shall I go and offer to help them, Mummy? Then they would not think it was me. Or would it be better if I were to kill myself?"

Hetty left him. Perhaps this time it would teach him a lesson.

On going up again, a few minutes later, to say that the fire was being beaten out, and what a fortunate boy he was that at least the garden fences had not been burnt down, she had not been able to find him.

Five minutes later she came upon him next door, sitting beside his Grannie and holding her wool for her, "as good as gold", Mamma said. How had he got there? The scullery door had been locked on the inside, and the chain was up on the front door. He had not gone through the sitting-room.

Hetty confided her troubles to her mother when Phillip had run off to play on the Hill, having washed his face and hands and smoothed his hair with water, to make him feel good. What made Sonny do such strange things? Hetty told Sarah how, after Dickie had left Hayling Island for his cycling tour, Sonny had spent two whole shillings on the Life Saving Apparatus, frightening the life out of her by riding down in all sorts of positions, upside down and inside out, until in the end he had arrived at the stopping place the wrong way round, and so bumped himself violently on the padded board and hurt himself so much that she had had to get Dr. Robartes to him. Dr. Robartes had ordered him to remain in bed; but that very afternoon he had got up and gone bathing and stayed in the sea so long that he had turned green in the face. He had just managed to crawl out on the shingle, and in the hired bathing tent he had lain in a shivering rigidity which had so frightened her, she had thought he was going to die. Brandy, followed by bed with hot-water bottles, had revived him.

"And would you believe it, Mamma, that very next day he stayed in the water over half-an-hour, ignoring my repeated requests that he should come out. Of course he was rigid again, with the need for more of Miss Barber's brandy, and hot-water bottles at his feet and stomach. Can you wonder at it that Miss Barber said that she would not have us again the next year, when we came to leave? Oh dear, I do not know what I shall do if he annoys his father as he does any more, for it is almost beyond me."

"I will make some tea, dear; you rest awhile. We must trust in One Above, Hetty, that is our only consolation."

Tea certainly helped to restore Hetty's equanimity: and optimistically she declared that perhaps, when Sonny had won a scholarship, the new life might alter things. Meanwhile, she told Sarah, she did not like punishing him, and it could never be said that Dickie had been lenient with him, except at first. In those early days he had loved his little son, and found pride in his original ways. Dickie had been delighted when Sonny had tried to smoke his pipe, to use his garden tools, even to put on his boots. Once when Dickie was away on a cycling holiday in the Norfolk Broads, hoping to see the Swallowtail and Large Copper butterflies, Sonny had insisted on taking one of "Daddy's boos" to bed with him, which surely showed that he was not entirely lacking, as Dickie had recently said, in a capacity for affection. "He is an entirely selfish child," were Dickie's words.

Certainly it did seem at times that Sonny had no regard or affection for anyone else, perhaps not even for himself. Why else should he go out of his way, so often, to cause himself such trouble and unhappiness? The setting on fire of the Backfield was typical. If God had not answered her prayers, he might by now be in a Reformatory. Hughie's explanation that he was "just a little devil" was really not applicable, for he never got any pleasure out of what he did, so far as she could see, but only anxiety and distress.

"Do not worry, dear," said Sarah Turney. "Things will come out all right in the end, I am sure."

The very next day Phillip took his father's chisels and mallet from the workroom, in order to hack off the lower end of a lead pipe leading from the scullery next door into the drain below the back steps. He managed to cut off about four inches of the pipe before the edges of the two chisels were rendered serrate by being struck upon surrounding brickwork. He wanted the lead to make weights for fishing, and also to carve a length of it into the shape of a small fish, for spinning with some triangular hooks his father had given him. A boy had told Phillip of a monster pike in the Randisbourne, and this, together with a reading in an old book on fishing by Cholmondeley-Pennell from the mahogany, glass-fronted bookcase, had inspired the necessity for strips of lead.

Worse than that, was the awful thing he had done to Mr. Bigge's little glasshouse, or plantarium. He had found out where Dickie had hidden his air-gun, and all one morning had been in the garden, watching for sparrows on the roof. Unable to hit any, he had turned his attention to objects about the garden, shooting at the clothes hanging on the line, then at the fence. Seeing the marks of the pellets in the creosoted wood, Hetty had told him that his father would be bound to see them, and since that would mean another thrashing, she had ordered him to return the gun immediately to the clothes cupboard from where he had taken it. At once he had climbed up the elm tree and, sitting in the top, taken pot shots into Hugh's room, the french windows of which were open. Not content with this, he had, saying that he was a sharpshooter in the rigging of a wooden battleship, shot at Mr. Bigge's glasshouse down below, over the fence. When at last he came down, a score of little starred holes showed irregularly along the coloured glass border which Mr. Bigge had made with such care.

"How dare you do such a thing! And to Mr. Bigge, who has always been so very very kind to you! You are no son of mine!"

"I don't care."

Mr. Bigge had not said a word about the matter, nor had Mrs. Bigge, though of course they had seen the damage done. She had felt dreadfully ashamed about it; and when the thrashing for the damaged chisels had inevitably come, for once she had not felt that Dickie was being too severe. And the very next day he had set fire to the grass in the Backfield.

At the beginning of the new term, he had been moved up into Standard Four, under a strict disciplinarian, Mr. Twine. Ever anxious for his success, Hetty had gone again to see Mr. Groat, at "Chatsworth". Mr. Groat had very kindly agreed to continue his coaching two evenings a week, but he had stipulated that the tasks set to be done in-between the boy's visits must be done, otherwise, he said, the boy would be wasting the time of all concerned.

Invariably the boy returned from "Chatsworth" with tear marks on his face. He seemed unable to learn at all, reported Mr. Groat; he seemed to have not the least idea of figures—Mr. Groat was coaching the boy in arithmetic, the subject in which he was very weak. It was essential, Mr. Groat had said, to show some proficiency in this subject if the boy were to qualify for one of the scholarships available annually from Wakenham Road School. Since Christ's Hospital was out of the question now, Hetty hoped that Sonny would be able to get into the Merchant Taylors' School, or perhaps the City of London School. Westminster School, next to the Abbey, was a beautiful school, but that too, like the Bluecoat, was out of the question.

What made it worse was that Mr. Groat had very kindly consented to coach Sonny without any fee, though Hetty had of course offered to pay in the first place. Mr. Groat was doing it all for nothing, as she had explained to Sonny many times, without any effect, she had to admit sorrowfully to herself.

Hetty wrote to Theodora about her problem. Dora replied at some length, saying that in her own experience of teaching, the old proverb that you could "take a horse to water, but could not make it drink" had to some extent been proved true. What was wanted was an entirely new system of teaching, which would never come about until women had the franchise.

Theodora's letter contained unhappy news of her own venture as a schoolmistress. Two things, she wrote, had combined to bring the school to a close: her partner Rechenda Baggot's insistence in having her sick sister in the house had given the school a bad advertisement, since she had died there of phthisis; while her own activities, though they had been kept strictly apart from the school, in the Women's Social and Political Union, had inevitably been misrepresented and distorted. Parents had removed their daughters.

"Well, Dora has only got what she asked for," was Richard's comment. He had no sympathy with Suffragettes. In the pages of *The Daily Trident* he had often read out to Hetty derisory accounts of their goings-on, to which she had had to agree for the sake of peace.

"It has long been obvious to me that Dora would spoil her chances of building up a stabilised school, with her cranky ideas. Hilary called in the office to-day, and tells me that it is being closed down. Well, it's her capital, not mine. I've seen that sort of thing happen with my own father when I was a boy. Dora has only herself to blame."

No avian shrieks accompanied Richard's voice from the Sportsman armchair nowadays. The parrot cage stood empty on its table. Hetty always saw its emptiness with some relief, since it was connected with a rarely happy incident between father and son.

One Sunday afternoon, following on the usual walk with the children to Cutler's Pond and back, and a dinner of roast mutton which, thank goodness, had not gone wrong, Dickie had said, "I wonder if Polly would enjoy climbing about the tree? He knows us well enough now to know which side his bread is buttered. So what do you say, Phillip, shall we let him out to stretch his wings?"

Before this, Richard had told the children the story of their Grandfather Maddison's tame partridges. It had been wonderful for Hetty to feel the happiness in the room. Phillip particularly had stared at his father, his eyes shining. Dickie had looked years younger as he talked of his old home in the country.

After dinner Dickie had taken the cage into Mavis's bedroom, which was at the back, and opened the window wide, as well as the cage door. After a while the grey and pink parrot had climbed out, and pulled itself to the top of the wire dome. There were some elm-trees down below in the gardens of Charlotte Road, and eventually the bird had flown away to them, uttering raucous cries. It had perched in the top of one, and, at sunset, had flown back to its cage.

The next Sunday afternoon Richard had let Polly out again, this time in the garden. The parrot had flown up into their own tree; but it had not come back. The next morning Richard had seen it in the elms on top of the Hill, perching up near the old nests, now abandoned by the rooks for the summer. Later, he had seen it flying with rooks over the grass. He walked daily over the Hill to the station, for after an interval of years he had returned to the London, Brighton and South Coast Railway, the quarterly season ticket to London Bridge being cheaper. The old feeling of embarrassment at the possibility of meeting anyone at the Tennis Club or Antiquarian Society had by now gone.

In the autumn the rooks came back at their tree tops, the African parrot with them. Phillip had seen it with the black birds on the grass. A rook was feeding it, he declared.

"Well," said Richard, "Polly is happier like that, it no longer has to go to an office every morning," and Phillip wondered what Father meant, seeing no connection. He was not the only one in "Lindenheim" unable to connect one event with another.

Phillip's reluctance to start early for school every morning, otherwise his chronic lateness which puzzled Hetty, was in part due to fear of arriving in the playground before the bell rang for the classes to line up before going into their classrooms. He was afraid of being seen by Mildenhall and his gang as he passed by Comfort Road, where Mildenhall lived. So Phillip went as late as possible to school, hoping to arrive at the gate just as Mr. Scrivenor was about to toll the bell. For the same reason he stayed behind in the classroom, pretending to look for a lost pencil on the floor, until it was empty. Then he could steal out, unobserved, to the gate, after making sure that Mildenhall was not about.

Phillip was still in Standard Four, where most of the boys, their hair clipped close upon the skull with a fringe left upon the brow, wore white rubber collars and long black stockings held up by garters above the knee. Standard Four was in charge of the disciplinarian, Mr. Twine. Mr. Twine was also the football master for the bigger boys in Standards Five, Six and Seven. He inspired a kind of fear different from that of "Gussy". Known as "Twiney", he was a man of twenty-six or seven years of age, tall and thin, with dark piercing eyes, a big brown moustache, and in the *Union Jack Library* he would have been described as hatchet-faced. Boys caught whispering, or even looking up from their books, were called out in front and usually told to hold out their hands, to receive two or three strokes of the cane on each palm. Phillip had not had the cane yet, but he lived in subdued terror of Mr. Twine.

There was a poor boy in Standard Four named Cranmer, who sat in the front row. He lived in Skerritt Road, nearly opposite the boys' playground. Hetty had forbidden Phillip ever to go down Skerritt Road. It was a slum, she said. The people living there were the lowest of the low. Cranmer certainly looked as though he could hardly be any lower. He had no boots or stockings on his feet, which were always dirty. His trousers flapped about him, having been made for a man. They were ragged below the knee. His jacket was too big, like his trousers. He had no shirt or vest underneath, the jacket being tied across his middle with string. His white flesh was sometimes visible when the string slipped.

Cranmer was often caned by Mr. Twine, for he could not learn anything, and Mr. Twine said he did not try, but he would show him who was master; so Cranmer's face was permanently stained with tears, wet and dry. Cranmer had a cropped head, some of his teeth were all rotten in front. He wriggled a lot in his seat, when his face was not lying in his arms on the desk. Sometimes he grinned at the other boys, and at the girls on the far side of the class. When he smiled at the girls, and was found out, Cranmer was always given the cane.

Mr. Twine pulled him out of the desk by his jacket. Cranmer cried out not to be caned, but Mr. Twine made him touch his toes out in front of the class. Mr. Twine hit with all his strength, the cane swooshing down. Cranmer burst into tears and seemed to drop all of a heap on the floor. Sometimes Cranmer prayed to Mr. Twine not to hit him any more, on his knees on the floor, but it made no difference.

Mr. Twine made Cranmer stand up, he never pulled him up; once he was out in front of the class, he made him stand up, then said, "Bend down again!" and swoosh! he brought down the cane again with all his strength, his eyes fierce and angry, and his jaw clenched tight. Twiney would give Cranmer eight or nine like that, standing well away from Cranmer and, on his toes, hitting with all his strength.

For the rest of the morning Cranmer would cry at his desk, his cropped head in the arms of his ragged coat, and in the afternoon he would play truant, and perhaps not be seen at school again for several days. Phillip once saw Cranmer raking in a dustbin, and eating crusts of bread wet with tea-leaves, out of the dustbin. He felt no pity for Cranmer, as Cranmer was not like other boys, for he lived in Skerritt Road, and was one of the lowest of the low.

Sometimes Mr. Twine, while the boys were writing or otherwise working in their exercise books, called a boy out in front to watch for any boy talking while Mr. Twine was taking the girls on the other side of the glass partition. The partition ended at the front row of desks, so that those boys in the lowest seats could sometimes exchange glances with the girls who sat in the front row, level with them. Cranmer was the only boy in the front row who dared to smile.

Mr. Twine's manner towards the female half of Standard Four was in sharp contrast to his attitude towards the male. He was gentle, often smiling, and soft-spoken with his "little women", as he called them. Always neatly dressed in a blue serge suit, with brown boots polished, and tall starched linen collar clean, Mr. Twine was determined to raise the standards of behaviour and intellect among the working classes, from which he himself had arisen. This could only be done by the spreading of knowledge through education, and the principle that cleanliness was next to Godliness; both were to be served only by an effort of the will, of discipline. Cranmer was a perpetual manifestation before this idealist of what was not to be tolerated.

The boy, called out to stand in front to watch for delinquents, was, of course, himself nervous and uneasy, since he shared the massed fear of Mr. Twine. There were no reprisals against him afterwards; the fear of "Twiney" was too deep to permit of any particular thought about it. The boy, whoever he was, picked to

detect any movement of lip, or even eye, was impersonal, to himself, to the other boys, and to Mr. Twine.

Phillip knew that he must never catch the boy's eye. If this
were to happen, a sort of helplessness might extend between
them, to be broken only by the mention of a name, his name,
Maddison. What would he be able to do if Mr. Twine looked
at him for the cane? He could no⁺ contemplate it—beyond the
incipient thought was a flash, a disintegration, the end of the
world.

So Phillip kept his eyes downwards, sometimes upon his work
of Sums, Geography, History, or Composition, but more often
upon the small two-column print of a *Pluck*, a *Union Jack*, or a
Boy's Life. Under the open desk was a small ledge, where you
were allowed to keep your things, such as pens, pencil box, cap,
scarf, and even a roller skate if you were lucky enough to own
one.   Here, instantly, could be placed, without movement of
upper arm or guilty glance upwards, and certainly without rustle,
the illicit literature. If Mr. Twine asked what you were doing, if
you said, "Thinking, sir", Mr. Twine never said anything back,
for only by thinking, Mr. Twine often said, could man better
himself in all directions.

The pens used in Mr. Twine's class, at least in the male section,
had one characteristic in common, in addition to the stains of
ink upon these brown wooden fluted holders of steel nibs, property
of the London County Council. Their tops were bitten to shreds
by little boys whose only other escape (apart from the illicit
reading of "bloods" under the desk) in the classroom from the
unspeakable problems confronting the mind was by chewing the
uneatable. At least, a reformer of the type of Theodora Maddison
would, and did, see in the frayed top of her nephew Phillip's pen
such an implication; while another, such as Thomas Turney,
would, and did, dismiss such an advanced theory with the remark
that chewing of wood by the young of *homo sapiens* denoted only
the need for a harder, more natural diet in an age of increasing
softness and "spoon-feeding".

Chapter 28

FAMILY DISTRACTION

The Sunday walks to Cutler's Pond, with Father and Mavis, by way of Randiswell, over the bridge and down the path through St. Mary's churchyard, and up the High Street, were some compensation for winter and the general dullness of life during that time of fogs and rain. In the long evenings there was nothing to do except to sit in the sitting-room and do homework, afterwards to play draughts with Father, or dominoes, snakes-and-ladders, halma, and tiddlywinks with Mavis and Doris. The front room piano might resound on occasion, Hetty playing the *Highland Schottische*, or any accompaniment for one of the children's songs. The fire was lit only on Sunday afternoons, so that Father might have the sitting-room to himself, and what he called a snooze if he wanted one.

Richard's Sunday afternoons were sacred, as far as the sitting-room was concerned. There must be no entry into what he called his *sanctum*; no noise from any other part of the house must penetrate there during the hours between Sunday dinner and Sunday tea. It was the only time of the week he could be sure of the room to himself, except the half hour of peace and quiet he allowed himself every night, after Hetty had gone up to bed. Then he could lie in his armchair, slippered feet to the fire, and think his own thoughts: or lighting a pipe, read his newspaper in self-expansiveness.

On Sunday afternoons he read *The Weekly Courier*, a newspaper which was reputed to be the oldest of its kind in Britain. The columns of the *Courier* carried a minimum of scandalous news of the kind which Richard considered was debasing the public, the gutter press with its pandering to the lowest instincts of the people: police court reports of rapes, seductions, child violation, and other sexual offences. Richard did not agree with the printing of that sort of thing, so, just to make sure, every Sunday when *The Weekly Courier* came through the letter-box, about half past nine in the morning, he put it away for Sunday afternoon

359

perusal, out of reach of Phillip. When Richard had read it, and seen nothing injurious in its pages, then the boy might have it.

Richard had a secret book hidden in the sitting-room, a book of which it was unthinkable that Phillip should ever get so much as one glimpse. It was a quarto, entitled *The Parisian Artists' Sketch Book of Models*, printed on glossy clay paper in Paris and exported specially for the London market.

Richard, alone in the sitting-room late at night or on Sunday afternoons, would sometimes unlock his roll-top desk and take out *The Parisian Artists' Sketch Book of Models*, and fancy himself among its young and sylph-like females in the nude, posing in various light-hearted attitudes permitted by the law of Britain, in the sense that a common informer, alleging that the British public, through him, had been obscenely libelled, would not have won his case. The *Sketch Book* was not pornographic; Richard drew the line at that; once he had been revolted by a photograph shown to him by a colleague in his early days of Doggett's in the Strand.

Richard had been surprised that such an apparently gentlemanly young fellow should, without the slightest reason, fail to keep his distance. *The Parisian Artists' Sketch Book of Models*—all of them drawn by black-and-white artists in London, though Richard was not to know that—was itself a model of decorum, as far as the habituées of Leicester Square were concerned. In that rather wicked place, seeing the book in the window of a bookseller, Richard had purchased a copy. On sudden impulse one Saturday, after leaving the Moon Fire Office, Richard had decided not to hurry for the 1.35 from London Bridge, but to walk westwards.

Pleased with himself that he had broken away from habit, he had gone past St. Paul's, down to Ludgate Circus, and so to Fleet Street and the Strand, remembering every detail of the last occasion when he had been that way, on the never-to-be-forgotten-ride in Hilary's Panhard et Lavassor. With a sense of the adventurous, he had gone into a strange A.B.C. teashop, and eaten a bath bun with a glass of milk; and thus fortified, had begun to enjoy the sights of Trafalgar Square, wondering why he had not done this sort of thing more often in the past.

From Trafalgar Square, with Nelson high up on his column—renewing boyhood regrets for the Navy—Richard had strolled up St. Martin's Lane, and then through narrow courts and by-ways to the centre of London's gay life, where stood the Empire with its Promenade, the Alhambra, and the pigeon-splashed statue of William Shakespeare. There was not, however, complete freedom for the mind here; for already upon the streets and on the seats under the plane trees of the railed-off Square itself, were some of the women of whom he had a deep instinctive fear. It was this fear which was the basis of his dislike, of more than dislike, his dread and horror, of the presence of his brother-in-law, Hugh Turney, who had locomotor ataxy.

While he was wandering aloofly past the Alhambra, wondering if he dared? if he ought to? could he afford it?—*should* he go in and see a matinee?—no, if Phillip failed in the scholarship, as he obviously would, there would be school-fees to be considered. No, theatres were not for him: a poor man could not afford such luxuries. There was no harm, however, in looking at the photographs before the theatre.

While he was passing on from a scrutiny of the unattainable, Richard saw that his boot-lace was undone. He stooped to do it up, and a young woman walking past slowly said, "My word, if I catch you bending!" while continuing on her way, her skirt held up to show her ankles.

Richard ignored the obvious solicitation, though he had been attracted by the pleasant voice, with its faint Scots accent. Rising to his feet, he saw that she had red hair, like Miranda MacIntosh, of Amazonian memories at St. Simon's Tennis Club. Nothing was further from his thoughts, he told himself as he rose upright, than that he should ever speak to such a personage. Even so, she was dashed attractive! He was wondering whether there could be any harm in, at most, passing her again, and merely exchanging the time of day, when a familiar figure walked by, without recognising him. It was George Lemon, the husband of his sister Victoria. What was he doing all by himself in Leicester Square?

Richard was soon to know. George raised his silk hat to the red-haired one; and after a brief conversation, the two walked slowly away, side by side. George Lemon, the respectable member of a firm of Lincoln's Inn solicitors!

When Richard arrived home that afternoon at tea-time, *The Parisian Artists' Sketch Book of Models* was concealed under his coat. Thereafter it remained under cover of the roll-top desk, the secret sharer of his dreams and longings—and of his son's too, since Phillip had discovered that one of the keys on his mother's bunch fitted, and opened, the lock of the roll-top desk.

For Richard Maddison, the allure of the nude young women, whether leaping (back turned), stretching arms gladly to the sky (profile), or sitting sideways on floor, couch, settee, or edge of bed, was as recurrent as their figures were ideal. They smiled, they offered bliss unattainable by sedentary, respectable, metro-politan, Faustian man: their winsome attitudes, their tip-tilted breasts, their charming hair, foreheads, noses, and chins, the gentle feminity of their shoulders, mid-riffs, flanks, and feet, stirred deep longing for subliminal dissolution in maternal gentleness, safety, and peace.

Yet contemplation of the unattainable, a wishful secret sharing by imagination of the delights of love, of unreserved abandon to the cave-man's instincts, brought reaction in moods of self-despising, and after each occasion of frustration, a determi-nation to burn the book. Shiny clay-paper, however, burned dully and with an offensive smell; so back it went under the slatted curve of the desk: the keys jingled; normal life resumed itself, with reflections upon the wretched isolation of his life, his every impulse to make things in his home better being baulked by the weakness and indifference of his wife. She did not want him as a husband; his pride prevented him from appealing any more to her, while thinking himself into a small boy, as though he were but substitute for her son!

Richard thought of himself as turned of forty—the current phrase *too old at forty* often came into his mind with an accompany-ing physical sigh. If only he had had the good fortune to have married an intelligent and vital woman, such as Mrs. Gerard Rolls who lived at the top of the road, or Miranda MacIntosh, who since the death of Mrs. Mundy had married Mr. Mundy. No wonder the vicar of St. Simon's was always in such a happy, hail-fellow-well-met frame of mind, though he was turned of sixty! If he had not married Hetty, as he now realised, for her maternal qualities, being caught on the rebound from his mother's death—he would not now be the failure he was.

Oh well, thought Richard, as he took up *The Weekly Courier*.

That Sunday afternoon, towards gas-lighting time, it being nearly five o'clock, Hetty came down from the front room and opening the door of the sitting-room quietly, in case he was asleep, peeped round the jamb. Seeing him awake, she went in, and putting on a cheerful air, which was not hard to do, as she had been happy for the past two hours with the children (who for once had not squabbled), she asked him if he was ready for her to lay the tea.

"Why do you not get the children to do it? It's time they did something to help you, instead of lazing about, expecting everything to be done for them."

"They do help, Dickie, quite often. They have their Saturday chores; and Sonny is working for his scholarship so hard. I can do it just as easily, in fact, to tell you the truth, I prefer to do it."

"There you go, making excuses, as usual. You are a slave to that boy of yours. What's he doing now?"

"I left him quietly reading, dear."

"One of his penny blood and thunders, I expect. I suppose he thinks I don't know when he reads them, when he is supposed to be doing his homework?"

"He is learning his Collect, Dickie. And tonight he is coming with me to St. Simon's; he likes to hear the anthem."

"Oh well, we'll see how he shapes in that precious scholarship examination. But don't blame me if he fails to pass."

"Would you like bloater paste with your toast for tea, Dickie, or some of your favourite patum peperium?"

"If there's any left after your best boy has been at the pot, you mean. Anyway, the fire here is not good enough for toast. What is it like in the front room?"

"It's a bit smoky yet, I am afraid."

Richard did not approve of using the gas for toast when there was a fire in the house. Economy was to be practised for its own sake, quite apart from the threatened rise in income tax to a shilling in the pound if the Liberals got in at the forthcoming general election.

"You might at least have seen to it, while I have my only rest of the week, that there was a decent fire for toast," complained Richard. "Well, we shall have to have bread and butter, that's all. This fire will do for the kettle, anyway. Send Phillip in with it, will you?"

"Yes dear, certainly."

Phillip obediently carried the kettle from the kitchen. Richard set it on the hob, after poking the fire to make a vent for the gas to turn into flame.

Back in the front room, Hetty asked Mavis to fetch some cut bread from the kitchen. Dickie liked hot toast for his Sunday tea, and the front room fire might, if the bread were held to one side, well clear of the smoky flame, be suitable after all, for toast.

Mavis was entrusted with this task, while Hetty carried down the tea tray. Richard had resigned himself to bread and butter and patum peperium; it was just as nice, really, indeed it was a better flavour on bread than on toast. Richard had taken down a book from his shelves for re-reading, Captain Cook's *Adventures in the South Seas*.

It was a slight shock for Richard to find, twenty minutes later, a plateful of toast brought to the table by Hetty, who was hoping that her little surprise would please him.

In her haste to get the tea, to be ready to start at six o'clock for the walk over the hill for evening service at St. Simon's, she had forgotten to wipe the bottom of the plate. A slight black, or rather grey, ring was imposited on the tablecloth. Richard had the observant eye that he had passed on to Phillip. When Hetty put the plate on the cloth, and it was lifted again to be offered to him, immediately he saw the slight mark.

The consequent conversation, or monologue, only added to Richard's sense of grievance when fed by Hetty's conciliatoriness. The final exasperation arose when the toast was found to be tainted by coal tar; and the whole tea, to which he had so looked forward, was spoiled. Richard's disappointment became the more vocal, based as it was on his recent sense of guilt. Did not such practice impair the brain?

Phillip was sitting at one side of the table, perched upon his old wooden horse on wheels. This had been a birthday present from his grandfather two years previously. It was a special Sunday tea privilege to be allowed to sit on the horse instead of a chair, and to read a book. Sunday tea was thereby a pleasurable occasion to look forward to, for Father usually read his book as well, and if the toast was well made, and no rings or tea-stains made on the tablecloth, it usually passed peacefully.

On the other side of the table sat Mavis, next to her father, and Doris next to her mother. Phillip was sitting on Dobbin, who had a knot on his wooden barrel, from which in the past the boy had declared he could extract cocoa. While Father was going on at Mother, Phillip was waiting with his usual dull quietude for Father to stop; the boy was deeply sensitive to his Mother's distress, and being young and overshadowed, was able only to endure silently in the hope that it would soon cease.

The previous Sunday Father had gone on like that, because during the afternoon Uncle Hugh had come into the front room. Father had been angry, saying he had again and again ordered that Hugh Turney was not to be allowed in the house where there were young children. Phillip did not know what this meant; nor did he wonder about it; he accepted it as being part of his life.

Perched quiet on Dobbin, Phillip saw that Mother was trying hard not to cry. He could only look with desperate challenge at Mavis, the silly fool who had allowed the black smelly moustache of the coal flame to touch the toast on the fork. He had warned her of this in the front room, but all she had said was "Mind your own biz, Donkey Boy". If the sitting-room door had not been open, so that Father would hear if she yelped, he would have pinched her hard for saucing him. So the smoky toast was her fault, and not Mother's. But Father would never blame Mavis, who was his favourite, often sitting on his knee while he stroked her hair, and kissed her. He never kissed Doris, who did not like him at all.

Father went on about the dirty plate, and the smoky toast, until Mummie was crying.

Suddenly Doris said a very strange thing, and hearing it, Phillip looked up in a kind of terror at Father's face turning round in the armchair to stare at Doris. For Doris, who was round-faced and always following Mummy about the house, looked at Father, pointed her finger at him, and said, slowly:

"If you make my Mummy cry, I will kill you. I have been meaning to kill you for a long time. I have a long knife hidden to kill you with."

Father jumped up in a rage. He smacked down Doris's finger and got hold of her and turned her up in her chair, so that her new white drawers were uppermost as she hung head down while Father held her legs under one arm and beat her hard with his other hand on her behind, hitting her again and again, before lifting her up and sitting her down again, and shouting at her: "How dare you speak like that to me! Hetty, this is your doing!! You have set the child against me!! I shall inform the police if you do not at once say you are sorry, young woman! Do you hear me?"

Phillip sat still and void. Doris, who had never once cried out when Father had beaten her, though her face was very red, would not say she was sorry.

Phillip knew Doris had not got a knife to kill their father but was only saying it to protect Mummy. But Father believed it, else he would not tell the police. Father stood over her and shouted in a rage:

"Say that you are sorry this instant, or I will punish you some more!"

Pointing her finger at him, Doris said slowly:

"You—leave—my—Mummy—alone."

Mother cried when Father smacked Doris some more. But Doris did not cry even then. Doris never cried. Once when she thought a burglar was in the house, hearing movement overhead when she was in her room, Doris had cried out in a deep voice "You had better be careful, and go away at once, Mr. Burglar, for I am a big strong man!" The noise was only himself exploring the loft over the trap-door in the bathroom ceiling, but Doris had thought it was a real burglar. Phillip wished he was brave like Doris, who was only five. Doris held herself like someone holding breath, and would not say to Father she was sorry.

"If you do not say you are sorry, I shall not answer for the consequences!" cried Father, so loud that Mother said, "Oh, Dickie, please, please! They will hear you next door!"

"Let them hear me!" shouted Father loudly, his face like a very thin lion's face. "Let them know what your daughter has just threatened me with! Unnatural child, unnatural wife! What sort of a life have I here in this blasted household?"

Phillip had never heard Father swear before, and it shocked him, as it also surprised him to hear what Father was saying to Mummy.

"If I had had any sense I would have left years ago, instead of remaining in a completely false position! Yes, that is what I feel about it! What sort of people are you Turneys, to insult a

man as I was insulted in the past? Who then seek to insinuate
themselves into his home, with never so much as an apology,
never a hint of any regret for the disastrous effect of caddish
behaviour towards me years ago? I know very well who was at
the back of the loss of my billet at Doggett's years ago! What was
my crime, can you answer me that? I was a young fellow making
my way in the world, and you yourself encouraged me in my suit!
Therefore, as is usual and honourable in such circumstances, at
least among my own sort of people, I presented myself to Mr.
Turney to ask his permission to pay my addresses to his daughter!
And what was the result? Disgusting insinuations, unbearable
insults! And then that laughter from an upper room in the house
as I left it, from your youngest brother! *That's* the sort of people
you are! Now you know what I think of you all!" and Father
went out of the room. Soon afterwards they heard the front door
shut.

Hetty's surprise at this outburst stopped her flow of tears. She
had always admired her husband for his restraint in the matter
of the way he had been treated by Papa. She had always been
ashamed of Papa's behaviour, but had tried never to show that
she was ashamed. She had always been conscious of the difference between the Maddisons and the Turneys, and from the very
first had realised that gentlemen to the manner born, like Richard,
had a power of restraint denied to other men who had not had
their advantages in upbringing and education. Now she was
shocked to realise there was little or no difference. All the time
Dickie had been keeping back his real feelings! She could see
now that he hated Papa, and Hugh, and all the others, except
perhaps Mamma, whom nobody could very well dislike, as she
never affronted another living soul. Did Dickie hate her, as well,
his wife who had devoted her life to him and to the children?
At least it seemed clear that he no longer loved her, if he had ever
done so. He was an unhappy man, always had been and always
would be; and it was her duty to continue to try, always, to do
her best to please him, for the sake of her little children.

Mavis and Phillip were now crying. Hetty said to a stoical, or
frozen, Doris:

"You are a naughty girl, Doris, to say such wicked things to
your Father. After all, he *is* your Father, you know! Wherever

do you get such ideas from, about long sharp knives? I am sure you don't hear of them from me."

"You can't sharpen a knife, Mummy, can you?" said Phillip. He was the anxious small boy again, talking to attract her away from grief. "You don't know the proper way to use the steel, do you? You take the edge off! Only Father knows how, doesn't he?"

"Mummy, Phillip told Doris and me a story about a robber with a long knife, with which he disbolled his victims! That's where Doris got the long knife from. It's those *Plucks* Phillip reads all the time!"

"Huh, fool!" retorted Phillip. "Any fool knows the *Pluck Library* is Jack Valiant and Co. The long knife story was out of *Chums* if you want to know. So sucks to you, you dreamy filthy toast-maker!"

"Sonny! Phillip I will not have you speaking to Mavis like that! I have told you before!"

"Children, children, please; we have had enough quarrelling for one afternoon———" replied Phillip, imitating his mother's voice.

Doris was sent to bed for a punishment by Hetty. The stoical five-year-old went up without a word, and put herself to bed. There, in some safety with her doll, she cried without a sound, after refusing to speak to her mother.

When Richard returned, he was induced to eat some bread and butter with patum on it. Hetty cleared the table, with the help of a docile Phillip. Mavis remained in the room with her father, engaged with her paint-box upon a friend's Confession book, both laid on an old sheet of newspaper. Richard settled down with Captain Cook's *Adventures*.

Hetty and Phillip got ready for church, and departed. They sat in the left-hand gallery, their usual place. Mr. Mundy, thought Hetty, preached a beautiful sermon on tolerance, which was a quality, he said, based on the endurance of all trials and tribulations. The sermon restored her faith; while the anthem *O, for the wings of a Dove* gave her back her hope. Oh, things would be better when Phillip had won his scholarship!

It was something to look forward to after church, to go to supper with Gran'pa, though Gran'pa had one bad habit in

Phillip's eyes—a habit of suddenly putting on his plate a snippet held between knife and fork off his own plate which Gran'pa could not chew himself, owing to his teeth, he said. Why should he have to eat anyone's left-overs? There was no need to eat these tough bits, with the cat waiting for them under the table; still, it was not nice to be told "Eat that," off anyone else's knife and fork. But then, Gran'pa was a Turney.

There was wine for supper on Sundays, with water of course, but this though red was never sweet. Phillip was given it for his health as his grandfather said he was too pale. Port was nicer, but boys were not allowed any; so if he wanted any he had to take a swig out of the decanter after supper, when no one was looking.

Father never came in to supper, though Grandma always included him in the invitation, said Mother; but he never came, which was a good thing. It was always much nicer without Father. Gran'pa never stopped you doing anything, though you had to be quiet while he read Shakespeare afterwards, but Shakespeare was better than Psalms or Collects.

Sometimes Uncle Hugh played his violin, or a cigarbox one with a brass horn sticking out of it. This made sad music, nice to listen to when you could think about old times, so long as you hid your face in case Mavis would taunt and say "Look, Phillip is crying, there is a tear in his eye!"

Sometimes cousin Ralph came to supper, and Gerry, then there was some sport afterwards in Uncle Hugh's room, where they all smoked Ogden's Guinea Gold cigarettes or Player's Weights, and talked of the things they would like to do. Ralph was soon to leave the school on the Hill, to go to work in London. He would have to sleep with other apprentices in the top of a building in High Holborn, where there were many beds in a row. It was a big shop of many floors underneath, where he would have to work in the daytime selling clothes and other things to customers, and so work his way up, said Gran'pa, who had shares in the business, to be a director.

Hell to that for a tale, said Ralph, he was clearing out to join Uncle Charley in the goldfields of the Rand as soon as he could save up passage money.

Hell to London life, said Gerry, he was going to sea as soon as he could. Phillip thought of the Redskins of Fenimore Cooper, the pirates of Ballantyne, the white hunters of Rider Haggard, and as soon as he had saved up enough pocket money he too would be off.

Hell to Twiney and Mildenhall! He thought of thinking hell to Father, too, but shied away from the idea, for he was wicked even to think of nearly thinking it of Father.

Sunday was always a dull day, because you had to wear your best clothes and be very quiet, though going for a walk with Father in the morning to Cutler's Pond was better than going to church. All sorts of interesting things were to be seen on the walks of Sunday morning, when it was fine. Along the main road into Kent were traps, dogcarts, brakes, occasional coaches and cabs, and, sometimes, a coster's cart driven by a man in pearl button'd cap and coat, and his wife in many feathers. In the morning all were going one way, to booze in the pubs, said Father.

Passing the horse-pulled vehicles were different sorts of motor-cars, driven by men with caps turned round the wrong way, with goggles in case there was dust, though in winter the grey road was usually moist, or at least damp. Phillip, ever since the ride in Uncle Hilary's Panhard, had been interested in motorcars. Some drivers wore fur coats, and ladies with them wore such coats too, with hats covered with veils, and fur gloves. One morning he found a big nut in the roadway, and Father said someone in a hole, or a tight corner, might be very pleased to give half-a-crown for such a thing, should he, Phillip, be in the right place. Phillip put the nut in his pocket, wondering how he could find the right person in a hole, or a tight corner; but though he carried it with him for several Sundays, he never found such a driver, and thought of trying to disguise the nut in a conker, to be the champion at school with it.

There was a police trap along the road, hidden, said Father, from ordinary mortals like themselves, and not affecting them, since they were pedestrians; but if Phillip kept his eyes open, he would see the signs of it when next a motorcar passed by them at that particular stretch, where the trap was.

They waited, and when an old Mors motorcar rattled along, a man standing beside the road held up a white dinner plate high above his head, then saluted the motorist, who saluted back. The man with the white dinner plate looked like a soldier, for he wore a khaki uniform, and Father said he was warning the motorist of the trap. There were hidden policemen with stop-watches, timing the speed of the motorcar; and if it exceeded twenty miles an hour, they would stop the driver and fine him a lot of money for being a road-hog.

"That old Mors couldn't do twenty miles an hour, I bet!" said Phillip; and certainly it passed through the trap, wheezing away.

One Sunday all the empty shops in the High Street were seen to be filled with posters, for, said Father, there was soon to be a General Election. Phillip understood that one side was decent and right, and told the truth, while the other was disreputable and wrong, and told lies. On the way home they counted the shops with the truthful and lying posters in the windows, from the Bull Inn to St. Mary's Church, on both sides of the High Street. There were nineteen altogether. You could tell which were the liars by colours. The right party colours were purple and primrose. The wrong party was so obviously wrong, for the right posters showed them up for what they were. Their Free Trade, for instance, meant free food, and this in turn meant that in China pigs were fed on human corpses—there the pictures were, showing great gaunt hogs eating dead men in a waste land—and the hogs became bacon which was sold by the Free Traders in shops like those in Skerritt Road. Tariff Reform, said Father, would put that right. The Unionists, or Conservatives had been in power for many years, and they ought to be put back, to stop tainted bacon being dumped in England. They were all the same, the Radicals, whether they called themselves Progressives, Liberals, or Free Traders, it was the same old evil of Radicalism, said Father. And later in some of the windows of Hillside Road there appeared cards with a photograph on them of the only decent man to vote for, Major Coates. Father said that as the ballot was secret, it behoved people to keep their choice to themselves; that's why he had refused to put one in the window.

Along Charlotte Road lived inferior people who put the other candidate's photographs in their windows. There was only one thing to do, said Gerry, on the way home from school, to teach them a lesson; to knock down Ginger on every one of them.

Gerry showed promptly what this meant. You crept up to the front door, gave the knocker a tremendous bang, then ran away. In the flats in Charlotte Road you could, by being quick, knock a group of four knockers at once, and you would be well away on your charger before anyone could give chase. It was wonderful fun, much better than setting fire to the Backfield, for if you got away no one could prove anything, said Gerry.

One morning on the way home to dinner Phillip knocked down a ginger and almost at once the door opened and a saturnine man appeared. He might have been a criminal by his face, which was thin, dark, and with a thin black moustache, and a bowler hat on top. He gave a snarling cry. The flat was one near the new church of St. Cyprian, and there being a path up to the Hill opposite, Phillip ran up it, arriving puffed at the top by the grammar school.

Something told him that the man would come after him. Crossing to where Father used to fly his kites, he ran down it and was about to climb over the hurdles, and so down through the thorns above the gully, when he saw the thin man rapidly walking up the gully, darting his head to left and to right like a snake's. *He wore a straw hat.* On seeing him crouching behind the hurdle, the man who looked like one of a disguised gang of criminals, cried "Ah ha!" in a sinister voice, and immediately started to climb the low railing.

In fear, Phillip ran towards the Backfield, meaning to climb over the spiked railings at the boundary of the Hill. You had to be careful doing this, first jumping up, then kneeling, then carefully putting a foot between the spikes, which were flattened half-way down, making it treacherous if you jumped and your boot caught there, for then you might break your leg and hang down and perhaps bleed to death.

The man was sprinting over the grass, having leapt the hurdles, as Phillip had seen in a terrified backward glance. He must be an athlete. Phillip wore his winter coat. Trembling, he sprang up with his hands on the top of the fence. He must be steady: with beating heart he told himself to be calm, and not to think of the man running to catch him. He got over without mishap, and plunged down through the long grass, wondering if he should drop into one of the big cracks down the slope, and hide, or run on down past the red ballast heap to the fence behind the gardens of the new road. He decided to do this, and jumping over the cracks, splashed through the level plashes below, and so to the fence. Here he paused, and saw with relief that the man was standing on the other side of the spiked railings. He was safe.

However, he had to be cunning, to throw him off the scent. He ran down the lane between the two fences, showing himself at the turn into an alley leading to the road itself; then dropping on his hands, he doubled on his tracks and when he came to the fence, he ran to the other end of the passage, bent double. This brought him to the site of the marn pits, beside where the elms had stood. Waiting until the man had gone, he crept on all fours to the edge of the thicket of elm suckers growing around the stumps of the parent trees, and following a run used by dogs and cats and members of his Band, reached the back fence under cover.

After dinner he went to school by a roundabout way, down Charlotte Road to Randiswell, then up the lane and round the south side of the cemetery to Skerritt Road, hurrying through that straight street of bad repute and arriving at school, with Cranmer beside him, half a minute before the bell rang.

After school Cranmer was waiting for him. Phillip went home by way of Skerritt Road, with his new friend who walked beside him almost without speaking, after the first shy request by the Boys' entrance, "Shall us walk together?" They said goodbye outside the lower entrance of the Cemetery.

The next morning, avoiding the house of the sinister Ha-ha man who had changed a bowler hat to a white straw to disguise himself, Phillip went the long way round to school, and found Cranmer awaiting him before the gates of the cemetery. With a shy grin the boy walked beside him, offering to carry his satchel. Phillip said "No thank you"—for some reason he felt very good and polite when he was with Cranmer—because Cranmer might have the germs of disease on him.

He was pleased to have someone who looked up to him, and who was trying, he knew, to copy him. The two talked about things unconnected with the school as they walked beside one another every day. Knowing that Cranmer's father was out of work, Phillip did not ask him what his father did, in case Cranmer was ashamed. He took some bread and dripping with him one day, and asked Cranmer to have some; but "No fanks" said Cranmer, "I mustn't take your food, reely."

"I've had a lot already. Besides, we're friends aren't we? Have this piece, go on."

"Are you sure voo don' mind? Straight, don' voo want it?"

By the way Cranmer wolfed the bread and dripping it was the first food he had had for a long time. Phillip took him a slice of bread and dripping every day.

Cranmer had a great liking for Phillip, and spent most of his time out of school hanging about in the hope of seeing him in the distance, even. Once Phillip saw Cranmer on the Hill, but Cranmer hid in the bushes. He thought of Phillip as very rich, and therefore a superior being to himself altogether. When later Phillip went the other way home, he used to look back sometimes along the High Road to wave to Cranmer, for always the poor boy would be waiting there until he was out of sight. He gave him a sweet now and again, when he had some, and Cranmer would push cigarette cards into his hands, which all the boys were collecting, and then shyly run off to another part of the playground.

On Sunday afternoons there was excitement on the Hill, or that area by the Socialist Oak where men stood on camp stools and boxes they had carried up, and spouted. Phillip and Gerry went there specially to see the fun, hoping there would be fighting, and with great luck, the mounted police be called out to charge the Socialists. These were funny, very nearly unreal, men who stood by their red flags and talked about revolution, altruism, bloated capitalists, and one of them, Mr. Chivers, an old gentleman, very thin, who wore a straw hat and no overcoat (though it was winter) spoke mildly about utopia to a very few listeners, and was, as Gerry said, mad but harmless.

The best fun of all could be got from a very small man, almost a dwarf, in a frock coat, top hat, and thick spectacles which made his eyes look like frogs' eggs when the tadpole was just beginning to grow in the jelly. He had recently returned from prison, where he had been sent for resisting arrest after a fight when his hat had been knocked off by someone in the crowd who had called him a "Little Englander" for saying that the Boers had had justice on their side in the recent war. He had demanded an apology from the hat-knocker, and in the scrap following, the little man, who had lost his glasses and was blind without them, had inadvertently pushed a constable, and so was frog-marched down to Randiswell Police Station, to the jeers and boos of the crowd following this anarchist. Now he was out of Wormwood Scrubs, and the centre of attraction once more beside the Socialist Oak.

Standing on his portable stool, the fuzzy-grey-haired man in the top hat and, Uncle Hugh had said, low centre of gravity, was now shouting about the need for prison reform. He had, he said, saved a piece of bread from his daily diet, to show his fellow Britons, in the Land of Free Speech, Magna Carta, and the Bill of Rights, just how the inmates of His Majesty's prisons were treated.

A froth like shaving soap lather was in the corners of his mouth as he slapped the piece of bread in one hand, to illustrate how hard it was, how poor in quality, being yellow instead of white.

"And that, ladies and gentlemen, is in the twentieth century of so-called reform and progress, when men, and women, have to be fed on food which the beasts of the field would refuse!"

This well-known agitator lived in the High Road, in the basement of a house where he repaired boots and shoes for a living. Mr. Kings-Lynn, for that was his name, yelled from the stool on which he stood, holding his unrolled umbrella on his arm, "You won't find me standing for Parliament, ladies and gentlemen! I would not pollute myself, or my wife and children, or my neighbours, or the fair name of Kings-Lynn, by appearing in that Temple of Unrighteousness! In that collaboration of Sodom and Gomorrah! That Upas Tree of Hypocrisy that poisons all in its purlieus! That combination of Midas and Mephistopheles! That conspiracy of Shylock and the Golden Calf! No, my friends!" screamed the little man, raising face and arms, showing celluloid cuffs, to the sky, "YOU WILL NEVER FIND ME IN THE SELLING PLATE FOR THE GADARENE STAKES!!"

His head dropped. His arms fell by his sides. He was spent. He let out a long sigh, and wiped his lips. Looking up, almost in a whisper he said, "History points only too clearly where the prophet ends up!"

With a sparrow-like detachment the speaker then raised his silk hat and scratched his head. Having set his shiner square on his head once more, he felt for the hard piece of bread which only a few moments before he had put back in the pocket behind the tails of his frock coat. Holding the bread aloft, as though it had given him renewed inspiration, he said in a voice of plaintive winsomeness, as he leaned forward confidentially,

"Do you know where you will soon probably be finding me, ladies and gentlemen?" He shook the square of yellow bread round the skyline. "Not in the cesspit of the House of Commons! You can have my head examined if ever you find me there! No!"

Abruptly changing his tone, Mr. Kings-Lynn declared sternly, as he shook a finger at an imaginary Bench of Magistrates in Greenwich Police Court, "I will tell you where I shall be! I shall most probably be found, after what I am going to say to you this afternoon, in——"

"—in your basement banging old boots!" shouted Phillip in his treble voice, and ducking down, he ran away through the laughing people.

The story got about; Mrs. Feeney heard it; and the next day she repeated it to Hetty, who laughed until the tears came in her eyes—for she had sometimes listened to the funny little figure who spoke every Sunday afternoon by the Socialist Oak—and then went in next door to tell Papa the joke, because he had the same sense of humour as herself. She told Dickie, when the children were in bed, and he, too, laughed.

"That fellow's a wind-bag," he said. "Kings-Lynn, what a name he has picked for himself! Why didn't he call himself Norfolk-Broads while he was about it?" and Richard laughed again, this time at his own joke.

Politics were in the air. Just before election day there was a meeting at night in the Randiswell Baths, and Richard took Phillip to hear the Unionist candidate, Major Coates, speak. When they got there the doors were closed, the meeting was full. However, as they waited outside, a window opened in the red brick tower above and the top half of Major Coates looked down. White starched cuffs showed below his sleeves, a bunch of flowers in the lapel of his frock coat, his cravat under big winged collar only less small than the big white moustachios. The Candidate beamed down.

"My friends——" he got so far as saying, in the rich, easy voice of a real gentleman, when boos and cries and counter-cheers broke out from the faces assembled below.

Phillip shouted "Hurray! Hurray!" as loud as he could.

Major Coates, leaning his elbows complacently on the window sill, and showing three inches of starched cuff with diamond links, waited until the noise subsided, then held up a hand and said, with a wide smile,

"My friends, I see below me a schoolboy. Now I will give him a very good reason why he should hope for tariff reform, because the Unionists would put a tax on all imported birches!" and waving his hand, the well-fed figure disappeared, leaving Phillip unhappy as he stood silent beside Father, for he had cheered *for* Tariff Reform and Major Coates, not against them.

When he told Cranmer the next day, Cranmer said he was Unionist too.

"Though if my hold man finds hout he'll belt me, for all ar street is fer t'other bloke, Wassiznaime."

Chapter 29

THE BLACK LINE

THE red and grey African parrot lived through the winter, accompanying the rooks to the potato and cabbage fields, the grass of the recreation grounds, and the other immemorial feeding areas of what was left upon the face of Kent north of the Crystal Palace.

There were other interesting things for Phillip to see and talk about at that time. After the general election new works were put in hand by the Progressives, among them the felling of the old elms along the High Road leading to and beyond Wakenham School. Gangs of navvies, with them Cranmer's father, who had been out of work for more than a year, dug out the roots after the timber had been thrown and hauled away. The High Road was being widened and prepared for the coming of the new electric trams of the London County Council.

It was the same in the High Street. The old trees lining the turnpike along which Julius Cæsar had marched with his legions, and Henry the Fifth had returned from Agincourt, and which had seen many another historical scene—"And this will particularly appeal to you, old chap, where Dick Turpin the highwayman often must have galloped"—were sacrificed to the idea of progress, said Father. Well, they were going to complete the ruin of England.

Phillip was used to hearing Father talk like that, as Father sat in his armchair evening after evening, reading from *The Daily Trident*, often with snorts and other expressions of disgust, while Phillip did his homework at the table behind the greying paternal head, in such a position that he could not be observed reading the brown *Pluck Library*, or maybe the magenta *Union Jack* on his lap. Father had taken the gas mantle from off his bedroom light, to stop him reading in bed; and he had to go up every night at half-past-eight, to conserve his energy for the coming scholarship examination. Phillip was no longer allowed to lock the lavatory door, and occupy the seat for an hour at a time.

But Phillip had not always to go in there to read. He had gone to try and ease the awful itch in a place he dare not tell even Mummy about. He was too ashamed. Once, feeling the itch which would not go, he had seen lots of wriggling little white worms. He sat for hours on the pan, trying to get rid of them, but there were too many.

One afternoon Phillip came home from school and sat at the kitchen table doing his homework before tea, in so quiet an attitude that Hetty wondered what had happened now. Leaning over him to stroke his dark hair—a thing which he always tried to avoid from his mother nowadays—she saw that he was looking studiously at his homework book. There, on the open double page, was the purple circle of a rubber stamp, with a smaller circle inside, and the words LONDON COUNTY COUNCIL printed around the rim, with *Wakenham Road School*. In the centre of the circle, which was about as big as the crown piece Dickie had given her for safe-keeping during the days of their secret betrothal, were the initials *A.G* above the printed word *EXCELLENT*.

"Oh Sonny, what have you done, dear, to deserve that?" Hetty was so surprised that she did not think of the oddness of her remark. "Did you really get that from Mr. Garstang, dear?"

"Yes, Mum. For Composition. I thought I was going to get the stick," he said, nonchalantly. "Instead, Mr. Garstang stamped my paper."

"An 'Excellent'! Oh Sonny, I can't tell you how glad I am! For Composition, you say? May I read it?"

"No, it isn't any good, really."

"What did you write about?"

"Oh, nothing."

He sat on the exercise book, pulled a new *Pluck* from his pocket, and began to read it.

"Can I have some dripping toast for tea, Mum? I'm rather worn-out."

"Of course you shall, dear! Only I think a little mouse must have been at my dripping bowl. Look at this!" and Hetty took the bowl from the larder. Knife thrusts had lifted out half of it. "And a little mouse has been cutting himself some extra slices of bread, too, I fancy. You can always ask, you know, dear, if you are hungry."

The next afternoon, being a fine sunny day, Hetty put on her best frock, with its trailing edge to the skirt, and bodice with flounces at the neck and sleeves, her hat with its upturned brim like a shallow oval truck holding artificial flowers, and with sunshade to complete the effect, walked to the school to see Mr. Garstang.

She was saddened to see the gaps where the elms had stood for so long, and the wide white squares of concrete piled for the new pavements, and heaps of dark wood blocks for the new road-way; still, it would mean an end to muddy boots for the mothers.

Entering the school by the Girls' and Infants' playground, she went through a swing door, passing a classroom hurriedly when little heads craned up from desks within to observe her going by. Coming to the hall, she saw a small and solitary figure in blue serge Norfolk jacket and knickerbockers standing at the foot of the pitch-pine stairs leading up to Mr. Garstang's study. It was Phillip, standing on the Black Line.

"Oh Sonny," she whispered. "What are you doing there?"

"I don't know," he said, in a whisper, as he rubbed his palms on his coat. He had been keeping them moist with spit, as that was supposed to deaden the sting of the cane.

About half-an-hour previously, while he was sitting quietly at his desk, a boy had come into Standard Four, and said to Mr. Twine, "Please sir, can Phillip Maddison come to see the Head Master," and Phillip had followed him out in trepidation into the hall, to see Mr. Garstang there, with about fifty boys standing silently in a semicircle about him. Mr. Garstang looked gravely at the newcomer and said, in his deep voice,

"Well, my friend! And who told you the story of Rubber Balls, which seems to have gone the rounds of the school?"

The words and tone struck terror into Phillip. He could not speak. He stared unwinking at the face above him.

"Have you lost your tongue, my friend?"

Phillip tried to speak, but only a dry Adam's-apple click came from his throat.

"Come, speak up! You were vocal enough in recounting the story, I am sure. Now tell me, who told it to you?"

It was an awful story. Cranmer had told him, and it had seemed very funny when he had heard it, as they had been walking together to the cemetery gate, where Cranmer had turned back with a smile saying, "So long, mate, see you to-morrow. 'Ere?" The story had been about an old woman who had fainted in the High Street and her daughter had cried out, "Oh, what shall I do? What shall I do?" A deaf pedlar standing in the gutter with a tray just then cried out his wares, "Rubber balls! Rubber balls!"

"Well, Phillip," said Mr. Garstang again, "you see before you all the boys who have repeated the silly story, one to another. I have called you all out together to tell you that it *is* a silly story, and that such things should not be repeated in this school. I want to trace it to its source. Now, my friend, who told you?"

Phillip stared in fear at Mr. Garstang. Would he be caned, with all the others? Moisture ran into his mouth. He felt cold drips under his arms. Jack Valiant in the *Pluck Library* would never peach.

"Come on, speak up."

"I d-d-don't know, sir."

Mr. Garstang looked at him intently. After a pause he said, "Then you are the boy who brought the story into Wakenham Road School, are you? I am surprised, Phillip, for you are the son of a gentleman, and should be the one to set a good, not a bad, example."

Phillip hung his head, and began to cry. He would never be given a scholarship now.

"Very well, my friend, go you and stand on the Black Line! You other boys now go back to your classes, and do not let me catch any one of you repeating such stories again! I shall see you later, my friend!" and Mr. Garstang climbed the stairs in silence as the last tiptoe blakey ceased to clink on the wooden floor.

Phillip had been standing there about half-an-hour when his mother arrived. She had not been in the school more than half a minute when the door above the stairs opened, and Mr. Garstang came down.

"Ah, Mrs. Maddison," he said, holding out his hand. "You have come at an opportune moment. I was about to write to you about the progress of Phillip. Will you come upstairs to my study? Phillip, as you can see, has been allowed time for a little meditation. Now you may go to your classroom, my boy, and apply yourself to your work, so that we may be proud of you in time to come. For you have considerable ability, if you care to use it in the proper direction."

Gratefully Phillip hurried away back into Standard Four, feeling such relief that only with difficulty did he stop himself from giving a loud shout, which would go right through the glass of the partition and make all the panes crack.

Up in the Head Master's room Hetty was telling Mr. Garstang that it was true about the African parrot being let out of its cage, and flying off with the rooks on the Hill.

"Well, Mrs. Maddison, in my fairly long experience as a master, I do not think I have ever been so impressed with any child's composition. Phillip wrote a nearly perfect description of the parrot, how it flew away and how it came back again; and then the details, which were so remarkable, showing keen observation, of the difference in the parrot's way of walking through the grass, and the rooks'. Did you not think so yourself?"

"I am afraid I have not seen it yet, Mr. Garstang. Phillip is rather reserved in some things, as he is unreserved in other directions, so I have not been allowed to see it." Hetty spoke lightly, with a smile, and the other realised that she was a little hurt.

"I can send for it now, if you would care to read it, Mrs. Maddison? It is only a matter of pressing the bell——"

"Oh no, I would not have him think I want to compel him in any way," replied Hetty, conscious of expressing herself badly. "But thank you very much indeed, all the same, I am sure." She laughed lightly again.

Mr. Garstang could see that Phillip was the apple of her eye, and that already the imperious little boy had imposed his conditions of living upon the mother. Mr. Garstang had noticed more of Phillip than Phillip was aware. Mr. Garstang knew of his friendship with Cranmer, for example, another boy in whom he had thought to see much good, if only it could be encouraged in the right way. It was through Mr. Garstang, a member of the Borough Council, that Cranmer's father had been found work under the new plans for the development of the High Road. Mr. Garstang had four grown sons of his own, all of them out in the world, and doing well; he was convinced that a happy home life was the only basis for the making of a good citizen. A man must have work, and children must be fed. Hungry children could never learn.

This essentially gentle, thoughtful man often wondered about the Maddison household. He was a little surprised that Mr. Maddison had not taken any steps to see him, as the Head Master of the school to which he had sent his boy. It was not to be expected, of course, from the general run of parents; but from what he had heard of Mr. Maddison from the vicar of St. Simon's he would have thought that such a matter of punctilio would be observed by him.

Mr. Garstang and Mr. Mundy were friends of long standing. They had both been members of the Board of Works, now abolished and replaced by the Borough Council; while for many years they had met with the Antiquarian Society. The vicar had described Maddison as an aloof man, with an inclination to stiltedness, due to loneliness and pride, a man who needed to be drawn out of himself.

By Mrs. Maddison's vaguely strained attitude under her friendly manner Mr. Garstang thought that perhaps all was not well between husband and wife in the home; in which case the children would be the first to show the effects of such an atmosphere. A mother wrapped up in her son, however much she might try and dissemble or make light of her obsession—if that was not too strong a word—was usually a *femmé manquée* towards her husband. Mr. Garstang noticed, for the first time, that the nails of her ungloved hand were bitten.

"Well, the season of scholarships will be upon us soon, Mrs. Maddison. This year our scholars will sit for the examination in Bereshill School."

"Will there be very many sitting? I suppose there are bound to be a great many?" said Hetty, hoping she was not revealing her anxiety.

"We have eighteen provided schools in the borough," replied Mr. Garstang, "and in all they supply nearly twenty thousand school seats. The scholarship scheme provides for the transfer of a large number of children to the Secondary Schools, but the exact number is not revealed. We are sending just over thirty candidates from here, and eight to ten may be successful."

"I see," said Hetty. "Well, I must hope for the best, I suppose. In any event, I shall always be very grateful to you, Mr. Garstang, for your great kindness to Phillip, and for the help and encouragement you have given in the matter." With these words Hetty said good-bye.

The examination was to be held in March of the new year. As the time approached, Hetty became more unhappy about Sonny's prospects of being one of the eight or ten mentioned by Mr. Garstang. After the Christmas holidays, the twice-weekly coachings by Mr. Groat were resumed. They were not satisfactory meetings for either the heavy-bearded man with steel-framed spectacles and massive squat body, whose questions the boy found unanswerable, or for the boy himself, whom Mr. Groat considered to be without normal intelligence, with a weakness for facile tears.

Long periods of silence, broken only by phrases of "Come on, surely you have not forgotten what I told you last time", or "If you won't make some effort yourself, how can you expect me to help you?" were passed while the BB pencil, having made so many crossings-out on Phillip's trial examination papers taken in by the boy after hurried last-minute work in the kitchen, occupied itself until the end of the prescribed half-hour by drawing weird shapes all over the margins of the paper. Usually Phillip went down the steps of Mr. Groat's home sniffing and wiping away with his hand the last of his bi-weekly tears in the gas-light.

There was a lamp-post just outside the gate of "Chatsworth", and one evening, coming out into chilly fog, Phillip thought he would be unobserved if he imitated a dog; and he was relieving himself against the fluted iron post, painted cream, when the familiar click of his own garden gate gave warning, but too late; for even as he saw Father's form against the halo of lamp-light at the top of the road, so his own movement was perceptible. In contemptuous anger Richard hauled him home by the arm, shaking him and calling him a dirty little beast; and the front door having been opened to the jingle of keys, Phillip was ordered upstairs, and to take down his trousers immediately. Pleas for pardon and reiterated apologies greeted the arrival of the parental cane. By the post at the bottom of the stairs Hetty stood, holding her hands to her heart, while near-hysterical shrieks came from the bedroom.

Hetty had a saying which she uttered on occasion with a little laugh—"There is no peace for the wicked"—meaning herself. Why were such trials sent to her? What was the *reason* of it all?

"Sonny, Sonny, what *will* your father say when he finds out this time? Oh, you wicked boy. You'll break my heart, Sonny. *Why* did you do it, dear? Don't you ever *think* what you are doing?"

These words were uttered a few minutes after a loud report in the back garden one Saturday morning had brought her down from the bathroom, where she was washing out handkerchiefs. Saturday night was bath night. The fire being lit in the kitchen range after breakfast, Hetty took advantage of the hot water to get all the small washing of the week done before Dickie came home at two o'clock.

Sonny had his Saturday task, or chores as they were called, as well as Mavis and Doris. His work was the polishing of the brass, the burnishing of fire irons, and the cleaning of boots. Hetty had fondly supposed, as she told Mamma afterwards, that he was busily engaged on this work, which brought a reward of two-pence a week—one half of which had to go into his money-box for the Post Office Savings account for a bicycle one day—when a bang bigger than that of the largest Chinese Cracker startled her at the bathroom basin. Running into the back bedroom, she saw the boy crouching down behind the fence dividing the Bigges' garden from their own, while a cloud of blue smoke hung above his head, and a voice that she recognised as Mrs. Groat's called out, "I saw you fire that pistol, Phillip, and as soon as Mr. Groat comes home I shall ask him to come and see your father! You have deliberately broken the whole of this window!" There followed the sound of a window being shut, and a tinkling of small glass.

"Where did you get that awful thing?"

The awful thing was a percussion cap horse pistol, with a barrel seven inches long, and a bore of three-quarters of an inch.

"I bought it in Sprunts', Mother."

"But it is highly dangerous! Are you mad, my son? Is that the reason why you do such wicked things?" Standing in the garden, Hetty looked at the bedroom window of "Chatsworth", the lower pane of which showed a large black jagged hole.

"It was only a cork, Mother, not a bullet. It had no right to go where it did. I fired into the air, and it just went that way. It's only a pop gun really, a sort of firework. It's as safe as houses, really. It's an antique."

"How long have you had it?"

"I bought it last night, on my way to the dancing class at St. Cyprian's Hall, with Mavis."

"So that's what you do when you are trusted to go dancing!"

To try and use up some of his energy in the right direction, Hetty had persuaded Phillip to join the dancing class once a week, from six till eight on Fridays. The new church hall was near Sprunt's, the pawnbroker's at the end of Comfort Road. His shop was distinguished from the others by three large gilt balls suspended above it. For days Phillip had coveted a horse pistol lying in the dusty window, seeing himself keeping off Mildenhall with it, among other Dick Turpinal enthusiasms. The pistol lay among an assembly of old ivory chessmen and brass cornets, flutes, dress button-boots, hockey sticks, javelins, coconuts carved and painted as ugly masks, a fiddle or two, a concertina, a clarionette, silver-mounted walking-sticks, sets of china (most of it cracked and mended with little metal rivets), sets of books, and a bric-à-bac of faded jewellery and old silver on shelves.

From Mr. Sprunt, who had a passion for natural history, Phillip had bought for his father's birthday a small silver tobacco or snuff box, engraved with flowers, and fairly heavy, for one shilling and sixpence; but on seeing the pistol, a week or so before the birthday, he had, after much hesitation, gone into the pawnshop, after taking Mavis to the class in the hall, and enquired the price.

Mr. Sprunt, a seedy individual who looked as though he had been in pawn most of his life, as indeed he had, told him the price was ninepence. Thereupon Phillip, feeling daring and important, had produced the silver box in which he carried his swops since Mum had given him a stamp book for Christmas, and pawned it for ninepence. With the money he had bought the pistol.

The next midday he had bought some black gunpowder at the ironmongers', and a little round tin of copper percussion caps, with money extracted from his money box with a knife. He had gone on the Hill, and having first made sure that neither the Lanky Keeper nor Skullface were about, he had poured about a thimbleful of powder into the pistol, rammed some news-paper in, hard down, put a cap on the nipple, fully cocked the hammer, pointed up into the elms, and, eyes shut, pulled the trigger. A report followed, and a lovely fireworky smell of blue-white smoke. The paper went to shreds in the air, and when picked up, was seen to be edged with black where it had been torn by the explosion. It really worked! He ran home to find some tintacks, meaning to stalk sparrows in the Backfield. He would bake them in clay in his fire in a hidden hollow behind the Ballast Heap, and eat them, thus doing better than Arthur who won the day.

In Grandpa's back garden Phillip had found a nice fat cork with a bulging tin head, marked *champagne*. Thinking that this might make an extra loud report, he had fitted it into the muzzle of the pistol, whence by some ballastical aberration it had moved at a tangent over Mr. Bigge's fruit trees, his arch of jasmine and yellow ivy, his lower fence, and so to Mr. Groat's sash-window, shattering the glass of the lower half. There the cork was, partly blackened by powder, waiting on the front-room table of "Chatsworth" as evidence when Mr. Groat should arrive home from his weekly hot bath (economy being the order of the day at "Chatsworth") in Randiswell Baths.

Having obtained possession of the horse pistol, Hetty went into Mrs. Groat's, and begged her not to say anything about it, adding that of course it was only right that Phillip should be punished by having to pay for the damage out of his Post Office Savings Account.

"He is a very naughty boy indeed, and I am very much ashamed of him, he does not seem to be my son sometimes," said Hetty. "I can only tender you my sincere apologies, and I would not ask you to keep it a matter between us, Mrs. Groat, were it not for the fact that the scholarship exam. is so very very near. Mr. Groat has been so very very good in every way, and if Phillip has any success, it will be entirely due to what Mr. Groat has done for him."

Hetty did not dare to look Mrs. Groat in the face. She could never be sure which eye she ought to look at, which was the glass one and which the real one. Hetty hoped Mrs. Groat would not think she was looking at her worn carpet too much.

Mrs. Groat did some thinking, while tapping her toe on the carpet, then she said, "It is dangerous to allow a small boy to have such a weapon. Look at my eye, Mrs. Maddison!" and then Hetty had to look up into Mrs. Groat's face. Which eye ought she to look at? Fortunately the matter was soon taken out of her hands, for pointing to what Hetty had thought to be the real eye, Mrs. Groat said, "I lost this eye, Mrs. Maddison, because a boy, very much like Phillip, never did what his parents told him, and one day, pretending to be Robin Hood, he fired an arrow at me, with the result that I lost the sight of the eye forever."

Mrs. Groat spoke in a doleful voice, and Hetty made a sympathetic double-click with her tongue.

"And I've had to wear a glass eye ever since, because of one little boy's wildness. A nice thing it would have been for me, just think, if I had happened to be looking out of the window just now, and had got this right in my other eye, wouldn't it?"

Mrs. Groat picked up the offending cork.

"Yes, you are quite right, Mrs. Groat. I will see to it that Phillip never has such a dangerous weapon again."

"I think I understand all your feelings in the matter, Mrs. Maddison."

"Thank you, Mrs. Groat. Phillip is such a worry, he never means any harm, I am sure, but he is always up to mischief. When he gets his scholarship, and Mr. Garstang is very pleased with his Composition, which I am sure is largely due to Mr. Groat's coaching, I am hoping it will make a great change in him. May I send him down to Randiswell at once, to send up the glazier, Mrs. Groat? Of course, I shall ask him to let me have the bill."

"Very well, Mrs. Maddison, just for this once. But if he fires it off again, it will be my duty to tell Mr. Groat, for we cannot have that sort of thing as a habit, you know. Our lives may be in peril."

On hearing of his lucky escape, Phillip ran down at full speed to the sweep in Randiswell, urging him to come at once, for double pay. His khaki-coloured Savings Book that afternoon was stamped by a withdrawal of ten shillings, duly handed over to Mr. Nightingale. Later in the afternoon the pistol went in Hetty's handbag to Mr. Sprunt's, where it was exchanged for a ticket and sixpence.

On the following Monday a quantity of deal planking was delivered at "Montrose", and stored in the passage below the fence, near Mr. Bigge's upper conservatory. Phillip wondered what it was for. He soon learned; for the next day two carpenters arrived, and raised the fence by another three feet, thus concealing all but the blank part of the passage, where there were no windows or fixed lights, from the garden of No. 11.

"There, you see what you have done, Phillip!" said Hetty, looking at him intently. "Oh, I feel so utterly ashamed!"

"Hark" said Phillip. "I can hear old Josie at his harp again, and I expect Old Mother Bigge is going to cook tripe and onions tonight. Ugh! Beastly stuff."

Chapter 30

OLD HULK AT SEA

THE WEEK before the examination arrived. Day by day the
dreaded Saturday came nearer, while Phillip felt colder and
colder inside whenever he thought of it. He went to bed early
on the Friday night, to rest his brain, as Father said; he spent the
slow hours until long after his parents had gone to bed in trying
to find a cool place on his pillow, in pulling up the sheet which
had somehow got twisted round his knees in a lump, in trying
to stop the quicksilvery rush of jumbled pictures through his
head.

When they slowed down, other figments moved down from
the fluid dark, to resolve themselves into great ugly faces
before his shut eyes, flowing up and shaping themselves like the
colours when stirred in the tanks of Grandpa's factory in Sparhawk Street, where they made the end papers of ledgers and
account books in blue, red, black and brown. He saw the
factory in Sparhawk Street, with its iron stairs and crowded
printing machines, shafts and wheels, and bands turning; in
other rooms lithograph stones with men in aprons making wet
pictures on them, also in colours. Over two hundred men and
girls worked there, Mr. Mallard said, then asked him if he
would like to go into the Firm one day. Then Mother took
them to Madame Tussaud's, which Uncle Hugh had said was
full of great glaring dolls. Some of their faces now came up and
became like rotten cabbages, and all sorts of awful things
looked at him, with lips bulging and pulled down and skulls
and lots of white worms wriggled and grinned at him, and he
went down a dark tunnel deep into the earth, and he could not
breathe and the white worms were going to eat him alive and
he shrieked and shrieked and his voice made no sound as he
tried to run and his feet were like those of a fly on flypaper
and then a light was jabbing his eyes and he heard himself
cry out Save me! Save me! and Mother was there, and Father
in his white nightshirt.

Father held a candle and said, "It's all right, old chap, it's only Mother and Father. You've only had a nightmare."

He was wet all over, and Mother held his hand, while Father went away and brought back a glass of water and put some fizzy stuff in the glass, and said, "Drink this, old chap, it will make you better; it's bromide of potassium, and will make you sleep."

Phillip began to cry.

"What's the matter now, old chap? Got a bit of a tummy-ache? What have you been eating?"

"I'll never get a scholarship," wailed Phillip. "I won't, I know I won't. I can't do it, I can't do it. I know I won't get a scholarship. I'm an old hulk, worn out."

"You'll feel all right in the morning, old chap. Just try and keep calm. Why, Mother tells me you got full marks for your English paper, and about our parrot, too! Well done, Phillip. Everyone feels like you feel before a race, or a fight, or an examination, everyone in the world. Now just you let Mother make your bed, and settle yourself down. Anyway, if you don't get a scholarship, we shall have to find ways and means to circumvent that. Plenty of time to think of that afterwards. Some boys, you know, have to lose. They can't all win. I bet everyone to-night is worrying himself sick about it. So don't you worry any more, old fellow, will you now? Promise me?"

"Yes, Father, thank you."

"That's a sensible fellow. Remember how you swung on the Life Saving Cable at Hayling Island? You did all right, didn't you? And you'll find you will be able to do the papers to-morrow. Now we must all get some sleep. You wait till you get a bicycle, Phil, I'll take you some grand rides into the country. It will be spiffing fun, having your own cycle. Good night, old chap, and don't worry any more," and giving his son a pat on the head, Richard went out of the room.

Tucked in neatly and securely, Phillip kissed his mother. "I want to be very proud of you," she whispered, and he replied, "Don't shut the door, will you, please? Good night. I feel very nice now, with that fizzy drink. Like the brandy—lovely!"

The next morning Hetty took him to Bereshill School, dressed in his best suit with a wide linen starched collar sitting upon the shoulders of his blue serge Norfolk suit. She left him there with an aching heart, he looked so pale and anxious.

The hall had desks in it, spaced out, where silent and apprehensive boys sat down. Phillip waited with dry throat while the man came and put the printed arithmetic paper on his desk. He read the questions, and tried to grasp them against a silent rushing something in the room which took away all thought. Clamped to the seat, he saw the clock hand moving onwards to the dreaded hour when the papers would be collected.

At last, after a fatal pause during which the air rushed silently with the brown wood of the roof and the maps and portraits on the walls about him, he gripped his hands and made himself read the questions again. He copied the figures of the first of the set sums upon his ruled foolscap paper. His hand seemed of wood and the nib jerked like the teeth of the big saw when the two men cut down the elms in the Backfield. The clock had moved an awful lot when he had done the sums. Hurriedly he read the Part Two problems.

There was the same man wanting to paper the walls of a room, to whom Mr. Groat had often introduced to him: wallpaper which must not be pasted on doors and windows, the spaces to be allowed for. There were the two familiar trains approaching each other at different speeds; while the third and last problem was to work out how many ounce packets could be made out of two-and-a-half tons of ground coconut. Phillip tried to deal with the wallpaper, while remembering what Mother had told him had happened when she and Father had tried to paper the bedroom in their first house. Father put the flour-and-water paste on the strip of paper before putting it on the wall, and as he mounted the steps the paper stuck to his face and tried to cling to his trousers. Then the next bit curled up when he pasted it on the floor, and licked his face. However hard Phillip tried to forget Father on the ladder, and Mother's laughter as she told him about it, he could not put it out of mind. With a stifled cry he turned to No. 5 question, the two trains.

Phillip saw only the trains rushing with rapid thuds of pistons and screaming whistles upon one another. In despair, with glances at the fatal clock, he crossed out his figures of No. 5 and started No. 6, while fighting the sick feeling he remembered when Mr. Hern in the grocer's shop at the corner in Randiswell had given him some mouldy coconut powder to taste, rancid and tasting like soap. Try as he would, he could not get away from a jumbled picture of himself filling packet after packet, putting them in a great pile on Mr. Hern's shop floor, like a sand-castle being repaired as the tide came in. Sticky wallpaper got on the grey-white powder, and was smothering him, he would never, never escape. He could do the answers if only he did not itch so much and the clock would not move so quickly, and if only the boy in front of him would stop darting his tongue in and out as he wrote. Now he saw himself trying to widdle up against Mr. Groat's lamp-post in the fog, although his bladder was bursting and cousin Ralph had said that if it got into your blood you would turn yellow and die like the old man at the bottom house of the road who had had yellow fever, in spite of lots of straw being spread in front of his home to stop the noise of passing horses' hoofs and cartwheels.

It was all as he knew it would be, he *would never win a scholarship.* The clock was now at the hour, and his neck felt like an assegai was stuck in it. O, Mummy, Mummy, I told you I was an old hulk, unable to float, like the ones on the mud near Hayling Island.

He felt better when he had been to the lavatory, after a break-off of ten minutes. When the Composition paper was laid on his desk it looked nice and cool, and he saw Percy and the other boys, in their clean white collars, asking if their collars were clean after they had hunted eels under stones in the Satchville brook. Then one boy said that young robins pecked the breasts of the parent birds and killed them, as they liked the taste of blood and the old robins were red from the blood of the Cross, after trying to pull thorns from the brow of Jesus. So it was right to stick thorns through the nestlings, to kill them first. Father said it was not true, young robins did not kill their parents, and only village cads believed such rot.

Describe in your own words either (a) *A Walk by the side of a river, or* (b) *Which season of the year you like best, and why.*

Phillip saw the Brickhill Ponds, the blue sky shining below the reeds, and the Satchville brook beyond, where some of the wild duck belonging to the Duke nested in pollard hollow oaks by the path leading to the Duke's village over the moors. He heard Percy saying earnestly, Pray don't touch so much as one egg, there is a fine of five pounds for each egg. Percy did not dare even to look into a tree, much less to climb up, though there was nobody about. He himself had climbed up, and counted eighteen eggs in one nest, grey-green eggs with feathers around them. The duck which had flown out as he had climbed up flew round in the sky, making a soft noise like *quaz, quaz, quaz,* until he had got down and they had gone away again, along the footpath to the village, to buy some No. 2 bulleted breech caps for the saloon gun. In the Duke's village was a lamp-post with a tom-tit nesting in it. And on going home by the brook they saw many trout, looking thin and flat in the angle of the water, and pale-blue flowers of brooklime, and big yellow kingcups, and on some watercress which Percy called water-crease a red dragonfly was resting, near a curly skin out of which it had hatched.

In dread of the creeping black hand of the clock on the wall Phillip wrote of all he had seen, making the brook much wider, into a river, and putting swans on it, like on a real river, and the sunset beyond made it alike on fire, with the rings of rising trout breaking the smooth fire into ripples, to be carried away on the water, and the river was like life flowing past, never to return, and yet always there in flow. And he saw the blue eyes and fair hair of Helena Rolls smiling at him, and she was dead, she had died as a little child. She was his best friend who had asked him always to her parties, and now her spirit was in the water and the sky and in the singing of the birds, and he thought of her like Minnie, she was Minnie, and very near him as he walked alone by the river at sunset, and wherever he went on the seas or across the great spaces of the earth, she would be near him, for she loved him and love was God.

Phillip's eyes filled with tears as he wrote; they dropped on the paper, making some of the ink to run, but the black long hand was now ever so near the top of the clock, and the hour was nearly gone, and it was time to go home from the river and sit in the old farmhouse parlour, where the crickets played their little fish-bone violins in the cracks of the wall.

As the man came to take up his paper he was filled with fear, for what he had written was not composition at all, but all made up, and not true. O, he had lost his chance of a scholarship, and poor Mummy, it would make her cry, and Father would be cross, Father who had spoken so nicely to him and not been angry or punished him when he had had the nightmare. How could he go home, and tell Mummy the awful thing he had done? He was wicked, because Helena Rolls had not died at all, and he had never been asked to her house because he swore bad words, and he had not really tried to work for a scholarship but read about Jack Valiant and Sexton Blake instead.

When Phillip arrived home he was at first curt and rude to his mother. Later he cried when she asked him how he had got on. The days that followed were haunted with fear, for what the Examiners would say when they read the terrible, terrible all-made-up writing he had done on the walk by the river. And, in desperation, for now nothing mattered, when Mildenhall held up his fist at him in class one day, Phillip held up his fist to Mildenhall. After school he did not run away, but went out with Cranmer to the boys waiting in the playground, some calling out, "Ha, Donkey Boy! Two black eyes and a broken nose, a lift under the lug, and down 'e goes! Donkey Boy! Donkey Boy!"

White-faced, Phillip found himself in a crowd being pressed forward to the Woodwork Shop round the corner, out of sight of the main entrance to the school. Gerry came with him, and said, "Don't you be afraid of him, young Phil. I'll tell you what to do. Let him do your dags first, see, and take no notice. Stand quite still, as though you're funky. Then he'll do your cowardies. Now listen carefully. The moment he has done your cowardies, punch him one on the snout with your left hand. Don't square up to him. Just bang one in on the snout, then hit him with your right before he can recover. He won't fight, he's a funk, really, that's why he's always picked on you, because he knows you don't fight. But you're a game cock, young Phil. I'll stand by you, so don't let him take the spunk out of you."

The boys made a ring. Mildenhall stood looking at Phillip. Phillip was frightened. He felt sick, and no stronger than a piece of paper. Gerry put his arm on Phillip's back and urged him closer to the buck-toothed Mildenhall. Mildenhall said, in a low voice,

"You sauced me!"

"I didn't sauce you, ever."

"Yuss you did. Will you fight?"

"I didn't sauce you!" cried Phillip, unhappily.

"You did then! I can prove it. Call me a liar?"

Gerry whispered to Phillip, "Say yes."

With a quaver in his voice, Phillip said Mildenhall was a liar.

"Tell him he pinched your blood-alley," urged Gerry.

"And you took my blood-alley! My Father gave me that one!"

"Yah, Ole Tin Wills," said Mildenhall, urged on by his friends, who cried, "Go on, Mildy, do 'is dags! Paste 'im! Wears a starched collar, and parts 'is 'air at the side, fancyin' 'isself as a toff! Take 'im dahn, Mildy, go on!"

Mildenhall tapped Phillip with his fist on the left breast, in the traditional manner of the challenge.

"There's your dags," he said.

Phillip stood still, his hands unclenched by his stomach.

Mildenhall dapped him again, saying "There's your cowardies, as you won't fight." Shutting his eyes, Phillip poked out with his left hand. To his surprise and dismay, Mildenhall stepped back, holding his nose, which began to bleed.

"'it 'im!" cried the boys. "Go on Mildy, 'it 'im, 'it the sawny Donkey Boy!"

Mildenhall stood there, his mouth twisting as he tried not to cry. Blood ran down to his mouth.

"Go on, slosh him, you can fight him," urged Gerry, but Phillip, though he wanted to give Mildenhall a straight left, of the kind he had imagined a hundred times when reading the *Pluck Library*, found that he could not move. His arms would not lift up. He stared at the blood running down Mildenhall's chin, and was sorry for Mildenhall.

The fight was over. Phillip did not feel like the winner.

Mildenhall's friends jeered, and followed in a bunch, chanting "Donkey Boy! Yah! Donkey Boy! Thinks he's better'n us wearin' a white collar on!" as Phillip walked away with Cranmer and Gerry. There was a low cry of "Billo, Twiney!" as Mr. Twine looked out of the doorway. The shouting stopped immediately.

The three walked out of the side-gate, followed by the others, some saying "Funk!" as soon as they were out of sight behind the playground wall.

"Try again, Mildy, 'e 'it you when you warn't ready. I seed him, yah, Donkey Boy! Bah! Donkey's Ass, your farver fed you on donkey's piss, old Tin Wheels what got two boys dahn Pit Vale put away in quod fer nuffink, only a bit o' sport! Cowardy cowardy custard, eat your muvver's mustard, what comes aht'v 'er——"

In a fury Gerry turned the boy taunting Phillip and struck him two blows on the chest in quick succession, crying "Cowardies and Dags, come on!" and danced round the boy, then with a swing of his right hand struck him on the side of the head. The boy sat down, howling. "Any more?" cried Gerry, looking round with weaving fists. He caught Mildenhall by the coat collar.

"D'you give Maddison best, eh? Want to fight? Go on, Phil, paste him!"

Seeing that Mildenhall did not want to fight, Phillip, who was now beginning to enjoy himself, squared up to him, while the boys made a ring, shouting out, "A fight! A fight!" then "Billo! Twiney's coming!" whereupon the whole lot took to their heels, to Phillip's relief.

He had won a fight! His elation was slight, for he could not forget the sight of Mildenhall's nose bleeding. It must have hurt Mildenhall a lot, and it wasn't a real fight. If Mildenhall had done it to him, he would have had to cry more than Mildenhall.

The next day Mildenhall did not look at Phillip, but went home first. Soon the fight was forgotten, as the end of term drew on.

There were hot cross buns to look forward to on Good Friday, and best of all, they were going the following week to Aunt Liza's at Beau Brickhill. Phillip was thinking of fishing, of nesting in the fields and spinneys, of sleeping with Percy, of the wonderful talks they would have, in whispers, when they were in bed together, when the classroom door opened and Mr. Garstang stood there, looking straight in his direction.

Mr. Twine went to Mr. Garstang. They spoke together, while Phillip pretended to be working. He knew they were talking about him. Mr. Garstang had found out about his composition. His heart thudded in his ears.

"Phillip, come with me," said Mr. Garstang.

Phillip got up and saw himself following Mr. Garstang out of the classroom, into the hall, past the Black Line, up the stairs to the dreaded study with its glass doors. He waited by the open door, afraid to do the wrong thing, frightened of the room before him. Mr. Garstang turned his head and said in his deep voice, "Come in, my friend", and at the mode of address Phillip felt a colder, more ominous fear.

He was just aware that an old gentleman was sitting in a chair in the room. He had a pink thin face, and silver hair. He wore spectacles like Father's, with a thin gold frame. Phillip wondered why the old gentleman was smiling.

"This is the boy, Sir Park," said Mr. Garstang. Phillip recognized with a start that his composition paper was lying on Mr. Garstang's desk. He was found out. He was going to be expelled.

"Don't look so scared, Phillip," said Mr. Garstang, and when he smiled he seemed quite different from Mr. Garstang. Phillip smiled, but did not know what to do. He waited, with dry throat.

"Under some tension," said the old gentleman. "Now, with your permission, Headmaster, I will ask my questions. First, will you introduce to me your pupil."

"Phillip, Sir Park Gomme, of the London County Council, has come to tell me the results of the scholarships examination. This is Phillip Maddison, Sir Park."

At the phrase LONDON COUNTY COUNCIL Phillip went pale again. They were great big black words which ruled everything and were everything.

"How do you do, Phillip," said LONDON COUNTY COUNCIL, holding out a hand.

Phillip could not speak. A swallowed cluck, a voiceless tremor of the lips greeted Sir Park Gomme.

"You must not be afraid of me, I am the friend of all little children," said the old gentleman.

After swallowing, Phillip found he could speak.

"Considerable tension as a normal condition, I should say, Mr. Garstang."

"Quite well, thank you, Sir," said Phillip.

"That's right," said the old gentleman genially. "And so you speak German, Phillip. Your old nurse Minnie must have been a very good friend to you."

Phillip began to feel happy talking to the nice old gentleman of LONDON COUNTY COUNCIL.

"Yes, sir, only it was long ago, when I was little."

"And you love the countryside, do you?"

"Yes, sir, very much."

"Have you ever lived there?"

"I go holiday-making, to my cousins, sir, at Beau Brickhill, near the river, sir."

"And you wrote about Beau Brickhill; what a delightful place it must be."

"Yes, sir!"

"Well, your Headmaster has told me before that one of his boys had an uncommon gift for writing, and your English paper, that is to say your composition, certainly bears it out."

Phillip was still puzzled.

"Are you happy?" said the old gentleman, looking at him keenly.

"Yes, thank you, sir."

"Always?"

"Yes, sir."

"Well, I am delighted to have met you. I congratulate you again on your description of the walk by the river. Thank you, Headmaster." The old gentleman sat back, Phillip knew it was over, and he was all right.

"Now, Phillip," said Mr. Garstang, "you may return to the classroom. Give this note to Mr. Twine, with my compliments, and ask him to send the boys whose names are written there into the hall at once. Your name is among them," he smiled.

When Mr. Garstang had told the ten boys that each had won a scholarship, he said that they could have the rest of the day free, and he would trust them to go straight home to tell their mothers. Eagerly they set off, some turning north of the entrance to Wakenham School, others to the south, along the road now without the trees which had lined its way for centuries. East of the road lay the cemetry, once the Great Field of thirty acres, of Lammas or half-year land.

Here, under a yellow mound of clay not yet grown with grass, set with a single jam-jar whose flowers had long since withered, lay the very old man whose act in bringing a jug of ass's milk to Richard Maddison one morning eleven years before, when his baby son was dying, had saved the baby's life. The ancient man lay in a pauper's grave: in his own boyhood he had plowed, with a yoke of oxen, the land where now he rested: he had seen corn cut with the sickle on the Great Field when Napoleon was master of Europe; he was back where he began.

The boy who owed his life to the old man, and through him to his donkey, the boy who feared, almost as much as he dreaded physical pain, the stigma of his nickname, was passing the railings and the evergreen shrubs without knowledge of the grave's existence, and yet with such happiness for life in his breast it might well have been that in the moment's freedom a feeling of deep instinctive love had passed from the human relics in the soil to the medium of the boy's mind; since, for no reason known to him the boy suddenly stopped, peered through the shrubbery, and smiled in secret, to what he did not know: except that now he must hurry home to tell his mother news which he knew would bring her happiness.

November 1951—March 1952
Devon.

Printed in Great Britain
by Amazon.co.uk, Ltd.,
Marston Gate.